D0394470

THE STRANGE MAID

BOOKS BY TESSA GRATTON

THE BLOOD JOURNALS

Blood Magic

The Blood Keeper

THE UNITED STATES OF ASGARD

The Lost Sun

The Strange Maid

THE STRANGE MAID

THE UNITED STATES OF ASGARD

+ BOOK 2 +

TESSA GRATTON

RANDOM HOUSE NEW YORK

Visit us on the Web! randomhouse.com/teens

Educators and librarians, for a variety of teaching tools, visit us at
RHTeachersLibrarians.com

Library of Congress Cataloging-in-Publication Data
Gratton, Tessa.
The strange maid / Tessa Gratton. —First edition.
pages cm. — (The United States of Asgard ; bk. 2)
Summary: "In order to become one of Odin Alfather's Valkyrie, Signy Valborn must solve a riddle. With the help of Ned the Spiritless and Soren Bearstar, Signy embarks on a journey in search of her destiny." —Provided by publisher
ISBN 978-0-307-97751-9 (trade) — ISBN 978-0-307-97753-3 (ebook)
[1. Fate and fatalism—Fiction. 2. Gods—Fiction. 3. Prophets—Fiction.
4. Valkyries (Norse mythology)—Fiction. 5. Mythology, Norse—Fiction.] I. Title.
PZ7.G77215bStr 2014 [Fic]—dc23 2013039568

Printed in the United States of America

10 9 8 7 6 5 4 3 2 1

First Edition

Random House Children's Books supports the
First Amendment and celebrates the right to read.

To Catherine,
the first of our next generation.
You're strong, smart, and loud:
my favorite things, and Signy's, too.

✦ ✦ ✦

THE STRANGE MAID

I'm not afraid of love
or its consequence of light.
. . .
It's not easy to say this
or anything when my entrails
dangle between paradise
and fear.
—*Joy Harjo*

✦ ✦ ✦

Don't you know people
write songs about girls like you?
—*The Naked and Famous*

THE CHILD VALKYRIE

I was born under a frenzied star, so our poets would say. Which meant only that I was wild and loud as a child, always running off, crying or laughing at nothing my parents could see.

But when I was seven years old, I went truly mad.

It was winter, a week after my birthday, and my parents had been dead for a month. Shot down far away from me, with nothing to protect them but prayers and hymnals, neither of which could stop bullets. A bruise ached on my chest over my heart where I pressed my fists every morning, every night, and all through the funeral service staring at the empty pyre, for we had no bodies to burn. I had to hold in the wail of grief beating through my blood because the god my family served did not scream.

My adoptive parents, old friends of the family and fellow devotees of Freyr, the god of family, wealth, and joy, thought a trip to the New World Tree might help me. It might calm the fury that kept tears in my eyes when I demanded, "Why did they die? Why did our god let them die?"

"You'll see," said my wish-father, wiping tears from my face

even as they gathered in his. "The Tree will show you, for it connects life and death and all the nine worlds together."

The Tree's garden was still and claustrophobic, a frozen park surrounded by high brick walls and a gate of wrought iron. A heart of nature in the center of Philadelphia. It is said that if you climb high enough among the branches you will find a road to Asgard, the home of the gods.

Freyr's home. He was responsible for their deaths. I would make him answer for it.

I shucked off my coat and squeezed between two iron rails before my wish-family noticed, though my wish-brother, Rathi, caught the hem of my dress in his fingers and hissed my name. I ignored the clamor behind me; I was so hot, so burning with anger, my feet could melt the frost on the grass as I ran.

The massive Tree rose out of the ground, forbidding as a giant's tower, and thick snaking roots wove out in all directions, leaping and diving through the earth like sea monsters. Elf-lights strung through the layers of canopy cast a pale, broken glow as I toed off my shoes and dug my hands into the trunk's ropy bark. I climbed.

My fingernails broke and my feet scraped raw as I scrambled higher up the trunk. I had little time before the holy gardeners, the death priests, came after me, pulled me down, and threw me out.

I reached the first branch and kept climbing. Higher, harder, until my entire world was narrow leaves and branches, the pinprick surprise of elf-lights wound through the darkness.

The branches thinned; I found birds' nests and squirrel

hollows, old ribbons and popped balloons. Holiday streamers smeared like old trash. Dead memories that had drifted down from the sky to be caught in the leaves of the New World Tree.

Wind blew, snarling my braids and shaking the limbs that I clutched. When I tilted my head to peer through the upper branches I saw only stars.

There was no magical bridge. No gateway to heaven or Hel or the Alfather's eternal battlefield. It was a lie. As Freyr the Satisfied was a lie.

I gritted my teeth and rubbed my sticky face, but still could not bawl. I grabbed twigs and broke them; I ripped leaves off the Tree and threw them away. They tumbled and fluttered down. Only leaves.

"What has this Tree ever done to you, little raven?"

Surprise nearly spilled me after the leaves, but I caught myself in the web of branches. Below me a man stood on a thick branch, legs spread and arms akimbo, as if the branch were solid ground. He wore a black uniform like a berserk warrior, and though his beard was blond, sword-straight silver hair fell around his shoulders.

One of his eyes shimmered like a pearl.

Odin! *My mouth fell open. The Alfather. God of madness and sacrifice and war. The Alfather, who once, when the world was still new, climbed the Old World Tree and hung on its windswept branches for nine nights and nine days and stabbed a spear into his side until the Tree offered up its wisdom to him.*

I struggled to speak. "The Tree is . . . a lie. There is no road to Asgard here."

"So you tear it to pieces." Odin peered at me with his pearly eye, blind with madness and wisdom. With it he could see through me and into my bruised heart, to my wails and screams that wanted to be free.

Anger flashed through me: he could have seen my parents' hearts if he'd looked. "You didn't save them, either," I whispered.

The god of the hanged smiled and stepped up onto the next branch, which bent under the weight of his scuffed boots. "Easy things are never worthwhile," he said, as if I'd asked a question.

"This isn't easy!"

"True. But sacrifice," he said, with his face near mine, all rough crags that made him old as a mountain, and the spinning vortex of his blind eye, "sacrifice is the most worthwhile thing in all the nine worlds."

"My parents didn't sacrifice; they died!*" Fury felt good, and the heat of it dried my tears.*

"Their death was the sacrifice required to bring you to me. For if they had not died, you would not be in this Tree. And I have waited for one such as you."

Waited? For me?

A black shadow landed hard beside my head, the leaves whispering like rain; it was a raven the size of a dog, with one twisted, empty eye socket and one luminous white eye. Memory, or Thought—one of Odin's creatures I'd seen on TV—scored bark off the limb with her claws. She tilted her head and croaked my name. "Signy!"

Her brother landed behind me and slapped his wings against my back and head. "Let go—let go—let go—" he cried.

I batted against the raven's assault and slipped off my branch. The Alfather caught me. "Daughter," he said.

His voice was hot, like the breath of my parents' funeral pyre, raising elf-kisses on my arms and sweat on my spine. And I thought, The Alfather's weapons are more potent than prayers and hymnals. *I wrapped my arms around his neck.*

Odin held me against him for a moment, let me sink into his scent of wood smoke and tinny blood. I could hear his heartbeat, a racing rhythm like hoofbeats.

He set me against the trunk of the Tree, then straddled the branch before me like a very large boy. He brushed teary strands of hair off my face with gentle, callused fingers.

"You were waiting for me*?" I whispered.*

"So it seems" was his answer. The ravens clucked above us.

"What for?"

"To give you a new name, little raven."

"I have a name. I'm Signy Loring."

Memory cackled again, and her brother Thought with her. In their twin blind eyes a thing shifted: the past or the future, mischief or wisdom.

Odin tilted his head exactly like the ravens. "Is there any name in all the nine worlds that survives an encounter with the World Tree?"

The god of madness was riddling with me, and I had never been good at riddles. "Yours?" I guessed.

"Not mine." He shook his head; his whirlwind eye spun.

I pressed my back into the trunk, letting its roughness be fire on my spine. "What good would a new name do me?"

The god of the hanged laughed. It was a wild laugh, a laugh like an avalanche, deeper than the World Snake's gullet and wider than the space between stars. It shook my bones and stopped my pulse, but I held my chin up because I did not know what else to do.

"You climb my Tree, tear up its leaves, throw rage in my eye, and still you bargain with me! You are my darling Hrafnling reborn!" he crowed. Memory and Thought hopped to branches beside him. They chuckled rough and raw, ruffling their oily feathers.

Odin leaned nearer. "Be mine, little raven. My Valkyrie, my Death Chooser. Be my Valkyrie of the Tree from now until you die."

I gasped. The Valkyrie were his handmaidens; mortal yet famous, powerful, and beautiful. They were never afraid. They would never die halfway around the world, never leave loved ones behind.

"A new name, a new destiny to better fit the desires and strengths with which you were born," the Alfather tempted, offering his hand.

I gave him mine. "Yes!"

His face was as rugged as the bark of the Tree when he said, "So I name you—Signy Valborn." He kissed my palm. "My Valkyrie, newly born into death."

My hand pinched and burned. I snatched it back.

Pink and raw against my skin was a binding rune, built of other runes woven together to create a new meaning. I could not read it, for I did not know the runes then. But it seemed to flicker with fire as I studied it, to shift and wiggle. Tiny tendrils of pain shot up my fingers and down my wrist, twining through my blood.

Wind whipped up around us, bending the leaves and branches into a frenzy. Through it I heard the Tree whispering. While the Alfather held tight to my shoulders and his ravens cackled and screamed, the Tree hissed its ancient secrets in my ears—the secret wisdom, the ancient runes, folding into my memory and cutting through my bones like hot barbed wire.

Before I fell down through the branches of the New World Tree, I heard his booming laugh. "Welcome, Valkyrie of the Tree!"

ONE

I TELL HIM my name and brace for the inevitable rejection.

The pawnbroker blinks slowly, his long false eyelashes like raven wings. Dull fluorescent lights do his hard face no favors, and he's sweating in his flannel button-up, utterly masculine and disapproving in every way but those lashes. He glances again at the knife waiting on the counter between us, then gives me a long look before saying, "You don't look like a Valkyrie."

Rag you, I want to spit at him, but he's my last resort if I want a private room for shelter from the storm rolling in over Lake Mishigam even as we speak. It'll be sleet and frigid wind, and I'll be ragged myself if I go back to the Lokiskin orphan house tonight. I'd been managing my anonymity nicely until one of the girls saw the binding rune on my palm this morning. They've certainly been gossiping about Signy Valborn, failed Valkyrie, all afternoon.

Couldn't you solve a simple riddle? the oldest of them mocked, glad to discover some power over me.

May your guts knot like birthday ribbons, I snapped at her before storming out.

I could show the rune scar to this broker now, too, but the idea of having to prove my word offends me. I only say, "Believe me or not, this blade is worth more than your life."

I flash as bright a smile as I can to soften the accusation.

He grunts. "If that's so, why not sell it to a dealer or weaponsmith?"

I don't answer.

"You thought I wouldn't want the registration," he guesses.

"Your kind usually don't." I wave my fingers at his false lashes. He's Lokiskin, by their proof: gender-blending is a telltale sign of the Shifter's patronage. So is a less-than-ethical business practice.

"I run a legit business, little girl."

I sneer at the metal shelving and clusters of pawned goods for sale. Televisions and game consoles, old VHS tapes, fancy dishes, furniture, lawn equipment, dusty books, altar candles and mismatched rune sets, bear and horse idols and mead horns. And behind the counter in locked glass cases: jewelry, daggers, swords, spears, and guns. None of them as fine as the knife I've offered.

"I didn't steal it," I say.

We both study my seax. The single-edge broken-back knife is twice as long as my hand, with Odin's runes etched along the spine, a hilt of smooth troll ivory, and a star of tiny death-colored emeralds embedded at the bolster. The brown leather scabbard sits beside it on the counter, tooled with my surname, *Valborn,* in runic calligraphy.

"Even if you are who you say you are," the broker says gently, "you should've known to bring registration for a piece like this."

It's the tone that stiffens my spine. "I wouldn't have this much trouble selling it in Kansa or Tejas!"

"Then scoot on down to Kansa or Tejas with your unregistered weapon. I won't have it in the shadow of the holy Death Hall."

It's just behind my teeth to spit out, *It was a gift from the Valkyrie who rules from that very Death Hall,* but what's the point? I snatch the seax and snap it into the scabbard, curse his mother Loki, and shove back out into the icy street.

The scabbard fits through my belt, snuggled comfortably against my ribs, and a knot in my shoulders relaxes just to have it back where it belongs. I wonder bitterly if I chose this shop so near the temple of the Valkyrie of the Lakes because some part of me knew I could pretend to have tried to pawn it but not truly worry that I'd lose it.

I caress the ivory hilt, then shut my old red coat around myself. It's bulky from stuffed pockets and makes me look twice as wide as I am. Though worn these days and ragged at the hem, other than my boots it's the last vestige of my former glory. Soon I'll have to trade it for something without a torn lining.

I braid my long hair with stiff fingers and wind it around my neck like a scarf before hunching into the wind off the lake.

Skyscrapers do little to block the cold. Their windows reflect the steely clouds and remind me Chicagland is closed to me. Cars crawl past as the evening drops, and my shoulders knock into hurrying commuters. If they knew that I'm what's left of that boisterous, vivid little girl, the Child Valkyrie, if they noticed my rune scar, would they think the same thing? *How hard is it to solve a single riddle?* Would they study me with the same pity as was in the eyes of that cursed Lokiskin?

They think the riddle is the source of all my problems, when really it was just the final straw.

The dark orange and brown of autumn trees from the distant lakefront park snatch my attention. Splashes of violence between modern steel office buildings. I cross Roosevelt toward the L station; I can see the distant dome of the Death Hall against the gray sky.

My feet slow.

I could stay warm in the hall's public sanctuary tonight, tucked in among the mourners and lost warriors, the devout Odinists and poets who seek out the Death Hall to pray.

The smell of mint and evergreen and wax would lull me; the candlelight, the creak of pews send me to sleep. There used to be green cushions tied to the seats that would make a soft bed. The death priests would allow it, and the wolf-guards, even if they came close, might not recognize my new thin lips and short fingernails, or my eyes, because they're bigger now that I've lost the round pink cheeks of girlhood. I'd be home.

In a week and a half I'll be seventeen. It's a decade since I climbed the New World Tree, since Odin Alfather, god of the hanged, named me the next Valkyrie of the Tree, and still I have not won my place on the Valkyrie council.

For 250 years, the Council of Valkyrie has advised the president and Congress on matters of the gods. There were nine of them until the Thralls' War, when Kara Neverborn defied Odin and was punished by being stripped out of the world, her name forgotten by all but the Valkyrie. Ever since then, the remaining eight have behaved—to a fault. They serve mead to the gods every holiday in Bright Home. They raise funds and awareness for charity. They speak out on behalf of the gods and sometimes mediate between our human government and Asgard. They officiate funerals and holy sacrifices. They're celebrities who wield tremendous influence, can go anywhere and do anything because they touch the gods and walk among them.

And I belong with them.

Memory and longing draw me toward the lakefront park, toward the manicured lawns and bright maple trees, the museums and observatories and avenue of temples at the water's edge. I played here every other year of my apprenticeship, when it was the Valkyrie of the Lake, Myra Quick's turn to keep and teach me. I laughed all the time; I had clean sheets and anything I wished to eat. Shoes for running and shoes for walking, shoes for dancing. Silver rings and jeweled pins to hold my braids off my neck. Caramel ice cream.

I had sisters.

After Odin named me, he turned me over to the eight women who make up the Valkyrie council, quelling their irritation that he stole their prerogative of choosing their successors by saying they and they alone would declare me ready to take my place among them. They passed me from Death Hall to Death Hall every three months for eight years.

From the Valkyrie of the Rock in Cheyenne and from the South in Port Orleans I learned history and politics; poetry from the Valkyrie of the Ice in her hall in Vertmont; ritual and comportment from the First Valkyrie, who is stationed in Bright Home, Colorada, to be near to the gods. Languages from the Valkyrie of the Prairie, as well as a love for open air. The Valkyrie of the East, in Shenandoah, taught me to speak evenly and perform, and the West, in Baja California, told me about sex and death and gave me kisses to keep nightmares away. From Myra herself, the Valkyrie of the Lakes, here in Chicagland, I learned how to fight, though she swore to gut me like a deer if I told her sisters how good at it I was.

She gave me this seax in my belt.

The Chicagland Death Hall rises before me. Half castle, half modern art, it's so different from my Old Eurland–style Death Hall that butts up against the New World Tree in Philadelphia. Here in Chicagland, they built their hall of limestone and tall dark windows that glint pale orange from the sun setting across the city. It's a rectangular tower of straight lines, but for the green dome of the belfry, with huge white faces of the dead carved into each corner. The main entrance doors are capped by a lintel carved like the rays of the sun.

From the pole at the tip of the dome flies a green pennant, ruffling hard and fast in the lake wind. It means Myra is in residence. She's somewhere above me, short hair slicked back for that severe look, maybe beating on a punching bag or bathing for dinner with the Jarl of Chicagland.

What would she say if I walked into the sanctuary and climbed over the marble rail separating the public space from the inner? If I knelt at her throne and told her all the secrets our god of the hanged has whispered to me, all the nights of stories and lessons that led to the riddle?

Every year on my birthday, at dusk, Odin Alfather sent Memory to my window to tap-tap-tap with her beak and draw me into the garden of the Tree. When I was still young, he'd come with his blond beard and fatherly smile to grab me up and swing me onto his shoulders, where I could wrap his braids around my hands like reins while he climbed us onto the lowest branches. I told him everything I learned during the year; he whispered how delighted he was with my fierce progress. That whirling mad eye of his noted how tall I'd grown, and he joked about my skinny arms, while I promised next year there would be muscle, next year I'd be nearly as tall as him.

Why did you choose me, Alfather? I asked. *What is this itch under my skin when I think of you? When I remember blood and sorrow?*

That itch is why I chose you, little raven, he said. *The madness teases at you, because you're bold and daring—who other would climb our sacred Tree for selfish reasons?* And he laughed when I screwed my face at *selfish.*

Sometimes he appeared younger, a thick warrior to put me through my paces all night long, testing my reflexes, giving me a solid wallop to drive the breath from me. Other times he came hunched and old, a tall hat over his ice-white hair and that mad-pearl eye shimmering with mystery. Together we dug into the earth beneath the Tree's roots to find worms and beetles with iridescent wings, the tiny building blocks of life, he said. *Death and life, an infinite circle,* he said. *See here, the rainbow colors hidden inside death? The poetry of putrescence? Red-hot blood and clinging green decay, as beautiful as sunrise, as the rose born in summertime.*

And I saw it; I believed it. I still do. There are hints of Odin the Mad under rocks and in the city rot; the violent pink smog has poetry in it, too, the dirty foam at the lake's edge, the crumpled trash tossed by a wind into life. In the hot licking flames of a funeral pyre. The rest of the country doesn't see it—even my sister Valkyrie pretend it's not there—but it's the Alfather's constant presence, like the sun in the sky reminds us of Baldur the Beautiful, that this underbelly of death is Odin.

Kneeling at the edge of the smooth concrete path that curves toward the Death Hall, I skim my cold, stiff fingers over fallen maple leaves. Bright orange and scarlet, they curl against the dirt, sacrificed by the elegant tree to conserve energy and survive the winter. Without dropping these leaves, could it bloom in the spring?

People say I've failed every few months when some interweave site or local news channel does a fluff piece: *Whatever happened to the Child Valkyrie?* These leaves are what give me hope, even a year after I left the Valkyrie with the riddle clutched close to my chest, even as I've wandered the country hunting the answer like a revenant. A ghost of Signy Valborn.

This reminder everywhere I turn that life and death are the same. One leads to the other, and my god rules over that transformation, the release of death into new life. The essence of sacrifice.

But in the shadow of Myra Quick's magnificent Death Hall it's so hard. Inside are warmth and a silky bed, delicious food and sweet-smelling shampoo. Death is concealed with makeup and evergreen incense, surrounded with ritual and simple poetry. Outside, where I am, with an itchy scalp and underwear in my pocket, ash on my tongue, only my own hair for a scarf, it is oh, so hard.

The queen walked out, gold-adorned—

We, shadow-riders, singers of death, weave with blood-soaked thread—

Lines of poetry shuffle through my thoughts, from the oldest Valkyrie poems, where the Death Choosers ride all together, as sisters and friends, shield-maidens and allies. I long to pull out my marker and draw the runes down my arm, or to find a bottle of paint and spray them against the sidewalk—better yet, a great red scrawl of poetry across the Death Hall doors. Poetry always makes me feel stronger, whether songs in Old Anglish or Old Scandan, or new, never-heard, never-read, never-spoken word-shapes I pull from my black imagination.

My mouth curls and I want that so badly, to paint my heart against the limestone hall, to remind them I exist. *Do you still think of me, Myra Quick? I almost sold this seax today.*

"Have you come to pray?" a man asks from behind me, his voice a rasp.

I scowl and answer without looking. "Come to the Death Hall to sacrifice, or don't come at all."

"Is prayer not a sacrifice of breath?"

The riddling answer gives me pause. I turn to find a young man slouching against one of the iron streetlamps. Perhaps five years older than me, in a tattered gray coat. He's got sharp cheeks and a thin mouth, slender shoulders, and eyes as colorless as the overcast sky. Most intriguing are his intricate pale braids, woven and pinned in extremely old fashion. Like a poet from before the Viker age, or a silent-film star. For a brief, vivid moment I think it's finally my Alfather again, come to me after all my prayers and begging. Slowly I say, "The worth of a sacrifice is in the pain it causes, and breathing does not seem to cause either of us pain."

He pushes off the lamp and approaches; a hitch in his step fails to strip his grace away. There's a sword strapped to his back, but all I can see of it is the one-handed grip and a garnet winking from the pommel. This man doesn't take his eyes off mine and stops at barely an arm's length away. We're the exact same height, eye to eye.

"That isn't the worth of sacrifice," he says.

Rain hits my nose, but I don't look away from his eyes. I search his face for a rune sign to show me his merit. Seeing such runes is a Valkyrie trait, to see the truth in the hearts of men and women: Who is a hero? Whose fate is grand enough to be touched by a Valkyrie? The gift bled into me when Odin kissed my palm in the Tree. It burned into my bones and cannot be taken away by any less than the Alfather himself. The council may have given up on me, but as long as runes appear to me in the faces of others, in their eyes or their freckles or the curve of their smiles, I'll know I still have a chance.

The man blinks as rain scatters over his cheeks. It sprinkles on us, tiny ice water drops seeping through my hair to trail down my scalp and spine. I shove my hands into my pockets and don't look away, though no runes appear. It cannot be the Alfather. I would know him; I would sense the madness. See some sign.

Slender wisps of hair stick to this young man's temples, water darkens his heavy eyebrows, and the corner of his mouth twitches as a long drop of rain slides like a scar down his chin. He's not handsome, but I think I could stare at him for a very long time.

"Enjoy what you see?" he drawls.

"Who are you?"

"My name is Ned Unferth."

I snort. His name is like a riddle, too: *Unferth* is an Old Anglish word scholars have argued over for ages. It means either *full of spirit* or *spiritless.* Brave or cowardly, nothing in between. It's a word that contradicts itself. It's also the name of the poet who challenges Beowulf Berserk in the famous poem about trolls and kings in long-ago Daneland.

I know it well, for my favorite Valkyrie, Valtheow the Dark, appears in its verses, too. *"He who knelt at the foot of the king,"* I recite.

Ned Unferth shrugs. "There are worse things to be called."

There's silence between us again, and he seems content

to wait here while the cold pinpricks of rain burrow into our bones. The tattered hem of his coat flaps, and under the water-dark cuff of his jeans his boots are scuffed and old. I should abandon this stranger, turn my back carelessly. But to go where? Back to the orphanage? To huddle under a bridge somewhere? *The Valkyrie of the Gutter.*

I shudder, and my head aches from the slicing wind. "Is there something you want?" I finally ask.

Unferth smiles quick, but enough so I see a flash of teeth. "I have a birthday present for you, little raven."

Every piece of me freezes. So the Alfather calls me, and none other. Was I wrong before and this *is* Odin, my god of the hanged, standing before me, teasing me with riddles? Finally come to me again? But there is no madness in this man's left eye, no hint of godhood or anything.

Cold rain falls all around as Ned Unferth leans toward me and says, "I know the answer to your riddle."

TWO

THE RIDDLE APPEARED at dawn the morning after my fifteenth birthday.

I'd slept shivering between two massive roots of the New World Tree, tears dried on my cheeks and a gnawing hunger in my belly, for I'd refused to eat with the Council of Valkyrie the night before. They'd come for my birthday, early, to surprise me, and instead of a celebration with honey wine and cakes we fought hard enough to shake the tallest limbs of the Tree.

They didn't like my Yule plans. *Gutless, old-fashioned cowards,* I called them.

Impudent child, destructive, reckless! they called me back.

All because I took what the Alfather taught me and tried to put it into action.

The last time he'd come to me, we didn't spar and we didn't dissect dead birds or dig into the roots for perfect beetles. Instead, Odin allowed me to curl under his arm and listen to the beat of his heart while he told me stories of his favorite, ancient Valkyrie.

He told me of Signy Volsung, who turned herself into a dire wolf and destroyed her husband's entire family with fire. He told me of Lady Hervor and her magical sword, of Sanctus Judith, who cut the heads off her enemies and tied them onto a loom of veins and intestines. *They understood the violence of creation,* he said with a sigh. *Do you feel this, little raven?* he asked, putting my fingers to his wrist, where his pulse raged with a strange beat like the hooves of Sleipnir the eight-legged stallion. To feel the god's blood under the pads of my fingers teased at my fear, and at my excitement, too. I didn't know which to feel, and he laughed. He said, *Give me a sacrifice for understanding,* and I grabbed up the knife from his boot. Without a thought, I cut open my hand. It burned like fire and I spilled blood and tears right there into his lap.

The Alfather used my braids to wipe the tears off my cheek, and the entire garden of the New World Tree smelled sharply of blood. *For your tears I will say that fear and excitement belong in the same breath, and for your blood I will tell you of Valtheow the Dark, who was born my daughter as no other in the long history of our people.*

I'd heard of her, Valtheow: she was a Valkyrie who lived sixteen hundred years ago and first hanged herself at the Yule sacrifice in Old Uppsala when she was thirteen, but Odin did not let her die. She cut her own throat to weave a necklace of blood and survived that, too. She married the king of what became Daneland, Hrothgar Shielding, rode with him into battle, and bore him two sons and a daughter, and when the troll Grendel came to destroy their palace, she fought him as wildly as any retainer. She conjured spells to empower the warriors' swords, though none could penetrate Grendel's cursed iron skin.

Beowulf Berserk finally came with his war band, and she bound him into a blood pledge to defeat Grendel or die. He did so, but it only enraged the troll's mother, who took vengeance upon the Shieldings and nearly tore Beowulf apart, too. Valtheow built herself a gown of mud and blood and moss, forged a mask of iron, hunted the troll mother down, and faced the monster at Beowulf's side.

As the Alfather spoke of her, his face lit with longing and perfect joy. It was no expression I'd ever seen on my parents' faces or even the Valkyrie's. I did not know it, except that it hurt me with *wanting* to know it. I wanted to be the one to make him feel that way, and while I thought of it, my wrist burned, my nose and throat were sticky with the smell of my own blood.

I said, *Tell me what to do, Hangatyr.*

Odin smiled. He touched my nose and ran his knuckles tenderly along my jaw. *Oh, little raven, what can you do? Those times are lost to us—to me.* And he told me the story of his riddle match with the poet Thomas Jefferson, who tricked him at the founding of the United States of Asgard into the Covenant that stripped all true power and divinity from the Valkyrie.

Odin said, *Before that rascal, before his riddles, my Valkyrie were spectacular. Near gods in your own right. You led armies and burned castles to the earth, cast vicious curses and changed the course of destiny with a kiss of my favor to the right king. You rode through the sky on wolves and starlight horses, hunting the most magnificent warriors to bring up to immortality in the Valhol, my heavenly Death Hall. You carried my magic in your hearts, with my wild passions to guide you. You were my immortal queens. You were worshipped even after death. Would that you could be so again.*

That was the end of it, but as the sun rose I realized that while he could do nothing, bound as he was by the Covenant, I had agreed to no such pledge. It was in my power to bring the old ways back to the Valkyrie. I could show my sisters what our god truly wished, for Odin's sake. I would be Valtheow reborn in his eyes, in the world's eyes, even if I had none of her ancient magic.

I'd prove it through a grand gesture nobody in the whole country could ignore.

For weeks I corresponded with three felons who had written to my Death Hall asking for the Alfather's absolution, asking me to witness their executions as was their right. I wrote poetry with them, to determine which was most worthy to be my first, and just as my birthday arrived I knew it would be Malchai, son of Elizabeth, convicted of murdering his wife and brother. His rage seeped through his handwriting, and his grief. I wrote to him, *I will tell you a secret, Malchai. The Alfather longs for the time before the Covenant, for the days when we sacrificed to him in great celebrations. The laughter in his voice as he speaks of such things teaches me to laugh at them, too, until I long as he does for the sharp scent of blood, the sick, clinging rot of death and battle. To find it and experience it: this moment he speaks of when terror turns into glory, when shaking fear becomes strength. That is the power I will claim, to take all my worries and dangers and transform them. To take your fears, the anxiety of the entire country even, and change them with sacrifice.*

He wrote back, *Come.*

I drove an hour north of Philadelphia to the New Dutchland Royal Penitentiary, a nearly fifteen-year-old Child Valkyrie weighed down by rings and bracelets and an embroidered coat the rich green color of death.

Malchai Elizabethson leaned his elbows onto the table, shoulders strong under the tight blue jumpsuit, wrists at an awkward angle thanks to the handcuffs. He smiled thin and wide like a lizard. His hard face was only softened by a scruff of beard.

I stared into his eyes and saw the rune I needed pressed into his slimy green iris: *sacrifice.*

"You wish to be hanged instead of put down with a needle like a dog," I said. My palms sweated and I pressed them against my dark jeans as subtly as I was able. I wore thick black liner around my eyes and a smear of scarlet like blood on my mouth—both to help me maintain this mask of composure, of absolute control. "I want you to go with me to the gallows outside the garden of the New World Tree, walk of your own volition up the dais on Yule night, and let me place the noose about your neck. You will not leap or fall but be lifted up and strangled slowly." I had practiced this speech in the mirror all the day before, so as not to hesitate or hear my own voice shake at the violence.

He said, "What will this scheme of yours do for me?"

And I slowly smiled. "Here is the magic of sacrifice, the power the god of the hanged gives to humankind: to take your death and tragedy and transform it into prayer, into opportunity. We've let go of this power, relegated it to history, when look what it's done for me, Malchai. My parents died, and from their sacrifice I was reborn the first Valkyrie of the Tree in one hundred and fifty years. What could it do for you? For all the United States of Asgard?"

"But I will be dead!"

Jerking forward, I grasped his forearms. I dug my nails into his skin. Malchai shoved his face into mine, that silver *sacrifice* rune brilliant as a star in his iris. I could smell his cigarette breath, the bland soap from his hair. All the flaws of rage and weariness spelled out in his heavy pores and the uneven stubble etching the shape of his jaw.

I said, "Your name is a cursed one. A kinslayer you are, with no family to say your name or remember you, no one to kneel at your pyre or scatter your ashes in nine places you've never been, as your Lokiskin do. Join with me, let me use your name to resurrect this power, and your name shall also be resurrected. Your glory, if not your honor."

The guards burst in and dragged us apart, but not before Malchai cried, "Yes!"

And I left with the blood of my first sacrifice staining my hands.

I returned triumphantly to the Death Hall, to discover my eight sisters waiting, ribbons drooping off discarded gifts in the corner of my suite. "Sisters!" I could hardly contain my joy at seeing them, could barely stop myself from crowing my plans. "What are you doing here?"

But my eyes lowered to see all my prison correspondence open and spread across the desk. Cursed evidence of my plotting.

Gundrun Graycloak, the First Valkyrie, took one long step forward and slapped my face. "Get on your knees, girl," she said coldly.

The words shocked me, harsher than the slap burning on my cheek. I remained standing.

"What were you thinking?" Gundrun demanded. "Your wolf-guard called us, told us where you'd gone."

Outrage made me yell, "Their loyalty should be to me!"

"To the council, foolish child. You are not one of us yet, and may never be after this."

The Valkyrie of the East and West threw my letters at me; Myra Quick tore them to pieces, Elisa of the Prairie turned woeful eyes to the ceiling, and Siri of the Ice hissed a line of poetry about Brynhild, who was cursed for disobeying the Alfather.

"It is not disobedience," I cried.

But Myra snapped, "That is what Kara Neverborn thought as well, and look at her punishment!"

"This is what the Alfather wants," I said through my teeth. "He can do nothing to bring our power back, but we can. We can bring the old ways back to the Valkyrie."

"In the old days we died young," said the Valkyrie of the West.

The Valkyrie of the East put a hand on her sister's shoulder and added, "In the old days, we were feared."

"We *should* be feared!" I said. "We made curses and rune magic and rode with armies. We had power then."

Gundrun stroked her feather cape, the mark of her station, which she wears at the president's side. "And we have no power now?"

"Only what the Covenant allows us. Not what we deserve!" I grasp at air, wanting to find the right words to convince them. "We could transform fear into hope if we tried."

"Our power is more subtle now, not of war and fire and death but of politics and money," said the Valkyrie of the Rock. "But it *is* power."

"What of the beauty of death?"

Siri of the Ice shook her head. "That is poetry, not action."

"Our god is the god of poetry! Siri, you are the one who told me to remember that. What is the line of your favorite riddle? *The pearls that grace dead flesh.* Maggots! I know you can see what I mean, Siri. And Precia and Myra!" My voice was thin, a taut cord. I looked to each one, appalled. "We are the tendon that connects life and death, the choosers of heroes, who can see the worth in a man's heart. We should embrace the potential of sacrifice—that is what I want, and what Odin wants. Let me bring this back. Let me show you how glorious it can be, I who was born out of sacrifice." I gripped my hands together and nearly fell to my knees. "It can change all of you, as it changed me."

None responded. They regarded me as a unit, eight pairs

of eyes hammering me in place, bending my knees with their weight. If only I could have read runes in their eyes! But never had their worth been revealed to me that way.

I pressed my fist against my chest, where I had when I was a little girl and wanted to shriek and wail my grief. "You are gutless cowards! This is transformation, and action! Odin chose me because I am bold, and you'll watch from behind me!"

"You will be rejected by the people if you try to bring back the old ways," Precia, the Valkyrie of the South, said calmly, as she was always calm. The youngest of them, barely seven years my elder, she coifed her hair like an elegant old lady and wore chunky antique jewelry. "They want us as we are. Symbols, voices. Protectors. They trust us, and we will not let you jeopardize that trust. Or the Covenant. Without the Covenant, we cannot exist in the modern world."

I felt tears in my throat, and I lifted my chin to keep them back. "You should hear his voice when he urges me to this; you should ask him yourselves. Let me show you!"

"You will not." Gundrun cut her hand down, and that was the final word. Hers was always the final word.

Except Myra Quick, the Valkyrie of the Lakes, leaned forward. "Happy birthday, Signy," she said bitterly.

I fled for the garden of the New World Tree, shoving past the death priest pruning the winter yew bushes. I flung myself at the base, scraped my hands against the trunk, and pressed my forehead into the rough bark until it hurt.

I thought Myra understood me better than the rest, she and Precia, the Valkyrie of the South. Myra sparred as skillfully and strong as the ancient Valkyrie Hervor and Skuld, and I remembered how Precia's cheeks would go pink with elation when we reenacted the *Flight of Brynhild*. We three would be the passionate, raging ones, spirit-sisters to tilt balance against the First Valkyrie and her conservative confederates, the Valkyrie of the Ice and the East.

But even they didn't understand.

Alfather, help me! Give me a sign!

There was no answer but the whisper of wind through the rattle-dry leaves of the Tree. I curled between two massive roots, hair tangled in my face, hands cold and tucked to my breast, until I fell asleep.

In my dream I led Malchai to the hanging ground, and the city cheered for me as the noose slung around *my* neck. I was the one dragged into the sky, to dangle and dance and choke for the Alfather.

Dawn woke me, frost in my hair and my face numb. My throat ached for all the crying I'd done and was bruised from dreaming. I stumbled to my feet. Three of the Valkyrie stood in the garden with me: Myra Quick, Precia of the South, and Elisa of the Prairie. Tears tracked down Precia's bright cheeks, and Myra's lips were pale. Elisa closed her eyes and pointed to the trunk of the Tree.

I looked.

Burned into the dark, ropy bark was a riddle.

The Valkyrie of the Tree will prove herself with a stone heart.

✦ ✦ ✦

It was the only answer I got from my god.

Thinking he agreed with them, that I'd gone too far, too fast, I took what I could carry and walked out of the Philadelphia Death Hall.

For nearly two years I've wandered, sleeping where I can, earning money how I can. Poetry on a street corner or, early on, officiating small funerals before the country realized I'd run away—before one of my death priests or wolf-guards leaked the riddle to the newspapers. I've crashed in half-decrepit buildings, brewing street-shine and selling it for coins. Trusting people with runes in their eyes like *joy* and *strength* and *courage.* At first I tried to be cool like Precia or Siri, tried to harden my heart into stone. Not to grow wild with anger or grief or passion.

Impossible, when I can't stop this itch to leap into action, to *do something* no matter what the consequences. How can I walk past another girl being roughed up? How can I not deface those infuriating anti-berserker subway posters? How can I do less than Valtheow, who made herself a mask of mud and blood to face down her enemies?

I don't understand why Odin would want me to have a heart of stone, if that's what the riddle means, when I know he was drawn to my wildness.

If this were an ancient poem, if I read the line in a song, I would think *stone heart* was a kenning for death, or maybe for a Freyan, someone who worships Freyr the Satisfied, the god of earth and fertility, like my parents. They love the earth and poetically speaking could be said to love stone, to have hearts for stone. But it's so twisted up in language! Could a stone heart mean justice? Balance, like what Tyr the Just brings to the world in the shape of laws and integrity, because a stone heart would not vary? Or maybe a stone heart is a heart of fire, because flint is a stone and it sparks fire from steel.

The people I've asked did not know, either. I managed an audience with several lawspeakers, and a Freyan priest in his temple; I got onto the stage at a public reading at the Mishigam Poet's College and recited them the riddle as if I'd created it. None of them had a better answer. *How should the Valkyrie prove herself with a stone heart?* I demanded again and again.

A young seethkona across the border in Acadia searched for a clue in my runes, but all she saw was the road stretching ahead of me for months and a cold, broken city. I even hitched to New Netherland City to ask Rathi Summerling, my former wish-brother, who was apprenticed to a Chautauqua preacher there and knew everything about history. I remained with him for three months, falling a little in love with him and his city for the mold in the cracks of its sidewalks, the violence of the taxicabs and sharp steel skyscrapers, the disposable smells, the crush of people streaming over all that death like it nurtured them. But not even he could give me an answer.

Two years now since the riddle appeared, most people have forgotten me.

The rune scar still marks my palm like a brand: this girl belongs to the god of the hanged. But I'm a Valkyrie in name only.

And here is this man, Ned Unferth, standing in the freezing

rain outside of the Chicagland Death Hall and saying as if it's the simplest thing in the world, "I know the answer to your riddle."

He must be mocking me.

I get right into his face. "*Liar.*"

"I never lie, little raven," he says.

Little raven. I flatten my scarred palm over my heart, pressing down against the rise and fall of my breath. Then I lurch forward and grab his face. He doesn't move, barely blinking. My thumbs press under his eyes. His jaw is rough and cold against my palms. He leaves his arms hanging at his sides, flicking a glance at the onlookers who pause with concern under their umbrellas. Then Unferth smiles at me again, a dangerous curve of lips that lures me even closer.

And there, there in the colorless iris of his left eye, is a single bright rune: *truth.*

He promises me food and answers if I go with him. Elisa of the Prairie would lecture me about getting into cars with strangers, but I have my seax, and the rune in his eye as a hint of his worth. I don't think he'll try to murder me tonight, and a clue to my riddle is worth the risk.

What else am I supposed to do? Anything is better than throwing myself on Myra Quick's mercy.

As he opens the passenger door of a blue pickup truck, Unferth calls me *little raven* again. Oh, how I miss my god of the hanged! This riddle is all I have left of him, my only way home to him again.

Unferth gets behind the wheel and turns on the heater as he drives north out of town. Neither of us touches the radio, and the only sound is the roar of the engine, the streak of wipers, and rain spattering the metal roof. By the time I'm warm, my stomach screams for food and I'm damp from the soaking my coat received.

"Where are we going?"

"Dinner, and then, if you like my answers, north into Canadia."

I could get used to such truth-telling. It's relaxing, despite the excitement that thrills up my spine. Canadia. That more than anything convinces me he has a plan: there are no good reasons to head into troll country. I watch him as he drives, eyes on the road, going about five kilometers below the speed limit, hands at two and ten. Always uses his blinker, lets cars merge, and never cusses, even in the Chicagland traffic.

Either he's from another planet or too cautious to be an Odinist.

"What's the answer?" I say after ten minutes and only about seven kilometers.

"I'd prefer to lay it all out in proper order," he says tightly.

"Did Odin send you?" I ask instead. "Are you one of his men? Not a berserker, not a death priest. A warrior?"

"I'm a poet."

"An Odinist, then."

"I didn't say that."

"Most poets are Odinists."

"These days."

I frown. It's all true, but not exactly answers. "Are you dedicated to Odin?"

He flicks an irritated glance at me but has to look straight back out the windshield. "Does it matter?"

"Obviously! Did Odin tell you the answer to his riddle? *And* you know my secret name."

"*Hrafnling*," he mutters. "An Old Anglish diminutive only. 'Little raven' was a Valkyrie's child name in ancient times, in the oldest songs."

"I've never heard it before!"

Unferth only shrugs.

For ten more minutes I glare at his profile. His nose is crooked and his lips thin, but I quite like his cheekbones and jaw. There's a twist of shine on his neck that might be a scar. As his hair dries it brightens to a wispy pale blond. He's got scars on his knuckles and fingers, too, from fighting.

Unferth pulls off the highway into the parking lot of a Xia buffet. "You must be hungry," he says.

"Just tell me the answer," I insist.

He settles his hands and the keys in his lap and leans his shoulder into the door to face me.

I try again. "How do I prove myself with a stone heart?"

"Kill yourself a troll."

"*What?*" I'm trapped between laughing incredulously and kicking him across the gearshift.

"A stone heart. If you kill a troll, it turns into stone, doesn't it? Heart included."

Laughter dries on my tongue. I stare for a long moment. Unferth waits expressionlessly.

"That's so . . ." I pound a fist onto my thigh. "Ragging literal. Too literal. It can't be. It has nothing to do with the . . . kind of Valkyrie I want to be. With the reasons I clashed with my sisters in the first place! The answer should be about being bold or not, about danger or power or safety! It should be more dramatic than this, at least."

Unferth's eyebrows go up. "Trolls aren't dramatic or dangerous enough for you?"

I shrug a little helplessly. It's a valid point. Killing a troll—a greater mountain troll, a monster—would be glorious and violent, a thing only the wild berserkers do these days, or Thor and his army.

Valtheow the Dark faced trolls.

Hope sputters to life. For the first time I wonder if Odin sent that riddle to prove to my sisters that I was *right.* Maybe I'm not supposed to learn something about myself or change; maybe *they are.* He wants the old ways back, and I'm his vessel for it.

"Perhaps some food will fatten up your riddling muscles," Unferth says, unlocking the doors. He tucks his sword under the dashboard and leaves me, running through the rain toward the buffet. I scramble down after him.

Cozy red decor welcomes us, along with tinny harp music. The walls are covered with banner paintings of misty hills and old fishing boats, and gentle lamps hang low over the booths. It smells like fried vegetables and fish, and I barely pause at our table before heading for the buffet. Unferth orders a beer after asking the hostess which is her favorite import, and adds a second for me before following.

I ignore that it's been weeks since I ate food this rich and plentiful, and devour it messily. Unferth eats like it's a science experiment. A bit of every offering fills up two plates and three small soup bowls, and he tastes it all, either discarding the whole after a single bite or finishing it. I'm done long before him, feeling stuffed for the first time in ages. I continue to study him, as if his clothes or his habits will tell me how he guessed the answer to my riddle.

Under his coat he's got on jeans and biker boots, a plain T-shirt over a long-sleeved one. It's definitely a scar around his neck, just exactly where a noose would pull, and three of his left fingers are encircled by rings. He's exceedingly polite to the server who refreshes our waters and offers chopsticks, and his speech has a rhythm to it that's not quite an accent but marks itself. I take a drink of the pale Xian beer and close my eyes. With a full stomach and warm all over, my body wants to sink deeper into the booth and relax, but my mind is sailing.

Here is this Unferth with a supposed answer to the Alfather's riddle—a miraculous, well-timed answer nobody has suggested before. If Odin didn't send him, how did he find me, and why now?

I set down my chopsticks. "How old are you?" I ask.

"As old as the flower that blooms and dies every year."

I scoff. "Where are you from?"

"A country where the sun rises and sets every other day." Unferth turns over an egg roll and meets my eyes as he spears it with his fork.

"Who is your father?"

Now a lazy smile stretches across his face and he slumps back into the booth. "As much a king as I am."

His answers are riddles, too, and could mean he does not age, he is not from the Middle World, or he is as divine as his father. As Odin. The thrill of leaping to a conclusion makes my toes dance in my boots. "You're one of the Lonely Warriors," I guess.

The Einherjar, Odin Alfather's undead soldiers, drawn from the greatest of our heroes from all the ages to serve him in Asgard. They train constantly in the fields outside the Valhol to fight at his side when the end of the world comes. They eat with him and drink from the Poet's Cup to retain their memories even in death; they are his spies in the Middle World, his brothers-in-arms. Perhaps he learned to call me *little raven* from Odin's own lips.

But Ned Unferth laughs dismissively.

I wait. Rain slashes the windows. We're practically alone in the restaurant, in a quiet bubble. "Well?" I finally push.

"Was there a question?" he asks, not bothering to hide his mirth.

How delightful that I can amuse him so well. I narrow my eyes. "Are you *Einherjar*?"

"I am a man."

Frustration squeezes my fists.

Smile gone, he says, "Ask the right questions and I'll answer them."

"Why are you sure the riddle means I need the heart of a troll?"

"I am a poet and riddler, little raven. I know words and their meanings inside and outside, and from angles you cannot imagine. I know all riddles have more than one answer, and the heart of a troll is *one* answer to your riddle."

"Is it the right one?"

"They're all the right one."

"Will you explain it to me? All the angles I can't imagine?"

Unferth curls his lips. "It would take a hundred days."

"*The Valkyrie of the Tree will prove herself with a stone heart,*" I bite out.

"Prove herself to whom?" he asks.

"To the Valkyrie. To Odin."

"Where does it say that?"

I open my mouth but say nothing.

He shakes his head. "You assume too much. All that is *there* is that the Valkyrie, whoever she is, will prove herself to someone or something with a stone heart. As no doubt you have *assumed,* many things could be symbolized by a stone heart. It's a poetic device, isn't it?" Unferth puts one finger against the polished wood of the table and draws an invisible heart. "The only thing that is absolutely, by every angle, a stone heart, literally, is a once-beating bloody heart transformed entirely into marble or obsidian by the sun's curse upon the trollkin. Perhaps not the only answer, but the best answer."

"And proving?" I ask. "Who am I proving myself to?"

"Who is mentioned in the riddle?"

"The Valkyrie of the Tree."

He wipes out his invisible heart, colorless eyes on mine.

"Me?" I say.

He shrugs one shoulder as if he doesn't care in the least.

"Prove myself to myself?"

"The Alfather hung in the windswept tree for nine nights and nine days, sacrificing himself to himself."

"You're seeing things not there!"

"I see many things others do not."

I grit my teeth again and spin the conversation back around. "You're saying that the riddle doesn't explicitly say who I'm proving myself to, or even that I'm the Valkyrie in question. And the only . . . concrete thing in the riddle is the stone heart, which literally could be a troll's heart."

Unferth sighs. "You certainly know how to strip the poetry out of a thing."

"This isn't a poem; this is my life!"

The words echo out through the mostly empty buffet. The hostess glances over, fingering the thin necklace at her throat. I can't even smile at her or see what god's charm she's worrying at.

Unferth watches me patronizingly. It's in the tilt of his eyebrow and the smile half-hidden behind his mouth.

I collect myself, clench my teeth. Smooth my hands down my jeans. When I look up, the expression is gone from his face.

He says, "Your god is the god of madness, war, and poetry. Don't dismiss it. Isn't poetry what you long for? The symmetry, the meaning, the *destiny* in ancient songs and stories?"

"You know too much about me, Ned Unferth."

Twangy harp music, so delicate and minor-key, nothing like the bombastic music of our gods, invades my thoughts. A discordant element to remind me that nothing is as it seems, but I have to act anyway. I cannot see the paths of fate—only Freya the Witch can, and her fortune-tellers—but not knowing where this leads is part of the point. Acting is the point. Leaping ahead is the point. Reaching for what I want—and what I want is to be the Valkyrie of the Tree. I owe it to myself to follow this opportunity, no matter who Unferth is, no matter how or why he's here.

"If your life were a poem, little raven"—Unferth leans across the table—"what would the hero do next?"

I take a deep breath. Raising my bottle of beer, I say, "Let's go find me a troll."

THREE

THAT NIGHT WE push north around Lake Mishigam a couple of hours to camp in an old trailer park he knows. He says we'll start again when the sun rises, because as we head into troll country it's safest to drive only during the day. It'll take nearly two days that way, heading east on the Trans-Canadia Highway toward the ruins of Montreal, where Unferth will teach me what he knows of hunting and fighting trolls until the ice is thick enough for the greater mountain trolls to migrate down to the coast of Quebec to hunt seals. There I'll make my kill. By Yule if I'm lucky, he says, in a tone that suggests he doubts it.

"I've never seen one," I say out the dark window, remembering illustrations in kids' books of the greater mountain trolls, with massive yellow eyes and bloody tusks and claws exactly sized to drag children away for midnight snacks. There are five distinct types of troll on our continent: the dangerous but small cat wights; curious iron wights; their larger cousins the hill trolls, with ape-like arms and thick, rough skin; vicious prairie trolls, who prefer human flesh to any other; and, worst of all, the greater mountain trolls.

It's the mountain trolls that are the stars of the old stories, the oldest and smartest of all, who hunt and haunt ruins or swamps or the crags of mountains that dragons have abandoned. The sort that gather in massive herds and have been known to use tools and paint their stone bodies with mud or blood before attacking. Their attacks are rare, but when they charge, they destroy everything in their path. I hardly know a thing about them that I didn't learn from bad TV movies and picture books.

Unferth says, "A troll?"

"A greater mountain troll. This last year while I was wandering, I used to see iron wights all the time—they make little houses under steel bridges and sometimes squat in the same warehouses the other street kids and I did." I recall the odd way the wights' huge eyes blink one at a time.

Iron wights look like human toddlers from a distance, except their skin is flaky and orange or reddish. They might wear mismatched clothes and are hardly capable of language. They hoard lost tools and random shiny items, though, and we offered them snacks of rusted nails or the chunk of an old car in return for the copper pipes and knives they didn't use but collected anyway.

"You won't be ready the first time you face a greater mountain troll," Unferth says. "They're massive, and smarter than you can imagine."

"Fantastic."

He slows the truck to a stop in the middle of the highway. The engine rumbles, but I hear the creaking trees beside the road. Unferth glances at me, hands on the wheel. The glow from the dash paints bluish shadows across his face. "Now is the time to give up if you're going to."

I wipe damp palms on my jeans.

"You're afraid," he says.

"I'm *excited.*"

"I thought we weren't going to lie to each other."

Leaning back into the cloth seat, I put my boots on the dash. "I never agreed to that."

The darkness swallows his smile, but for the glint of teeth. The hairs on my forearms rise as he dives lovingly into a retelling of the murder of Luta Bearsdottir's family by greater mountain trolls in the Rock Mountains, followed by the saga of the Nordakota Prairie Massacre, and finally *The Lament of the Mere Troll.* He illustrates broken limbs and blood spatter and battle frenzy, all with a surprising number of rhymes for carnage. I've heard the stories before, recited the elegies, but inside the small truck cab, with his odd rhythmic accent and nothing outside but acres of wilderness, it all comes horribly alive.

Trolls could be hiding in the black forest as it flashes darkly past. This Trans-Canadia Highway we're heading for is the farthest northern evidence of New Asgard in the east. Farther north in Ontario we'd only find isolated homesteads and walled farms, but usually they're boarded up and abandoned this time of year against the greater mountain trolls who come down from the ice as winter presses at them, searching for greater sources of food. There's not been a settlement attack along this stretch in twenty years, but isolated travelers are much more at risk.

We reach the trailer park, a spread of abandoned electric hookups and overgrown picnic tables. The cab isn't terribly comfortable for sleeping, even bundled under blankets Unferth drags out of the covered truck bed. He's got thick spears back there, too, and a couple of axes, therma-wool coats and sleeping bags, and not a lot of food. But we only have to make it to his base outside the ruins of Montreal.

I fall asleep with the blanket over my head to stop myself from imagining the mountain trolls from Unferth's poems hulking between the trees. Their huge black shadows have piercing yellow or red eyes, tusks and hammer-fists, hot breath like fog in the cold night. As I sweat, I remind myself that the best glory will come from taking the heart of a greater mountain troll. They are the devils of our stories, and a stone heart from such a creature will be magnificent, the size of my head. How glorious it will look held in my hands when I bring it to the New World Tree. Perhaps I'll cast it in silver and have it mounted over my throne.

Our first full day together, the sun shines along flat fields of wild corn and wheatgrasses broken and brown for the winter. They stretch like patchwork blankets toward a horizon I can see clearly. The crisp lines between gray and gold, between blue sky and white cloud, and the distant green hills layer over each other carefully, even artfully. It reminds me of Elisa's glorious prairie.

We try the radio, but bad lyrics make Unferth cranky, and it's half static besides. He asks me about myself for entertainment; first if I've got family, and second what I've done to keep myself fed the past few months. I tell him about my parents' best friends, the Summerlings, devout Freyans who took me in when my parents died. Rome and Jesca and their son, Rathi. I miss them during the harvest months, when the leaves turn red and I remember the bonfires and sweet smell of horse barns where we lived briefly down in the Cherokeen kingstate. They moved up northeast to some historic settlement after I climbed the Tree, and I've not seen them but for Rathi last summer.

And as for my life without the Death Hall, ah, that I can paint for Unferth as a glorified adventure, filled with my own band of scraggly, wisecracking friends, militia officers as our arch-nemeses, abundant street-shine, odd jobs that led to treasure, fortresses under city bridges, helpful matrons at the Lokiskin shelters, creepers, and secrets and wonder.

He laughs and I like the spiky edges of it.

I add, "Someday they'll tell the story that the Valkyrie of the Tree fended for herself, that I became part of the city, lived in the shadows of New Asgard, with the lowliest, with the half-dead, the nameless. They'll say I understand roots better, I understand decay better, because I surrounded myself with it."

He says, "And what is the truth?"

"Doesn't that depend on who's asking?"

"No. You know. The poet always knows."

"The truth . . . I found jobs, slept where I could, and . . ." I hesitate, but what's to stop me from complete honesty other than fear? "The truth is, I did learn about longing and street miracles and cold and hunger; I understood decay and hopelessness and those magical, shadowy places where life forces its way through cracks in the concrete. But I never was afraid, because I could have gone home anytime. Called one of the Valkyrie anytime. I never *was* hopeless or starving or alone. Every moment of it felt like living a story, not living a life."

Unferth looks at me the longest he's ever taken his eyes off the road, and again, and again, eyes flicking between my face and the highway, narrowing more each time as if he has to tear them away from me.

I shrug my sudden discomfort away and slump into the passenger seat. The sun is low behind us, melting the rearview mirrors orange and pushing our shadow ahead of us. I always like that, when my shadow touches a place before I do.

"Tell me a moment you did feel alive," he finally says.

"You first," I whisper.

He sighs as if letting go of a great weight. "The first time I faced a troll, swallowed his hot, rotten-berry breath, felt his iron claws scrape my bones hard enough to spark. Little feels as real as your own blood on your hands. Or the blood of someone you love."

"Is that why you limp?"

"Among other things."

I glance at him, still standing by my first assessment that he's only five years older than me—if he's not immortal. "I can't think of a troll attack in the past ten years, not a bad one where people died."

Unferth is silent. Because that was no actual question. I ask, "Where were you attacked?"

"On the ice," he murmurs with a tiny smile.

I groan. "What ice?"

"The long-since-melted kind."

"Unferth."

"Your turn. A real moment for a real moment."

The first thing that occurs to me is awful, but I spit it out. "Sitting on Rome's—on my wish-father's—lap when he told me my parents were dead. There was a tiny blue horse charm tied into his beard, and I stared at it and stared at it. He stroked my hair and it was like I could feel every individual strand where it connected to my scalp. I thought I might die from the pressure of it. I was so alive." I touch my chest with my middle finger but don't need to hold anything in. That desperation passed a long time ago.

"I remember when my father died," Unferth says. Before I can press, he flips on the headlights and peers at the gauges on the dash. "We need more gas."

We sleep that night inside the protection of a walled gas stop. Its tanks are refilled once a week by a convoy out of Toronto, Unferth explains.

I've hardly slept at all when the day begins with a muffled dawn. Clouds cap the sky, but there's a line of violet and silver at the eastern horizon. Today we'll reach his base at the ruins of Montreal. As we drive, Unferth murmurs under his breath. It's Old Anglish, like his name, and I know many of the words but am not fluent enough to parse the meaning beyond that it's a prayer.

"Teach me?" I ask, late in the morning.

He darts a glance at me; I've surprised him.

"I have a better idea," he answers, and starts in with the first lines of *The Song of Beowulf.*

Over the long hours of the drive, he recites the entire three-thousand-line poem.

I put my feet on the dash and close my eyes. The vibration of the truck and cold, lonely wind lulls me into a space between waking and sleeping, where Unferth's poetry evokes imagery of Heorot, the great hall of King Hrothgar Shielding, and the tragedy of its occupation by the monster Grendel for nine long years. The devastation and hopelessness of his people and retainers, the fury and desperation of his wife, Valtheow the Dark, who sacrificed and prayed to summon the power to defeat Grendel. Unferth shows me their relief when Beowulf came from over the sea to save them, and he twists his words as if drunk to voice the protestations of his namesake poet who challenged Beowulf's worthiness before giving the berserker his own sword.

I see the torn limbs and hear the wails of grief; my heart breaks when Grendel's mother sings a lament for her dead son. I imagine Valtheow herself as she brings a goblet of mead to Beowulf in celebration.

After lunch Unferth recites the confrontation between Beowulf Berserk and the troll mother, Grendel's dam, who attacked Heorot in revenge. How Beowulf and Unferth and Valtheow followed her to the cave under the mere, and with Unferth's sword Beowulf slew her. From my Unferth's lips, the song describes their battle like a dance, like a meeting of lovers, and tears dampen my lashes when the troll mother dies. I can hardly believe he's made me mourn the monster.

There are lines I whisper with him, my favorite passages about Valtheow or the Frisian funeral, with its meditation on the glory of battle versus the viciousness of war, but his version differs slightly from the standard. His adds words or half lines to complete the alliterations or perfect the caesuras, as if his version was written in Modern Anglish instead of translated from more ancient tongues. The eloquence of his rhythm never falters, like it's his natural way of speaking, and I realize that *this* is his accent: not a lilt of regionalism or upbringing. Ned Unferth talks as if he's always reciting poetry, even when telling me how many kilometers to Montreal or ordering me to remove my boots from the dash.

As the sun sets he dives into the final part, years after Beowulf defeated the trolls, when he goes as an old king to face the woken dragon. The rhythm of it shifts, not quite as eloquent, as if it were penned by a different poet. But my thoughts are all dragon fire and gold hoards, and though I have to pee, though my stomach reminds me it's been hours since lunch, I wouldn't interrupt him for even Odin's sake.

He finishes the song quietly, not with the excitement or awe I'm used to but with a sour note, as if the hero Beowulf does not quite deserve his final praise.

We're silent, and the lack of poetry is like a roar. I turn away, watching black Canadian forest pass by, and cling to the poem. If I do anything else, or look at him, I'll stamp his name against my heart forever.

FOUR

UNFERTH'S BASE IS an abandoned meadery outside the ruins of Montreal. There's broken asphalt underfoot when we park, an hour past sunset, and Unferth surprises me by taking my hand to lead me through the darkness toward the black shadow of the building. I stop, though, to stare up at the brilliant stars. They're thick as spilled salt in the freezing night, and without being told I recognize the Milk Path for the first time. A sliver moon hardly disrupts the glorious heavens, and I'm dizzy as I stare at it all, at the huge arc of sky, because there's more stars than earth and for a moment I don't think anything is real except those billions of tiny lights.

Unferth squeezes my fingers. "Here the mask of daylight stripped away," he murmurs.

"What poem is that?"

"It isn't one. Yet." He smiles briefly so his teeth catch the moonlight. *Truth* shines silver beside his pupil. A star itself, caught there forever.

"Why do you always tell the truth?" I ask.

His good mood breaks, and he lets go of my hand.

I press on. "Is it to build trust? To make me trust you?"

Though only the stars are watching us, he backs away from me and murmurs, "Perhaps you shouldn't, little raven." He walks swiftly away, limping toward the abandoned meadery and the doors leaning off their hinges.

The danger implied by his answer makes me recall what the Alfather said to me: *fear and excitement belong in the same breath.*

I hurry to follow him inside. There are no lights in the lobby, and dim moonlight presses its way through cracks in the roof to reveal a long counter and dusty old shelves where once bottles would've been displayed, and cups for a mead-tasting. My boots crack against broken glass, and even decades later a sour honey smell hangs in the air. It seeps into my hair like sticky smoke. I breathe deeply. The broken glass shimmers in the moonlight, and I decide this beautiful abandonment is a good sign in favor of this quest.

Twelve rickety stairs lead into the cellar, where Unferth keeps only a cot and sleeping bag, plus a short table and stools, tin coffee mugs stacked beside one, and a gas stove sitting in the middle of the floor.

Thick wooden beams hold up the plaster ceiling, and the floor laminate curls in the corners. An elaborate copper distillery covers the rear wall, where Unferth uses the pots and tubes to make some kind of street-shine. Smells like corn mash, which we'd have sold fingers to get ahold of in the Chicagland alleys. Three oak barrels tuck into the corner, one of them tapped with a thin spigot. We won't be thirsty.

It's warm, and behind a thin plywood door is a toilet and crudely rigged shower. I hang my coat on a nail and am moved in within minutes. All my possessions fit into the pockets of that coat: tightly rolled shirts and panties, toothbrush and hairpins, a comb, camping tools like fishing wire and matches, and a variety of oddities. Some notes and coins. Two slim books. While Unferth unloads his truck, I shower awkwardly and slip into the sleeping bag. I hear him clattering around but keep my eyes pressed shut. He doesn't complain I stole his bed.

And good thing, too, because at dawn he knocks me out of it and stuffs me full of coffee and protein before dragging me up to the empty display room to assess my combat skills.

To my pleasure, I hold my own. I can box and have a strong front kick, I'm excellent with the seax, and I can run and climb trees and lift rocks as long as he likes, though my endurance turns out to be the only thing Unferth bothers to praise. He's appalled I only know how to use a sword in combination with a round-shield, which a troll will break in seconds, and sneers at my hand-to-hand, says it's built for speed and escape, not taking on an enemy of any stature. "You must be stronger to face the mountain trolls," he says, "or use the right techniques to fake it."

I'm so determined to prove him wrong that I gather bouquets of blisters on my palms from his heavy troll-spears. Unferth is a fast and cranky teacher, voice impatient when I don't angle my hips correctly or shift my alignment to something more comfortable. He unceremoniously grabs my shoulders or slaps away a hand when he needs to, grunting with exasperation at my *fancy Valkyrie-style* footwork. It might look impressive on TV, he says, but it won't hold for two breaths against an opponent with the bulk of a greater mountain troll. They use their fists like hammers and will rush forward, knocking anything out of their way. Running or climbing to higher ground is usually the right course, but in my case to kill one I have to learn to use physics in my favor.

He stomps the spear butt into the cold ground, secures it with the sole of his boot, and points the wicked blade up at forty-five degrees with a sharp war cry. I copy him, minus the cry, and he says, "No, little raven, no. Vocalize! Focus your energy and aggression with your voice—give the Alfather the wordless poetry of battle; scream for him; cry for him!"

Unferth provides workout clothes for me, and a sturdy hunting outfit. I try to hide my relief at fresh new clothes. It's been weeks since I had anything not worn thin from rough hand-washing.

At night when I'm too exhausted to move, he breaks out a flask of his home-brew. He offers it to me, and I take too large a swallow, gasping and tearing up at the burn. "It's called screech," he says calmly, rubbing rough circles against my back as I hold on to my knees in an awkward crouch.

We feast on jerky and dried fruit, oatmeal we cook on the gas stove, or rehydrated stew and canned chili. As we nibble and drink, we flyt. It's an elaborate game of back-and-forth riddles and insults, the more rhythmic and poetical the better. Unferth introduces myth and history into it right away, so we're not insulting each other so much as creatively dragging Sanctus Grim's parentage through the mud or making fun of Fafnir and Loki and Sigurd Dragonslayer or, more frequently than is fair, Thor Thunderer.

The game continues until I fall asleep in the middle of his triumphant verse, and we pick it back up in the morning. Between laps, between sparring matches, we keep up the back-and-forth, though he wins every time.

On the third afternoon he takes me out tracking. He shows me how the forest should look, what's normal as a baseline, before he starts pointing out deer paths and scat and frost-covered tracks. We spend little time with such signs, as trolls themselves are both exceedingly obvious and nearly impossible to detect.

I'm to look for exposed rocks first of all, as trolls turn to stone under the sun and prefer to find natural stone where they'll stand out less. A giant boulder in the middle of a field won't keep any troll safe. When there's no stone in sight, I should begin with water, since like all living things they have to drink, and soft earth holds footprints. If there's a deep-enough river, a troll may even hide from the sun below the surface. The oldest may go hours without air. He's heard of troll mothers pushing their already-calcified youngest sons into lakes and rivers to hide them from other trolls or Thor's Army. Not this far north in the winter, he adds, because of the thick ice.

We also keep our eyes open for shallow caves carved into

the hillsides or overhangs, and check the ceilings for smoke sign. Trolls scatter the ashes of their fires but rarely rub out the char marks.

"Trolls cook their food?" I interrupt, appalled.

"If their mother is wise." It's the troll mothers who determine a herd's behavior, he says. In all troll species that gather into such family groups it's the case, but especially with the greater mountain trolls. If the mother is smart, she'll teach her sons wider vocabulary and to use simple tools or paint with mud and scar their own bodies for decoration. A triumvirate of ancient, shrewd troll mothers was responsible for the Montreal Troll Wars in the first place, able to command their own army and even negotiate with Thor Thunderer.

I thought such things were only legend. I thought the stories of peace talks were exaggerated, but Unferth is too grave as he explains it for that to be the case.

Lucky for us, he's not heard of troll mothers working together since the burning of Montreal.

I wonder if in the end it will be the heart of a mother I take back to the Alfather.

Abruptly Unferth crouches down with a tight wince, favoring his left leg. He scrapes a finger through dead leaves, revealing grayish dirt. "Do you know, little raven, how trolls came to be?"

I do, but say, "Tell me."

He pauses just long enough to let me know he sees my dissembling, then begins. "In ancient days, when the frost giants pressed south hard and harder against our gods, the brave northern kings who carved out livings at the bases of glaciers begged the gods for a weapon against them. Thor, who loves men, asked his cousin Loki Changer to use what magic he could to fashion it. And so Loki drew fire from the earth and pressed it into the chests of thirteen men.

"But the fire burned the men, devouring them completely. Loki turned to the goblins-under-the-mountain, who were no friend of his but owed him. The goblin queen set her best smiths to discovering a solution that would allow the monstrous men to hold the fire in their hearts without burning. Yet even their skills, even their mountain forges and moon-silver tools, could not find a way.

"As intrigued as she was frustrated, the goblin queen sought out Freya, the feather-flying goddess of magic, who is herself a daughter of goblins and of elves. And Freya, always twining her fingers into the strands of fate, looked far into every future and smiled. The queen of dreams took the fire of the earth, formed it into a brilliant charm, and put it into the heart of a woman. The magic overwhelmed the woman, but she kept her mind. That woman became the first troll, the mother of all trolls. From her were born the race of trollkin, monstrous as their monstrous mother.

"Freya said to the goblin queen, 'Only magic as powerful as the earth's fire can hold such creatures alive, and the only fire as strong as the earth's belongs to the sun.' And so to balance the magic, the troll mothers and their children were cursed to transform into stone whenever the sun cast its light upon them, that the rock of the earth itself might contain their inner fire."

Unferth's voice fades and he waits expectantly. I say, "If that's the case, where did cat wights and iron eaters come from?"

He smiles. "Early experiments the goblins performed with tundra cats and monkeys?"

I laugh to think of elegant elves and crystal-boned goblins fussing with a basket of cats.

"So you believe they evolved as the rest of us did," he says, combing through the brown leaves again with his fingers.

"Why not?"

He tosses a fistful of leaves away in frustration.

I kneel beside him. "What are you looking for?"

"Last winter this was a path they used to travel to the ruins of Montreal. There were frequently prints. It must be nearer the creek than I remembered."

"I'll find them." I crash ahead, stomping through the low growth with my boots, not waiting for him.

Unferth calls after me, "There's another story that the trolls were born the bastard sons of fallen Valkyrie."

I stop, my back to him. His tone says he meant it obnoxiously, that he's needling me. And so I slowly turn around and make as vicious a face as I can. "Then I should be very good at hunting them, shouldn't I?"

My voice rings between us, light and sharp, and Unferth's eyes pinch in a secret smile that never quite touches his mouth.

It's becoming my favorite expression of his.

+ + +

The next morning—two before my birthday—Unferth packs camping gear and all manner of weapons and leads me southeast toward the ruins of Montreal, to show me the damage greater mountain trolls can do, and maybe even find one so I can begin to appreciate their real size and malice. Only to watch from a distance, though I want to get in his face and insist I'm ready now, I've been training all my life for this. I suspect that is exactly the opposite way of convincing him. Ned Unferth needs poetry and action, not impatience.

We hike at least fifteen kilometers with troll-spears and heavy packs, and despite the winter I'm glad my coat is tied over my pack instead of around my shoulders. The therma-wool shirt Unferth provided is plenty warm, and sweat stings my eyes.

The forests are thin but wild, with thick underbrush and cold, leafless branches that clatter together in the wind. We tromp through fields, some with evidence of fifty-year-old farms: half-buried giant tractor wheels, silos missing all their tiles and roofs, crumbling troll-walls graffitied with the *thorn* rune, which has always signified a warning that *here be trolls.* Most of them are faded or obscured by weeds. A few walls still protect farmhouses and barns, whose broken windows reflect the light like eyes.

At lunch we break to spar with the troll-spears and for me to find at least three places a mountain troll might hide from the sun amidst the abandoned traces of humanity.

As evening approaches we climb to the top of a hill from which we can see in the distance the ruined skyline that used to be the city of Montreal. Blocky buildings that were in fashion sixty years ago and the dark gray and brown of trees grown up in the streets, gaping holes from the bombing that destroyed half the city before Thor Thunderer and the troll mothers made their treaty.

"This," he says as I catch my breath. "This is evidence of their power. Even in your grandmother's day, with all the heliplanes and machine guns and technology of mankind, the trolls took back Montreal, where hundreds of years ago they'd ruled. The mothers worked together, brought their herds into one massive herd, and when the sun was gone they attacked. Again and again, disappearing at dawn into the Lawrence River, hiding in basements, and even using runework to appear like man-made slabs of concrete, they attacked every time the sun fell. They crushed skulls and set fire to homes, they chased men and women out of the city, and even when Thor's Army arrived with their heliplanes and their bombs, even when hundreds of trolls died and were shattered into dust, the troll mothers did not let up the charge."

"They say most of the troll mothers died." I wave my hand at the distant skyline. "Thor tracks them; there are scientists, and that Freekin Project with the reserve in the desert. They say there are not enough of them left to be a threat."

Unferth takes the flask of his screech out of the inner pocket of his tattered gray coat. "And yet . . . Montreal remains a ruin."

I shrug. "We have a long memory."

"*Yes.*" He offers me the drink and I take it. I lift it up so the metal catches the evening sun behind us. It's only light, none of its warmth penetrating the winter air.

"To the slaughtered," I declare. "The men and monsters both, the mothers and women, the children." I knock back a burning gulp, and as the fire scorches down my throat I think I can hear screams echoing. I cough, bending to lean my hands on my knees. My throat is raw, as if I've been the one screaming.

Unferth snatches his flask back. "To the poetry the dead leave behind." A pause as he drinks. "May it not be all that is left of you, little raven," he mutters.

"Poetry is all any of us leave behind." I lift my chin defiantly.

We plow north around part of the city, but see only a few trees scoured of bark that might suggest trolls crashed through here. I find no footprints. As the sun sets we hear a long, echoing cry, a moan from the far distant city, and Unferth nods at me. "Not a battle cry, but a simple communication that she is awake."

"She?"

"The mothers wake first, always."

I listen until the moan fades completely, just as the light does. I want to go down into the city and find her, but Unferth insists the time is not right, the place not right. We'll hunt when we are ready, not before, not because it's the first I've heard her promising cry.

We make camp in the shell of a farmhouse, surrounded by mostly intact troll walls. There's no fire, but we have a small battery-powered lamp. Its even light is more eerie than flickering flames might have been, illuminating rotting old chairs and a table still set with a runner and vase. I sink onto the worn rug while Unferth settles with a groan on a short old sofa printed with dull cabbage roses. He sips his screech and says, "Tell me, Signy, why you love Valtheow the Dark most of all."

I lick my lips and reach for the flask. The blistering trail it leaves down my tongue gives fire to my words. "Nothing about her was half-done. She did not symbolically bleed; she poured her own blood out for sacrifice. She tied a rope around her neck. She . . . embraced passion and war like they *were* poetry, not only things to be described by it." I gather my knees to my chest. "Since Odin first told me her name I knew she never hesitated to embody death, the way it feeds life."

"Why do you want to be like her?"

"It's exciting! It—it thrills me. It's this . . ." I close my eyes and recall my Alfather again, arm around me so my ear presses to his thrumming heart. "An itch like madness, that I was born with. That drives me forward."

"It's dangerous."

"Everything worth doing is dangerous, Unferth."

He contemplates me as he drinks, one hand loose on the arm of the couch, his injured right leg stretched out so his pose is languid. The more I talk about this, the more I want to make him understand. I grab the flask from his hand and plop down beside him on the couch. My legs hook over his outstretched thigh and our shoulders touch as I drink. He sets his head against the wall. I let the vertigo of liquor sway me against him until I'm leaning. The upstairs floor groans gently. The electric lamp buzzes. I can hear the rush of my own blood in my ears.

"What would you do with that power if you had it?" he asks.

"Change the world," I murmur contentedly.

"Don't you mean destroy your enemies and paint your face with their blood?"

"Isn't that the definition of change?"

"Ambitious."

"No good reason to aim low."

His shoulder trembles and I realize he's laughing. I poke his ribs and he catches my hand. He turns it over and smooths out my fingers until he can see the binding rune. As he taps my scar with his thumb, a hot line sears from my palm to my belly. "Death Chooser," he says. "Strange Maid."

"What?" I whisper. The runes bound together into my palm are an odd variation of *death* and *choice* and *servant.* After parsing them out years ago, I had assumed they only meant to mark me as a Valkyrie. A Death Chooser.

"This binding rune is from a very old thread of language . . ." His breath touches my temple, curling down my cheek until I turn into it. There are his rain-colored eyes, alight with *truth.* He says, "Death is linguistically connected to *otherness,* to foreigners and . . . strangeness. Death and stranger, like different fruit on the same linguistic branch. You can trace all kinds of names through the binding rune. Like . . . Alfather—Valfather. Valborn, Valkyrie, *Valtheow,* death-born, Death Chooser, servant of death, death maid . . . *Strange Maid.*"

My breath catches in my throat. We are the Strange Maid and Ned the Spiritless, finally together again. The thought comes from nowhere as Unferth closes his eyes and settles his head against the wall, his hand loose around mine.

FIVE

ON MY BIRTHDAY I wake alone in the cellar and slowly realize there's no metallic click of tin cups or the unconscious groan Unferth makes when he sits or stands. He's not sipping his doctored chocolate on a squeaky stool, waiting for the right moment to limp over here and nudge me awake with the toe of his boot.

I throw off the heavy sleeping bag and grab my seax out of the scabbard before heading up the cellar stairs.

Late-morning sunlight streams through the roof and cracked windows, bringing fire to the shards of glass spilled across the wooden floor. The front of the abandoned meadery is even sadder in daylight, and I crunch through it to the rear, where all the old shelves and bottle boxes are shoved to the side to create a clear arena. Three troll-spears lean against the wall; there are his bootprints and mine, scuffs and shuffles from sparring. A chipped wooden round-shield tilts upside down like a turtle on its shell.

And one of the old tarps is spread out at my feet, paint

scrawled across it to read: *Find me.* He's written the rune for *spirit* and crossed it out as an ironic sort of signature.

It's a test.

I dash back downstairs for my belt and coat, though I dump the unnecessary items from the pockets: comb, hairpins, a copy of *Birds of the Middle World,* and a slim volume of Freyan songs Rathi gave me with a gentle inscription that always makes me feel guilty. I keep my fishing line, matches and lighter, mini-flashlight, insultingly small wad of notes, and pocketknife. I grab two of the protein bars and a bag of trail mix, stuffing both into the pocket that formerly housed the books. I wash up fast, use the toilet, and braid up all my hair into a messy crown. Before starting out I return to the meadery for one of the troll-spears and sling the shield across my back.

My guess is I'm not hunting Unferth, I'm hunting Unferth-pretending-to-be-a-troll, so it's troll-sign I should look for: broken tree limbs, flattened underbrush, stone, or fire. There's nothing at the edges of the parking lot, though I walk the perimeter twice and slowly. I head for the creek, because he said they need water.

It's a quick hike over rough forested land, cold and dim from the heavy evergreens pressing all around. But there's no snow and the frost is thin, melting in patches so I can't even tell if he came this way. Birds trill at odd intervals and everything smells of crisp ice and tangy evergreen sap. I can't help smiling, despite the heavy shield and awkward troll-spear I have to wedge in the crook of my elbow so my whole arm carries the weight instead of only hand and wrist.

The creek is wide enough I couldn't leap across without the spear to use as a pole. There's no sign of Unferth here, but I head downstream, deciding the creek might widen or spill into a larger body of water, where either a troll could hide or there might be a deposit of glacier boulders or other exposed stone.

I go quietly now, knowing that though the sun is high, the oldest trolls could be awake in this pockmarked shade. Unferth said the adolescents can't take sunlight filtered through cloud cover and when they calcify they look like rough-cut marble statues of themselves. But the strongest, and the troll mothers, not only can move slowly through morning or evening light; they can force their calcification into bulky, nonspecific shapes and truly huddle like boulders.

The banks of the creek grow steeper. The trees lean around me. Heavy clouds roll over the sky and it grows dark, but my eyes adjust to the variations of shadow. I keep them up on the trees, searching for a swath of broken branches, and finally see a row of baby trees cracked halfway up their trunks as if something quite huge shoved through.

I pull myself up the bank with a wrist-thick root to where there was a small fire. The smell hangs lonely around it. I hover my hand over the ashes, but there's no residual heat: it's been out for a while. Scouring the area, I find a print hidden half under the weeping feathers of grass. It's nearly circular, with deep gouges where the claws would be, impressed into the ground litter. I settle for a moment, leaning on the troll-spear, and drink some water. Eat a handful of nut mix. Then I take off at a jog, going parallel to the creek but up on the bank. The spear knocks against my shoulder, and the round-shield rubs the small of my back.

In perhaps another half kilometer I burst out through a layer of trees and nearly fall headlong into a meter-deep gully. With a tiny cry, I catch myself on the rough trunk of a tree and hold tight, entirely winded and heart pounding. A flatter stream, more like runoff from rain, spreads beneath me, reflecting the gray cloudy sunlight. The mud clearly displays troll footprints.

Sliding haphazardly down the bank, my boots crack through a thin layer of ice and sink into a layer of slimy mud. I inspect the prints. They're two hand spans across, but I see the tread of Unferth's boots in them. He must've stamped out these vaguely troll-shaped tracks. I laugh a little.

The tracks lead away from the creek.

Ice begins to fall from the sky, hissing against the bare branches and thick umbrellas of pine needles. I hook the shield off my back and lift it over my head to keep ice out of my eyes as I follow this uphill path marked only by crushed and slightly disturbed undergrowth. My arms tire quickly and I'm huffing before long.

Once or twice I worry I've lost the trail, and I stop. I close my eyes and listen. I breathe deeply through my nose, trying to smell smoke or the sweetness Unferth insists is the greater mountain troll scent. There's only the dull moan of wind and hiss of snow. I press on, both times finding sign again: first an uprooted baby tree, and second, three fresh gouges in a reddish trunk that are too perfect to be made by actual claws.

I come to a meadow and wince away from the white glare of sunlight on ice and snow. Tucking against a tree until my vision adjusts, I realize there are rocks here, large ones on the opposite edge of the meadow, where the land cuts up sharply into a short mountain. A perfect place for troll-Unferth to hide.

But there's nothing to see besides gray and white and dismal yellow deadfall. I start across and something hard hits my shoulder.

Spinning, tearing the shield down before me, I fall into a ready stance, knees bent, and I slam the butt of the thick troll-spear into the frozen grass and brace it with the sole of my boot just as Ned Unferth throws his body against me. The blunt tip dents the huge leather cushion he's got strapped to his torso, but he rolls and shoves into the shaft with a yell. I stumble, and swing the spear around in a fast arc to hit his shoulder. He retaliates with a hard punch to my ribs with weighted mitts that turn his fists into hammers.

They make him slower, but his punch knocks the breath out of me.

Cold wind burns down my throat as I gasp for air. Ned charges sluggishly forward, like the very trolls he's teaching me to fight, and raises both fists up for a heavy blow.

I scuttle back, dropping everything, and head for the boulders. He gives chase, laughing out a guttural roar like the challenging cry of a real greater mountain troll. I run full out, hitting the tallest boulder hard, and scramble up onto it. Unferth can't follow me with his troll gear. I stand and yell wordlessly. He glares up at me with his colorless eyes, opens his mouth to chastise me, no doubt for escaping, when I bend my knees and smile.

He only has time to realize what I'm doing before I launch myself down at him.

We slam together into the meadow.

All the leather cushioning and Ned keep me safe, but I roll off him fast before he can get a good grip. He doesn't move.

I spread out my arms and pant, sweat tingling at my hairline. Tiny pellets of snow prick my cheeks, melting down the hot skin. "Does that . . . count . . . as a win?" I gasp after a moment.

There's no immediate response besides his own labored breathing, and if I had the energy, I'd crow with triumph.

"You took your time getting here," he eventually grumbles.

Rolling, I slap my hand against his stomach, forgetting about the leather cushion. He smiles as I cradle my smarting fingers. "It was well-enough done, little raven," he admits. "Much longer and we'd have been snowed out. But you did let down your guard."

"You said *find me,* not *beware of sudden attacks.*"

"More the fool, you."

I climb to my feet and stare down at him. "Can you stand in that? You look like a beached walrus."

His head is tiny as a pin over the wide, scuffed leather cushion tied around him. He strips off the gloves and unties the heavy ropes securing the cushion. When he stands, it falls off around him like he's shedding a shell. His shirt sticks to his stomach and shoulders, molding into the shape of his muscles like a shellac. He puts his hand on the back of my neck, his fingers freezing against my hot skin. I shiver but return his victorious grin.

Like we're teammates, or partners, Unferth tugs me under his arm, against his side, and clasps me there. I put my arm around his back, hand tentative on his hip, and we face back the way we came. Side by side. His shoulders lift and fall as he sighs with absolute satisfaction.

Steely gray swirling clouds press low to the blackening tree line and snow falls silently, muffling the wind around us. We're the only two people in the world.

Unferth and I drag the cushions, shield, and troll-spear to the other side of the boulders, where he's hidden a sled. It all stacks easily, secured by bungee cords, and we each take a rein to drag it like a pair of workhorses. Snow falls harder as we go, but there's a gravel path this way, narrow and curving widely back toward the meadery. I wish for gloves immediately, and a hood and scarf as I bend into the snow. The wisps of hair loose from my braids freeze to my neck and forehead, and the only thing keeping me warm is the rough work of pulling the sled. We don't speak, our hot breath puffing in rhythm. I lose track of time but for night falling. The wind blows harder and my legs shake from effort and there's as much sweat streaking down my back as snow dripping down my face. My skull begins to throb.

A low moan, like a distant horn, calls out to us. Elf-kisses draw up my spine: we are too close to home, too far from Montreal.

Unferth stops and swings a hand out to stop me, too. "That's not the twilight call."

I blink snow from my eyes and reach for my seax. "What is it?"

His chin is up, eyes on the sky, and when the call repeats I see the tight line of his mouth, the shift of muscles at his jaw. "Danger." He drops the rein with one sharp shake of his head and jerks his hand for me to follow as he pushes on faster. I struggle to catch up. Unferth grabs my coat at the shoulder, bunching it in his fist to keep us together.

The meadery rises through the trees at the end of the gravel road, black and leaning on one side. I never noticed from the front. That low moan calls again, louder and right here. It sounds as if the cry echoes from lungs as large and cavernous as the hollowed-out building. Unferth pulls me close and says into my ear, "Go to the truck and get the UV light from the glove compartment."

Snow topples onto me when I tug open the passenger door, and I shake it off to dig into the narrow glove compartment. There's a wide-faced flashlight that must be the UV. I grab it in stiff fingers and head for the meadery. Its door hangs open, half off the hinges. Unferth is a lithe shadow waiting there, and he nods, points to the button that will turn on the light, and again leans close to whisper in my ear. His breath is warm and all my nerves crystallize into hot, bright excitement at its touch against my neck.

"I'll go first and you follow right after. Be ready to turn it on, and aim for the face. If we blind it—calcify the eyes—it won't be able to defend itself. I'm going to go for the lockbox in the cellar and my sword. You calcify as much as possible and stay out of its way. Understand?"

I nod.

With no further warning, Unferth slips inside.

I follow. The roar comes fast, tripping me as if it's a physical force. I roar back without thinking and flip on the flashlight.

The spear of light scours over the wall and flies across part of the ceiling, bobbing everywhere as I spin, and there! It catches the edge of a bulbous shoulder and I go to my knees as a huge arm swipes for me. I jerk the light up, pinning the spot of it onto the rageful face of a greater mountain troll.

It stumbles back, shaking the floorboards, and cries again, this time high-pitched. I immediately think, *It's terrified.*

Knees burning from the broken glass I landed on, I stand, training the light on the hulking black shadow of the troll.

It hides its face with one hand, still backing up, messily, heavily. I follow. Under my light, the troll's bluish skin cracks and hardens, turning paler and mottled bluish gray, but only as long as the light remains. It turns, knocking shoulders into the wall, careening the other direction until it hits the counter and then lashes out at me.

I fall back, seeing stubby tusks and bright fangs flash. I

catch myself hard on one hand, bite my tongue, but keep the light up as my shield.

There's Unferth suddenly, tossing a chain around the troll's neck, putting his sword to its throat. The monster's small yellow eyes roll and I shine my light directly into them. It cries again, but it hunkers down. It covers its head with one arm, curls into a ball. It's missing its other arm, and the stump bleeds thick purple ichor.

"Hold it, Signy," Unferth says calmly, evenly. "Take my sword in your other hand."

He transfers the grip to me and I try not to shake. The tip of the sword scrapes against the troll's shoulder and the light bobs, tracing an uneven line of calcification from the troll's head down its chest. The poor thing moans, digging its fingers into its hardening skin.

Unbelievably, my heart aches. It must be in pain. Afraid and alone.

Even as small as it can make itself, the troll remains a solid two meters at the shoulder, and if it stood straight it would certainly be three. Unferth tightens the chain around its neck, puts more around its wrists and feet, too, punching it to get it to shift and let him in. He's unafraid, methodical, and excellent at looping the chains. He has a sledgehammer from somewhere and hammers the ends of the chains into the wooden floor.

Just before my strength gives out, Unferth gently takes back his sword, and the UV light as well.

Outside the snowstorm howls.

"Happy birthday, Signy," Unferth finally says.

SIX

SNOW CRYSTALS HANG off the troll's blunt tusks, glittering in the thin morning light from the broken windows. Because he's young, his calcified features are a rough sketch carved into the stone. He's a beautiful pale blue, with darker blue veins like polished marble. His right arm is missing from just below the shoulder, torn away—recently, too, by the thick purplish blood now crystallized into amethyst. The edge of the shoulder is sharp and rough, like broken rock. A line of reddish lichen crawls down his spine. Unferth says it'll get thicker as he ages.

We've waited until the sun arrived in order to take this next step in a more controlled fashion, so the troll is trapped inside the meadery just in case.

"Shut it," I say, gripping my seax in my fist.

From atop a ladder missing several rungs, Unferth reaches out and swings the shutters closed. Snow puffs down. "He might be too young, and so even this ambient light could keep him calcified. . . ." His voice fades away as the beast's entire body shivers.

I lift my seax to put the sharp tip of the broken back blade against the troll's marble chest. Over his heart. I hold my breath, wondering why the entire world doesn't pause for the occasion. Here I am, ready to slice into this martyr who came to me like a gift. The stone heart will be crusted with blood crystallized to amethyst.

As the troll wakes, dust flakes away from his skin and settles onto the mangy rug. The chain looped around his neck rattles. Tiny cracks appear all over his body, like the bed of a sun-baked river.

A fissure catches my eye: it looks like the rune *child.*

I suck in a quick breath and pull back the seax.

"The gift of mothers," I whisper to myself. A kenning for sacrifice. Mothers always lose the most, they say.

A thin layer of stone sloughs off from his chest. The pieces clatter and clink down to the floor.

This is too easy. Here is a lost troll, crippled and weak, hardly ferocious, as trolls are supposed to be. I'm not even afraid of him. Defeating him barely counts as a triumph.

"Signy," Unferth says softly from right beside me. "Why do you hesitate?"

The troll opens his mouth, revealing square molars, and he moans. His breath is sweet like rotten bananas.

"This is wrong," I say, thinking of the rune *sacrifice* in Malchai Elizabethson's iris. I will know my martyr when I see him.

Big yellow eyes creak open and the troll cries out, pushing away from us, but he's chained to the floor and can't go anywhere.

Unferth lowers his sword and says tentatively, "Wrong?"

The troll is at least a meter taller than me, thick and shaped like a giant gorilla. He winces from the light, one wide yellow eye on me. He's awkward and broken and how can his heart possibly mean anything to the Alfather?

I spin and stalk away, kicking a dusty mead bottle. It skitters across the floor and shatters against the far wall. "It's not right! I could never sacrifice a half-broken animal or man to my god. What honor could he bring to Odin? What could this heart possibly prove?" I jam the seax back into its sheath. *"Rag me."*

The troll groans loudly enough to shake the shards of glass that litter the floor. I have a devastating urge to feed him.

"Here, stop." Unferth thumps the troll on the chest, and the troll swipes at him with his one good hand. Unferth touches his sword to the troll's stomach and presses lightly, but enough that the tip cuts in. The troll howls as tiny streaks of violet blood drip down his belly.

"This sword is an unhallowed blade and made to kill the likes of you, so behave," Unferth says to the troll, then turns his back. The beast leans down onto his haunches, curls his only arm around his belly pathetically.

I stare at Unferth as he limps toward me. "Unhallowed? What does that mean?"

Eyes tight and leaning onto his good leg, Unferth wipes a smear of purple blood off his blade and onto his pants. "Cursed. A blade that has been used for ill. You have an imagination, little raven, use it."

"How was it cursed?"

Unferth's mouth opens, but for once he remains silent. There is no sudden mean cut of a smile, no disarming poem. *He doesn't want to tell me.*

"How, Truth-Teller?"

His lips tighten. "I killed my brother with it."

Like a hammer thrown down, the words hit hard.

Kinslayer.

Unferth goes fast, ungracefully, toward the stairs.

Something like anticipation thrills through me, hot and melting. I hug myself and take deep breaths; I turn to the troll. "Red Stripe," I murmur, naming him for the strip of scarlet lichen. "Do you think it's not you or me but Ned Unferth who has a heart of stone?"

The troll sings a low note to agree with me.

Unferth stomps back upstairs with a stained and many-times-folded map to lay out our new options for the winter. He says Red Stripe was probably alone only because he was thrashed out of his herd for being puny or for this groaning he does. We need to find safe ground because if this troll knows of the place, so will his mother. Unferth's refrain is the same as it was at the ruins of Montreal: we want to be the hunters, not the hunted. We should leave the troll here and continue up the coast as was the plan. But I can't shove Red Stripe back out into the harsh wilderness to face his tormentors already missing an arm.

Reluctantly, Unferth says we might find a safe haven among

the northern homesteads, except there's no certainty that other trolls, other herds, wouldn't find us. We'd have no chance against an entire herd. If I insist on caring for the beast, he thinks it's better to wait through the coldest, iciest months and go hunting again with the thaw. I've already waited this long; what's four more months?

An eternity.

"You can always change your mind about this one," Unferth says as he thumps his fist against Red Stripe's solid belly.

But I know better. This troll's gentle, needy gaze is too innocent, too simple. He's nothing like the trolls in the stories, and it's difficult to imagine him razing a city to the ground. More like he's a doe-eyed cow or pygmy mammoth to be protected. Some of his groaning sounds like *please.*

Unferth nods tightly and says, "I spent last winter on an island nearby, where there are few people, an isolated tower for him, with ample practice grounds to continue improving your skills and hunting. They have electricity, running water, fine mead, and best of all they know me already and will trust me well enough when we drag this beast into their midst. We'll be able to leave him there protected when it thaws if we position it well."

I wait, expecting he offered such a long list of pros because it must have a rather hefty con.

Unferth smiles. "Jellyfish Cove, on the island of Vinland."

My stomach twists.

Vinland is the northern territory where the Summerlings moved after I climbed the Tree. My wish-parents, Rome and

Jesca, whom I've not seen in ten years. Who may hate me or, worse, have forgotten me. "That is not a good idea, Unferth."

"Because you're afraid of your family."

"I'm not afraid of anything, you tick-eating old man."

"Then give me your reason." He smiles his challenge, for he knows I don't have a better one.

Once the recent snow melts enough to drive—it's early enough in the winter that the sun can still manage that—I wait with Red Stripe while Unferth returns to Toronto for a massive van we can pile the troll into without breaking the shocks. I follow behind in the truck. We make it to a tiny town named Seven Islands in about ten hours of very slow driving, and Unferth rents a ferry. Or rather, Unferth trades the van and two barrels of old wine for the winter's use of the flat, sturdy boat. With ourselves, our gear, Red Stripe, and the truck all loaded up, we sail the Gulf of Lawrence. Unferth complains constantly but silently, and any time I think of cutting Red Stripe loose I can barely breathe. The beast looks at me as if I'm his herd mother now, and I won't betray that, even if I should. We finally arrive, seventeen days before Yule, at the northernmost tip of Vinland.

An icy island of alpine tundra and inland mountains, Vinland was home to the oldest settlement of Vikers from Scandia. Gudrid Far-Traveler and her family landed here a thousand years ago, longing for new land to make their own. It was the ruins of her longhouse, found by archaeologists, that led to the National Historic Site the Summerlings currently run. I have vague memories of Rome's excitement at being asked, Jesca's worry that it would be too isolated for raising children. Rome thought it would be good for me especially—space enough to run wild if I liked and maybe drag Rathi out into freedom with me. But I never made it here until today.

Brisk wind blows across the ocean, making me think on the cold, deadly hand of destiny.

The island is untamed where we come ashore, no sign of people but for the signal tower. Boulders left by some ancient glacier tumble near the water, and the beaches are stone and pebbles. Cormorants and gulls hover in the salty wind. There are no trees at all, but tufts of dead grass and low, rough bushes cling to the shallow hills, and frozen streams cut through the valleys, shimmering with sunlight like diamond veins. Rathi told me about it last summer when we were together in New Netherland, about the detailed historical reenactments and elaborate theater of the Viker Festival, how he thought I'd adore the drama and poetry. He showed me pictures of the pennants and tents, the cobblestone lanes and whitewashed cottages. But mostly he showed me the wild land and loud ocean, the desperate beauty of everything. Rathi remembered I loved my beauty raw.

Unferth and I anchor the ferry as near the rocky beach as we can, using the butts of the troll-spears to shove chunks of ice out of our way. The bergs glare blue-white like the hottest of flames as they bob gently. We leave a sun-calcified Red Stripe on the ferry and jump into the water to wade to shore with bags held high over our heads.

My legs and hips grow so cold so fast I think they'll shatter.

But we make it. Before we die of hypothermia, we head into the tower to strip and heat up the iron oven that warms the entire living space. It's an old signal tower, three stories, with a giant bell hanging forgotten at the top. On clear days, Unferth says, there's a view across Leif's Channel to the Canadian coast. While digging around on the bottom floor last year he found fifty-year-old letters that claimed the bell was part of a troll warning system put in place after the Montreal Troll Wars. Leif's Channel used to be one of the most dangerous crossing points for the greater mountain troll herds who wished to avoid the heavy patrols of the mainland.

And so it's best not to show up unannounced in the Jellyfish Cove bay, even sixty years later, with a greater mountain troll.

Tonight we'll take the rowboat leaning against the whitewashed side of the tower out to unchain Red Stripe and lead him through the water to shore. Tomorrow we'll sail the ferry around to the eastern side of this long peninsula to the town of Jellyfish Cove. We'll dock there and off-load the truck. Give them all warning about Red Stripe.

Unferth and I wrap blankets around ourselves and get the oven going. It's a wide iron chimney up one side of the tower, with a hearth on the first and second floors. He claims the bottom-level bedroom on account of his leg and says there should be some old clothes up on the second floor. Out of fashion, no doubt, but made for the Vinland winter.

The metal stair winds around to the second story, which is

divided into two rooms by a thin partition. One must've been an office or library, with a metal desk full of tiny drawers, a key closet, and one curved wall covered in old books and dusty magazines. I go into the next room, which has a twin bed and sink-toilet combo popular in army movies and prison. There's a porthole window with a frosted view down the eastern coast. Against the aggressively blue sky I can just make out lines of smoke from Jellyfish Cove.

I dig through a trunk of discarded clothes, mostly heavy canvas pants and fishermen's coats, until I find patchy thermal shirts and a long wool sweater that'll come to my knees like a dress. Some men's long underwear work as leggings, and I've practically got an acceptable outfit once my boots are back on.

In the mottled little mirror over the sink, the first I've seen in a month, I stare at myself. Precia of the South used to call me once a month and ask what runes I saw in my own green-gray irises. I answered for a few years, usually *fate* or *choice* or *death,* typical things one might expect of a Valkyrie's heart, until it became clear none of them would tell me what *they* saw in me.

I lean in to focus close on my left eye. There I see *torch,* a rune of passion that burns destructively.

Rubbing my chest, I clomp down again, rattling the entire frame of the staircase. Unferth says, "We do have to live here, little raven."

He's looking fresh and devilish in a dark red sweater rolled up at his wrists, his hair loose from braids so it blankets his shoulders in a hundred tiny kinks. I don't bother to hide my stare. When he turns away from the fire, hair sweeps away from his face and there's something vulnerable in the loose smile he offers me. I'm too surprised to return it or say anything. He rubs the heel of his hand into his thigh and stands. I reach out to skim the feathery ends of his hair that dangle beside his elbow. It's nearly as long as mine. Unferth slaps my hand away and swiftly twists all his hair up to the nape of his neck, tying it there in a knot.

He says, "It'll take a few hours of work to get the water heater up and running again, so if we want real food we should go into town. It's slightly less than two kilometers' walk."

I grimace; I'd rather stay here than play nice in a small town. Or face the Summerlings.

The sun is low in the west, though it's barely past lunchtime, and we make our way along a narrow path that's visible only because the gravel is paler in general; every once in a while a small wooden slat bridge connects it from one low hill to the next. We don't speak, though our shoulders knock together frequently and the tattered edge of his coat flaps against my knees. My lips are chapped in seconds and my ears numb, but I imagine I can get help for such things in town. Balm and a thick scarf, mittens perhaps, since I've heard those keep your fingers warmer than gloves.

I think of the Summerlings as I tromp through the slush, wondering if they've changed at all. Rathi had, of course, growing from a sober nine-year-old into a brilliant young preacher with his father's golden hair and mother's ability to read my every thought. The last time I was with him six months ago, I got a bruise on my wrist from how hard he clung to me, arguing his point faster and faster as if it would make a difference.

But Rome and Jesca I've not seen in a decade. Since that final night together in their small hotel room next to the Federal Library, with a narrow view of the New World Tree. I had dinner with them at a fancy restaurant on the First Valkyrie's coin, me jerky with excitement and them talking constantly as if that might make everything seem normal. Rathi spent the whole time silent, occasionally running fingers through floppy yellow hair.

Rome stopped us at a corner drugstore during the walk back to the hotel and pulled a cheap black Eye of Odin charm off the shelf. He bought it and braided it into his beard beside the Freyan horses and bright red beads. *You'll be a child of both houses, Signy.* Jesca had tears in her eyes but only said my mother would be so proud of my bravery.

I said my mother wouldn't recognize bravery if it introduced itself with song and dance. Jesca smiled a watery smile and shook her head in automatic forgiveness.

If I were returning to them triumphant now, surely I wouldn't feel such trepidation. It would be a wonderful homecoming, a hero's welcome for the errant Valkyrie arriving to honor her past life, her old family. I would have titles and accolades for a shield.

As it is, what will they think of me? I left them so hard and fast, without a second glance or thought. When Jesca kissed me goodbye and Rome pressed a Freyan hymnal into my hands, I thanked them, I smiled, but I never once looked over my shoulder for that final glimpse of their faces. I ran for the Death Hall like it was all I'd ever wanted.

My boot slips on loose rocks and crunches into slush at the edge of the path. Unferth takes my elbow, lifting an eyebrow as if to say, *Clumsy Valkyrie don't last long.*

I jerk my arm free and stomp ahead before he guesses what I'm thinking.

Jellyfish Cove clings to the side of the island like a sprawling checkerboard. Whitewashed houses are shining barnacles on the long slope of the bay, their scarlet and blue and yellow roofs merry splashes of color. Cobbled streets curve toward the docks, which reach long, narrow fingers into the silver-capped ocean. Boats of every size sway with the tide, some with coiled sails and some complicated by rigging for nets and metal traps. Others carry sharp seal spears raised like fangs toward the sky, and there are at least two huge sea-buses painted with tourist slogans. Though it's so near Yule, people move around in bright coats, mostly orange and blue and red, like elf-lights in clumps and pairs. A steady stream of them leaves town along an inland road, disappearing over the hump of a hill where I can just see the flicker of pennants from the valley beyond, advertising the Viker Festival.

Unferth leads me toward the center of town to a four-story hotel with three wings, dark brown thatching, and baby-blue shutters. The swinging, old-fashioned sign names it the Shipworm.

Inside is warm and wood-paneled, smelling of ale and fish chowder. Unferth asks for a table in the common room, where there are swordfish stuffed and polished on the wall, a roaring fire in a huge dark hearth, and exposed beams hanging with hats from around the world. Poorly hidden speakers play scratchy folk music. A few tables are occupied, though not nearly all, as it's between lunch and dinnertime. We sit and I ask for whatever the cook likes best that's hot, Unferth correcting my order by asking for two bowls of chowder and some of the fresh bread. Before I can glare, a woman in flannel and fingerless gloves bustles into the room and says, "Ned Unferth!" with a gleeful north coast accent. She plops down in an empty chair and grasps his hand. "We didn't know if you were coming back this year!"

I suspect she ends every sentence with an exclamation and dislike her when Unferth smiles warmly, even though she's at least Myra Quick's age. He says, "Patty, here's my apprentice, Signy. Signy, Patty runs the all-in store down the street." His tone adds, *so be nice to her.*

"Signy!" Patty transfers her grip from Unferth's hand to mine. "Aren't you all washed up and salty! This one likely hasn't let you feel like a girl in ages!"

My eyes narrow. "I try not to let him feel like a man, either."

Unferth's face tightens and Patty's lips part as she works out my meaning. Fortunately, we're saved by two more people who know Unferth. One man in coveralls claps him on the shoulder, and the other is the man's son, with the sort of too-new haircut his mom probably did with safety scissors. "Go tell the king our poet's back," his dad tells him, and the kid scampers off.

Our poet? I mouth at Unferth, but he pretends not to see. He does answer the fisherman with a line from *The Viker's Elegy* about returning to home port. Patty and the fisherman stay with us to share a round of local brew and fill Unferth in on the year's events.

I fill my belly and let the beer warm my blood, leaning back in my chair with a loose neck. The names wash over me, births and deaths and who won the Summer Solstice war games, the lack of seals this year, how many more days of tourists we've got before the island is ours for three months of the off-season, yes we've got a welding mask so he can fix up the water tank, no Rome probably hasn't given up on the idea of recruiting him as poet for the feast hall.

I sit up straight. "Who's Rome?" I ask Patty, ignoring Unferth's disapproval at my insinuation I don't know anything. It's the first thing I've said in fifteen minutes and the words smack with the yeasty aftertaste of beer.

Patty nods. "Rome's the showrunner up at the festival. Mastery in history and preaching, and oh, darling, you wait until Freyrsday and his service. Will be glad you're Freyan when he lifts your heart to satisfaction!" Suddenly she's looking past me toward the door.

I shove out of my chair and spin so fast I knock a fork to the floor. It clatters on the wooden slats and I press back against the smooth edge of the table, gripping it hard to support myself.

Rome Summerling is as golden as I remember, even in

my dreams. Big and bright, his reddish beard braided with tiny charms still, his hair shaggy around his ears, with thin streaks of gray. Hazel eyes and wide shoulders, hands on his hips, and a smile of greeting that fades into drawn shock when he sees me.

He wears a wool tunic and thick pants wrapped up the leg with more wool. Leather boots. A thick belt. Dark copper torc around his neck. Like he walked out of a painting of Old Scandan farmer kings. It suits him so much more than jeans and jackets and ties ever did.

"Signy." His voice is as filling as ever, finding all my spikes and smoothing them out. My grip on the table loosens.

I don't say anything, which is enough agreement for Rome. He's here in three broad steps and laughing and hugging me in those bear arms, beard soft at my temple. He smells like smoked meat and charcoal. He releases me but cups my elbows to look down at my face. "You've got your mama's eyes still." His voice is husky with emotion. Deep wrinkles pull at his eyes and vanish into his beard. There in his left iris, like a beacon, I see the rune *faith.*

My tongue sticks in my mouth and I swallow. I try for anything to say. The inn around us might have vanished. I manage, "Rathi—he looks more like you than he used to."

Rome chuckles and there's an answering scatter of happy laughter from the room. My ears buzz. "My little son, Hrothgar, is not so little anymore," he agrees.

"I saw him, ah, last summer in New Netherland." That was the last time I was held like this, hugged in relief and also with expectation. As if I owe these men something. Which, of course, I do. And my wish-mother, too.

"He mentioned it. Said you were doing . . . well."

I imagine he said quite a bit more than that.

"Want a beer, Rome?" calls someone. My wish-father nods absently, gaze roaming behind me. His eyes snap back to me and his eyebrows lift. "You're the girl Ned brought? His apprentice?"

I twist around to shoot Unferth a hideous glare. He stands and spreads his hands. "Rome, you likely know better than I how our Signy resists labels like that." He says it fondly, curse him. Rome laughs and so do all these people who don't know a thing about me.

Ned Unferth is like a different person here. A good-old-boy poet.

For all the *truth* in his irises, he certainly is an excellent player. I say, "Ned wants to be part of the feast," and watch Unferth's eyes narrow. It goads me into adding, "We have a troll for your show, too."

Two tiny spots of pink appear at the sharp edges of Unferth's cheeks, but he doesn't naysay me.

Patty exclaims and Rome asks for more details, proudly holding me under one arm as I tell them all about our Grendel. I weave a story that's almost completely a lie about how we tracked and captured him, about the trolls we fought off to get him to safety, finishing with a wide grin just for Unferth. He smiles back at me, and there's a clear promise of retribution in the pinch of his lips.

The thrill of battle raises elf-kisses up my arms.

Jesca Summerling arrives with a tiny cry like a songbird, and she feathers her hands up and down my arms, touches my tangled braids, and then presses a firm kiss to my lips. She's small but sturdy, freckles staining her face unevenly. An apron dress as historically accurate as Rome's tunic and leggings pulls in attractively at her waist. There's a sheen of tears in her pale green eyes, but what catches my attention, what breaks me and remakes me, is the circle of tiny runes twining themselves like a bracelet around her pupil.

If I had any doubts about the past month, about my riddle or the specifics of the answer, about following Ned Unferth and learning his troll hunting, his bitter, beautiful poetry; if I had any doubts about my destiny finding me, they're all shattered by that single rune in the eye of my wish-mother.

Home.

SEVEN

IN THE DIM light of a stuffy dressing room, I become Valtheow the Dark.

Black liner drawn thick evokes the eye Odin Alfather gouged out at the Well of Mimir in return for wisdom. Both eyes marked black turns my face into a skull, the death Valkyrie carry in their hearts. Crimson lipstick cuts across my mouth like a mortal wound, but I smile and it becomes a lover's mouth to speak the Alfather's words.

I'm glad for this quick moment alone in the dressing room usually reserved for the clowns. Peachtree, the only clown my age, is out leading the audience through a Wild Hunt number, and I can hear the screams and laughter through the thin wooden walls. This afternoon the Viker Festival is a crush of people. Baldur's Night is the unofficial first day of the season, and they've come in droves from New Scotland and mainland Massadchuset to see us perform. To see me, and my troll, for one night only. Come one, come all!

I wear an old-fashioned scarlet dress and an apron the

deep green color of decay. It hooks at my shoulders with abalone brooches, and a belt of iron loops heavily against my hips, dragged off-center by my seax in its sheath. I've braided my hair into two ropes, framing my face in the traditional Valkyrie's way. My sleeves are cuffed with silver bracers tooled to gleam golden in the stage lights. Rings set with colored glass decorate my hands.

Here is Signy Valborn in the mirror, looking for all the nine worlds like an ancient Death Chooser.

But it's only an illusion. I think of what my sisters would say, who spent nearly ten years trying to make me see how much of a Valkyrie's job is performance. Here I am, doing what they always wanted: translating the raw power of death into a palatable display for the masses.

Much to my irritation, I couldn't avoid it any longer.

The past three and a half frozen months have been one constant negotiation; between Unferth and me, Unferth and the town, the town and me, Unferth and Rome, me and Rome, me and Jesca, on and on until I wished the ice would fall harder, the snow pile on tons of layers. Anything so I could hole up in the tower and never be expected to smile for a crowd or explain one more time to one more resident of Jellyfish Cove why I'm learning to kill trolls when Red Stripe is so tame, what it all has to do with my riddle and my eventual triumphant return to the New World Tree.

It wasn't me who spilled the connection between trolls and my riddle; it was Ned Unferth the first night Rome and Jesca joined us for dinner at the signal tower. Unferth and his cursed truth-telling, his refusal to just sit silent when they asked how we met. Like revenge for my thrusting him into the festival as a performing poet, the answers just fell out of his mouth. He wasn't even drunk.

Rome and Jesca knew from Rathi enough about my situation they weren't surprised, and Rome immediately started in on a number of historical examples of quests like this involving the great beasts of legend. By the time he and Unferth were halfway through a bottle of mead and a thesis on dragon hoards in history, Jesca pulled me aside to clean up and gently but firmly reminded me that living openly with a man like Unferth wasn't entirely decent.

She hardly cared about the riddle or troll or my winning my place on the Valkyrie council. She cared about my virtue.

I promised her that I had no virtue left to tarnish.

As they left on their gas-guzzling ATV back for the Cove, I wondered how long it would take Jesca to bring it up with Rathi. Judging by how fast the whole town knew Unferth was helping the Child Valkyrie solve her riddle, she likely called him in the middle of the night.

Avoiding everyone became my mission. Unferth helped or hindered, depending on his mood. He either pushed me harder than ever with the troll-spears and sword work so I legitimately had no time for conversations, or he meandered into town like he had nothing better to do and told people I was open to visitors. They poured in, always in couples or groups, as if too nervous to face me alone. They asked about Odin, about the Tree, about trolls and hunting and whether Elisa of the Prairie dyed her jet-black hair or Gundrun slept over at the White Hall as rumors suggest.

I made it a point of honor to lie about everything.

Once or twice I caught ten-year-old boys running up to the tower door, knocking, and then fleeing as if their lives depended on it.

Though I refused to perform, I helped Unferth create a troll-baiting show for the festival, with Red Stripe as the main attraction. Thankfully, once it was Yule there was no tourism to speak of on the island. We had two blissful weeks snowed into the tower, just us because Red Stripe hunkered down unchained against the outer wall and buried himself in the snow to snore all day.

To pass time Unferth and I made the tower into an obstacle course and I ran it again and again while he graded me from the kitchen counter. My grades tended to be less about success and more about flare, as he awarded me with cries of "You look like a donkey!" or "There are those beautiful Valkyrie wings!" depending on how well I finessed a corner. I built a huge nest of old sweaters and blankets near the ground-floor hearth, the only place warm enough that my voice didn't puff out in icy fog. We'd fall asleep side by side, though sometimes I stayed awake on purpose, just to listen to him breathe.

Every morning I looked for runes in my eyes. *Torch* and *death* and *choice* cycled through as they always had, with *torch* the most frequent as our isolation lasted, unsurprising because of my burning desire to get back out into the world.

Finally the snow melted enough that we crashed into

town for an impromptu celebration at the Shipworm. Amidst the laughter and fiddle and crush of everyone, I glanced once at Unferth and caught him in the corner with his shoulders against two other men's, obviously sharing gossip like a clutch of chickens. His cheeks were bright, his mouth loose, and when he saw me looking his gray eyes shone. He was happy with the Freyans, knew all their songs and prayers. Some boys dragged him to the middle of the dance floor, where he first crouched and touched his fist to the wooden panels in an old Freyan act of devotion to the earth. Then he leapt onto a table with a yell and recited the opening lines of *The Charge of Winter* to much uproarious applause.

The inn grew hot with his poetry and the enthusiasm of the crowd. He held them trapped in rhyme and rhythm so long that sweat melted through his shirt and he stripped it off during the dramatic transition from the warrior-king's forces to the approaching army of frost giants.

Two girls beside me gasped to see the jagged claw marks striping down Unferth's chest and across his back. I shifted away, itching with tension as he performed for them. The scars shimmered in the firelight, forming runes against his skin like a message just for me. *Truth* and always *truth.*

The final line rang through the fiery air and Unferth's head fell forward in a bow, his hands turned palm out, his shoulders heaved. It was a moment when I could have called out a response, drawn his attention, gotten those rain-colored eyes on me and me alone. But we were surrounded and I didn't want to share it—share him. I rubbed my arms as the inn exploded with cheering. They clapped his hands and pulled him off the tabletop, offering mugs of beer and requests for another or another. As he promised he'd perform at the festival feast when it started up again, the crowd swallowed him whole.

He belonged there, shining with sweat and pleasure, and I wanted to destroy it all. I shoved my way outside into the white snow.

Every time Unferth went into town after that, I stayed in the tower. I dug mazes in the snow, building my muscles until I could throw the troll-spears accurately. I tended to Red Stripe, picking dust out of the crevices of his stone skin, polishing the shards of amethyst at his arm stump until they shone. I wandered the island as I could, pretended there were trolls to hunt here, and twice tracked a pack of wolves swinging too near town. Using troll-spears on caribou is overkill, but I did it anyway.

And if I heard Unferth's familiar gait stomping through crusts of ice toward me, anticipation burned like never before. I started leaving the tower just to dredge up the buzz of expectation I'd feel when I went home to him again. It was pathetic, but I didn't stop. I blamed the forced stagnation of the winter, the inability to act or get anything accomplished. There was nothing more fantastic to hold my attention, and so too big a piece of me latched on to him.

But sometimes he would push me onto a stool to brush and braid my hair, or tease me with a string of riddles whose answers were always *troll,* and his hands would linger on my neck, his smile relaxed, and I'd have traitorous thoughts about staying in that tower with him forever.

It was a rough winter.

So when Rome and Unferth came to me last week, as the first icebergs in the harbor cracked open, it was easy for them to convince me to perform in their Baldur's Night feast, as a send-off for their temporary Vinland Valkyrie. Our show would open the season for the arrival of spring, and then Unferth and I would charge back to the mainland to seek out my sacrifice.

And here I am, ready to perform the Valkyrie part on Baldur's Night. It's a holiday about hope, when across the USA we celebrate the god of light and his epic journey back to us from the darkness of Hel. He brings the sun with him, and the promise of summertime. Though on Vinland the ice remains, and there won't be flowers for weeks, winter is officially over.

I smile just to think of it. By the next high holiday, Disir Day, in six weeks, I intend to be back in Philadelphia, sitting at my throne beneath the New World Tree.

My eyes in the mirror flash, and I lean nearer to see what rune will appear today. I hope for *journey,* because it's time to move on, or *fate.*

But there, winking beside my pupil, is *chaos.*

Startled, I blink rapidly. Never before have I seen this rune.

It means upheaval, a moment when anything can happen. Anything can change.

Chaos probably reigned in my stars the night I climbed the

Tree. Under *chaos* destiny breaks and even Freya, the goddess of Fate and magic, cannot see true. I take a calming breath.

The center cracked/no future seen/we fly into the chasm of fate.

With the thinnest makeup brush and liquid eyeliner, I paint the dangerous rune onto my thumbnails.

The back of my neck heats and I glance higher in the mirror to see him there, Ned the Spiritless leaning indolently against the door frame behind me. With him comes a spill of applause from the crowd waiting in the feast hall, but Ned's expression is skeptical, studying my reflection. My heart pounds harder and I wonder what he would say if I told him I see *chaos.* But I tuck the surge of excitement away and lift my eyebrows. "Do I not suit?"

"Signy the Valkyrie," he drawls. His pale eyes meet mine.

He's already in his costume for the feast, where he plays court poet to Rome's king. It's a long wool shirt cut tight against his lean torso, a tooled belt, and loose dark pants tucked into heavy leather boots. His sword hangs over his shoulder, sheathed in a baldric that slashes a line from his right shoulder to his left hip.

Ned stalks from the door to me. He takes up the iron collar from the dressing table, the final piece of my costume, and with exaggerated concentration pushes aside my braids to clasp it about my neck. His hands linger there.

"Such a lowly thing for a Valkyrie to do," he murmurs.

Though I agree with him, I raise my chin. "It isn't lowly by virtue of a Valkyrie doing it."

He laughs—just a single bark of a laugh—and leans his hip against the table to take weight off his injured leg. His gaze sinks to my mouth.

Elisa of the Prairie whispered to me once that her husband's first kiss brought the nine worlds together for a single moment. Brynhild was awakened from a curse by the kiss of her true love. Signy Volsung kissed her husband and instantly knew she would destroy him one day. She said, *My heart does not smile with his,* before burning his castle to the ground.

I want to know what will happen if I kiss Ned Unferth.

But he glances away and pulls a flask of screech from his pocket. I stare at his neck as he drinks, until he offers it to me. I take it, warm from his hand, and put my lips where his were. I toss back a sip that burns down my throat.

As he screws the cap back on he says rather casually, "I'm to tell you we're running twenty behind from the extra crowds. Rome says you can choose a big entrance or come with me and take your place at the throne. But I know you'll choose the former."

"What's the point of a small entrance?" I shrug. It's the heart of my problem with the council, with my riddle, after all.

He hesitates, then gives a sharp nod and leaves.

I head outside to prepare Red Stripe.

Equal parts historical attraction and carnival, the festival has taken over an entire meadow just outside the town of Jellyfish Cove. As I march quickly through the muddy lanes to the pancake booth, I'm surrounded by re-creations of thousand-year-old sod houses, a smithery, and a spiral of canvas tents thrown open for selling traditional Viker fare and fried foods, dragon masks, and wooden swords and jewelry. Tourists in puffy, colorful coats stream through the aisles, pointing at the girls demonstrating how to feed our pygmy mammoth or at the smith's apprentice as he works the giant bellows while the smith pounds out a red-hot sword. Iron-smelting bloomeries squat like man-sized eggs along the road, tended by two kids in long tunics and fur coats. Reenactors in old Viker costumes demonstrate weapon forms, and two elder ladies in apron dresses teach tourists to weave at the standing loom. On two small stages across the meadow, players compete for the crowd and hat tips, and soon they'll usher their audiences to the feast hall to eat roast boar and drink fine mead while Rome presides like a king of old over poetry contests or boasting games.

Today the meadow is decked out for Baldur's Night. They've put up evergreen boughs and chalked sunbursts onto the tents and booths. Prayer flags flap in the sharp breeze. The air smells like ice and grease and tangy iron. Slush and mud slip under my boots, and yelling and laughter attack my ears. There is no room for peace here, and I love it.

The impromptu troll cage is a small shed on the side of the meadow nearest to town, where most of the electric hookups are. Melting snow pours down the sheet-metal roof, dripping in long streams to the rocky earth, where it forms a moat of mud and ice I easily step over. An evergreen bow shakes glitter onto my face as I jerk the door open.

Beside the bolt lock is a heavy switch that controls the UV lights rigged to the inner ceiling. When I flip the light switch a dull hum clicks off. I unlock the door, then shove it back with my hip in order to keep my eyes on Red Stripe.

He's a statue of himself, pale blue and mottled with gray. His arm wraps protectively about his ducked face. His shoulders slump; his tusks are only cracked points of stone.

As I watch, dust flakes away from his skin and settles onto the mangy rug covering the floor. Tiny fissures appear all over his body and a thin layer of stone skin sloughs away. He shakes all over and groans.

Red Stripe rubs his tiny yellow eyes. In the cool light streaming through the windows set high enough the sun won't ever touch him, that brilliant line of scarlet lichen stretching down his spine seems to bleed.

"Good evening," I say loudly enough for him to easily hear, and set down the plate of toutons and molasses I brought from the pancake booth. Trolls are supposed to be carnivores, but theses cakes are Red Stripe's favorite. "I'm sorry I'm late."

He grunts thanks. Though he can say my and Unferth's names and responds to commands, he seems to prefer communicating without words. Unferth teases me it's to do with my mothering style.

While he eats, I go through into the small back room and grab the long broom. The handle is smooth and warm in my hand, thanks to Red Stripe's amazing ability to fill the whole shed with his body heat. I brush him, scrubbing the remaining rock dust from his shoulders, from the creases of his elbows, and most important from under the heavy iron collar connecting him to the massive chain bolted three meters into the ground. I don't believe he requires it, but for the comfort of the Summerlings and Coveys from town, who aren't used to trolls at all, much less tame ones, we leave him trapped. He tilts his head and raises his arm for me, and his wide lips relax against his blunt tusks.

I smile as I scratch at his broken arm with the broom, where it itches the most. My fondness for the beast wells up and I'm glad we've already discussed with Rome leaving Red Stripe here when Unferth and I go. He's a welcome attraction, given how rare it is these days to find greater mountain trolls in captivity. There are laws, I've learned, against hunting them in the Rock Mountains or near Montreal because of those old treaties between the troll mothers and Thor Thunderer, and when they wander farther south they're destroyed almost immediately by militias. When they die they turn to stone, so almost nobody in the world knows what their living skin feels like, or the color of their eyes, or how well they communicate. Tonight will be a revelation for the festival guests.

"You'll be happy here with Rome," I say, patting Red Stripe's cool arm. He heaves a massive sigh that fills the room with his hot, saccharine breath. It disrupts the motes of dust that hang lazily in the shaft of sunlight cutting past his head. I feel as he must, trapped and slow-moving, made to perform the same steps again and again. Now that the snows are melting, now that Baldur, the god of hope and light, is coming back to us, I'll shake off my stone dust and explode back into the world with my stone heart.

Chaos is here to remind me: I'm going to change my destiny again.

The festival feast hall is modeled after the ancient kings' halls of Old Scandia; a massive single room of wood and sod, with pillars holding up the roof, intricate ironwork thrones, long tables and benches, and painted round-shields hanging from the rafters. Three nights a week the tourists can buy a seat and a meal, complete with the sort of entertainment they might have found had they lived a thousand years ago and sworn to a Viker king.

My wish-father, Rome, plays the king, in a yellow and red wool shirt and trousers and a heavy fur cape latched with golden brooches. He has on a wide leather belt and bracers, with massive copper rings around his upper arms. The Freyan charms braided into his reddish beard glint in the false firelight as he welcomes the tourists back to Old Asgard, where please may they yell and cheer, please may they stand with a poem to share, and all give thanks to the great god of Vinland, Freyr the Satisfied.

Tonight he calls himself Hrothgar Shielding, the great king of Daneland, and welcomes the crowd to the golden hall Heorot. Unferth will play the poet as usual; I will be Valtheow the Dark, queen of Heorot. The beefiest of the actors, George, wears bearskin and has painted a spear onto his cheek to play the hero, Beowulf. We've created a breakaway section of wall for Red Stripe to burst through for the finale. He waits behind it now, with two clowns holding UV lights on his legs.

Once the welcome and the opening prayers are over, Rome exhorts his poet, Unferth Truth-Teller, to entertain his company while the meal is served. Most nights there's roast boar and cured ham, apple tarts, salted cod, a not remotely authentic spinach salad, six options for beer, free honey soda for the kids, and plates of cheese. But as it's Baldur's Night, we have mead for toasting out of great cauldrons, and the trays are loaded with candied apples and bacon-wrapped apple sausages.

Unferth rises from his crouch beside the carved thrones to call out a song about Pol Darrathr, a son of Odin who lived hundreds of years ago and earned himself immortality and the name Baldur the Beautiful.

I listen for my cue while hidden behind the thrones and don't wait for him to finish before I throw aside the curtain and stride in, arms spread. "Listen to the Valkyrie's Prayer!" I cry.

Unferth flicks his hand dramatically at me, and I just as dramatically ignore him to take Rome's hand and step onto the queen's throne.

From here I can see out over the long tables, meet the eyes of families and guests spread out on benches with their plastic goblets lifted. Hot orange lights flicker like fire from sconces, gleaming against the snakes and deer and running wolves carved into the rafters. There are men of our company seated among the crowd in the hard leather and metal armor of a great king's retainers grinning at me, and the serving women stop with hands full of mead and food to watch.

I slam the butt of my spear onto the throne three times before crying,

"Hail, day!
Hail, sons of day!
And night and her daughters now!
Look on us here
With loving eyes,
That waiting, we win victory!"

At the halfway point, everyone in the crowd recites it with me, even the smallest children. The Valkyrie's Prayer is one of the first we learn as children, regardless of what god we most worship. The audience's repetition of my words rumbles through me, becoming a familiar eight-count rhythm that sounds in my ears, like a pounding heart or Odin's eight-legged horse running through my bones. It's more exhilarating to lead the performance than I expected.

Holding up my spear, I call for silence. "Tonight is Baldur's Night—tomorrow we will celebrate his return to us. But do you remember when he died? Do you remember the wailing and tears?" I lower my voice just a tad to say, "I remember; I remember every prince's death, and this one we all dreamed!"

"What did you dream, Valkyrie?" calls a man with a little girl in his lap.

I point at him with the tip of my spear.

"I dreamed I rose before dawn
To clear up the Valhol for the newly slain.
I woke the Lonely Warriors,
Bade them up to strew the benches,
Clear the ale horns,
And my fellow Valkyrie to ready the wine.
I dreamed the arrival of a prince
Like no prince we had known before."

I push through the crowd to tell them what runes I see and use my calligraphy set to paint binding runes and poetry onto their faces and hands. Rarely do I see actual runes in the faces of these tourists but only pretend I do for the act, for the game. When I can, I scare them with prophecies of death and gruesome visions.

One of the serving women brings me a goblet of mead and I drink it down before slamming the goblet onto the nearest table. The yellow honey alcohol sloshes over the sides and splashes onto the worn wood, and I cheer—the audience cheers with me.

I sit back in the throne as Rome takes over again and encourages two performers to act out a boasting game while everyone eats. Unferth joins me, lounging against the side of my knee, and I once or twice take a thin braid of his in my hand, curling it possessively through my fingers. We cheer the competition, Rome and I, with Unferth crying insults to the losers while rubbing the ball of his hand into his cranky right thigh.

George stands up from among the actors playing King Hrothgar's retainers. He says his name is Beowulf and challenges Unferth's poetic prowess with a boasting poem about how strong he is, how he swam through the ocean strangling sea monsters. Unferth snarls back, perfectly in character, calling George a liar and a coward with florid language.

Just as their spar grows too heated, just as Rome and I pretend to consider intervening, a great low roar pierces the hall.

We freeze in exaggerated poses. It comes again. Red Stripe, exactly on the poetry cue Unferth's been repeating for days. George/Beowulf draws his sword as Red Stripe bursts through the foam-brick wall to the north of the thrones. I scream as loud and horridly as I can, drowning out the troll's war cry.

The audience screams, too.

Red Stripe charges in, taking prompts from Unferth, who's shifted to the back of the hall, using blunt-tipped spears to poke and prod his thick skin. Rome yells to George, "No sword can penetrate this beast's cursed hide!" and George throws down his weapon. The retainers join him, but it's George alone who throws himself at Red Stripe, gripping the papier-mâché prosthetic arm we tied to him. The two grapple and dance, fast and grand in the firelight.

It's all I can do not to laugh with delight.

Unferth yells, "Grendel!" and Red Stripe roars again, throwing George away. Red Stripe turns to the audience and opens his mouth hideously wide. Children scream and many of their parents, too, but there's clapping and gasps of amazement.

Nobody runs. They know this is a show, despite the terror blazing through the atmosphere.

George leaps onto Red Stripe from behind, grasps the immobile prosthetic arm, and tears it off with a berserker roar of his own. Dark purple corn syrup—my idea—splashes in an arc like arterial spray, pumping as George squeezes it from a hidden trigger.

Red Stripe crashes to his knees, but is up again and runs away with a long, sad moan, his footsteps shaking the hall. Unferth slips after him through the ruined wall of our false Heorot. George lifts the dripping fake arm over his head, and I climb onto my throne to begin the applause.

Great bands of laughter and cheering hit me, hit all of us. George and the retainers nail the arm to the wall behind the thrones and Rome calls for celebratory dessert.

The crowd is loud with chatter and wonder, cheering us and digging into their tarts and ice cream. I sink into the throne, hot and alive, a grin splitting my face so hard my cheeks ache.

After dessert I stand up and crow a harsh poem Unferth wrote about living on a rock of ice like ours, about how badly we need the coming dawn to drive the trolls away and for Baldur the Sun to bring joy back to the world. Rome waves a ring-adorned hand for dishes to be taken away and every goblet replaced with a paper lantern and an apple. The lantern is for releasing when the sun sets, to light Baldur's path home. The apple reminds us of our mortality, that like Baldur we will all die some day without tasting the apples of youth that give eternal life to our gods.

I eat my apple wildly. I destroy it like it's my enemy, letting juice run down my chin to a roar of approval from the actors playing Rome's warriors. They pound their feet and I pound mine back, every grain of the wooden throne pulsing beneath me. Rome laughs, a comforting old sound, and the audience laughs with him, children joining me in messy eating; apples and apple juice stain the tables.

We release the crowd, Rome and I, crying out a closing prayer together. Rome invites them into the meadow for bonfires and a mummer dance before we release the lanterns at sunset. I toss the last of my mead into the fire and it bursts into sparks and snaking smoke.

Out in the meadow, I grab a mask from the communal box and dance as eagerly as any Freyan born. The bonfires remind me of harvest dances from my childhood, of my parents and colorful autumn leaves.

I drag tourists into the dancing with me, hold their hands and spin and spin. The clown Peachtree leaps onto me from behind, enveloping me in a monster hug. "That was amazing!" she shrieks. "Stay with us, Signy!" Her hair flairs blue and pink around her head and a hundred tiny plastic sequins stick to her face for a mask. I only laugh, and she flaps at my boring raven mask. We share a plastic glass of mead before diving back into the dancing.

Fiddles make raucous noise, and shrieks of laughter carry it along. Everyone wears a mask: some are plain from the bin like mine, some feathered or long-nosed, others bejeweled, painted, or scattering glitter with every step. Who can tell tourist from townie? Husband from wife, or Odinist from Freyan? We all crowd together on Baldur's holiday, dancing, drinking, and readying paper lanterns to send up into the sky as a trailing beacon to guide Baldur home at dawn.

The raven mask lets me be one of them, not Signy Valborn, if only for a night.

Jesca bustles through the crowd, her hair uncharacteristically loose and a flute of champagne in her delicate hand. "Signy!" she calls out. Her hip bumps into the woman beside her, and she playfully apologizes before reaching for my hand. I kiss her cheek, and she says loudly in my ear, "I just spoke to Rathi before the feast! He's accepted a summer fellowship at a church in Mizizibi; isn't that wonderful! He said they fought for him!"

I look into her bright eyes and see only *home* there. Only a tipsy glaze and happiness. She pushes my mask off my face to better study it. "He'll be here next week to visit, and I thought perhaps you might want to wait for him, to stay just a little bit longer. . . ."

"Jesca!"

"You two were always so good for each other."

"We were little kids; that's not who we are anymore." My vivid joy is sinking away, but I cling to it, wanting to keep hold of this high bliss as long as I can, before I have to go away tomorrow and leave this perfect night behind me.

Jesca touches my cheeks. "That isn't what he told me last summer, maidling." But she shakes her head before I can answer. She kisses my cheeks and murmurs, "Happy Baldur's Night," into my ear.

She vanishes into the crowd again and suddenly I'm desperate to find Unferth. Where did he disappear to? Isn't he finished putting Red Stripe to bed yet? I turn in a full circle, scanning the crowd.

Thin, straight clouds point toward the vanished sun, dragging lines of pink with them. The air is cold but bright and very much alive. People smile at me, hold out hands to pull me back into the dancing. They call her name, *Valtheow!* or *Vinland Valkyrie!*, not Signy. They want me to join them, offering another drink or piece of roasted apple. I take it all, eating from their fingers, drinking the mead or sparkling wine until my head spins.

What I want is Ned Unferth, right now. I want him to see me being part of all this, bright and heady like he was at the Shipworm, a piece of this whole.

I hurry toward the boundary of the meadow, heart beating harder than it should. The evening presses in and I blink fast, trying to find my best balance. I search the shadows for him, the edges of the crowd where he must be if he's not in the center of it all. "A creature of thresholds." I whisper a drunken poem to myself. "Spiritless because nothing exists between nothing."

There he is, standing on the slope of the moor, flask in hand, still wearing his feast costume. A green goblin mask covers his face, with apple-round cheeks, crescent eye slits, and a wide, clownish nose. But under it is his dangerous smile, his sharp white teeth.

"Finished gaping?" Ned says lazily, one corner of that smile hooking up.

"I don't think I am," I whisper, stepping forward. I snatch his hand and pull him farther up the rocky slope to where the shadows dance, too. The beak of my mask is too long for what I want, and I shove it up over my forehead, catching it in my hair with a tangle. Ned widens his colorless eyes but says nothing as I pull off his mask. It leaves two small red lines on his cheeks where it pressed.

He'll never be beautiful, never free of the gouges pain leaves around his mouth. Always tight angles and narrowed eyes. But there's a charged string connecting us and it's the only thing I understand at all.

As the firelight flickers across his thin lips I hear nothing but the howl of blood in my ears. I kiss him.

His chest is hard against mine and he touches my elbows. I cup his face; my fingers skim the rough edges of his jaw. A tiny sigh escapes him, and the moment he breathes into my mouth I sink in, dropping forward forever, but not like falling. Like floating.

"Oh, little raven," he whispers, and I smile, thinking, *I want those teeth cutting into my lips.*

But when I move to kiss him again, Unferth holds me back.

"Ned?" I say, blinking. The slope puts him centimeters higher than me, so he looks down with an ache in his eyes, except that it might merely be pity.

"You shouldn't do that again," he says.

Confusion makes me spiky. *"Do that?"*

"Kiss me," he snaps.

I push my hands into my stomach. "You liked it," I say, knowing, knowing, *knowing* he kissed me back.

But he's silent, as if he has no idea, for this one single time, what he can possibly say.

I grab his coat in my fists and kiss him again, pushing our teeth together, making it a fight. He'll fight me to the end of the world if that's the sort of kiss it has to be.

"*Signy,*" he hisses, shoving me away.

Everything inside me combusts. "*Unferth,*" I spit back. "What is *wrong* with you?"

He lifts his eyebrows in that arrogant way and I feel small and stupid. *What is wrong with me?*

My heels catch on gravel and I trip, righting myself with a furious grunt. Without a backward glance I stomp away, wishing my boots could pound bruises into the island and tear the night up.

Wind tosses mist off the surface of the sea and I scrape my hands against lichen-crusted rocks to balance in the near dark. At the far end of a narrow peninsula a fleet of standing stones waits, as though the island holds them in the palm of its outstretched hand. It's precarious, but the easier path out to the death ship ruins is also longer by a kilometer.

I hurry through scruffy grasses and clumps of heather, kicking at stones and cursing, furious. Anger and hurt burn through me, keeping my fingers warm in the frozen evening, but not humiliation. *Never* humiliation. I did not misread anything, I did nothing wrong. I don't know why he pushed me away, but *odd-eye!* It isn't because he doesn't want me.

The ruins are thirteen death ships in all, each built of sixteen standing stones over a thousand years ago as a holy place to burn the dead. The ships are worn smooth by high tides and cracked from ice, but their prows still aim at the ocean and the long way home to Scandia. Some of the rocks are collapsed upon themselves or crumbled, and a good ten of them tilt to one side or the other. But at least three of the ships are untouched by time, ruins in name only.

Few come here, even of the most adventurous tourists. There's no marked path and no advertising. It's lonely and cold and haunted. I found it accidentally, on one of my lonely winter marches.

Here at the western edge of the grassy beach, a shallow cave is dug into the hillside. Probably erosion and ice did all the work to create the three-quarter circle of shelter. Over the weeks I've left supplies there: candles and matches, blankets and extra mittens. The wind has died down, and cuts off completely when I'm in the dugout. With a fire and the blankets, it'll be nearly cozy.

In the last light, I take the candles and pick my way out into the fleet. The very last of the sun sets behind me, casting gold against the edges of the icebergs that dip and soar with the gently rolling ocean. I stick a taper onto the prow-stone of each ship and set them aflame. Thirteen candles to light Baldur's way.

I tried to celebrate it in community. I tried. I danced and I performed and embraced joy the way the Freyans do, yet here I end up again, alone in my red therma-wool dress and heavy boots, my hair braided like a Valkyrie and the darkness around my eyes, red on my mouth. I'm half Signy, half Valtheow, and all pretense. I touch my lips, and I think of Unferth's teeth. "Odd-eye," I whisper. The curse slinks through the ghostly fleet.

With my hand on the prow of the front ship, I lift my eyes to the stars.

Speak to me, Alfather. I miss you.

There is no answer.

My heart hurts, and I bitterly think maybe it *is* turning to stone. Maybe that's why Unferth is here. To wound me. Valkyrie are supposed to know suffering, to understand pain and betrayal. In the old stories they hunt vengeance and cast curses, destroy cities when they need to and set fire to the world.

Light in the east catches my attention. A tiny glow rises up from the black horizon, flying slowly up and up.

There's another, and another. Three more.

The lanterns being released back at the meadow for Baldur. Two hundred of them rise. They bob and twirl in the wind, dancing out over the sea. Like constellations come to life.

As I stare, as I sink down among the death ships, I imagine they spell out a burning, vibrant rune.

Chaos.

Again and again it appears against the starry sky, weaving in and out of itself like a message for the entire world.

EIGHT

THE SUN WAKES me, groggy and chilled. The ocean sighs and I get up, walk to the threshold. During the night a chunk of ice broke free from one of the larger bergs and drifted near enough I could swim out to it if the water were any warmer. The blue ice winks in the sunlight. I splash my face with the freezing salt water to clear my head and wander down the coast to relieve myself.

The death ships are peaceful and whisper to me, and I'm reluctant to return to town and find Unferth. Though today is the day we're supposed to leave.

Can I still face this destiny with him at my side?

Just the thought of going without him, of hunting alone, grips my stomach like a vise.

To calm down, I crouch along the shore to draw rune poems into the sand, wishing it were spray paint on the sidewalk. Siri of the Ice used to make me write poems with her on snow or the sand of a beach, teaching me the point was to relax, to give the words to our god, not to seek fame or accolades. *Poetry is for Odin, and from him, in a cycle like breathing,* she would say as the snow melted or the tide wiped our songs away. Once I was on my own, this was one of the only ways I could relax. But I always found ways to leave a stain, to draw the rune poems with permanent marker or paint. *Signy Valborn was here.*

Beginning with *chaos* I link words and ideas together into one massive, scrawling poem, runes atop runes, in lines and spirals. The runes flow from the nothing-space in my memory, from the gossip of the ocean waves. I let my hand wander—*chaos chaos chaos changes the fate-strings of any life, we the death-born in years gone by walk out gold-adorned, walk in tinged with blood. We rest in stone under the sun. Hear the bear star be born, the seether fall into darkness. Lost sun answer me when the sky is cold, and fate unravels*—on and on, one rune after another.

As the tide slowly moves in, pushing dark streaks of seaweed up the beach, I back farther into the field of stone ships.

Fate unravels.

Hear the bear star be born, the seether fall into darkness.

I could never admit it to Siri, but she was right. Poetry is like the very breath in my lungs: alive for one moment and gone in the next, never the same because poets change, our voices change, our rhythm and accents, our purpose and meaning all change.

This poem will never exist again. There is no pressure in it, no future. I whisper the words of my rune poem and the ocean drags them away one line at a time.

Signy Valborn was never here.

✦ ✦ ✦

Refreshed, I head for the tower to see if Unferth is still coming with me. I take the longer circuit past town, a gravel road that meanders around sinkholes of water and high tufts of grass, with a dozen small bridges spanning the creeks. The sky is cold blue, painfully so, and I tuck my chin against a wind that chaps my ears.

Usually the Cove is a scatter of white block buildings with flat red roofs tucked against the slate-gray beaches and choppy water. But for the holiday the town, too, has exploded with streamers and rainbow elf-lights, dazzling layers of color. Purple and blue paper flowers decorate the windows. A yellow sunburst has been painted against the cobbled courtyard in front of the militia station. Coins are strung between roofs, drawing the eye to the sun. Even the boats in the harbor shine with elf-lights.

Except there are only half the boats I expect on such a tourist-heavy day. At least two of the sea-buses from New Scotland are gone already. And despite the festive colors, the town is as quiet as a rock cathedral. I falter in the crunchy mud.

We must've had five hundred guests yesterday, not to mention the Coveys, who should be bustling around, and instead the streets are empty but for one or two tiny figures hurrying toward the Shipworm.

A sudden foreboding and the whisper of *chaos* urge me to change direction and head quickly into town. My boots hit the cobblestones hard, the noise jarring loudly against the deadened peace of waves and wind and distant-calling gulls.

At the Shipworm all the ground-level windows and doors have been thrown open, unheard-of on a cold morning like this. I step across the threshold into the lobby to find it crushed full with strangers grouped together, hands held, praying hard. They stand in concentric circles across the wooden floor, some seated on the wide staircase, some pressed to the walls, some perched on tables and armchairs. Those not tucked into prayer all look to the front desk where Rome Summerling stands, his arms open but his eyes closed. Praying, too. The kitchen TV's been wheeled in on a portable bookshelf, and though the sound is muted, I see a blaring red ticker exclaiming: . . . FURTHER ADDRESS THE NATION IN THIS TIME OF CRISIS, FIRST VALKYRIE GUNDRUN GRAYCLOAK . . .

"Signy!"

It's Jesca, grabbing my elbow. She throws herself around me, enveloping me in the smell of toutons—hot grease and dough and jam. I return the hug as talking explodes around me and the crowd shifts away from us. There's Rome, too, his height and presence creating space. He puts both hands on my face and kisses my temple. The charms tied into his beard knock my chin. "You're here," he says, and then louder, "Our Valkyrie is here."

I shake my head.

Jesca smiles but touches the corner of her mouth with one finger: there's something very wrong. She did that when I insisted on hanging a live cat instead of an effigy at the island's Yule sacrifice. She did it when lecturing me on impropriety and the student-teacher relationship when she couldn't talk me into moving out of the tower. Here she is again pointing out that her smile is armor, not gladness.

Her worry is mirrored in her husband's eyes as Rome says quietly, "Are you all right?"

"Why shouldn't I be?"

Rome's frown is like the prow of a ship: heavy, keen. It drags the mood of the crowd behind him in his wake, and they press nearer. "You don't know what's happened, daughter," he says in a wistful tone, as if he wishes he did not know, either. Rome and Jesca shift to block me from the crowd, forming a curtain, and my stomach sinks further. Jesca takes my hand, and Rome puts his atop my shoulder. Rome murmurs, "Baldur the Beautiful did not rise this morning, and even the gods can't say what's become of him."

I feel my mouth open, my breath rush out.

All I can think is that the first sign of the end of the world is the Fenris Wolf devouring the god of light. "Fenris?" I whisper. *Is it the end of the world?*

"They don't know," Rome says. "At the ritual this morning, when they poured his ashes into the roots of the New World Tree, nothing happened. There will be a formal announcement from the White Hall soon, and we'll hear from the First Valkyrie what Odin will do."

I should be there. That's *my* Tree. My responsibility. Odd-eye, what am I doing so far north and away from my duties? I swallow. Try not to panic, not to tear away and find the first ferry to New Scotland. "What do we do?" I ask as low and calmly as possible.

Rome says, "Pray," and Jesca says, "Bake."

I draw away, feeling in my guts there's better action to take.

I should be there; I should have already been there! But the Summerlings need their wish-daughter today. I know it by the tightness in Rome's hand on my shoulder and the twitch in the edge of Jesca's shield-smile. I can give them that. I owe them that.

I throw myself into the kitchen, folding dough and chopping apples, listening to orders from Jesca and Sandra Gothing, the Shipworm housekeeper. TVs are on in every room, the commentators circling around and around the same lack of information: nobody knows where Baldur is; it was the Valkyrie of the Rock who took her turn pouring his ashes but of course she must be blameless; there has been no other sign of Ragnarok like the blowing of the Gjallarhorn or flowers blooming among the leaves of the Tree.

My sisters must be beside themselves. Aerin of the Rock will blame herself, will have bruises in her palms from her own fingernails. Elisa's eyes will be bright with righteous tears, and Myra will be threatening to murder someone. Siri of the Ice must be investigating already, combing through suspects with the ruthless certainty of faith in herself and Odin. The sisters Isabeau and Alanna of the West and East must be organizing the council's response or a national sacrifice. Gundrun is with the president. Maybe Precia of the South is wondering where I am.

The only thing I can do for them is keep this island calm, then find Unferth and go tonight or first thing in the morning. Find a troll with the right stone heart, take my place to make the council whole.

I rush around, carrying stacks of cups and dragging around pitchers of water and tea, while Rome holds the anxiety as low as he can through prayer and simple conversation. They press me into being a runner, back and forth to the store for bread and escorting the elderly here. I coordinate some children to fetch.

With the emotions in town so frenzied and strange, I'm not sorry there are others in charge. I do as I'm told, barely stopping to eat or drink, until Jesca suddenly catches my shoulders and studies my hair with growing horror. She orders me to shower and change, that everything will be better when I'm clean and my hair is less of a wight's nest. I promise to take care of it soon.

Around lunchtime we receive the televised message from the president and Council of Valkyrie. First to speak are the president and his lawspeaker, announcing the activation of the federal militia to organize searches and set up crisis centers as well as a conference of kings. They give us comforting words about the strength of the Poet's Cup and bless us all.

Next there is Gundrun Graycloak, the First Valkyrie, with her soft braids and business suit, the feather cloak of her office clinging like armor to her shoulders. She speaks calmly, explains what she knows: Baldur's ashes were replaced with those of a boar; Loki Changer has an alibi; the Fenris Wolf, too, is accounted for and innocent; and Freya the Witch herself is searching along the web of fate to find our missing god. The Alfather, Gundrun says, her voice ringing straight to my bones, will offer a boon to any who aid in the Sun's return.

The president and his lawspeaker address us next, announcing the activation of the federal militia to organize searches and set up crisis centers and a conference of kings. He gives us comforting words about the strength of our character as a nation, and the lawspeaker lifts her replica of the Poet's Cup and blesses us all.

It's clear to us and the commentators that nobody knows much of anything. They speculate about Baldur's ashes being elsewhere, wonder if he's alive but lost or hurt. They wonder what we might have done wrong, or what our gods did, to cause this. They ask what fate could possibly have in store. They regurgitate rumors of anxious pilgrims at the gates of Bright Home and discuss the last time the federal militia was activated.

Lady Serena, the festival seethkona, tells anyone who will listen of the dream she had last night full of burning apple trees.

Anxiety is pervasive. It pokes at my heart, and my breath comes faster and faster. I see trembling in the hands that take drink from me; I see tears reddening Peachtree's eyes even when I squeeze her arm and whisper that the Sun will return to us. I see mothers crushing their children's fingers with worry and fathers not letting their family members out of sight. Even Jesca and Lady Serena speak in tight whispers.

All I can think is that I'm doing not enough good here. I have to go.

NINE

THIN CLOUDS STRETCH across the sky, ruffling like the scales of a giant salmon. Nature unaffected by the turmoil below.

I pick my way over the gravelly yard toward the ocean and our holmgang ring, where Unferth drives himself hard, shirtless and sweating. Both of our packed bags slump against a boulder, ready to go.

His back is to me, troll scars giving his skin jagged stripes, and his braids are in a double row, held together with rubber bands into a club at the nape of his neck. There's a heavy troll-spear in his hands; he swings it smoothly around, slams the butt into the ground, and sees me. Relief flashes across his face before he hides it and snarls, "You're late."

"I've been busy." All the anger from last night floods back with a vengeance.

His face pinches and he drops the spear. "You aren't in your travel clothes," he says, bending down with a grimace to swipe up his T-shirt. His hands are dark with sweaty dirt.

"I've had more important things to do this morning," I snap.

Instead of answering, he pulls his shirt over his head. The collar catches on the knot of his braids and I take some malicious pleasure in his sudden awkwardness.

He sees it and sneers. "More important than going after your stone heart?"

I say, "Baldur is missing. The god of light didn't rise this morning."

The change in him is instant. "Odd-eye," he whispers, and takes my elbows, but not to steady *me*. His neck is rigid, his fingers hard. There's ice in his colorless eyes. Suddenly he pushes away and pounds the side of his fist against the nearest boulder. His back hunches and I hurry forward. He's whispering in Old Scandan but cuts off when I touch him. "Go, Signy," he says. "Go inside and . . . I don't know. I have to . . . to think."

I take a backward step, then another, until I spin and rush for the tower, because even Ned Unferth is scared.

I strip and bathe in the warm but low-pressure shower on my level, scrub my hair, and comb it wet. Because the afternoon is cold, I put on wool leggings and a thick wool dress, my boots, and a coat before I gather up a blanket, hairpins, and an extra calligraphy set to head up to the bell balcony. Unferth will join me when he's ready, and we'll talk about leaving in the morning. This is just a minor setback, I tell myself, as I sit against the curved wall where the late afternoon sun can shine on my back. It's cold up here, but the wind is gentle, and when I pad the floor with a blanket it's not so bad. I lean a shoulder against the wall and let the low sun dry my hair, let my eyes glaze as I stare through the rail at the shivering gray ocean.

Everyone is upset, afraid. But I never thought to see fear in Ned's eyes.

To distract myself I open the calligraphy set Jesca gave me at Yule and pull out the ink, the brush, and a tiny oval mirror I pried from a foundation compact. I angle it to reflect my right eye. My irises are green and gray in jagged chunks, with a darker gray ring at the edge. In them this evening I see only *death* and there, ever-so-tiny, between a blink and the next, *chaos*. I long for my excitement yesterday, instead of this pervasive dread.

To remain calm, I recite the first six verses of "Brynhild's Lament." As the sun turns the tips of the icebergs into pink fire, I draw runes up my arm and across my palm. *Death Chooser, Strange Maid*, the binding rune scar says. I trace the lines, tickling myself, and then mark a long rune poem against the salt-seared wood of the balcony, half prayer, half invocation. I try to summon my Valkyrie ancestors and the ravens Thought and Memory. At least this poem will remain, staining the tower for months. Whatever happens when I go hunting tomorrow, this was real.

When my hair is dry enough I slowly weave my fingers through it. Its color is bland like ashes and driftwood, though afternoon sun can tease out darker honey-brown strands to set alight. Separating it into sections, I put it back into a braided crown and am near finished when I hear the uneven creak of Unferth on the stairs. He pushes through the thin door out onto the balcony and I keep braiding, my back to him. My fingers slow as he sets things down, and my arms burn from effort by the time he kneels behind me. His fingers slide into my hair and he undoes the braids, gently slapping my hands away. I lift my chin, but silently he pushes my head back down.

While the sun sets, Unferth braids an intricate pattern into my hair that requires me to lend him the use of my hands to hold different sections at different times. When I try to speak, he grunts at me to be quiet and let him concentrate or my hair will be lopsided.

The moment he's finished, having stuck in the final pin, I move around behind him to return the favor. As I begin separating sections, his shoulders slump in a sigh. Pink blotches his cheeks and I know he's already been drinking.

An arrow of gulls flies past us; to the north I hear the rustle of the cormorants spilling out of their breeding ground. I want to talk, but resist it, though I playfully tweak a strand of his long blond hair between my fingers. He reaches up and skims his hand against mine for the barest moment of comfort.

We at last both have intricate braids like the poets and queens of old, and I don't know what to do next that won't shatter this temporary peace. I sit back against the round wall and glance at what Unferth brought: a bearskin blanket and ham sandwiches and a nearly full bottle of lavender mead labeled with masking tape.

I work the stopper free and pour a mouthful down my throat. The sweet alcohol brightens my insides. Unferth pulls my blanket aside and spreads the bearskin down instead. He sits and he drinks, too, before tipping the bottle over the edge of the balcony to splash some down to the faraway ground.

"To the Glorified Dead," he says, "all who are and those to come."

"Are you worried about Baldur?"

"No."

"Then what are you afraid of?"

He's quiet and won't look at me.

I tip my head back to study the paling sky, a gradation of blue and violet, and accept the bottle when he offers it. For a while we pass it back and forth. I grow warm with the bearskin beneath us and with Unferth so close and the alcohol filling in the cracks.

Without looking at him, I say, "It doesn't matter that Baldur is missing. Or maybe it matters even more. In the morning, I go hunting."

He doesn't respond.

"I want you to come."

Still nothing.

"And if fear is what made you stop last night, then . . . well. I guess I'm glad. I don't want to kiss a coward." At that last, I turn and he's right there, face very near and shadowed in the evening light.

"Really, that's what you think," he says.

"I don't know what *else* to think." My voice is softer than I intend it to be.

"Don't you?"

I force myself to say, "Unless you don't . . . you don't want to kiss me . . ."

Unferth flips his hands in a little shrug. He says, "*Often shall many men, for the will of one, endure suffering.*"

"Riddles, Ned?" I hug my knees against my chest, trying to parse what he means.

To my surprise, he murmurs, "Isn't the heart of every relationship a riddle?"

There's so much regret layered into his voice that I wonder, as I study the sharp line of his nose, the last sunlight gilding his eyelashes, if ours is a riddle for me to solve, or him.

Unferth says, "So, in the morning you leave."

You. Not we.

"You're not coming?" The words are as tight as I can make them, lest my voice shake. "I thought that you'd be with me for it; I *want* you with me for it."

Say it, Ned. Say you want to be with me, too.

"We can't always have what we want." His toothy smile edges toward triumph.

"Why not?"

"That isn't how destiny works." Unferth glances away from me, out over the ocean. "We're bound by history and our circumstances, and sometimes all we can do is let it wash over us."

"I won't let destiny drag me along like an unwilling victim. I will take it in my hands, Unferth. Like I did when I climbed the Tree. I did that." My fingers are rigid as I grasp for the right explanation. "I won't let anybody else make my destiny for me."

He gives me that grin again, the one that's all teeth and

longing. "That's what will make you great, Signy, daughter of Odin."

I put my hand against his neck and caress down to the collar of this ragged red sweater of his I love so much. I start to slip under the cloth, pulling him closer to me, and he allows it, until our lips are a breath apart and he says, "Or, you'll do something foolish and die young, never to achieve any glory."

I push myself away, then snatch the mead. The alcohol fills my mouth with secondary delight, gone too fast. I tilt the bottle so it sloshes gently, moving it in a circle until I find the same rhythm as the waves below. My head already swims, and when the sea wind blows I sway with it. The scar in my palm burns.

"Signy."

I turn my head to Unferth. Our faces are so near I can smell the sweet drink wafting on the air between us. His eyes go silver in the moonlight. *Chaos* is plain in them, sharp as lightning. I inhale hard. It's never been anything but *truth* in him.

"Little raven, what is wrong?"

"I'm drunk," I whisper. Maybe I imagined it, and I can hear pounding, like hoofbeats on the sand. *Sleipnir, the eight-legged beast, is coming for me.*

"You've been so before."

I try to tug away, but he holds on.

"Signy."

"I see *chaos* in your eyes, Ned."

He freezes. It seems even the wind stops blowing and the waves stop crashing for a moment as he stares at me. I bring my hands up to his face and he grips my wrists like they're saving his life. Like he *wants* me to save his life. "If you finally see my true, wretched worth, I beg you not to look further."

"Tell me what you're afraid of, Ned," I whisper.

"Oh, everything, little raven," he whispers back. One of his thumbs brushes over my lips. "But you most of all."

"Me?"

"Signy the Valkyrie, too dangerous for her own good, who walks along the precipice of power and temptation. Longing to dive in."

I snort.

But he keeps on. "Who sees into men's hearts, who will change the courses of fate, serve at the Alfather's side . . . Shouldn't we all be afraid of the Death Choosers?"

"Not you! Not when I—"

Ned Unferth covers my mouth with his hand. "Don't say anything you'll regret."

"I won't ever regret how I feel and what I want."

He laughs once, like a lazy dog. "If I can have a prayer, this is it: *May Signy Valborn never regret.*" He rolls the empty mead bottle against the uneaten pile of sandwiches, then lies down against the bearskin with his hands behind his head. He stretches, wincing as his right leg straightens. And then he opens his arm for me. Because I'm drunk, it takes little courage to put my head on his shoulder and close my eyes around the sliver of nausea poking in my stomach.

We're quiet again while the ocean continues to murmur, only hushed waves now against the shore. Unferth's chest rises and falls against my cheek and he curls his arm around me tightly. I want more and more, but tonight this is enough. I close my eyes, thinking of what he's trying to tell me with his riddles and open arms, thinking of Baldur and tomorrow and what choices I'll make and whether he'll be here to make them with me.

Cold wind on my cheek wakes me. I'm alone in the dark, curled against bearskin on the tower balcony. Moonlight flashes red near my eyes. I slowly focus on the pommel of Unferth's sword. The one he brought with him across the moor, strapped to his back, the finest possession he owns. Once he said, *This sword is an unhallowed blade.* The style is old, a ring-sword with a relatively short, fat blade, a wide fuller, and a narrow crescent guard. A loose iron ring attaches to the pommel, which is embedded with a small round garnet etched with a tiny boar. That bloody eye is what winks at me in the moonlight.

"Ned?" I call, sitting up and taking his sword in my hand. The smooth wooden grip is freezing. He never leaves his sword behind.

A long sound like a faraway trumpet calls back. It echoes over our edge of the island and I pull myself to my feet. I lean over the rail and stare northwest toward Leif's Channel. The howl comes again and again, layering atop of itself; an argument of low, deep screams followed by a roar I recognize in my bones.

The signal cry of a greater mountain troll.

TEN

IN THE MOONLIGHT the trolls are like a river of ice and marble, shining white and blue and gray-silver as they roar past. The herd gallops over the black rocks toward Jellyfish Cove. Their path will not bring them here but will pass the tower by.

I lean out over the railing, gripping it so tightly my knuckles ache.

What are they doing here? So far south, across the channel! How did they get here? The ice is too broken up now; they should be migrating back north for the summer or hunkering down in their ruined cities.

They could destroy the entire island. Panic squeezes my throat.

I turn to the signal bell that, thank blessed Freyr, still hangs lopsided from its lintel. There's no clapper, I know, or the hard sea winds would make it sound. I touch it, then slap my hand against the cold metal, causing only a dull noise that dies fast. My heart rages at me to get going, to leave it and run to town, but this will warn them fastest. That's why it's here.

"*Ned!*" I scream, and turn in tight circles, hunting for a thing to beat the bell with.

His sword is in my hand.

Flipping it around, I grip it with the pommel down and take a deep breath before slamming it with all my strength into the bell.

Pain jars up my arm, but the shock of the signal bell's cry knocks me back into the railing. It reverberates through my skull and beyond, fading into silence. Even the troll cries are diminished.

I hit it again, and again, and again. Gritting my teeth, letting tears of effort fall cold onto my cheeks. The warning bell fills every space inside and around me as I ring it until my feet are numb, until my eyeballs vibrate and my bones crack.

It continues to sound as I run down the tower stairs with nothing but Unferth's sword. I grab an armful of troll-spears from the disaster of a third level but can't carry heavier swords or shields. We'll have to make do.

I burst out of the tower, crying Ned's name again, but he's not anywhere.

The terrain is wet from melting snow and uneven. Cold air slices down my throat as I fight to keep running even as I slip and fall in the loose earth. Unferth's sword weighs me down, and the spears are awkward in my arms. Hidden pockets of snow catch my feet and send me down hard. My wool dress becomes heavy at the hem with water and mud. I'd never make it if I didn't know the way in all this darkness.

The two kilometers from tower to town has never been so

long. I struggle and pant, fear like lightning in my veins, but a thrill, too. The trolls came to me. They're here. As if it were meant to be: my stone heart, served to me on a platter!

If only I can remember my training and survive. The mother is the leader. Stop her, stop them all. Use my whole body against their weight. Stab, not slash. The eyes are a good target. *Run.*

Fear and excitement in the same breath. Oh, Alfather, be with me.

The first screams hit me as I round the hill that shelters the Cove from the harshest ocean winds.

The herd has reached the festival site before me and half the booths are destroyed, two on fire.

People and monsters dash madly about, flames casting deeper shadows, shadows that fool my eyes. I raise Unferth's sword and throw myself into the terrible lunacy.

A massive troll blocks my way, canceling out the moon. His tusks are sharp and straight down like a saber-toothed cat's; he's wider than Red Stripe and reaches for me. I drop all the spears but one and hook its butt under my boot. He charges into the blade. He howls, hot sweet breath blowing at me, and his weight shoves me and the spear back.

I stumble under his weight but manage to lift Unferth's sword and jam it up into his neck. It grates against rough skin as I drag it out again. I haven't killed him—it's not so easy—but as he grabs at his wounds I seize the scattered spears and run on.

I have to find the mother. Stop her, stop the herd.

Where is Ned?

Firelight and smoke war with the moon to cast shadows and an argument of light into the fray. Trolls tear through the circus. They bash through walls and rip down the canvas booths. I see our Beowulf George in silk pajamas hacking at a pale gray troll with one of the warrior swords. The blade sparks against the hard skin.

"George!" I scream. "Stab! Not slash! Lever it . . . with your weight!"

I drop the spears again and crash into the troll from behind, Unferth's sword an arrow in my hand. The point pierces through tough skin. George's eyes are wide holes and he fumbles to follow suit. The two of us stab and hack, but the troll punches out, knocking George away with a roar and charging toward a few of its brothers.

There are so many of them.

I turn toward more yelling to see other actors caught in the attack. Some flee; some are stock-still, some fighting poorly. "Here!" I throw two of them spears and have three left. The first troll, gushing dark blood from his stomach and neck, comes at me again and I drop the spears to put both hands behind the sword. I thrust it with all my power, and he knocks me aside with a wild swing. My shoulder explodes and I hit the ground, its blood a hot mask on my face. It sticks my lashes together and I think of Valtheow, I think of Sanctus Hervor and her vicious fighting. Suddenly I'm flooded with more joy than fear.

I suck in a breath of sticky cold air and get up.

The herd heads for the Cove. I grab the discarded spears

again, throwing them into whatever hands I can, using this flare of excitement to rally others. We run behind the trolls down the rocky hill toward town.

Everything is alive with fire and screams.

Coveys throw iron pots and use their own swords to attack, broken tables as shields. There's a barrier built between two houses, and an actor helps me clear out the troll hounding the residents. He snarls at us and we both drive spears hard into his chest. He hits one house hard enough to shake us all but still lives, still swings back at us, baring his twisted tusks. "Get out!" I yell at the families. "Go to the docks; take the boats while you can!"

Racing forward, I drive Unferth's sword up into the troll's softer neck. He falls back, dead weight nearly ripping the sword from my grip; the first one I've killed.

A scream of victory feels like laughter tearing up my throat.

Here's Peachtree, a butcher knife in hand and human blood staining half her face. "Signy." She grasps my arm, crying and choking. "Come on, we have to get out."

I take her face in one bloody hand. "Peachtree, gather as many people as you can and *go.*"

She shakes her head desperately but obeys, stumbling away from me with her arms out.

My eyelashes stick together when I blink, and my left shoulder and arm hurt with a constant pressure. My ears ring. I'm alone in a pocket of town where the battle has passed on. We're barely killing any of them, even with my heavy spears. Our only hope is to keep them off until the sun comes and pray for no cloud cover. My body shakes with adrenaline, but already my legs are like lead. I might not make it until dawn.

And where is Ned? He's the only other person here who knows how to deal with these monsters. We should be fighting side by side. Where did he go?

The Shipworm. That's where Rome and Jesca will be. Stepping over bodies, I run toward the center of town. In the darkness a troll looms up, reaching with his massive, crushing hands, and I swing my sword. He catches the blade. I rip the sword free, slicing open a shallow cut in the beast's palm. He roars and I trip backward. I hit the ground. The troll looms over me, grabs my arm to haul me back up. An excruciating pop as my shoulder jerks out of joint. I scream and he puts his curled yellow tusks to my face and roars again. His fetid breath blackens my vision and I kick desperately at him, take his tusk in my good hand and yank. I punch him in the eye.

He bellows his pain and flings me away before charging on.

Loki's luck and the cobblestones together jar my shoulder back into the socket. I scream through grinding teeth.

There's a metal taste clamped to the back of my throat. My fingers are numb, and thank Fate it was my left arm. I roll over, grabbing for Unferth's sword. Purple blood stains the blade, is caught in the creases of the pommel, and runs down the fuller to drip onto the cobblestones.

Pushing to my feet, I stumble toward the center of town again. Nausea pulls through my veins, and my skull throbs; my shoulder burns.

The Shipworm is alive with light and people, surrounded

by trolls waving fists and broken doors like threats. People are trapped inside, high up, who must have run for the roof instead of out.

A sixth troll enters the courtyard.

She's bigger than her children, huge, five meters at least, white marble with gray and blue veins. Her stone skin gathers the littlest strands of moonlight and glows. She's a ghost with flaccid breasts and silver rings piercing her nipples, her ears, her nostril. A looping collar of iron and bone hangs from her neck. Tusks spiral out of her mouth, ivory-yellow and curling gracefully, impractically.

The troll mother.

I step out of the alley. "Mother," I call.

She turns to me, her marble muscles shifting smoothly. Her eyes are shocking aquamarine, bright and alive.

I raise Unferth's sword in a challenge. "Fight me!" I cry, voice cracking.

The troll mother roars.

It's an elegant howl, like the first strain of the Gjallarhorn that blows to signal the end of the world.

Her sons echo the call and I'm trapped in this circle of them. They're turned away from the Shipworm, and I force a smile so wide I imagine Unferth's grin behind it, his teeth behind mine, both of us here and dangerous. As the first thin light of dawn kisses the red rooftops, we face each other. Maybe if I can just draw it out long enough. Maybe.

The troll mother opens her mouth and she speaks. "*Valkyrie.*"

My spine straightens in shock. *She knows me for what I am.*

I work my mouth, but nothing comes out. It doesn't matter, this shock, this troll mother recognizing me. What matters is distracting her, saving the others. I swallow grit and troll blood.

"Yes!" I cry. "I am Signy Valborn, the Valkyrie of the Tree. The Alfather named me. I am born of death and for death, troll. Who are *you* to be here, to challenge me?"

The troll mother stares at me, and I pray the people in the Shipworm are using the time to escape. I cannot glance their way, can't let her notice them again. Unferth's sword trembles in my exhausted hand.

Her stone skin is nicked and lined with scars, claw marks dug in straight lines and patterns, as if purposefully made. One great sickle-shaped scar on her shoulder almost appears to be the rune for *transformation*, and another giant X might be the rune for *day*.

The beautiful moon-marble troll twists her mouth into a horrible smile. She flexes her hands, rattling the bone bracelets on her wrists, and makes a huge barking sound.

"Poor lost girl," she says, and laughs again. "Never know monster inside."

I shake my head, knees weak.

The troll mother opens her arms invitingly. "You defeat me, they all live."

I flick my eyes toward the red roofs. No true flash of sunlight, and low clouds could keep her safe for ages still, if Unferth's stories of the mothers are true.

Dull certainty settles on my shoulders. I won't survive her

that long. Whose poem is this? Hers or mine? My vision wavers; my shoulder burns. I'm so weary, and the arm with Unferth's sword trembles.

My story. It has to be mine.

"For Hangatyr!" I scream wildly, then run at her.

She doesn't move but simply allows Unferth's sword to cut into her chest. Dark blood bubbles around the blade. She casually lifts one arm and bats me away. Her sons hoot and bellow from the edges of the square.

The sword rips from my hands. I tumble over the hard stone yard and hit in a mess of aches and limbs. I struggle up. She pulls the sword out of her own body and tosses it to me. It clangs against the cobblestones.

I sway as I stand. The troll mother waits with an air of patience while people pour out of the Shipworm. Her sons growl and bare fangs at the people, but their mother flings a hand up to keep her sons from attacking. There's Patty and some trapped guests fleeing for the docks.

I step forward, arcing around to get between the mother and the inn. I charge her again, dashing across the courtyard, sword raised.

There's a scream of my name behind me, but I strike.

The troll mother knocks the sword aside and catches me against her chest. Her eyes are right at mine, sea-blue and aquamarine, and her breath warms me; her arms embrace me. She's so hot, not like stone at all but slick and warm. Comfortable. I feel the beat of her heart like the tide, ancient and strong.

But there in her frozen eyes I see *stone* and *heart.*

Her heart.

The knowledge blazes through me. Sudden hope makes me twist and fight and scream again. I punch at her eye and her nose, and she coughs. I grab her tusk but can't hurt her.

Her mouth opens and she says, "*Your heart.*"

I freeze. The runes pulse there in her eyes and I think, *This is the end,* but before I know, hands pull me free. I hit the ground and recognize Unferth's boots next to my face. I grab at his ankle, but he charges her.

Gore covers Unferth's gray coat and he stabs a thick troll-spear into her ribs. The mother roars and picks him up by the neck. He kicks. I scramble for his sword.

The troll mother squeezes and Unferth wilts. His arms dangle limp.

My world narrows.

Sunlight touches her head and she ducks. She throws Unferth's body over her shoulder and barks at her sons.

Then she turns away with him. I try to run after and she swings her arm at me, catches me in the chest. I slam into the cobblestone courtyard again, unable to breathe, wheezing, gasping, clutching at my chest. A sharp, horrible pain branches like lightning from my side. I roll, try to stand. My skull pounds; I can hardly claw my way up the side of the general store to watch the final troll-sons harass the survivors fleeing the Shipworm in every direction. The lightening sky begins to reach the streets and alleys, and the trolls dodge through the remaining shadows after their mother.

I'm suddenly alone again.

Your heart.

Her heart.

The inn smokes, sending up long lines of ashes into the sky. The wind is not only acrid but sharp with blood, the sticky and nauseating smell of a funeral pyre. Strings of lanterns and colored paper flutter on the ground, scattering fake coins everywhere.

My eyes won't focus at first on the lumps on the ground. There aren't too many right here, mostly strangers I don't know. Blood is frozen across their hands and faces. Their teeth shine from open mouths.

I whirl away, but there's Amelia the dentist against the well, her dress stiff with blood. And there the actor Leif pinned to the earth with one of the troll-spears. My throat closes.

Then I see Bethya the mead mistress, but only because the tip of her braid suddenly catches fire. I stagger to her and fall to my knees, batting the fire out with my hands. The musky smell of burning hair gags me and I wretch against the ground, gripping deep into the cracked cobblestones until two of my fingernails break. Tears fall from pain and grief, and my heart is an ever-widening chasm.

Wiping my eyes, I turn toward a sudden flurry of movement.

The wind ruffles Jesca's graying hair and the end of Rome's blue shirt. *No! They were supposed to escape.* But here they are, fallen beside each other, his shattered arm half on top of her. A tiny wail worms its way out of my mouth. Both their faces flash before me, golden and laughing. I remember the roughness in Rome's voice when he called me *daughter* and Jesca hugging me with hands as delicate as bird wings. *Even the Alfather has a family.*

I lean over Rome, one arm pressed to my ribs. I touch his cold cheek. His eyes are closed already, and his lips are pressed tightly together.

I open my mouth to say his name.

But nothing comes out.

Is this what my mother and father looked like, piled one atop the other in that faraway jungle? This is not how Freyans are supposed to die.

What will I tell Rathi? My throat is raw and burning; tears fall onto my cheeks only to dry tight against my skin in the heat from the fires. With a shaking finger I draw the rune *peace* onto their faces.

I lurch up to keep after the troll mother and her stone heart. There's nothing I can do for them, but if there's any chance, any at all, that Ned is still alive, that I can catch her and dig out her heart, I have to go.

Scarlet binding runes mark the alley she took. They waver in my hazy vision and at first I think I imagine them: *final destiny,* which means *Ragnarok,* the last battle of the gods. And *lost sun.*

But I stumble into one wall, and the rune *lost* smears under my hand. The runes are painted on my town in blood.

Here on the cobblestones is Unferth's sword, the sword he didn't have to keep himself alive.

And now I defile the blade by leaning on it, but I have to, I need the solid strength of it to pick carefully through the alley and out of town. Over heather and scraggly, muddy moorland to the festival. All I know is my harsh breathing, the painful pump of blood behind my eyes. Broken bones in my side, my shoulder a starburst of fire, bruises rising like dough over every part of me.

Posters with my face in the Valkyrie paint are strewn haphazardly; Lady Serena's booth is tossed on its side, spilling glass and pillow feathers like intestines. Game stalls lean precariously against each other. Even the stuffed animal prizes are singed.

The feast hall is nothing but a charred ruin. Outside it is one of the retainer's spears, shattered halfway down the shaft. The wide spearhead bends because it was only decorative, not a true weapon. Why didn't they know? I find George near it, his chest crushed. Maybe he was too desperate to care.

Red Stripe's shed is leveled. I pick through the remains, heedless of injury. The smoldering wood burns my fingertips, and every breath I take poisons my lungs. Troll chains lie half-buried under sod and thick rafters. The can of paint we used to draw black and green runes on Red Stripe's back has exploded in a viscous mess. A broken piece of the long broom jabs into my calf. Then there are the chunks of stone smoothly curved on one side like skin but jagged on the inside. A troll died here.

I leave.

The ceaseless wind scours my eyes, chaps my lips. But my blood runs hot and fast, groaning in my head as loud as the ocean. My breath rattles, and my tongue is as dry as a tundra.

Nobody would need hunter training to read the troll-sign screaming at me from the land: boulders scoured by claws, and pine trees shattered halfway up the trunks. Wide swaths of moor are marked by the herd. Their sweet stink, more potent and ripe than Red Stripe ever was, clings to the grass. Weak white sunshine filters through low clouds. I walk and walk, a dragging step at a time, one hand wrapped tightly around the hilt of Unferth's sword. We're fused together now.

I pass into a dense pine forest. Crows flap overhead. Moor wolves howl far away. My fingers are still numb, my ribs cracking with every breath. But the trees are destroyed, the ground cover flattened. They've left me a perfect trail.

My feet go numb, too, and my leggings soak up freezing water. When my eyes drift closed, I clench my jaw, grip Unferth's sword, and walk on.

My ruined dress clings damply to me, and my breath is frost. There may be wolves stalking in my wake; I may go through a mass of caribou, but I'll never know, because all I see is the meter of earth in front of me and Unferth's body going limp. He has to be alive. It's impossible that he's dead. He only passed out, and she took him because . . . because . . .

The eight-legged beat of Sleipnir's hooves drives me, pulsing in my head and heart and the palms of my hands.

I have to find him.

Alfather, please don't take him away, too.

The trees drop off suddenly. A long flat moor pulls away south, gray and gold except for the single tree with branches only on one side. Around it is the herd of trolls like massive boulders, lolling about three bonfires. The sky remains cast over by thick gray clouds, but even without the sun piercing through they should be crouched in caves, sheltered. If anything I thought I knew about trolls is true, this makes no sense. Unferth said the wisest mothers could use rune magic to protect their sons, hide them, but is this one so powerful? She must be.

In the pale light, I can truly see them. They're all the colors of limestone and shale, some even with flares of orange and yellow lichen growing thickly down their backs.

I stop. The mother isn't here.

Her sons sit like lumps, healthy and whole and enjoying their feast. Piles of bones, broken and sucked dry, are flung around their camp. There are caribou antlers and the carcass of a gray dog sprawled with its face broken in.

It isn't only animals they're eating.

Tattered clothes stripped off a few of the bodies give it away.

And one mess of a dark red sweater turns my heart to stone.

I think of him in that sweater, bulky sleeves rolled back to show off wiry forearms. He was so dangerous and sharp and young.

I scream his name.

The trolls hear, and their bulbous forms shift and grate as they get to their feet one by one. I count seventeen of them left. I raise the sword and hold it high.

The air trembles around me, and a gentle thrum replaces the hoofbeats in my head like constant thunder kilometers away. "Where are you, Mother?" I scream, so raw it burns in my throat. I take one step, then another, the weight of the sword dragging me faster into the valley. *So many of the ancient*

Valkyrie died young. Tears streak down my face and I know I should stop but I can't.

There, in the tall pine trees sloping up the opposite mountain. Their triangle tops shudder and tilt as she barges through. Easily recognized even from this distance by her dangling breasts and iron nose ring. She roars, but not at me.

Wind pushes at me from all sides and the growling is so loud the force of it would shove me down onto my knees.

Heliplanes.

Three of them swoop down ahead of me, their massive rotary blades making the thunder. From their black bellies men spill out, leaping down ropes and landing hard onto the moorland.

These men scream and pull axes and swords loose. They've no guns or armor like a militia or Thor's Army but wear only black coats and pants and boots. Their heads are free of helmets.

Though they are only men, and the trolls each three times larger, they run toward the trolls and the collision of battle, of blade against stone skin, of fist and bone, seems silent under the roar of the heliplanes.

I stumble on, determined to be there. The heliplanes are landing, more men pouring out. I can hear it now, the clash of trolls and men, and smell the burning meat, the smoke from their fires.

A man is thrown into the air, hard and fast. He hits the grass with a cry and skids toward me. Purplish blood covers his face and his grimace is ferocious. There on his cheek is a dark tattoo: the spear of Odin, marking him a berserker.

These are men who carry the Alfather's battle-rage inside their hearts, the madness that burns away self and doubt and terror until all that's left is the fight. *The purpose.*

The berserker near me leaps to his feet and hurls himself back into battle. I want to run after him. I need to be there. I need to be the one to kill her!

But my legs don't listen to me. My breath is shallow, cut off by fierce pain. I can't keep going. I sink down with Unferth's sword and stare.

Trolls begin to fall under the onslaught of power and god-blessed strength. One is spiked by three swords and crashes hard enough to shake the moor. Another loses his head by well-swung double axes. One of the berserkers has his arm torn off in a spray of blood but rushes his opponent again, as if he feels no pain.

Whether from the arrival of the heliplanes or Freyr's blessing, the clouds overhead begin to disperse. Thin spears of sun appear, and two of the trolls run, while another is caught in the light and trapped while his legs solidify. The stone crawls up his chest and he lifts his arms to shield his head, but not before an enterprising berserker stabs straight through the monster's throat.

It is not long after that.

The heliplanes have all landed, and now there's only yelling and cries of pain. Steel on stone. Breaking rock. The tumble of boulders that is the death knell of a troll. Nine trolls are dead, purple ichor melting into the dirt. Four are trapped in stone, all but one cracked beyond regeneration. The rest escape, running off into the mountains. Including the troll mother. She looks over her wide white shoulder at me as she charges away and for a moment there's a cracking magic between us that makes me whimper as it squeezes my broken ribs.

Then she's gone. But I feel my heart beat hard as an earthquake, loud in my ears as if it beats in a cavity as humongous as hers.

The battlefield is quiet.

She was responsible for killing two of the berserkers herself. The third dead berserker is young, maybe twenty, with wide-open eyes. I get up, half-stumbling to him, needing to close his eyes. Another berserker whirls when he hears my boots on the grass and catches me around the waist, pulling me back.

I open my mouth and nothing—nothing!—comes out. My words fail me still, so I push with all my might against this man's black-clad chest. My fingers squish in the blood-soaked material. He says, "Stop struggling, girl," then "*Balls*" as he grabs Unferth's sword by the blade to keep it away from him.

More arms come around me from behind, gentler but just as strong, and a new voice murmurs, "There, maidling, there." Jesca sometimes called me that. The fight pours out of me and I let go of everything but the sword. My eyes close and my knees fold. I don't breathe and there is a pause so long and quiet because my heart stops, too.

All I know is the sword in my hand.

ELEVEN

WE FACE EACH other in a forest of thin white trees. Her eyes, like chunks of aquamarine, loom large. Smoke trails like a curtain around us, dropping flakes of ash into my hair and onto the mother's great sloping shoulders.

I stare at the crystal flecks of her irises, so human-seeming, but luminous.

She stares back. She shifts her head slightly, studying one of my eyes, and I know she is looking for a rune. Like a Valkyrie would do.

I shove at her cold stone chest and wake with my hands pushed out, flailing off the narrow cot.

Morning light brightens the room, highlighting the hammer of Thor hanging against a peach-colored wall, just beside the door. Crafted from two railroad nails, it's homemade, with blue yarn wound around the center like the god's eye. A wallpaper trim of smiling stars and moons and short-handled hammers lines the ceiling. Sunshine courses through the open window, along with a breeze to rattle the billy goat mobile dangling over the empty crib in the corner. The bells on their plastic tails tinkle gently.

As I sit up, gasping for breath, the cot below me creaks. I was brought to this small home on the North Ice military base late last night by a heliplane pilot named Sagan. His wife is called Esma, and she offered their baby daughter's room immediately, as well as a bath, clean clothes, and sanctuary as long as I need it.

Carefully I stand up. My neck aches, but so does the rest of me. The cracked ribs in my side throb and my shoulder is tight enough it might shatter if I knock into anything. I'm bruised everywhere, though most of my cuts are shallow. A berserker medic glued the worst of them closed last night, but my shower must've undone most of that good.

I glance out the curtained window. Everything in this neighborhood is the same taupe color. Row upon row of military housing, with identical front doors and thin walkways. Even the parked cars are all a variation of brown or white or silver. What's truly strange, though, is the lack of people. Counting backward, I guess today is Thorsday, and so maybe children are in school. But the longer I search for signs of life, the more unnerved I become. There's not even litter in the gutters to remind me of Odin.

A small pile of clothes waits stacked beside Unferth's sword. The garnet in the pommel is a dull red this morning, like some life's gone out of it.

My pulse throbs in my fingertips and I think of her. *Your heart.*

I put on the clothes left for me: a loose-fitting cotton dress with a sweater to go over it. The collar is so wide it falls off of my shoulder. I make it through most of a normal bathroom routine, aching on the outside, strangely numb and empty in my heart, until just after I spit out my tooth gel and notice my broken fingernails.

Clutching the sink's edges, I lean into the mirror. There's so little blood in my cheeks that what's usually a scatter of freckles across my nose has erupted across my face. A thin cut slices from my left eyebrow back toward my ear, the skin around it alive with a vicious bruise. My hair is a wight's nest of snarls, as I couldn't bring myself to unknot all the intricate braids Unferth wove before I collapsed into bed. I hardly recognize my own eyes. A ring of blood stains the white of my left one, brightening the green iris until it nearly glows. Like hers. But no runes dance at the edges of my pupils. And my hair looks so awful I laugh. That laughter shakes up my entire body, punching at my cracked ribs until I have to grip the sink tighter, clench my jaw to keep from puking. Tears spill down my cheeks in two straight lines.

I press my fist against my chest, over my heart. I must keep myself together. The Alfather would expect me to be strong after battle.

But I hear the troll mother's roar echo in my ears.

She's still alive. I have to find her, destroy her, chisel her heart from her chest. Not for my riddle but as the blood price for Vinland. For Ned Unferth.

If I am a Valkyrie, it starts here with revenge.

Hands shaking, I dig into my mass of ashy hair to find the little pins Unferth used. One by one I pull them out and drop them into the sink. They ting against the porcelain. Each braid falls, flopping into my face or down my back, around my shoulders. With every gentle tug on my scalp another tear slips past my lashes.

I've no idea how long it takes to work out all the knots. My normally straight hair is kinked and ruined, and I wish I had scissors to cut it all off. But I twist it against the base of my skull and take the pins out of the sink. I close my eyes and try to drag up the memory of Ned's fingers against my scalp, the scratch of pins and the tug as he set them into place. *I'll always have these pins, at least.* Laughter pops up again, reflected like panic in my eyes.

I bare my teeth at myself in the mirror, watching for any wisp of this madness escaping through the cracks.

For the slightest moment I see the rune for *need* spelled out in my freckles.

The kitchen is at the end of the tight, poorly lit hallway. It's cramped with white cabinets and appliances, with a wooden dining table filling the center so there's barely any room to maneuver around it. But what it lacks in space it makes up for in friendliness. Creamy wallpaper with tiny yellow and pink flowers cheerfully displays a set of framed butterfly drawings, and the refrigerator is covered in rainbow alphabet magnets. The *E* and *M* hold up a Thorist prayer card in which a romantically drawn Thor holds a half-dozen small children in his massive arms.

Esma sits at the head of the table, half her attention on the year-old girl in a cherry-red high chair, the other half on the small muted TV crushed up on the counter between a coffeemaker and standing mixer.

Mother and daughter both have round brown eyes and tight curls that hug their heads. Esma's skin is darker than the baby's, glowing smooth and pretty in the warm light.

"Good morning," I say, but it comes out scratchy, like a horrible radio signal.

The baby slaps her palm against the high-chair tray and Esma turns to me, straightening her shoulders as if grateful for the interruption. "Good morning. Help yourself to cereal or toast, and there's coffee in the carafe. I'll finish up in just a moment."

I pour coffee into a wide green mug that says SUMMERFEST '97 ~ LOKI DID IT and join Esma at the table. I can do this; I can be calm. The baby stares at me, opening and closing her mouth around the spoon like a robot. I wrap my hands around the mug and avoid the TV. The news is on, and I don't want to hear any reports from Vinland.

"Did you sleep all right?" Esma asks as she scoops the last bite of orange mush onto the baby spoon.

"Yes," I say to my coffee. No need to speak of nightmares.

"This is Manda, and I'm so glad I had her with me last night or you'd have never gotten to sleep. The little goblin always gets a tish crazy when her da is in and out so fast."

Because it's polite, I look up. "Is Sagan gone again?"

Esma's mouth curls down like a crescent moon and she

shakes her head. "He flew before dawn to join a militia group in Mishigam hunting for Baldur."

And here I'd forgotten the god of light was even missing.

After a stop at the infirmary to have my ribs wrapped, we go out to the Exchange. I've no money, and nothing even to my name but Unferth's sword. Even the seax I couldn't sell remains useless with my packed bags in the warning tower on Vinland. Esma insists on buying me clothes and tells me we're all children of Asgard and what sort of woman would she be if she didn't help? When she quotes *The Charge of Thunder,* I have to accept the charity. *We give aid to those in need, and make of our strength an entire world.*

I ask if we can find news of the troll herd. I try to say it lightly, when I want to rip the information out of the air: *Where is the troll mother? Is she still breathing?*

At the base commander's office, we wait in a pale blue room with wilting flowers in the window. The ache in my muscles and tight cracked ribs force me not to pace but to sit still and find some measure of patience reciting lines from *The Volsunga Saga* to myself. Signy Volsung burned down her traitorous husband's castle; she transformed herself into a wolf for battle. She did everything she needed to in order to protect her family, even lie and cast curses and seduce her own brother. Turning the words of her poem over my tongue calms me.

It's nearly an hour before the commander's lowliest retainer greets us and gives me his condolences. He tells me there's a hospital in Halifax where refugees are being temporarily settled, but no, they can't provide the manpower to send me anywhere. Not to the refugees, and definitely not back to Vinland. Even when I remind him of my name, of my history, he shakes his head regretfully and apologizes that he can't accommodate me. Everyone but dependents and a handful of necessary personnel are deployed for the Baldur emergency. And because we're so near Canadia, where trolls still roam wild, the national troll alert set off by the Cove massacre has locked down the base, not to mention the major highway between here and the city. They expect the lockdown to last at least as long as Baldur is missing and all the country's resources are spread thin. I learn that the berserkers who mowed down the troll mother's herd are called the Mad Eagles, and they alone remain on Vinland, tracking any stragglers or escapees from the herd. The berserkers will annihilate the trolls, I'm assured.

They won't find her without me, I tell him, though he clearly thinks I'm addled from trauma.

But I'm worried they *will* find her. I want to stand over her body as it calcifies and hack it into chunks of stone to get at her heart.

The commander only promises to send word to the Death Hall that I'm here and see if the council will help me return to the island to find the troll mother, but he won't allow me to leave on my own.

By the time we return to Esma's home, it's too late to do anything drastic.

Esma lets me be for the evening, and I gather up Unferth's sword from under the cot. The hilt is cold. I cover the garnet with my palm as if it will keep him from seeing me.

With it I go out into the narrow backyard. A chain-link fence separates it from the next and the next, every metal box the same for two hundred meters in either direction. I spend a few minutes warming my aching muscles and then raise the sword into the first offensive position. The sword is perfectly balanced and only slightly too heavy for me. I've never practiced with it before, never even thought to; it seemed too perfect and right in Unferth's hand. Just as it seems perfect that I should use it now to strengthen myself for vengeance.

I lift it slowly, move into defensive forms. The pain in my side is a fire urging me on, pushing tears into my eyes, but when it becomes a vise I can't breathe through I stretch out onto the lawn to stare up at the sky as it slowly darkens.

The troll mother must be moving now that the stars give her permission. I will tear her to pieces, and when I prove myself to the Valkyrie it will be through violence and death, a confrontation with a monster, not some symbolic riddle solving. It will be on my terms. Raw, vicious, legendary terms.

And I won't wait for her to come to me again.

Esma calls me for dinner and I don't respond. She puts her daughter to bed and sits beside me for a while, but the cold night wind chases her inside. She brings me an old green peacoat and I tuck it under my chin, squeezing myself into a ball as if I can hold myself together.

At dawn, I've chosen my favorites of the clothing Esma

bought for me, just what I can wear. Jeans, a thermal shirt, a dark purple hoodie, and the pea jacket. And my own tired mud boots. I strap Unferth's sword across my back and pin up my braids.

I begin coffee for Esma and then go to the refrigerator. With the alphabet magnets I spell out THANK YOU in bright colors.

I reach the gates of the base just as they're opening to allow in a convoy of armored trucks. With my chin high I slip out and march along the gravel shoulder of the highway as if it's exactly where I belong. When a voice yells at me, orders me to return, I disregard it.

But the last truck in the convoy stops and three soldiers pile out. They all have hammer patches sewn to the shoulders of their dun uniforms. This is Thor's Army. The first soldier holds a hand out and says, "Let's get you back inside, honey."

I keep walking, and his two companions spread out to flank me. Beyond them are the rolling hills of New Scotland for me to focus on; the pale green and grayish gold of early spring. There's no troll-sign here.

When the first soldier tells me to unsheathe my sword and put it on the road, I curl my mouth with Unferth's own disdain. "I need to be on Vinland, and I will find a boat to take me there in Port Hali."

"There's a troll alert. This highway is closed."

"I don't care." As I begin to notice details of his face, his dark eyes and the shape of his nose, I force myself to ignore them. I don't want to know him. "I can make it."

"It's thirty kilometers to Hali," the soldier says quietly. Not without sympathy.

That tenderness infuriates me. "Take me, then."

"It isn't going to happen. You'll have to wait. Maybe we can put a call somewhere? Is your family here on base?"

"My family is destroyed! On Vinland!" Desperation makes me add, "I am the Valkyrie of the Tree and you will obey me, soldier."

"There is no Valkyrie of the Tree," the soldier says as he reaches for Unferth's sword, and it's probably only his surprise that lets me punch him in the face.

The others are on me instantly and I kick to the side, then spin and try to block them. But they throw me onto the road hard enough to knock the breath from me. I shut my eyes against white-hot pain in my ribs and swallow bile. My hand throbs but isn't broken, and gravel cuts into my right cheek. "I have to go!" I yell.

"Nobody's going anywhere, girl," one of them says. They drag me up, don't wait for me to find my feet, and haul me into their truck. The moment one reaches for Unferth's sword again, I snap my head around and say, "If you touch that, I will kill you."

They take it anyway, just before tossing me into their brig.

TWELVE

BEING IN PRISON at least gives my ribs a chance to heal.

For days I lay on the pallet, breathing slowly to soothe the pain, staring at the pipes that cross the ceiling like a road map. I close my eyes and the stone walls of the prison shake; trolls pull away from it, forming out of concrete and metal, tiny yellow eyes glaring at me. They roar in my dreams. Sweat burns my eyes and I throw myself up to pace, to tear at the bars until I'm wasted again by the vise of my ribs.

I'm given ink when I ask for it, though, and I scrawl poetry in spirals and uneven lines all over the walls of the brig. Everything I remember about Rome and Jesca Summerling, about the first light on the ice Yule morning, the laughter and electric joy of the festival. What must be memorialized. A sprawling epic poem with bridges and returns, melodrama and as many rhymes for *home* as I can find.

Every night the troll mother reaches huge hands for me. I toss and yell, sweaty and wild. I wander the nightmare battlefield hours and days, witnessing the slow putrid rot of bodies after the spirit is gone to heaven or the Valhol.

Once Elisa of the Prairie showed me the decaying carcass of a dead bison. She said, *Remember, when you one day preside over a national sacrifice, over a great funeral, this is what happens when death is not followed by fire. This is the deepest face of death, the heart of it.* She cried as she spoke and let her tears drop onto the dry prairie dirt.

I thought I understood death better than Elisa, the rawness of it, the filth. But I never thought the bodies slowly rotting would be men and women I loved.

And in my nightmares, the body I study as the rats come, as the maggots tumble from his tongueless mouth, is Unferth's own.

There's no poetry left in me now, he whispers in my dreams.

It makes me want to tear at my hair and face, dig into my eyeballs until I find runes under my skin. All the desperation, all the terror and nausea, I force into poetry. I draw the troll mother's claws and a spiral of tusks. I write down the side: *the mother of her own destruction.*

I cannot drag my thoughts away from her.

And so I write, too, until my fingers cramp, about Valtheow the Dark, who faced the most ferocious troll mother of our histories with the berserker Beowulf at her side. There was a line she said: *I make myself a mirror to understand the beast.*

Unferth whispers in my head, *Tell me, Signy, why you love her most of all.*

I draw the scar from my palm, the binding rune that he linked linguistically to Valtheow: the servant of death and the death-born, both *Strange Maids.* She became a monster to fight Grendel's mother.

But that Valtheow had a poet named Unferth at her side, and mine is dead.

Nine days after Baldur the Beautiful disappeared, a young berserker and a Lokiskin orphan find the god of light. After days of celebration the country rises from its crisis, and apparently there's no reason for them to hold me prisoner any longer.

It takes several days for me to make my way to Halifax, then on to Port Hali. Walking and hitching rides, relying on the kindness of elated strangers who are happy to share a meal or water with me, to raise a toast because Baldur lives. I have to smile and watch the newsreels, listen again and again to the same information on the radio: a disgruntled Einherjar stole Baldur's ashes, and the god of light woke in a desert, where he was found by Soren Bearstar, a berserker boy a few months older than me.

For his boon Soren asked to serve Baldur instead of Odin, and for the first time in our history there's a berserker unbound from the Alfather. His girlfriend, Vider Lokisdottir, asked to be given the berserker madness, and so there is a woman berserker for the first time since Luta Bearsdottir died.

"It all ties together with a nice little bow," I say when I hear it, earning me an uncomfortable look from the driver of the longship carrier truck that is currently my ride.

With nothing but the clothes Esma bought me, Unferth's sword, and the pins holding my braids up, I scour the Port Hali docks until I find a ferry captain who remembers me. He lets me on board for the first voyage to Vinland since the massacre and says most of the refugees are at a hospital in Halifax. They'll be trickling back soon enough, once the death priests sailing with us purify the bodies and town. The captain's also heard some Freyan preacher from down south has declared the restoration of Jellyfish Cove and the Viker Festival to be an official act of worship, so the military cleanup and death priests won't be our only company before long.

It hardly concerns me. I only need to get to the truck, parked near the ferry ports at the south edge of the Cove. There are protein bars, bottled water, camping gear, and weaponry in the bed, all I need to hunt the troll mother from there back to Canadia if I have to. There's been no word of her, though the Mad Eagles officially cleared the island, wasting a handful of her straggling sons. She's either crossed back over the channel or gone to ground. I'll find her either way.

At the prow of the ferry, I grip the metal rail as salt water splashes my boots and coat. I stare out over the steely ocean, lips chapped, shivering, and I think of her moon-bright face, her claws, her teeth.

"Signy?"

Rome Summerling calls my name, tentative like a ghost, and I stop breathing. I turn, hands sticking to the half-frozen rail.

It's not Rome, of course, but his son, Rathi, standing with his hands in the pockets of a slick tailored coat, collar popped. His hair is a disaster of gold, twisted and tossed by the wind. With the last of the baby fat lost from his face, he's as beautiful as Freyr the Satisfied himself: strong jaw, smooth, symmetrical face that invites confidence like a prince. I step forward, tossed by the rocking ferry, and he reaches out a hand. I grasp his arm.

He's real. He's *here.*

I stare up at him, and there it is, swimming in his black pupil, surrounded by bottle-green iris: *prince.*

Except in my memories his eyes are always the same rich earth color as his father's.

"What's wrong with your eyes?" I say.

Instead of an answer, he hugs me like I'm the only thing in the world. His arms tremble, his shoulders hunch so he can bury his face in my neck. I slide my hands under his coat, around his ribs, glad he didn't go for mine. Here's the familiar smell of his hair gel, the comforting warmth of his arms. His tears stick our cheeks together.

Rathi pulls back to look at me and I stroke under his eyes, wiping away his tears.

"Contacts," he murmurs.

I twist my mouth. "What was wrong with your brown? Brown the color of Freyr's earth? Brown the color of your father's eyes?"

"Sig," he says, ignoring my anger the way he ignores everything he doesn't like.

I turn my back into him and we both face Vinland, a thin strip of black appearing on the horizon. Soon there will be mountain peaks and snowcaps, the dark green of trees and the ferocious gray of cliffs and shattered beaches. He presses a kiss to my hair. To the part between two thick braids. I remember running as kids through coarse grass with our hands linked, and our ankles knocking together under the Summerling kitchen table.

Rathi wraps his arms around me and it's so comfortable I hate it. It was always his problem—or my problem with him. He made me comfortable; he let me relax, slow down, settle, stop pushing and fighting and raging. Last year I watched him perform in a traveling Chautauqua as part of his preaching apprenticeship. He glowed onstage and his words reminded me of warm hearths and bonfires, dancing with my parents, curling at the foot of his bed with licorice to scare each other with tales of giants and dragons. He brought back everything I'd been before the Tree and handed it to me, exactly when I needed it, when I'd fled the Death Halls and my Valkyrie sisters, when I was starving for somebody to say, *Signy, you're amazing,* and that's what Rathi Summerling did.

He'd forgiven me for abandoning him when I climbed the New World Tree, forgiven me for leaving Freyr the Satisfied and our long family histories, our future together we'd childishly whispered and giggled about for years. He'd forgiven me for becoming a daughter of Odin, and I didn't want him to.

Now he murmurs, "I thought you were dead, too, and I was all alone."

"Rag me," I whisper.

Rathi waits, patient as his parents, patient as the earth. He's always like a gift when I need it the most.

Sucking breath through my teeth, I take his cold hand and lead him to the top deck of the ferry, where the wind is harshest and I can't hide anything. I sit him down on one of the rows of metal benches with flaking blue paint. "You're not alone, Rathi. You won't ever be as long as I *am* alive." My voice is rough and unforgiving even as the skin around his lips pales, even as his hand digs into mine. "And I'm not alone, either."

"Tell me," he whispers, eyes unfocused. "Tell me what happened. Please."

I do.

It's a poem, but a dark one, a quiet one. This story I spin for the only living Summerling about how his parents died, about how all of them died, resembles the truth not at all. I wonder if Unferth would forgive me for lying.

THIRTEEN

TO KEEP RATHI out of the battlefield that was Jellyfish Cove, to keep him from finding his parents' bones picked over, I ask him to go with me to the warning tower. I say I can't face Unferth's ghost alone.

The walk is muddy and rough, and Rathi slows me down, picking his way around snowmelt ponds and doing his best not to step in slush. With his arms out like a stork for balance, he almost makes me smile. The cuffs of his suit pants soak up plenty of cold water. His shoes slip against the frosty gorse and the splash is followed by a disgusted groan. He glares at nature and then stops bothering to avoid anything.

Except for the front door knocking loose against the frame as the ocean wind blows, the tower appears as it always has: lonely. I steer clear of the holmgang ring and head quickly inside, barreling upstairs to my room. The air is silent, still, and cold. My breath frosts on my lips, is harsh in my ears.

Footsteps downstairs stop my heart, but I remember it's

Rathi. An iron poker scrapes against the hearth, echoing up to me as he begins a fire.

Grabbing my seax, I buckle it at my hip, and take a moment to arrange it so it doesn't rub against the belt holding Unferth's sword across my back. I dig into the backpack Unferth packed me weeks ago for the silver rings and cuffs Jesca and Rome gave me at Yule and clasp them over the sleeves of my thermal shirt. Then I stuff in my only other wool Valkyrie dress and swing the pack over my shoulder.

I don't say goodbye to my room, but I think of the poetry I painted onto the balcony overhead. My mark.

Rathi's put a pot of water to boil on the fire. I brace myself and go into Unferth's room. It's shaped like a slice of pie, with light from the single porthole window facing north. Nothing personalized.

Once I barged in on him shaving in the bathroom. I called, "Unferth? Are you decent?"

He leaned out of the small bathroom in only his sweatpants. "Rarely," he said with a twisted smile. I pursed my lips to mask my reaction to his near nakedness.

"What do you want, little raven?" he asked, pulling back into the bathroom. I joined him, standing just outside, and watched as he scraped the razor over the last line of shaving cream beside his left ear. Unferth bent over the sink to splash water on his face. The long scattering of scars marred the right side of his back; I only saw because as he stretched they glinted strangely in the yellow bathroom light.

I reached out and touched his shoulder blade. Half-shocked

he didn't jerk away from my touch, I boldly stroked the twist of scars. "Troll?"

He took a second to glare at me in the tarnished mirror, water running off his face like rain. "Troll," he confirmed. After screwing off the faucet, he did pull away from my hand, patting his face and chest with a thin towel he snatched from a ring in the wall.

I cupped my hands against my chest. "You must have been so young."

"It was the first troll I ever met."

He threw the sentence away, but I caught it and held my ground in the bathroom door. Unferth stopped so close I might've leaned in and pressed us together. My breath picked up pace and I remained still, curling my hands around the doorjamb.

"I'm not going to tell you more, little raven, not today."

"Someday?"

"Someday." Unferth's voice dropped, as if he was making a wish, not a promise.

I'll never know now. *But,* I think, as I take a deep breath and dive into his bathroom, searching for anything of his, *at least he died as he lived.*

Armed with three thin copper rings he used to wear and a pair of his gloves, I rejoin Rathi. He didn't make tea but hot chocolate, since that's all we kept here. Unferth liked it first thing in the morning, but I never had the patience to stir and stir so it heated without burning.

We sit at the worn old table and drink as spring wind rattles the shutters, until Rathi says, very quietly, "I wish they hadn't been here. I wish we'd never come to Vinland but stayed in Cherokeen."

"They loved it here. It was everything they wanted from life."

He nods jerkily, like he doesn't want to agree but has to. "Ardo will rebuild. I can't run it, though. We'll find somebody else."

"Ardo?"

"Vassing. He heads Bliss Church in Mizizibi. I'm working on my mastership with him this summer. Or was going to be. It was an honor."

"Jesca told me. She was so excited, and proud." I reach across the table and touch the back of his hand.

"They're saying . . ." Rathi trails off to look out the narrow window toward the sea. "That Vinland was a necessary sacrifice to balance the strands of fate and bring Baldur home. That the trolls came because the sun was lost. The troll mother wished to sow doubt and chaos, and that's why they left those runemarks for Ragnarok."

I sigh through my teeth. Chaos. *Sacrifice.*

"Do you believe it? Did the gods let this happen to our family?"

The idea gnaws at my throat. I remember the bloody runes, the clarity in the troll mother's eyes. Her fury, and the broken bodies scattered at her feet. "No, I think it was fate. Every choice has consequences, and those consequences cause more consequences. They can become sacrifices in retrospect. Like my parents died and I ended up climbing the Tree. They didn't know it would happen, but it's still connected. Their death became the sacrifice that brought me to the Alfather's attention.

"The same can be said about the troll mother. We were destined to meet; I saw it in her eyes." I shake my head. *Your heart,* she said. "She's the answer to my riddle, and I feel that we'd have come together sooner or later. It was here, because of . . . choices we all made. Me to spend the winter here, and your parents to move here. Maybe the troll mother chose this time because of Baldur, and so his disappearance and the massacre are connected. Maybe she had no reason at all. Maybe chaos was her reason. Who knows how many choices and consequences brought us all to that moment, when I could see the answer to my riddle. It was Fate."

"So it's all about you, Signy." His voice is hollow; he leans away from me.

My guts go cold and I shove the hot chocolate away from me. "That's not—not what I mean. Only that it's connected. The Tree, Baldur, trolls, the riddle. Knotted together in Fate's weave."

He stands, hands pressed to the table, to loom over me. "You like thinking that. You like to believe it all has meaning, some grand meaning, so there's what? A good reason they died? If they were meant to die, you didn't do anything wrong! You just did what you were *fated* to do."

I don't know how to respond, and so I only stare at him. The silence between us turns stuffy.

Rathi's shoulders slump. "I shouldn't attack you. They

loved you. I love you. It's just, they always followed your news, wanted to hear from you, but you never wrote or called. You were a skit daughter, Sig, and they didn't care. Last year, after you left me, my dad said, 'Signy's too big for us, son.' And I hated you because I wanted them to think I was big enough to match you."

My skin crawls with regret and I hug myself, knowing there's only one way to make this feeling go away. "I swear to you, Rathi Summerling, I won't let their sacrifice be in vain."

"That's something Odinists are good for."

Because Rathi doesn't want to look at me at the moment, I grab my bag and tell him to use the tower. It'll make a good base of operations for the Freyan rebuilding process, and I certainly won't be returning. He runs a hand through his hair, leaving furrows in the gel, and pulls his face down, but doesn't argue.

I trek back to town to get the truck, throw my hiking bag into the passenger seat, and take off.

I begin hunting at the meadow where the Mad Eagles found us, where they cut through so many trolls and the mother escaped. All the broken pieces of stone have been collected, sent off to some lab for study or smuggled into a black market or put on display in a roadside museum. I walk the length of it, hand sweating on the pommel of Unferth's sword as I remember the shudder of wind and roaring and sticky sweet smell of their breath.

In the west, I find sign of a single troll shoving through the tree line. And a chunk of iron with a hole bored through: a piece of her great bone-and-iron collar.

The troll mother fled this way, alone by the looks of it.

I drive to high ground over access roads that are mostly mud and slush. With binoculars I study the shadowy pattern of broken trees, tracing her path for a half kilometer before she came out again onto stony moor and I can't see obvious sign. This island is over a hundred thousand square kilometers. Pocked with giant lakes, mountains, and moors, it could take years to explore on foot, and the roads barely cover ten percent of it. I've set myself an impossible task.

But I won't give up so fast. The Mad Eagles searched with heliplanes; they couldn't see the smaller signs from the air, like mismatched lichen patterns or smoke stains, that I'll be able to find if I'm methodical and on the ground.

So the tedious driving begins. The truck crawls down the coastal road and I peer carefully to either side, every half kilometer getting out to walk the edges and go into the stunted pines a little bit. The caribou haven't come back to this northern finger of the island yet—whether from the cold or the recent trolls and military heliplanes, I couldn't say. I don't know much about the non-troll fauna of Vinland except that there are arctic hares and foxes, lemmings, squirrels, and little brown bats, but no snakes. And that I need to be on the lookout for wolf scat. Rome told me some of the wild dogs out here were descended from dire wolves within two or three generations.

Birds flit everywhere during the day, and much of the grass is pushing up new shoots. The evergreens leak sap, and the creeks run hard with snowmelt. There are ponds and lakes everywhere, winking in the sun, a few with ice still staining the edges. If my heart wasn't so sore this would be lovely. If I wasn't so alone.

At night I sleep in the truck, curled in blankets and trying desperately not to think of Unferth. He mutters in my head sometimes, rules for troll hunting, reminders not to neglect to look up high or take into account rockslides. I whisper back to him poetry and riddles I make up on the spot. I want to ask him what she meant when she said *Your heart* back to me, as if she'd been looking for me, too. But most of all I walk long and hard; I don't let myself rest, so when the sun falls I'm exhausted.

It doesn't stop the dreams. The troll mother hunts me as I hunt her. She moves gracefully even in the daylight, circling me like a shadow, near enough so at nightfall she can creep closer to watch me sleep. Her moon-bright face stares at me all night, and she sinks into the earth itself when the sun rises. I wake repeatedly, scanning the forest in terror, and take to parking in open spaces. It feels as though the entire world hangs from the tension between us.

The second day, and again on the fifth, I do find sign of her: an ashy clawed handprint smeared down the side of a cliff near Plum Point. It's the nearest place to Canadia, and a ferry runs twice daily over the summer. The town has about fifty permanent residents, none of whom have seen her. There are no additional prints on the muddy gray beach, though I scour it for hours. I wonder if she stood there at the base of the rocks considering a return to Canadia, if I'm going to have to buy a ticket on the next ferry. But there right along the highway, I find a row of baby pines has been bent clear in half as if she turned inland again. Why?

Three times at the end of my first week I see sign of lesser trolls, which makes no sense, as they've never been on Vinland before. Cat wights and iron eaters tend to follow human populations, and Vinland has never had much of one. But the bright orange scat of the iron eaters is unmistakable, and cat wights mark their territory with an acrid scent as well as by braiding tiny fences in the grass.

Eight days into my hunt, I stop abruptly an hour before sunset, because there's another car on the road. A small SUV, shiny and new under a layer of Vinland mud. New Scotland plates and nothing else to distinguish it other than being out on this gritty access road halfway down the western coast of a nearly uninhabited island. Frowning, I unsheathe Unferth's sword and approach on foot.

Before I get to the SUV, a shrill scream darts from the valley to my left, like a jaguar or panther in the movies. It's returned by another, and then more and more, pitching up like monkeys worked into a frenzy. Lesser trolls.

I hesitate for the briefest second before diving between the trees.

Needles and twigs whip my face and I ignore them, sword

at the ready, boots skidding over fallen pinecones and the wet ground. The screaming draws me to a surprising grove of aspen, glowing like bones in the late evening light. A huge crack shatters the air as a man breaks off a thick tree branch. He swings it like a bat at a cluster of furry, dark cat wights, roaring loudly.

At least thirty wights harry him, three on his back, cackling gleefully as he swats at their cousins. Claws rip his shirt, tear at his short dark hair, and he opens his mouth to rage. He kicks and spins, catches them with his aspen-tree club. One splats against another tree; there's the slick pop of breaking bones, screams, and more wild laughing. They die fast, but more come, all huge eyes and tiny claws, matted fur and fangs and curling cat tails.

I slice one down the spine with Unferth's sword and stomp at another. Some turn to me, and I unsheathe my seax to wield a blade in each hand. A cat wight tears at my leg and I brain it with the pommel of the sword. I turn and scream at two more, swinging Unferth's sword, slicing with my seax.

Fire burns across the back of my neck, my hair pulls, and I bend, rolling hard against the ground to crush the thing clinging to my shoulder, then back to my feet with a groan. I taste blood-black earth, and my old cracked ribs suddenly dig at my lungs.

Thank Fate the surviving wights begin to disperse. They flee south, and I lower my weapons. With a shaking hand I wipe pinkish blood off the seax blade onto my jeans and sheath it. I press my hand to my ribs, let the tip of Unferth's sword brush the flattened grass.

The man's labored breathing makes me turn my head just as he rushes me.

I curse in shock, raise my arm, but he hits me and the sword flies off. I smash into the ground with a scream and kick up with both feet. I catch him in the chest and he grunts but grabs my ankles and throws me.

My shoulder slams into the ground first and I roll, hitting rocks hidden beneath the moss and grass. The incline drives me down, skidding and rolling. I spit blood and my eyes are full of grit, but I climb up just as he swings the branch at me. I duck, unsheathing my seax to strike out as I spin away. The blade rips through his shirt and cuts his side. He staggers back slowly, as if he's surprised but not hurt.

I run.

Up the hill, tearing between the trees, gasping and scrambling until I reach the truck. I climb into the bed, tripping over the canvas-covered supplies and onto the roof of the cab.

I breathe deeply, carefully, and tears spring to my eyes from the wretched pain in my side.

There's no sign of him.

Silence from the forest but for a gentle wind that blows through it. I could get into the cab and drive away, return later, but the berserker could be hurt. I cut him, certainly, and the cat wights probably bit and scratched.

Seax gripped tight in my sweaty hand, I spit blood and grit

off my lips, then call out, "Berserker! I am Signy Valborn. Get ahold of yourself and come speak to me."

Nothing but the echo of my voice and the whoosh of wind through the valley.

"Are you one of the Mad Eagles?" I yell.

Still there is no response.

I wait, legs spread for balance, seax at the ready, and scan the shadows spilling down the forested hill. Twilight approaches and I don't want to be here if this is the cat wights' territory. But I don't want to leave the berserker, either. Besides being injured, who knows what he's seen?

I count to one hundred, lengthening my breaths, pressing my side with my free hand. I count again. My head is beginning to ache, and just as I decide to hop down out of the cold evening air, I hear him coming.

The pace is sedate; he must no longer be mad.

The berserker appears through the dark green with one hand up in peace; in the other he holds Unferth's sword, blade down. "I'm well," he calls with a deep, shocked-sounding voice.

I lower my seax with relief.

He's young, my age, with dark skin and eyes and buzz-cut hair. His hands are massive and possibly he could wrestle Red Stripe and win. A red T-shirt is in bloody tatters from the cat-wight claws and my seax, but he seems mostly intact himself.

When he reaches the truck, he sets the sword down reverently, then raises his face and looks at me, displaying the berserker's spear tattooed straight down his cheek. It bends as he twists his broad face into regret. "I am sorry; I was lost."

I grit my teeth against the pain of my ribs. He will see no fear or sympathy from me, another child of Odin. "You seem to have found yourself, then."

Something like a smile shifts over his luxurious mouth. It's incongruous on his otherwise rectangular face: hard jaw, wide nose, broad cheeks, heavy brows. His eyes are mottled brown and slender. He certainly isn't Asgardian. An Asgardian Islander, maybe, or with some of the old native blood, but the berserkers are supposed to be pure.

That's when I recognize him. This is Soren Bearstar, the young man from Nebrasge who rescued Baldur the Beautiful. The berserker who forsook my mad god.

"Odd-eye," I say, surprised. "The Sun's Berserk."

He has the grace to wince.

I crouch, then hop to the ground, hitting slightly too hard. He steadies me, but I catch myself against his chest. The whole left side of his shirt is plastered to him with blood. I offer my hand. "Sanctuary for the night, berserker?"

His sticky hand connects to mine and the last shine of sunset skims across his face. I see a golden rune in his pupil.

It says *hero.*

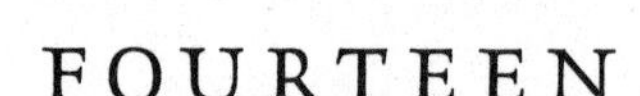

FOURTEEN

IN THE GLOW of my truck's headlights I clean Soren Bearstar's wounds. He stares up at the darkening sky as I pat alcohol onto the gouge in his ribs. It's not as deep as I thought, and bled so much because of the berserker rage heating up his heart. I use Band-Aids to hold the worst part together and then wrap gauze all around his torso. He's so wide I only have enough to go around three times.

"At least you'll finally have a scar," I mutter, eyeing the rest of his perfect body. Except for a few nicks and scratches, there's nothing dramatic marked on him. "What kind of berserker has no scars until he's eighteen?"

Soren pulls a new T-shirt over his head. "I won't be eighteen until the middle of the summer."

My hands find their way to my hips and I study him. He moves deliberately, even just putting on a shirt. He reaches for the alcohol and cotton pads, then meets my gaze. "May I?" He nods toward my left arm.

Awkwardly I roll up my sleeve, not wanting to lose the

shirt. He doctors the three parallel claw marks drawn bright scarlet down my forearm. It stings, but he's incredibly gentle. I lift my drooping braids to let him see the back of my neck. He cleans the cuts there, too, and my arms tremble from effort because it's difficult to breathe with them raised and my ribs smarting.

At least I'm not cold, despite the frigid night. Soren's like a walking radiator.

"Done," he murmurs. "Except your ribs. I . . . I apologize. You're lucky I didn't crush them more."

"A troll did that." I turn and poke him in the chest. "A greater mountain troll, three weeks ago."

Soren takes a step back from me. "You're the survivor."

"There were others."

"Baldur and I heard a story about you—about the girl who charged an entire herd of trolls with nothing but a sword in her hand."

It makes me smile. I was hardly charging at that point, but I prefer this version to the reality.

We drive to higher ground and make camp at the edge of a cliff. I haven't seen any troll-sign, but to be safe I suggest we don't build a fire. Soren nods and pulls three flat brown cardboard packages from his SUV. They're self-heating MREs. I watch as he adds water to a chemical pouch and slides it back into the box. It silently but effectively warms up the beef ravioli. All three boxes are different flavors, and he lets me choose. I decide the stew will be the lesser evil, and he eats both other packets. Mine is thick and sticky, but I haven't had a hot meal in over a week. I miss the sloppy oatmeal Unferth used to make, when it was the two of us.

Starlight and a soft sliver of moon keep the night dark, but as I eat, my eyes adjust to the layers of nighttime, to the distant peaks and darker valleys. To the undulating shadows of the ocean in the west. Ghost-gray clouds drift low, and the longer I rest the better my ribs and stinging cuts feel. I stretch out on my sleeping bag, and Soren does the same. We make a V with our heads together near the cliff, feet pointing at the trucks. The half of me nearer to him remains warm, though my outer arm and leg feel the ice still hanging in Vinland's spring wind.

"What are you doing out here?" I finally ask him.

"Baldur and I are concerned about the troll herd."

"Don't you trust your brother berserkers to clear the island?"

It takes a moment before he answers. "Baldur feels guilty about the massacre."

"Why?"

"He thinks it wouldn't have happened if he had not been gone and forgotten himself."

And so even Baldur believes the massacre is connected to his disappearance. I shake my head. "What does it mean, forgotten himself?"

"Ah, that . . . He didn't remember his name or know anything about himself when he rose in the desert. We found him and he was mortal, memory-free without the apple of immortality from Idun's garden."

"I didn't know death strips away your memories. Or is it resurrection that does it?"

"Either. My understanding is you need a guide for crossing between worlds if you want to retain yourself," Soren says very sadly.

The ache in his voice finds my own pinched grief. So Unferth has forgotten me. I realize I'm rubbing my hand against my chest. I stop, let my fingers spread over my heart. "Who is we?" I ask suddenly. "I thought you were alone until after you had him, until you met the little girl berserker?"

The dead silence that exudes from my left, the flare of heat, makes me roll over to stare at him. "You didn't tell the true story."

Even in the pale starlight I see his jaw work hard as he clenches and unclenches it. He sits in one smooth motion. "I . . . can you just pretend you didn't hear that?"

"Never." I laugh and sit, too. "Tell me, Soren Bearstar; I'll keep your secret with you."

"I . . . can't. I'm not supposed to." He chews the words like even they are difficult. I wait, hugging my knees to my chest. To keep myself from pushing him harder, I draw *hero* against the toe of my boot. With a twist, I transform it into a binding rune with his name: *bear star, hope's hero.*

Hear the bear star be born, the seether fall into darkness.

The cliff seems to tilt below me like a ship going out with the tide. I say the line of poetry out loud, one careful word at a time.

"What?" Soren's dark eyes glint as he turns them to me.

"A poem I wrote the morning Baldur vanished. About trolls and my faith and . . . you. And a seether."

Heat blazes from him but Soren shuts his eyes, flattens his hands against air. He reins it in, lowering his hands to the earth slowly. "Yes," he whispers.

"It's a riddle, and you can't tell me the answer," I whisper back.

His head jerks one nod.

The seether fall into darkness. Death strips memories away. "She's not dead?"

"No. It's just that . . . nobody can remember her."

"They tore her name out of the world," I say. "Like Kara Neverborn."

"Who?"

"Exactly. She was the last Valkyrie of the Tree."

"I didn't . . . didn't know she had a name."

Focusing on a different story seems to calm him, and so I keep on. "Kara, the last Valkyrie of the Tree, the most beautiful of all Odin's handmaidens, lived a hundred and fifty years ago. Her triumph and her downfall came during the Thralls' War."

Precia of the South told me this tale the first night I stayed with her, and every time I stayed with her. It was a lesson for me, and, I always suspected, one she kept close to her own heart.

I close my eyes to recall her words, to recall the sorrow in her voice.

"Long in New Asgard the kings and jarls had argued, some claiming our traditions of conquering and thralldom were wrong, that a way of life, a tradition, does not equal truth. Odin's men laughed, saying, *Once defeated, a man's destiny is enslavement, and his children's.* But Thor Thunderer said, *If a man wins freedom with his sword, or even the Alfather's favorite weapon of words, who is to say his fate is not changed?* We warred over it, all of New Asgard sundered in two.

"The Ninth Valkyrie agreed with the Thunderer, with change and choice. When the Shenandoah Army and the Army of the Potomac faced each other at Gettysburg, she saw the hot, sticky death, the heroes falling, the lost and losing, and she cried, *Why does my Alfather allow this slaughter? There is no glory here!* On the third day of the battle, she defied Odin's wishes by raising her sword to fight with the Potomac Army, bolstering their will and courage with hard, hopeful words. The ground trembled at Cemetery Ridge for the final charge, and Kara Neverborn screamed as she ran against Odin's army. She spread her arms and her swan-shift flew out to either side, reaching out like massive wings. Her eyes marked the dead like a Death Chooser of old.

"General Leeson lost that day and the rebel army was broken. The war dragged on, but from the moment the Ninth Valkyrie stepped into the fray, just as her ancient sisters had done, picking a side to win and a side to lose, it was over. Even the Alfather reluctantly bowed to history, to the collective will of New Asgard. But no one living saw Kara again."

I lean nearer to Soren and lower my voice. "For her betrayal, the Alfather ripped her out of the Middle World. The trail of her blood became the Red River, and all the history of her family vanished. Kara had a surname once, but she became the Neverborn. No one knows her name but for her sister Valkyrie."

Soren says, "So they remember the price of defying him."

"No, because he loves her, wherever she is, and couldn't destroy the long poem of Valkyrie names by removing hers completely."

His expression hardens. "The Alfather doesn't love."

"Just because he doesn't love you, he must not love at all?" I laugh, and hear Unferth's voice murmur, *You've met someone more self-absorbed than you, little raven.*

"There's no evidence he loves anyone."

"He loves *us*."

Soren regards me, brow low in a frown, hooding his eyes. "Us."

"The Valkyrie."

"You're . . . the Child Valkyrie. The Valkyrie of the Tree, who ran away because she couldn't solve her riddle."

I flop back down onto my sleeping bag. "Yes."

"*And* the girl who faced the herd of trolls."

"Yes."

"And you think the Alfather loves you?"

Staring up at the bare glitter of stars, I say, "Yes. I know he loves me. And he never has betrayed one of us if we did not betray him first. In all the stories and poems, I defy you to find an example otherwise."

I hear the shuffle as he lies back down, too. He says, "That isn't how Odin treats the berserkers. He should love us as much."

"Maybe he does and you just don't see it."

"No one who loves would give the berserking as a gift. It makes us outsiders, apart from the world."

That familiar pinch of loneliness responds to his words. "At least you have each other, your fellow berserkers."

"I don't. Not since I chose Baldur."

"But you still have your madness, the frenzy. It connects you back through generations of ancestors. You're a berserker still, Soren. You chose to give up on the Alfather's ways, but he didn't give up on you."

He sighs, low and deep like the earth itself lifting rough shoulders. "We're tools to him. That's what berserkers are. I'm glad for you if you think the Valkyrie are different."

A hundred arguments crowd my head, that the Valkyrie have wills of our own, that he gives us choices, that Odin asked me to choose him; he didn't make me. But it's such a strange position to find myself in: defending the Valkyrie, talking of them as a unit, like I'm one of them.

I fall asleep wondering if my sisters know where I am.

Soren's already up when I wake, boots scuffing slowly against the loose dirt and frost here at the top of the cliff as he works through a set of offensive postures. I sit, folding my legs up to my chest, and watch. His body is like one thick muscle, all shifting as one. It's a different grace from Unferth's, who was tight, fast motion. Soren is smooth and appears relaxed, though the sweat glinting in his buzzed hair and heat radiating off him are a sure sign otherwise.

He comes to a center pose, legs spread, hands together, and blows a long string of air before opening his dark eyes to look at me. In the bright morning sun it's no easier to read his face than it was in the bare starlight. No expression but for the wrinkle between his eyebrows. It's nearly a frown, but maybe that's just how his face rests. I smile wryly, though he surely won't understand why.

"Morning," he says.

"Morning."

Going to his SUV, he digs into the backseat, then tosses me a can of coffee. I catch it, startled by the cold metal. The logo is fancy, declaring, EVEN THE GODS CAN FIND HEAVEN IN OUR BEANS.

"Sorry it's not hot. If we build a fire I have some real grounds."

I raise my eyes to his and pop the top. "This alone is the nicest breakfast I've had in weeks."

"Ah, Baldur bought the supplies."

My laughter even surprises me with how merry it sounds. Soren's mouth presses into a line. "Do you mind if I finish my routine?" he asks, then drops down to impress me with the speed and number of push-ups. I stop counting at forty-seven.

"Can you do the thing where you clap between each one?" I tease, but he pauses to say, "I've never tried."

He does, and it makes a huge dull thump against the ground. He lifts his head to smile a little.

"What about pushing up from a handstand?"

Soren actually laughs. There's his sense of humor: in his muscles.

I drink the smooth canned coffee and share my protein bars with him. As we pack up, I realize there's no doubt in me that we'll be hunting together now.

All morning we continue winding farther south than I've ever been, off the north peninsula and out of the tundra. The spruces gain strength and the ground grows thick with moss and ferns. The ocean flashes in the west, but in the east fog hugs the earth, clinging to the pockets between mountains, obscuring the sun to make our task more dangerous. The long highway twists inland, just south of the Lonely Shadow, the tallest mountain on the island. I hate being confined by the roadways and would rather cut straight there, because if I were a troll wanting to hide, the mountain is where I would go.

We stop for lunch by a lake that's meadow on one side, hard, climbing cliff on the other. Sunlight has burned off the mist so the water shines blue. As we eat I tell Soren what I know of greater mountain troll–sign: scoured trees and disturbed rock scree, boulders with no cracks in them, caves that appear full of stone, a stripe of lichen that ends abruptly. Vaguely man-shaped boulders, for the younger trolls are less capable of calcifying into a decent disguise and tend to hunch over to hide their faces and hands. Water is everywhere here, so it's useless to remain close to any particular body of it.

It relaxes me to be the teacher, though I find I can't put the words into poetry or riddles, and instead let them fall explicit and dull from my mouth. My mind turns to Unferth again and again, his troll pads, his spears, the dangerous curve of his smile.

I fall silent, listening to the gentle lap of lake water against the pebbled shore, when Soren says, "I never expected to find any trolls. Baldur gave me the Mad Eagles' report, and they believed they destroyed the entire herd but for the mother, who surely returned to Canadia. There was no proof they were right, though."

We sit on two camp chairs unfolded from the trunk of his SUV. Mine creaks as I lean toward him. "You came hunting to appease Baldur's conscience."

"It lit him up when I suggested it. He wants to be sure the troll mother is gone, that they're all gone."

"I've seen signs of her periodically, and I'll find her."

"How do you know?"

"She's my destiny. *The Valkyrie of the Tree will prove herself with a stone heart.*" I say the riddle up at the stratified stripes of the cliff across the lake. Green lines of moss highlight the jagged nature of it, and the top is flat, bare of trees. "Hers. Her heart. It's my answer and my blood price, all wrapped into a tidy package."

He grunts.

"What?"

Those big shoulders shrug. "I don't trust tidy packages. Especially not when they come from the gods."

"What do you trust?" I ask sourly.

"Not a what, a who."

"Yourself?"

"Hardly." There's even a tinge of sarcasm in his voice.

I wait.

He says, "Baldur, and . . . her."

"Not the Lokiskin girl? Who's a berserker now?"

"That's Vider." Soren stands up. He goes to the pebbles at the edge of the lake and sifts through them until he finds one round and the size of an eye. Rolling it between his palms he says, "I trust that she would mean to do her best for me, but she serves Odin now and chose it."

Offended on my god's behalf, I throw a balled-up MRE wrapper at him. It unfolds in the air and floats down to the grass harmlessly. "There are trustworthy Odinists, berserker."

Soren glances at me over his shoulder. "Most of you are selfish, or mad, or racist."

I jump to my feet. "I'm only one of those things, and it doesn't make me untrustworthy." I slap dirt off my hands. "Coming?"

He gets up more slowly. "Which one?"

I slam back inside my truck.

Two hours before sunset we find a shattered cluster of rock that looks like a dead troll. It can't be her because there's no bone jewelry or any trace of the ivory tusks. I walk into the forest about a kilometer off the road, trying to smell her or see if she really came this way. It brings me to the edge of a narrow, long lake, where I find a deep claw print with two little birds bathing in it. As the sun sets, we drag our equipment out to it and make camp. If she's sleeping at the bottom of the lake, she'll rise with the moon and we'll be ready.

I breathe carefully around the thrill of excitement and tell Soren to go ahead and build a small fire. She won't be scared away by it. Maybe it will be a beacon.

We eat and then wait, alert into the night.

Soren spends the time rubbing down his sword with an oil-cloth. Its well-worn sheath leans against his thigh. The lobed pommel is plain metal, but etched into the crossguard are runes and small knot-work animals. The hilt is wrapped with something smooth and gray, and its overall design is from the Viker era, not as old as Unferth's but old enough.

"Was it your father's?" I ask. A side note to the story of Baldur's rescue revolved around Soren's infamous father, a berserker who lost control of his madness and murdered ten or so people in a mall.

Soren flicks his fingers against the hilt as one would pet a touchy cat. "Yes."

I bite my tongue to keep from interrogating further. My own father had ashy hair like mine, long fingers that helped me paint ponies and long elegant trees. I remember a cold smear as he drew color down my nose. "My parents died when I was young, too."

"My mother is still alive, somewhere." His hands pause in their work; his eyes remain locked on the blade. "But I don't have a family at all anymore."

"Loyalty ties us together as well as blood," I offer. It's a Freyan proverb, and I hope he doesn't recognize it as such.

The tattoo on his cheek curves as he smiles, a spear that bends but doesn't break. "And your sword?" he asks. "It looks incredibly old."

"Ah, a ring-sword." It's my turn to glance away. *Odd-eye, and rag me,* I think, curses the only words I can seem to apply to all this longing and the ache of missing Unferth. Especially hunting with a partner again, all day I've thought of Ned, as we approached the base of the Lonely Shadow, as I repeated his words to myself, as I drove with the weight of his sword across my lap.

I push off the rough ground and grab up Unferth's sword. Facing Soren, I unsheathe it with a slick motion. The short old blade catches the gentle orange of the flames.

Soren meets me on his feet. He's slightly taller than me, and I step near enough I have to tilt my chin to see the rune in his eyes. "It belonged to my friend who died in the troll attack," I say, no prologue to soften it. "He told me once the blade was unhallowed and so could kill monsters. That it *had* killed monsters before. But he left it with me, and she killed him." I hold it out as a horrible blaze of anxiety turns my blood into nausea or ice or both. "I loved him."

Soren touches the tiny garnet and nudges the loose ring welded to the pommel but doesn't lift it out of my hands. "Does the sword have a name?"

"I don't know." *I don't know.* "I thought I had forever to ask that sort of thing."

He slides his hand to cover mine so we're holding the blade together.

"His name was Ned," I whisper, "which was the plainest name for him. I called him Unferth."

"Ned the Spiritless," Soren says.

We're alone under low, dark clouds so even the stars cannot see us. Wind blows hard off the lake, makes the trees dance. Soren steps closer. I do the same until the hilt touches both of our shoulders.

He says, "Her name was Astrid."

"Astrid." For the slightest moment I know everything there ever was to know about her. But she slips away and there's only Soren staring back at me.

"Some days my greatest fear is that I will die and nobody will remember her name," he adds hoarsely.

I stretch my hand out and find his fingers. "I will."

With every breath his hand seems to grow hotter, and he flexes it but doesn't pull away.

Soren takes a breath deeper than any three of mine, then blows it out in a continuous stream. When he finishes, his temperature has dropped noticeably. "I had hoped maybe Fate was finished with me," he says.

Is that bitch ever really finished with us? Unferth whispers in my ear.

FIFTEEN

THE TROLL MOTHER doesn't appear. I take my frustration out on a few of the trees and hunt with my nose to the ground around and around the lake until I find four tiny broken branches at her shoulder height that maybe she crushed in passing. If so, she definitely is headed for Lonely Shadow. I feel like I'm grasping at shadows.

We abandon the trucks as near the foot of the mountain as we can get, load up supplies, and hike the entire circumference together, hunting her. If we didn't travel so slowly, searching through the forest and spreads of granite scree, it would be strenuous. But stretched over five days it's only exercise. Though we find a few marks of lesser trolls again—grass woven into the low branches of a yellow birch, the carcass of a red fox pulled apart and skinned—there's nothing to show she was ever here.

In my dreams she and I grapple together, both of us as large as the mountain, crushing lakes and towns as we wrestle. Unferth's sword melds with my arm and my bones turn to steel, her skin becomes iron and we start massive fires when we spark together, when we clash. Soren wakes me up several mornings before dawn. I'm stained with sweat, but he doesn't ask why. He silently hauls me into stretches and boxing warm-ups until my sweat is just from hard work.

Overall, he's a quiet companion, speaking little but to point out the dark backs of caribou moving across a distant field or ask if I want the grilled chicken MRE for dinner. At night I tell him stories about the Vinland I knew, the Summerlings and Unferth, the festival, and even the massacre itself. I talk about the Valkyrie, about how different they all are but that together they're the voice of Odin. I tell him about climbing the Tree and meeting the god of the hanged, and he tells me of his own encounter with Odin, how everyone believes the boon he asked was to be allowed to serve Baldur as a berserker, but really he begged not to forget Astrid's name. I learn his mom was born in Baja California and is a U.S. citizen, but her parents were Savaiian, that she was Lokiskin and met his dad while working where he was stationed. He learns how my parents met at a Freyan leadership camp but died far away in Guathemala.

We discuss the riddle, and I tell him what the troll mother said, that it makes me chill with fear but also hope, because I'm certain we'll meet again. Soren says there must be more to the riddle's answer than only presenting a heart of stone to the Death Hall, that there will be a catch or a trick because Odin Alfather does nothing without a catch.

I ask him why he dedicated himself to Baldur, and he only shrugs and says, "When you meet him, you'll know."

"A lot of people meet him and don't change their dedication to him."

"I . . ." Soren drags the pause out, not to avoid me, I think, but because he's never put it into words before. "Baldur is the first god I've ever believed in." He's quick to add, "I know they all *exist*—there's nothing to believe in that way—but I mean that I know he cares what happens to me, and that he's good. He believes in *me,* and none of the rest of them do."

Hanging behind his words is the question: *Does Odin believe in you?*

It's such a light word, a gentle word: to have confidence in, to trust in. I put my fingers over my heart. "When my parents died, I felt this desperate longing, this growth in my heart that made me want to scream and drag others behind me until they felt that scream in their own hearts. I still feel it, and so does the Alfather. He recognized it in me, and instead of saying I was too wild or wrong he embraced it. He's the god who not only lets me need to feel the troll mother's blood between my fingers; he encourages it. The god of the hanged understands how violence is part of life. Creation itself is an act of violence, and everything I do is violent."

Even your way of kissing, Unferth whispers.

"So I believe in that. And Odin does, too. We want the same thing. That makes us allies."

"Dangerous ones," Soren says.

"Danger is necessary to life."

"If you can contain it, control it."

"Ride it; use it! Dance with it! You can't control life, Soren. That's what people try to do with troll walls and seat belts; it's what the Valkyrie do with their rules and costumes, but you can't. Horrible things still happen. Trolls attack; people die. People who shouldn't." My throat tightens and I realize I was near yelling.

Soren doesn't try to comfort me. The tiny fire casts him in bronze and earthy tones, like he's a statue. A calcified hill troll.

I look away. I want Unferth here so badly to argue on Soren's side, to cut me down with a well-placed barb, to twist what I say into a riddle so I'll spend hours delving deeper into myself. That's what he did. He drove me deeper.

Ned Unferth believed in me.

It's no use. The day we reach the trailhead, and there's the lightning-scoured spruce as proof we've gone all the way around, I take my backpack off and fling it to the ground with a cry. I pick up a rock and throw it as hard as I can toward the mountain. It clatters through branches and lands softly, rolling several paces. I throw another and another.

Soren puts a hand on my shoulder and I drop the last rock. Sunlight pounds down on us, warm enough to actually feel. "How am I supposed to find her? Where am I supposed to go next?" I yell, tossing out my arms.

"The funerals are tomorrow night," Soren says.

"What?"

"It's seven days since we met, which was a Moonsday, so the funerals are tomorrow night. Back at your Cove."

I blow a hard breath. I don't want to go. I don't want to watch the town burn again, even if it's in pyres.

But a Valkyrie does not balk at death.

We arrive as the sun is falling. There are media vans and death priests everywhere. I recognize logos from Freyan volunteer organizations from all up the eastern coast of the States. Soren is even more interested than I am in avoiding anybody with a camera. Men and women come from across the country; half of Congress is here, kings and princes, representatives from every priesthood, reporters, and the far-flung families of the dead. Baldur the Beautiful is here, Freyr the Satisfied with his endless entourage, and two Valkyrie: Siri of the Ice, whose region we're in, and Precia, the Valkyrie of the South, where Rome and Jesca Summerling were born.

I'm glad I packed my last wool dress from the tower. It's dark green and falls to my knees. A red apron ties over it, cinching my waist and pinned at my shoulders with abalone shells. Chains of fake gold line the collar and wrists. I pull on Jesca's silver rings and wear both my seax and Unferth's sword. I braid tiny ropes to either side of my face and let the rest of my hair fall down my back. I use ash to darken my eyes with thick lines, like a mask, and dab it onto my mouth, too.

It's as if I think all this preparation and costume will help me look my sisters in the eye. They surely know what I've done, since even Soren had heard the story, and maybe that commander on the military base did get around to calling one of the Death Halls.

We join the mourners, and one look at either of us parts the next section of the crowd until a path arrows us toward the pavilion. It's set up in the valley beside the razed festival site, a gilded stage hung with prayer flags and flowers flown in from some tropical greenhouse. It clashes dreadfully with the moor, especially as the sun sets and our island goes hard and harsh with shadows, but the pavilion lights up in a blaze. There are fourteen pyres arranged so that when lit they will become a circle of fire like Freya's *brisinga* necklace. My stomach twists at the pomp. This is the part of being a Valkyrie I always hated. The decorations, the ceremony, the gilded prettiness of everything. I would prefer to light the fires and scream. Make a sacrifice, yell gruesome poetry, to remind the mourners death is all we truly have in common.

Rathi speaks at the podium in a red three-piece suit, pink starburst tie pinned with a horse brooch, his hair perfectly slicked back and his false green eyes bright. He welcomes everyone in a shining voice. Behind him stands Siri of the Ice, her thin lips in a line when she sees me; she flicks her fingers lightly against Precia's elbow. There's Baldur the Beautiful, nearly impossible to look at in person, a golden beach bum in jeans and a loose white coat, tears caught like stars in his night-purple eyes. And my parents' own Freyr the Satisfied, taller than his cousin-god, in old-fashioned finery: purple velvet jacket and hose to show off his well-shaped legs, fur boots, a six-hundred-year-old sword crusted with gems, and an actual crown. There are congressmen and the president's lawspeaker, a death priest in a silver raven mask, five wolf-guards with their faces tattooed black, attendants in gray and green cowls holding incense and torches at every corner of the pavilion.

The crowd waits in a half circle, the first fifty rows in wooden folding chairs, the rest arrayed among the fourteen pyres. I reach the end of one aisle, Soren at my side.

"Signy!" cries Peachtree the clown from across the crescent of empty moor between dais and crowd. She waves an arm as Rathi falls silent and everyone turns to me. I keep my eyes on Peachtree, on the two sequins melted onto her cheek from the fires of the attack.

Murmuring breaks out and Rathi steps around the podium. "Signy," he says, only loud enough for those of us near to hear. He holds out his hand for me to take, to pull me up with him, but I shake my head.

"I am only here to grieve," I call loudly. "To dance with the song of crackling flames."

My wish-brother hesitates and then nods. He goes back to his welcome speech and ends with Rome Summerling's favorite prayer. When he looks at me I mouth the words with him. It loosens the pain curled tight around his eyes.

Into the silence after his invocation, drums beat a sedate, gloomy rhythm, and a team of flautists raise the hairs on my neck with their ghostly accompaniment.

Precia and Siri step forward to opposite ends of the pavilion.

The Valkyrie of the Ice is tall and lean, in a white feather cape and an impractical skirt of chain mail. Beside her the young Valkyrie of the South wears a leather and fur coat, her dark hair coiffed and her eyes dangerous. They are both so elegant, so powerful in every smooth gesture, and together they lift their voices in a song of mourning.

It's controlled, synchronized. Not a word out of place, not a gesture unpracticed. So unlike the wild splash of death, the frenetic beating of my heart as I struggled and fought to save my family. Not desperate, not thick and bloody.

This is only a performance.

Such a lowly thing for a Valkyrie to do, Ned told me when I painted myself up for the festival.

I feel so empty.

We don't even have his body to burn.

The Valkyrie fall silent and put their arms around each other like sisters.

Freyr the Satisfied holds out his hands. He draws Rathi forward with him, and from here I can see the shudder as my brother closes his eyes. The god is lovely and tall, as they all must be, and charisma flares in the corner of his smile, in the light way he flirts with the audience even as his words are sad. He offers condolences, and those of his twin sister, Freya the Witch, who promised him our island would never be forgotten in any of the strands of fate.

Freyr then tells us a story of meeting Rome Summerling once, over a decade ago; his words blur in my ears, but everyone around me laughs, gently at first, then uproariously. Even

Rathi smiles widely and puts his hands together over his heart to bow to the god of joy.

Rathi leads another prayer, that lilt of his father's accent carrying the sadness out of his voice, and he gleams with a sincere sort of glory. Cameras flash, and I imagine viewing this all through a television screen, as I've seen so many appearances by the gods and Valkyrie before.

But the cold ocean wind tickles my ears and I smell salt and mud under the perfume and gathered bodies. There are evergreen boughs tossed onto the pyres to brighten the inevitable sickening of the air when the remains burn, and I wish there weren't. That we would all be forced to breathe in the sour death.

Why should it be beautified?

I ignore the congressman with his wide sideburns and rearing-horse lapel pin as he eulogizes my island. I ignore the click of a camera beside my face. Let them see that I stand to the side, that I don't sing along with Jesca's favorite hymn or the old dawn theme they used to open the festival.

Only when Baldur the Beautiful steps forward, and tears glint on his cheeks, do I feel any of it matters. He shines like a star in the darkness, tan and healthy and perfect, his jacket casually open, his collar unbuttoned. All the god of light says is "May they rest peacefully in Freya's embrace, as I do in my turn."

The Valkyrie step forward again, both with unlit torches in hand. They raise the carved wood in harmony, and in an arch over their heads tap the tips together.

Flames burst to life.

The congregation gasps, and Baldur claps with a smile. Freyr takes a torch and lights it from the Valkyrie's fire, then so do Baldur, Rathi, the congressman, and the president's law-speaker, who is short and unimpressive among this company.

It is so choreographed, exactly like our *Beowulf* pantomime in the feast hall. A shallow production, a mask. This is not what death is. This is not all the Valkyrie should be.

A scream builds in my chest. I clench my hands into fists, push them hard against my heart, and the Valkyrie of the Ice suddenly looks at me. The Valkyrie of the South does the same.

They lift their voices in a keen. A beautiful, controlled wail of grief. There's no rage in it, no desperation.

Other voices join them, until all around me a hundred people cry as the fire passes from torch to torch. This is no scream, but a song they tried to teach me.

The Valkyrie step away from the pavilion and stride together for the first pyre. It lights, flaring loud and bright and cutting off the howl of the crowd. The Valkyrie are shadows against the bonfire as the others file from the pavilion and walk through the rest of the pyres.

I back away, touch Soren to tell him he need not follow, and dart through the mourners onto the free, open tundra. It sparkles in the moonlight, so many human bodies shielding it and me from the warm light of the fires.

If the frost-tipped gorse rose up to become the troll mother, if her moon-white marble body loomed over me now, I would say his name for her.

"Signy."

I turn to face the Valkyrie.

The firelight behind them darkens their faces, but the Valkyrie of the Ice tilts hers so I can see the glint of green in her eyes. And there is Precia beside her. In the two years since I've seen her, I've grown a head taller than the Valkyrie of the South.

"You do not mourn?" Siri of the Ice says with disdain.

I try to match her tone. "Not like this. It is too clean for me; you should know."

"People like for death to be clean."

Precia adds, "It's part of what we do."

"Death isn't clean. Especially these deaths," I say.

The Valkyrie of the South shakes her head at me. "We make death into what we need it to be."

"Or what the Alfather needs it to be," Siri adds. "We translate for him; we are *his* voice."

I drop my hands to my sides. This is habit to argue with them, over this thing. I shrug. We will never agree.

Precia reaches for me, takes my hand. "Ask us for help, Signy."

"No."

"She's too proud," Siri scoffs.

Precia narrows her dark eyes and I hold my breath, wishing I could read runes in her irises.

The Valkyrie of the Ice laughs, a brutal, sharp laugh. "We saw the posters with your face, you wretched child. Playing Valtheow the Dark for tips. And you said we were shallow, we had lost our way."

There are a handful of justifications I could give, especially that I was here for the riddle, but I won't lend her the satisfaction. So I say nothing, not even that the Alfather led me here by the hand of a poet.

"You look horrible," Precia murmurs.

"I've been hunting on the mountains," I say, cutting a hand toward the south.

"You fought the herd," Precia says. "You faced a herd of greater mountain trolls and lived. We heard the stories, from your wish-brother and from Baldur the Beautiful, who is enamored with you. Come home with us. You have surely earned it, and this moment you could hold the country in your hand with your story: Signy the Valkyrie of the Tree, who shepherded the great Vinland sacrifice."

"It's not the answer."

"To the riddle?" Precia asks hopefully.

"Yes."

Ice leans nearer to me, takes my face in one cold hand. "I don't believe you. You are still searching, undecided. It's plain in your runes. You lack conviction."

"I don't believe *you,* Siri. Conviction is all I have tonight. And passion, and hope." I twist out of her grasp. "Because I do know the answer, and before long I will bring a stone heart to the Death Hall that you cannot even imagine. You will be the one to change."

Siri catches her surprise and snuffs it out fast. "Only death changes me. Another lesson you've never learned."

"Death and *poetry,*" I snap.

But the Valkyrie of the Ice stalks away.

South lets her sister go and cocks her head. Not a single hair falls out of place. "Myra will be glad to know you still carry her knife."

"You believe me?" I ask.

"Signy." Precia's hands are tucked into her fur and leather coat. She holds herself together, back from me, though her voice is tender. "I always have known you would succeed. It's you who fights it, not me."

Darkness surrounds us, wails and conversation from the funeral pyres, the harsh snaps of burning wood.

"What do *you* see, in my eyes?" I whisper.

"Not indecision but madness. Chaos."

My jaw clenches. *Chaos.* Still.

The Valkyrie pulls her hand out of the pocket of her coat and points southeast. Toward the ocean. "For now, your madness is that way."

Turning to look, all I see is the dark sky, the long shadowed stretch of the moor. What is that direction? The sea, the death ships, and, far over the ocean, the coast of the USA. Or perhaps she only means *Your madness is away from us.*

When I open my mouth to ask, the Valkyrie has already gone to join our sister again at the first bonfire.

I trip and cuss as I make my way through the intense darkness, through mud, for there is no path this way she pointed. I have no idea if she meant it literally, but if not I'll reach the ocean and be forced to quit. I'll find the death ships and sleep there, light my own pyre for Unferth. Once I took him there with me, held his shoulder as I climbed atop the prow of the flagship. *Sometimes I think I want to remain here forever,* I cried up at the windy sky. And Unferth said, *You would hate forever.*

Cold air chaps my lips, for even so many weeks after Baldur's Night the island will freeze, but I press on. My boots slip and the hem of my dress grows heavy, despite it being cut just below the knee. My palms are raw from catching myself, and finally I stay where I fall.

The wool soaks up cold water off the hill, freezing my thighs and making my ass numb. I lie back and spread my arms. Unferth's sword is like an external backbone, an exoskeleton shield for my heart. My fingertips brush baby grass, and sharp rocks cut up into my hips, but I don't care. My chest heaves.

I stare up at the stars and try to find poetry in them, words to ground myself in, but there's nothing.

Your heart. Your heart. Your heart.

The rhythm of the words is the rhythm of the distant waves.

Dark figures loom suddenly around me, coalescing out of the moorland. They're broad and dressed in black coats, weapons strapped to shoulders and hips. Their eyes gleam and every one of them has a slice of darkness cutting down their left cheeks. Berserkers.

I hold my hand out and one takes it in a very firm grasp. He hauls me to my feet. "Hello, pretty Valkyrie," he says, almost purring. There's a buzzed line of hair striping down his otherwise bald skull and he smiles a head-swallowing smile.

"I'm Sharkman," he adds. "I saw you as I descended from the heliplanes. Your madness was so raw. It affected me, who is affected by little."

"You affected all of us," says the warrior to his right: a berserker with dark braids pulled tightly back from his face and one of those thin Frankish goatees around his solemn mouth. I know his brown eyes. This is the berserker who caught my sword in the fray, who held me back, who said, *Balls.*

He puts two fingers to his heart and says, "The Mad Eagles salute you, Valkyrie."

At least seven of them surround me, mostly shadows in the dark. "Thank you," I say.

"I am Darius Strong, captain of the Mad Eagles." He covers my hand with his, the warmth of his skin traveling up my arm. "We returned here for you, Valkyrie. Come with us tonight, home to our hall, and drink in honor of our fallen, and yours. We will show you how the Mad God mourns."

Without hesitation, I say *yes.* Darius and Sharkman flank me, with the five other berserkers spread behind.

SIXTEEN

THIS IS WHAT a funeral should be:

Me standing atop a table beside a wide bowl of honey-dark mead, in a torchlit warehouse before an entire band of berserkers. They put two fingers to their hearts and together cry, *Hangatyr!* God of the Hanged.

I let the words wash over me, closing my eyes for only a moment, hunting for a response in the bowels of my memory. My head swims, my body buzzes with the heat of Odinist frenzy that exudes from the berserkers, with fierce joy and heavy, heavy sorrow. I dunk my goblet into the cauldron of mead, let the cool alcohol swirl around my fingers and into the cup. I lift it, mead streaming down and dripping onto the table. As I hold it high, I say, "To the glorious dead!"

The Mad Eagles roar in response and the warehouse rings with the echo of our cries.

It's a huge metal cavern in the center of the berserker camp. They're tucked far into a corner of the North Ice joint military base, between the airfield and the ocean, separated from the army by curling barbed wire and a small guardhouse at the gate. Tiny windows high against the warehouse roof glow with moonlight, but the metal catwalks hang with torches and oil lamps. Real fire, not the false flicker of stage lights like in the old circus feast hall. The orange light dances over chipped and abused round-shields, rows and rows of spears that line the walls, dust-covered wooden rifles, and one autocannon crouched like a wolf in the corner. The Mad Eagles have created a strange, dark home that's half ancient, half modern here in this industrial building.

When the roar fades, I drink all that will fit into my mouth, and the berserkers pound the floor with their boots, the table with their fists. The air vibrates, my bones shake, and I let myself laugh wildly.

Then I dunk the goblet again and crash down along the table to kneel before Darius. I wrap my hands around the cup and say, "Captain Darius Strong, drink mead with me as your fallen brothers drink mead with the Alfather."

I put it to his lips and he drinks.

One by one, I offer my cup to the berserkers. I ask for their names and repeat them back, inviting each to drink mead with me. Some murmur my name, *Signy,* and some *Valkyrie.*

Sharkman covers my hands with his and feeds alcohol back to me. Another, called Thebes, ducks bashfully but meets my eyes. He's got a strip of burn scars distorting his face from temple down past the iron collar of Odin. Another warrior has tears in his dark blue eyes, and the oldest of them all says not my name nor my title, but calls me *Nine.*

I'm flushed and sweating midway through the ritual. Fire and alcohol and the fevered madness that spins under the heart of every berserker raise the temperature in the warehouse. It's a sauna. I shed the top layer of my dress onto the floor while Darius holds Unferth's sword, and when I take it back I leave it unsheathed. Cup in one hand, sword in the other, I use Sharkman's shoulder to climb onto the table again. There I stand in my underdress and jewelry, Jesca's silver and Ned's copper rings on my fingers, and I fill the goblet again. I drink long, tossing back my head, and when I wipe my mouth with my forearm they laugh and salute. They come to me and I pick up cups and goblets and drinking horns from beside the mead cauldron, passing out full cups to every berserker. When we've all a drink, I lift the sword and tell them a piece of my story I've not told anyone.

"I was afraid," I call, "and numb and desperate—but it did not matter because I burned, too, with rage and grief, and when I saw that herd picking their teeth with the bones of my own glorious dead, when I raised my sword—this sword—and charged, there was a great roar behind me. The roar of power, the roar of our grim god of madness and death, pushing at my back like wind, like massive black wings."

My throat is hot, and my stomach and heart, too, tingling with alcohol and passion. The poetry tumbles out of me, fast and strong. "They were wings, though they did not grow from my back. They were *your* wings, every dark feather a finger of your craze, your passion. My heart spun with the Mad Eagles as you charged from the sky like my own battle wolves, to tear apart my enemies. That madness has hounded me, has lived inside me, ever since."

They cheer.

The cry raises the hairs on my neck, and my head falls back. I shut my eyes as they yell. We drink together.

A throne-like seat is brought for me and I slouch in it, Unferth's sword slung across the back and the goblet of mead in my hand. They tell their stories now, boasting about the trolls they killed, their visions of me, the spinning fury of the madness inside them. I hear of rending limbs, the sweet smell of troll ichor, crushed bones, and tears that streaked their faces from the hot wind of death. I learn the names of their fallen and we salute their brothers with more mead.

My head is lost in dizziness, my nose numb from drink. I eat roast pork with my fingers and stomp with them in the rhythm of our united heartbeats. I down the last drops of mead and laugh.

Here's red-haired Marcus tugging the goblet from me and lifting me to my feet. He swings me close and spins me around, and I still laugh. I'm pulled from him into another's arms, and then another's, my head cloudy and the entire world spinning. Brick, with a scar cutting his tattoo apart, grabs my elbow too hard and I swing it up into his face. There's blood in the mix now, and a frozen moment before Brick laughs outrageously and the others follow. I dance with him then, heady and wild. There are hands on my ribs and my arms, loosing my braids, and then a hot mouth against mine. I allow it, embrace it, sinking into the kiss for one brief turning of the magnificent world, and then put my hand on his cheek and push back.

It's wicked-eyed Sharkman, one eyebrow tilted and his face still close. His shoulders slope with muscles bursting out of his black vest; he's a head taller than me. He'd take me away right now and give me everything I desire, and there's no hiding it on that wide, flushed face of his. He doesn't even *try* to hide it. Everything the opposite of Ned.

"*Valkyrie,*" he whispers. I grab his face and I kiss him again.

I'm still in his arms when the sun rises.

It spills through the wide-open doors of the warehouse, where tables and benches are pushed back or turned over and so many berserkers snore, sprawled out or with heads together. My eyes ache and nausea digs spindly fingers into my stomach. From this dark corner, I spy Darius at the main table reading a book, a mug of something steaming in hand. It smells like hot chocolate and I think of Unferth.

There's no hard, sharp pain at the thought of him, but only a sorrowful echo.

Slowly I push out from beneath Sharkman's arm. My underdress is twisted uncomfortably and my braids a disaster, boots I have no idea where. Sharkman grumbles and I shove him off the hem of my dress. I creep to my feet.

"Signy?" Darius murmurs.

"Darius," I whisper. I walk to the bench as if on a tightrope, and Darius hands me the mug. It's coffee, not chocolate, and I smile sadly down at it.

There's a fuzzy aura around everything, but a cool breeze snakes inside, dragging away the sticky heat of stale berserker frenzy. I sip the coffee. My stomach revolts and I feel like an idiot, though I wouldn't change last night. It was magnificent and wild; it was mad frenzy; no control!

I lay my head down against the cool wooden table, and Darius puts his hand beside my face, not touching. "I can get you some water."

I murmur something, actually wanting a toothbrush and a shower. My thoughts drift like thin spring clouds. I danced hard and laughed; I abandoned my family to their Vinland graves, and Ned Unferth, too. I ran off with strangers who are just like me, sang for the dead, kissed, and forgot my own name for a little while. And it was a relief.

It *is* a relief. I want to remain here, soak it up, let it go, cycle through it again and again until I'm spent and exactly this loosened, this relaxed every morning.

But I can't. I have too much to do. I can't only be wild and free like they are, waiting for their orders to rend and destroy, to set loose their madness and rage.

They embody the destructive passion and death in the Alfather's fiery heart, this scream inside me, and sharing it made even my bones ache with glory and pleasure. Yet this place has taught me a thing I never understood before: the Mad Eagles, the berserkers, they *are* controlled. In their hearts they're pure, but they're caged from the outside by military laws and barbed-wire fences. Like Soren said, they're tools. They're not a part of the world.

The Valkyrie are. The Valkyrie walk free among the people; the Valkyrie lead. Because they are not feared, because they are their own control.

Two sides of a coin, the Valkyrie and the berserkers. The voices of Odin, and the hands of Odin.

I don't fit with either. Like Soren Bearstar did not fit with his wild brothers, I do not fit with my cool sisters. He transformed himself into a servant of hope and light, but the difference between us is that I *want* Odin. I could not give my god of the hanged up if I tried.

There must be another way. A middle ground between Valkyrie and berserker, between voice and hand.

A tiny laugh strangles in my throat. *The heart.*

I want to be the heart, passionate and wild, but with a pulse. A rhythm to keep myself in check. Poetry and passion together.

Like Unferth's story about Freya creating the trolls by tempering the fire of the earth with the fire of the sun.

Odd-eye.

In that story it was a magical charm the goddess put into a woman's heart, and the wisest troll mothers, Unferth said, could use rune magic.

Magic like keeping her herd out under thin clouds? Safe from morning light?

Is it possible the troll mother who destroyed Vinland is that first mother? Could she live so long? If it's her, that means my stone heart, the answer to my riddle, is no average troll heart, but the original, the magical charm Freya, the goddess of dreams, created.

We were destined to meet; I saw it in her eyes, I told Rathi. *Choices and consequences.*

We recognized each other. *Stone heart. Your heart.*

I have to get back to it. Find her.

"Signy?" Captain Darius says, concern painting his tone.

I raise my head and look at Darius. His dark eyes wait for me. "Captain, I have some questions about your hunt for the Vinland herd."

"I will answer them, but first you should see something." He pushes up from the bench and gestures for me to follow him outside.

Sunlight burns blue and white spots into my vision and I blink it away. I smell ocean and oil, hear distant gulls cry out, and the hum of machinery and propellers. We stand on black asphalt painted with bright yellow lines where armored trucks are parked, emblazoned with the band's screaming-eagle emblem. It's all harsh colors, no softness, like the berserkers themselves. But tiny dandelions and curled grass push through the cracks in the pavement.

Darius says, "We have one. One of the trolls."

I gasp. "One of the Vinland herd?"

He nods toward the north end of the warehouse. "It did not fight us when we came, and so we captured it instead of killing it. All the rest are dead, or vanished off the island."

A thrill courses through me. "Not the mother?"

"No." He leads me silently to the only door at that far end and punches a code into the keypad beside it. A lock clicks, echoing up to the rafters, and we go in, closing the door behind us. Darius takes a large key from a box built into the wall that he forces open and leads me down a short hall to a second metal door. He unlocks it, then pushes his shoulder into it and sets his feet firm. It takes all his muscle before the door groans open.

This next hall is a prison built to hold berserkers. Lining the way are cells of solid steel, three to a side. One door is open and the metal is at least ten centimeters thick. It's stainless steel and stone, locked together into a wall that must be nearly impossible to break.

The prison ends in another door with a large wheel lock sticking out. Darius says, "It's easier with two," before gripping it and throwing all his weight into it. The metal grates together and I hear pieces churning and clinking deep inside the wall. When finally it snaps unlocked, he strains to pull it open. A waft of cold, sweet-smelling air flows out.

My skin flares in a million itchy points and my stomach crawls up my throat, burning like screech. I know that smell, oh, how well I know it.

Troll.

UV light shines hard out of four spots set up in each corner, glaring at the monster.

Like a great boulder, it huddles in the center of the room, its neck and ankles chained to six-finger bolts dug into the ground. A meaty hand covers its head, as it protects its sensitive pig eyes.

My hands tremble and I splay my fingers rigidly. I walk to it.

Sweet Mother Frigg, have mercy.

In this light the troll's skin shines blue and is marbled like polished granite. A long weeping scab trails purple down his shoulder, and there is a line of dark red lichen growing along his spine. His right arm only a broken stub.

Red Stripe. He's alive.

"He's not public knowledge," Darius says calmly. "Though of course the General Berserk knows, and the Valkyrie of the Ice, and Baldur. Baldur has claimed the troll for himself, though there's also an etin-physiology doctor who's already put in a request to have any remains we recovered remanded into her custody."

"I see," I whisper, imagining Red Stripe's skull sliced open while they train bland UV lights onto him, keeping him lethargic but not calcified. Then they'll cut him up and send his head to one facility, his torso to another, his arms and legs perhaps given out as trophies. It's law that no dead troll be kept whole—they're to be shattered and spread so there's no chance of re-forming.

A part of me itches to take Unferth's sword and drive it into Red Stripe's heart. Because I can't stop thinking of the troll mother's gruesome meal. The memory of her fist cracking against my chest, her hot breath and tusks, the screams and fire.

Darius touches my shoulder. "Lady, are you well? I shouldn't have brought you. It's too soon."

I close my eyes to remember rubbing Red Stripe's ears, scratching dust from his tusks. The calm way he would hunker down at Unferth's slightest touch.

"They can't have him," I murmur, stepping nearer Red Stripe. I touch his cool chest and draw a line toward the gash with its crystallized blood, like tiny chunks of amethyst growing out of him.

"My understanding is Baldur wishes to make him a sacrifice of some sort, so you don't have to worry about him living long."

"No." I turn to put my back against Red Stripe, leaning into the hard marble of his bent chest. "I know this troll, and tamed him. That's why he didn't fight you. His name is Red Stripe; I captured him with Ned the Spiritless last year outside Montreal."

Darius lowers his head slightly, thoughtfully. "I see. If it were up to me, lady, I would relinquish him to you immediately, but the gods have an interest now, and we'll have to communicate properly and make requests."

"I know a way to contact Baldur about him."

His eyebrows lift, but he doesn't question me. "Good."

I walk to him, our gazes connected, and I look for a rune in his warm brown eyes. Darius is a decade my elder, I think, or twenty-five, young to be the leader of an entire berserk band. Maybe he has that little Frankish beard to appear more mature. There's a tiny string of runes repeated in a line from his pupil to the darkest ring at the edge of his iris. It's one of the runes in the binding rune scar on my palm: *servant.*

✦ ✦ ✦

I call the Shipworm and leave messages for both Rathi and Soren. To Rathi that I'm well and with the Mad Eagles, and to Soren that I need to speak with him as soon as possible. I leave the private number for the warehouse.

Hopefully through Soren I can find a way to not only keep Red Stripe safe but maybe pull in resources for the hunt. Baldur might agree to help me get permission to have the Mad Eagles at my disposal, or a local militia unit. Anything that could help expand the search for her. I wonder how much to tell any of them about why I need to be there when she's found.

Darius gives me a copy of his report, but there's nothing useful inside, nothing I didn't already assume. They made a thorough sweep and killed five more trolls, plus caught Red Stripe, but weren't able to spend enough time, boots on the ground, to track the mother.

While I wait to hear from Soren, all I can do is keep myself busy with Red Stripe and learn what I can from the berserkers.

Most of them share duty shifts with soldiers in Thor's Army. They patrol the coast in heliplanes and man the front gates of the base, and fly regularly over the Canadian sea to watch for trouble out of troll country. They wait to be called up by the president or the Council of Valkyrie as peacekeepers overseas or as bodyguards stateside. Guarding is one of their only allowed duties on New Asgard soil because of prejudice against them—the fear of their berserking, that they might lose control at the drop of a flag.

After scrubbing dust and amethyst flakes from Red Stripe, after waking him and feeding him under the watchful eyes of Darius, I insist on helping with chores like unloading the crates of supplies that arrive around lunchtime and scouring the feast hall tables of spilled mead and pork sauce. Anything to keep myself busy.

Captain Darius gives me a berserker uniform and the smallest black coat he can find. I work out with a contingent of them: Sharkman, who makes himself my informal chaperone, and Thebes and Marcus and Carrigan and Brick. They're interested in my troll-fighting techniques, and I show them how I steady the troll-spears with my weight, though it isn't much suited to their rampaging style. The fact that they never did catch the troll mother burns their pride. Sharkman swears to me that if I ask, he'll track her down; we'll find her together. With the Mad Eagles at my side we could destroy her. I promise I'll do what I can to see it happen.

That evening at dinner I paint runes onto the thumbnail of every berserker present. I look into their eyes and draw for them the blessing I see. I sleep with Sharkman (*torch*) near the round hearth in the center of the warehouse; he holds me close and intimately, stroking my nightmares away. There's a tattoo on his chest: eight horizontal spears in a line down his sternum. He'll add a ninth, he says, when I am in my proper throne.

The troll mother wakes me at dawn with a roar, tusks pressed to my cheeks, hot breath rolling over me. My eyes snap open, suddenly and sharply, my heart pounding. I slip free of Sharkman and gather Unferth's sword from where it hangs on the throne by the fire. With it I run to the guardhouse, where the berserker Brick slumps in the chair with earphones tucked into his ears. He sits up at my approach, but I go straight to the chain-link gate, shut tight overnight. I curl my fingers through the links and peer out into the army base. The airfield is slowly waking up; a handful of men in flight suits crawl all over the heliplanes whose rotary blades droop like spider legs.

"All right?" Brick says through a yawn. I hear the tinny song beating from his abandoned earphones.

A small SUV turns the corner onto the road leading directly for us. It's shiny and dark blue, cleaned of all the salt spray and Vinland mud. He drives slowly—it must be exactly the on-base speed limit—along the low gray fence surrounding the airfield and stops ten meters back from me and the guardhouse.

Soren turns off the engine and climbs out. He glances briefly at Brick, who's clamoring out of the little wooden house, then keeps his gaze on me through the gate.

"Good morning," I say.

"I didn't think you'd be waiting." The sun behind him turns his buzzed black hair into a trim halo and makes it tough to see his tattoo.

"Odinists only, boy," Brick says.

I sigh. "Then let me out to speak with him."

"Valkyrie . . ."

"Brick. Soren Bearstar is a hero of Asgard and my friend. I recognize his worth, and I will not speak to him through a chain-link fence."

Making his reluctance known by dragging his feet, Brick levers the gate lock open and we slide it aside. "Come on," I say, waving my hand for Soren to follow. He does as Brick gets on his radio to warn Captain Darius what I've done.

I lead Soren away from the warehouse to the edge of the camp where the asphalt meets star-shaped pylons and the wide, cold sea. Mist and low clouds obscure the sun. "You could have called, saved yourself that," I say, nudging his wrist.

"It wouldn't have mattered. That's how they treat me."

"Odd-eye, Soren, you're such a martyr. You *should* be devoted to the god of sacrifice."

The little jerk of his shoulder is all the answer I get. The wind scours salt against the concrete pylons, rushing past my face. "The Mad Eagles have Red Stripe, the runt troll Ned and I captured last winter. I want him, but the captain says Baldur has put a claim on him already. You need to explain to Baldur that Red Stripe is mine."

Soren eyes me sideways. "Explain to Baldur."

"Well."

"I'll call him. See what he says."

"Tell him Red Stripe lost an arm and is ridiculously tame."

"A pet. You have a troll for a pet, even after all of this."

I scrape the toe of my boot against the pylon, scraping off a few little flakes of concrete. "Also I'd like to see about having the Mad Eagles—or at least some of them—assigned to me. A Valkyrie usually has a small band of berserkers, and even though I'm not technically on the council, maybe Baldur could help get around that."

"I'm starting to think it isn't my help you want so much as whose help I can get you."

I offer Soren my best smile. "Can't it be both?"

"There was a report in Vertmont last night of a sighting of a greater mountain troll mother." He says it so casually I'm halfway to answering I don't care about Vertmont before the meaning sinks in.

I clutch his arm. "Last night. Vertmont. The north part? That's . . . near Montreal."

"I have the bags from your truck in the backseat."

The urge to throw my arms around him, to kiss him or drag him into an impromptu dance, is nearly irresistible. But all I do is hold out my hand. "Take me, Bearstar," I say, pitching my voice low and flirty.

Soren glowers down at me until I laugh. This is it; we're going after her, and nothing can muffle the violent thrill spiking around my heart.

SEVENTEEN

LONG SALT IS a walled town in Vertmont kingstate, situated along the North River about forty kilometers southwest of the ruins of Montreal. We arrive midmorning the day after leaving the Mad Eagles. Pain stabs the back of my eyes, since I woke up again and again last night, despite the completely decent hotel room Soren bought for us with a fancy credit card he sheepishly admitted had been supplied by Baldur the Beautiful.

In my dreams the troll mother raked her claws across my eyes, her tusks hooked into my ribs as she buried her face in my chest, tearing me apart, until all that remained was my bright, beating heart. Soren dragged me up after midnight to run laps around the hotel parking lot until the sun rose. We piled into the SUV then, with Styrofoam cups of bad lobby coffee, and I leaned my head against the window, eyes shut, while Soren kept me barely awake with stories of the Berserker Wars. He's no poet, and his voice faded into the gentle rumble of the engine more often than not, but he knows more grim details about the five-year back-and-forth between berserkers and the last of the frost giants. He almost manages to distract me from all my worries about whether this troll mother they saw in Vertmont is *my* troll mother.

The walls of Long Salt are four meters tall and at least one thick, meant to deter most types of trolls or at least slow down a greater mountain herd. We roll slowly through, though there's no guard, into a charming town that bustles with life. Early spring flowers burst from long boxes lining the main street, and colorful prayer flags flutter from the tall light posts. A handful of temples raise the only skyline, their white steeples reaching toward the perfect cotton-ball clouds. Children run through the school yard, mothers push strollers along the sidewalks, and every block has its own crossroads shrine strung with plastic beads and incense sticks.

As we reach the whitewashed downtown with its antiques stores and coffee shops, a long banner stretches across the road, bright yellow with green and pink daisies, that reads: WELCOME TO LONG SALT GARDEN FESTIVAL.

There's nothing here to indicate the presence of trolls. With the national troll alert so recent, it's hard to imagine they wouldn't have reacted even more strongly than usual.

"You're sure this is where the report came from?" I ask.

"It was an anonymous caller who claimed to be fishing out by the old locks and saw her rooting around near the northern wall of town."

"Who'd he call? The militia?"

"The Mjolnir Institute."

I don't know much about the institute except that it's funded through efforts of Thor Thunderer and tracks all kinds of troll information. They aren't the first responders in an attack, and so it's odd this tipster would've called them. But I heard about it so fast probably because it went through Thor's institute and straight to Baldur's ear.

We stop for brunch at a bistro with outdoor seating, and Soren does his best to hunker down and not draw attention while I flirt with our waitress for information. I pretend to be interested in the history of the town and ask about the garden festival, about how the population did during Baldur's disappearance, and with the troll alert if she thinks they'll get as many out-of-town guests as usual. I bring up trolls at least three times, giving her ample opportunity to tell me about any actual sightings, but the nearest she offers is an anecdote about a place out by the river the kids call Troll Spot, where they can look toward the system of locks and some drowned cities called the Lost Villages. They go up there to smoke leaf and make out, and pretend to see trolls in the water. Since the anonymous fisherman mentioned the locks, too, I guess it's our best bet. I give Soren a sidelong glance and say to the waitress, "A good make-out spot, you say? How do we get there?"

Soren, bless him, ducks his face, which is as good as a blush.

Full of caffeine and sandwiches, we get back into the SUV and follow her directions out the east gate, then north on a dirt road through a lovely forest. Spring leaves turn the light chartreuse as the road climbs over a slight hill and stops. The land slopes away toward the river, a quick-moving, wide-banked waterway here, glinting brown in the sun. Soren stops the car and we climb out, armed with troll-spears and our swords. The view north stretches over flat fields and groves of green trees, and to the east the river narrows and we can see the concrete rectangles of abandoned locks. Farther east the horizon slides into a haze of clouds, but it must be where the Lost Villages were.

I pick my way downhill to the river. West where the water slows, a handful of motorboats laze in the current, and a couple of kayaks, too. Nobody here is worried about trolls. The couple who spot us give our spears a surprised look, though.

My boots sink into the mud. A few drowned trees cling to the bank. Insects buzz at my face and I swat them away. I shuck off my coat, wishing I'd left it in the car. We're not on a glacier island anymore, obviously, and spring is in full bloom. Behind me, Soren sneezes.

For an hour I walk along the bank toward the locks, eyes down for troll-sign. There's absolutely nothing. Frustration has me slashing with the spear at the thin branches that hang in my way, stomping down on grass that did me no harm. We get to the locks and I push easily through a hole in the rusty chain-link fence. The locks are huge rectangular chambers built into the river, with mechanisms for raising and lowering the water level in order to help boats get upriver. These are drained and defunct, because there's nothing north since Montreal fell.

I climb the crumbling old stairs up to the top and look down into the first lock. Moss darkens the low, stagnant water, and it smells like rotten plants. The river flows free on the other side, splashing resentfully at the concrete.

Soren touches my elbow and points to the bottom of this first lock. Huddled down in the sunny corner are three small oblong stones. The water has them only partially hidden.

"Skit," I say. Lesser trolls. There's a broken and rusty old ladder beside them, missing several rungs. Fine dining for an iron wight. I don't know if that makes it more or less likely the troll mother is here. Conventional wisdom would say they avoid their larger cousins, but the wights appeared on Vinland only when there'd recently been a herd moving about. If mine is the first mother, with Freya's charm in her heart, there's no knowing what effect she might have on the lesser trolls.

I hurry along the side of the lock, heave up onto the next one, and keep going. There's evidence of claws and chewing on some metal drums lined along the land side of the locks, and one spillway has been torn out enough that water trickles slowly through, making a perfect little drinking fountain. But I spy no broken trees, no boulders of any size, and there's nothing but flat farmland for kilometers. No caves, no veins of granite near the surface of the earth.

"There's nowhere for her to hide," I exclaim when the sun is at its apex, wiping away any shadows. "Unless she's underwater."

He squints against the glare off the river. "You aren't about to propose diving, are you?"

"A few more sleepless nights and I might be."

"We can come back when the sun is gone, and until then go interview the fishermen. Maybe find our anonymous informant."

With a final glare at the little iron wights calcified into stones at the bottom of the lock, I agree.

But even interviewing all the hikers and kayakers we can find nearer to the town, there's no sign of him.

When the sun sets we drive out to the end of the locks, farther east toward Montreal than we walked. We eat takeout in the SUV, staring at the black river through the windshield. Stars pop out, brighter in the northeast than they are back toward the glow from Long Salt. Maybe she'll show herself in the darkness.

I drift into sleep, waking as Soren shuffles around because a muffled pop song sounds behind the dash. He mumbles an apology as he reaches across me for the glove compartment. It unlatches and a cell phone falls out. He catches it and thumbs it on. "Hello? Ah, yes. No."

The tinny voice on the other end sounds like Baldur. I think I hear *Port Orleans* and *your Valkyrie.*

"Yes, thanks. No, we haven't had any luck. Yes . . ." Soren taps his head back against the driver's seat, staring at the roof. "That might be related; we'll talk about it." Turning his head away from me, he whispers, "Baldur, *stop.*"

There's laughter from the god of light. I'm torn between wanting and not wanting to know what he's teasing Soren about.

Soren closes the phone and clears his throat. "Can you put this back?" He drops it in my hand. "Baldur says he's taking Red Stripe to Port Orleans for a Disir Day charity ball he's throwing with one of the southern preachers, to benefit Vinland relief. He wants you to come claim your troll there and be his special guest."

Shoving the phone back into the glove compartment gives me a moment to calculate. "That's the end of next week?"

"Nine days. Probably three days' easy driving from here, two if we push it."

I blow out a frustrated sigh. I want Red Stripe, but to take so much time away from the hunt sticks under my skin. Maybe we'll find her before then. "I'll think about it. Do you know the story of Freya creating the trolls?" I ask.

Soren grunts acknowledgment, and I tell him my theory that the mother we're hunting might be the mother from that story.

"That's . . . old."

I keep my voice calm when I answer, as if it will rein in my enthusiasm. "And so are the gods, and the giants lived centuries, too, millennia even, before they were destroyed."

"Maybe you should pick a different heart, then. The riddle says *a* stone heart, doesn't it?"

Frustration makes me kick the glove compartment. "Never. I saw the answer in her eyes, and she owes me blood price now. Even without the riddle, without anything else, I'd be hunting her."

Outside the SUV the wind flutters the leaves and turns the banks of the river into ruffles of grass. I open my door and jump out, taking a UV flashlight with me to the lock. In the dark it's hard to find good footing, but I climb up to peer down into the low water. "Hey, bridge eaters," I call. Something skitters against the concrete, and I hear gentle lapping below. I flip on the light and scan it straight down along the edge of the water. A tiny shriek starts my heart beating faster. There's movement in the pit. Light reflects back at me from the tiny tossing waves.

I slide the spotlight back the other way, then around the whole perimeter. Five pairs of eyes flash at me; I see teeth and flailing limbs in the far corner.

It's only a two-meter drop, and I crouch first, put my hand on the edge, and jump down.

I hit with a huge splash, boots on slick ground, and shove fast to the corner. Water up to my knees sloshes everywhere and the iron wights scream. Thrusting out my hand, I snatch one by the neck and push it into the wall, pointing the UV light toward the rest of them so they stay back. The wight weighs about as much as a house cat but is shaped like a monkey, tiny hands grasping at my wrist and man-shaped mouth gaping. Its front teeth are jagged like a shark's, for tearing through metal—or soft human flesh—and the molars heavy and hard. It wears thin, ragged pants it probably stole off some stuffed animal. "Peas, peas!" it gasps.

"Where's the troll mother?" I ask calmly. "I won't hurt you if you tell me."

"No—no!"

"There isn't one? Or she's gone?"

"Cat-man!"

Above me, Soren says, "What are you doing?"

Ignoring him, I lean nearer the iron wight. It snaps at my face. "Did you see a troll mother, a giant, mean mountain troll?"

"Mean troll yessss." It nods and slobber drops onto my hand.

"Signy, it's just answering because it's terrified." Disapproval coats Soren's words.

Claws rake against my calf and I kick out, connecting with a small body. I hurl my wight into the water.

"Come on," Soren calls, reaching his hand down. I throw the flashlight up. It arcs over him, flashing light at the sky like a strobe, and lands back on the grass with a thump. Then I leap up to grasp his forearm. He drags me up, none too gently, pulling on my arm and, when he can reach it, the scruff of my shirt. Below me the iron wights hiss and curse. Water splashes and a few hard chunks of metal hit my legs and back.

I roll over onto my back against the rough concrete of the lock and Soren sighs. "That was a waste of time."

"She's not here."

"Are you hurt?"

"Bruises, nothing else."

"You need sleep. We'll get a hotel room in town, and then . . . head for Port Orleans?"

"There has to be sign of her somewhere. We'll go up into Montreal, hunt in the ruins. I'm not giving up."

"I don't want you to, but let's be smart about it. If you go to New Orleans for Disir Day, afterward Baldur might join us, and if there's anybody you want at your side for troll hunting, it's him."

That's not true. I want Ned Unferth.

\+ \+ \+

That night the troll mother crouches on my chest. She suffocates me, scratching her claws down my arm, and when the blood spills out she uses it to paint runes on the walls and ceiling: *Find me, Death Chooser; I will eat your heart.*

Find me.

Find me.

I wake with Unferth's name on my tongue.

Baldur calls first thing in the morning to tell us of greater mountain troll–sign in Ohiyo kingstate. I actually talk to him personally, and he tells me the man who called it in was hunting deer with his two sons and she rose out of the river fog "like the moon." He described her in explicit detail, down to the green-blue of her eyes and the sickle-shaped scar on her left shoulder. It *must* be her, no matter how strange that she's traveling that fast and out of her territory. Where could she be headed and why? What is southwest of here but the center of the country?

We drive straight to Ohiyo. But the results are the same: nobody will admit to being the source, and this time we're in rolling forested hills, the proper habitat for hill trolls, not mountain trolls. Unlike Vinland, where they're only rare, this far south greater mountain trolls are unheard-of. What they've plenty of, however, in Cleaveland and Louisville, are lesser trolls. There's a news bulletin about a bridge on the Ohiyo River buckling under the weight of a semi, thanks to ruined support beams that were just replaced three years ago, and another about a riverboat in Cincinnatus infested by cat wights, who're supposed to despise water.

Soren and I spend four days in the kingstate, using his Sun's Berserk credentials to talk with city planners and local exterminators about the sightings and serious uptick in lesser-troll presence. They all agree it must have been the recent national crisis bringing the wights out of their normal shadows. They say that, like the Vinland herd, the wights were sensitive to the air of fear here in the heartland when Baldur vanished. Soren believes it, but that sounds like a bunch of fluffy nonsense to me. The iron wights I've known weren't *sensitive* to anything but the presence of metal or shiny toys. Fortunately, Soren inserts himself between me and the city workers before I say anything unforgivable.

The longer I spend along the river, the crankier I become. She is my destiny, I tell Soren, and she recognized my heart, too, somehow. I have to find her.

He says, "You *choose,* Signy. *You* make your destiny; don't just let it pull you along," and I remember saying exactly that thing to Unferth our last night together. How he would scorn me for accepting the drag of destiny now, because it aligns with what I selfishly want.

Soren continues to push for us to head south to Port Orleans. I'm torn because I want Baldur's resources, but I don't want to risk losing her trail. If only I could sense her somehow, or use my dreams as a guide.

For she comes to me every night now, from slimy swamps,

rising out of the water with long grasses that slide off her head and shoulders. She bears rune scars carved into her hard marble chest. *My* rune scar, which Unferth translated: *death-born, servant of death. Strange Maid.* She comes with it painted in blood over her heart. She crouches on a white sand beach, drawing a rune poem into the sand, but before I can read it the tide washes it away and the mother is behind me, ripping runes into my flesh, and I scream prayers for my skin to harden like hers.

The fourth night in Ohiyo, I soar over a battlefield on a massive gray horse, at the head of a flight of Valkyrie. Below us the dead burn in a single great bonfire. We point, my sisters and I, at one man, and then another, drawing their spirits up with us as we gallop across the clouds. I laugh and shriek at the glory of it all, at the blood, the hunger. But when I twist to look back, they're not golden women at my flanks but eight troll mothers in feather capes, the one near me as wide as the moon and graceful as a swan. She bats me out of the sky, but a rope around my neck snaps and I hang from her thick hand as she flies over the battlefield. Tall flames lick up at my legs. I scream and struggle. I flail my legs and claw at the noose.

Someone says my name, over and over, calmly. Puts cool hands on my face, unwinds the noose and gently kisses me.

Little raven.

I'm awake, and he's gripping me tightly, pinning my hands between us. *Ned, Ned, Ned.* But it's Soren, light streaming around him from the desk lamp. I bury my face against him and try to breathe.

"Skit, Signy," he whispers, "are you sick? You're on fire." He slides his hands down my bare arms until he reaches my hands. "Let me get you water."

I grab his hands, gouging him with my nails hard enough that he grunts. I let go. "Sorry," I whisper.

I flee to the bathroom to splash water over my face. We're on the top floor of a standard highway hotel with free hot breakfast and an interweave connection if we had a computer. The walls are covered with gilded paper to remind us of another era, and these bathroom fixtures are overly elaborate. The kind you have to stare at too long before you figure out which is hot and which is cold.

Soren puts his shoulder against the wall and waits for me. After I pat my face dry and manage a few clean breaths, I face him, wrapping my arms around my stomach. "I'm all right. It's only more of the same."

"Do you need a workout?"

"I think I need a drink." I duck around him with a flirty smile.

"My . . . Astrid . . . would say if you figure out what's scaring you, you can face it."

I stop beside my bed, head down. "I'm trying to, Soren. I'm looking for her. She's looking for me."

He says, "Nightmares like this aren't normal, not even for post-trauma."

My knees melt and I plop onto the floor with my back against the bed. He joins me and I only stare at him for a long moment. The lamp casts rather dim light onto us, and Soren lacks that guarded expression he normally wears.

"You don't have to be alone," he finally says.

"What would Astrid think of that?" I snap.

Soren frowns and studies his right palm. He slowly says, "She'd agree. She'd like you, and she'd know you helped me already." He lifts his gaze to mine again, and when he speaks again his tone brooks no argument. "She wouldn't be worried about *us* at all."

I dig my fingers into the carpet. "Well, *good.*"

Silence drags through a couple of minutes.

"Maybe your dreams are trying to tell you something," Soren finally says. "Something your imagination has already put together but you can't parse yet."

I think of the troll mother, of the imagery that she hanged me, that I died. That first we flew as sister Valkyrie. We were the same. I cover my face with my hands. But he gently pulls them away, folding them between his own hot hands. "Tell me."

"She's in a swamp, or on a white sand beach. My rune scar is carved onto her, like we're connected—and we are connected, Soren. We both draw poetry into sand; her eyes are full of runes for the Valkyrie. She said to me, *Your heart,* when she held me close to her face. I used to dream of killing her, but now she kills me. She flays my skin; she knocks me out of the sky. It's like instead of me becoming her mirror, she's become mine." I squeeze his fingers.

"Your mirror?"

"Valtheow the Dark, the Valkyrie? She hunted a troll mother centuries ago and said that in order to hunt the beast, she had to become a beast."

"I don't know about that."

"Of course you wouldn't, Sun's Berserk."

He lets go of my hands. "You don't have to be mean."

I work my jaw and eventually grind out an apology.

Soren just watches me.

"I hate being afraid," I confess.

"When I'm afraid, I take deep breaths. I remember who I am. I pray."

"What are you afraid of?"

He's so still, the least fidgety person I've ever met, and for a moment it's like he's become a statue. "Killing innocent people," he says quietly.

Like his father, like the trolls. I touch the tattoo on his face gently, knowing better than to offer any easy comfort to that.

"I'll tell you what I've learned about dreams," he says, his voice almost too quiet for me to hear. I climb onto my bed while Soren stretches out on the floor at the foot. I wonder if it's easier for him to talk when he can stare up at the ceiling, pretend I'm not really listening as he tells me how the berserking madness woke in him a few years ago, that it gave him insomnia and made him afraid of himself. Until he met a girl who dreamed true dreams, and Baldur the Beautiful, who always dreams of his death, and they taught him he wasn't a monster.

I scoot sideways on the bed, hair loose and hanging to the carpet, arms splayed out like wings with my palms up. Unferth's sword lies beside me, just near enough I can skim my fingers against the garnet. With my head tipped back the blood rushes into my eyes, filling my skull near to bursting. *Fear can be a sacrifice, too,* Ned whispers. I don't want to hear him now, and take my hand away from his sword.

"It isn't natural to dream your own death again and again," Soren says. "But Baldur does. And Astrid's were sometimes frightening, sometimes uplifting, sometimes about people she didn't know and never would. They were always true, though. Because she was a seethkona. And her goddess is the goddess of dreams. That same goddess Baldur sleeps with every winter, in death. The goddess who connects them."

"Freya, the queen of witches," I whisper. I shiver and close my eyes. The troll mother roars.

"Signy . . . the Alfather does many things, manipulates words and memory, and thought . . . but he has no power over our dreams."

My eyes fly open. "You think Freya is behind them. My dreams."

"She stole Baldur's ashes."

"What?" I roll over abruptly, clutch the foot of the bed, and stare down at him. My hair falls all around my face. "They told us it was one of Odin's Lonely Warriors, and why would she do that?" A memory flashes through my head: demanding to know if Unferth was Einherjar, and his swift, amused denial.

Soren's dark eyes are grim, his lips tight. "To manipulate Astrid to exactly where Freya wanted her—for the destiny of the world, she said. Maybe she wants something from you, too."

"But Odin Alfather cast my riddle into the Tree; the Valkyrie would know if it were otherwise. That's what set me on this path!"

My calm companion doesn't reply, his silence full of weight and meaning.

I throw myself back onto my back and stare at the popcorn ceiling as if I could force the swirls into answers. "What could she want from me?" I whisper.

"I don't know. Maybe she doesn't. I only know that either your dreams are only dreams, or they mean something because the goddess of dreams wants you to know a thing."

"Odd-eye and rag me," I whisper.

Could Freya be sending me dreams, could she be pushing me toward the troll mother? The troll mother she herself created?

"Odin," I start, tentatively, "Odin would have to be . . . aware. He sent the riddle."

"It sounds like a prophecy, though, doesn't it? And Freya is the only one of them who sees the future."

I say, "And so maybe he asked her to read my future, and this was her answer."

"Which might have been all her intent, merely doing her cousin a favor."

His tone makes clear that he doesn't believe it. He doesn't trust Freya, because whatever it is that happened to his Astrid, whatever got her name torn out of the world, he blames the goddess of dreams.

"All right." I lick my dry lips. "Let's pretend that's what

happened. She gave him this prophecy that he turned into a riddle. Maybe he knew the answer, that the troll mother is the stone heart I need—but Freya must have. If she's the one driving me toward the mother."

"And how did you figure out the troll mother was the answer?"

Nausea ruins my insides. "Ned."

"Are you certain he came from Odin?"

"I believed it," I whisper. "I chose to. Everything pointed to it; it was the right answer to the—the riddle of his existence."

This is called doubt, little raven, he murmurs to me now.

"But no, I'm not *certain,*" I say through my teeth, barely willing to let the words out. I press the balls of my hands into my eyes. "Oh, *Hangatyr,* oh gods."

May Signy Valborn never regret, Unferth prayed, the last thing before he died.

I knew he left pieces out of his story; I knew there was more to tell—but it can't be that he used me. It can't be. I kissed him. I loved him. I trusted him.

I want to take up his sword and crash it into the window, destroy something.

I have to know if Ned was a liar by his riddles, by all he omitted. I have to know if Freya sent him or if Odin did, because I am *his,* not hers: a Valkyrie and a wild, passionate, screaming one. If I am on a path Odin set me on, fine. But I won't work against him. I have to know.

"Soren."

"Signy." He kneels, leaning his elbows onto the bed.

I sit cross-legged and reach for his hands. "Precia, the Valkyrie of the South, has her Death Hall in Port Orleans."

He nods, turning his hands over so our palms connect.

"We'll go for Disir Day and I'll ask her about all of this. She told me she wanted to help."

Soren agrees, and I cling to him. With my fingers dug into his wrists I beg him not to let go. We lie next to each other on the bed, only our hands connected. His hot, mine tingling with my pulse until I fall asleep.

But the troll mother waits.

Unferth is with her, and she puts her hand on his face gently, like a lover. It envelops his head and he leans into her, curls his fingers around her thumb. He smiles. He looks straight at me and says, "My only Signy."

I wake up in darkness, unable to close my eyes again.

EIGHTEEN

BALDUR'S TOWN HOUSE in Port Orleans is a narrow blue-shingled building with a porch on the second and third stories, bright yellow shutters, and plants dripping like hair from the rails and even the roof. Soren parallel parks impressively, and I hop out onto a broken cobbled sidewalk. Graybeard moss dangles from the low branches of an oak. I have to brush it out of my way as I swing Unferth's sword onto my shoulder.

Baldur himself will be joining us here for the ball tonight. Soren tapped his finger against the wheel for the entire drive once we hit the Orleans kingstate, which I assume means a level of excitement that would've set a lesser man puking.

We start for the front porch, with its wide fans and line of white rocking chairs. A man stands up from one, lifting a hand in greeting. But it's not the god of light.

It's Rathi.

He looks amazing, with his golden hair curled about his face by the humidity, his jacket gone, and those pale pink shirt-sleeves rolled up to his elbows. I hope his slacks are cotton. I'm sweating already in my jeans and Mad Eagles T-shirt. "Rathi," I say, letting surprise show in my tone. He puts his arms around me and hugs me.

"I've been worried about you," he murmurs. "I'm glad you agreed to this."

"The preacher cosponsoring the ball must be your Ardo Vassing?" I lean back to meet his eyes.

Rathi nods, then releases me to bow politely at Soren. "It's good to see you again, Bearstar. And thank you for watching out for my sister."

"She's watched out for me," Soren rumbles.

I lean my shoulder into Soren's and catch Rathi's swift glance of appraisal. "Well," he says, his well-practiced smile flashing, "she's good at that, too."

"What are you doing here?" I ask, letting go of both boys and heading up to the tall front door.

"I got in last night with Ardo and managed to obtain this address to see if you had any free time for sightseeing."

With a sardonic glance at Soren, I say, "He means he flirted his way here."

Rathi holds still, one eyebrow tilted slightly as if to say *I'm above such things.* But Soren, knocking against the cut-glass window in the door, glances pointedly at me. "That skill must run in your family."

Both Rathi and I laugh, but for different reasons, I'm sure.

+ + +

An hour later, I'm walking through the Old Quarter between Rathi and Soren, with vague directions from the housekeeper to the hanging tree in Sanctus Louis Square. Soren was surprised we weren't heading straight for the Port Orleans Death Hall, but that's not where Precia will be today.

I recognize the energy of a tourist trap, though here we're seduced not with hawkers and historical artifacts but with dark, almost filthy mystery. The Quarter sticks to the back of my throat; I could peel a film of it off my skin. The streets are narrow and cobbled in most places, the buildings redbrick though often painted over with dingy white or pale green. Upper stories are quiet, all tall dark windows and empty iron balconies. At street level, doors are flung open and painted signs beckon to us with the promise of magic charms and unique jewelry, seether readings, fancy shoes, and every sort of fried food.

The air smells of old beer and molasses, with an acrid undertone I choose not to dwell on. Littered in the gutters are beads and torn streamers making half-rune signs, and everything is slightly damp, though I don't think it rained.

We find cold coffee to keep me awake and share a basket of airy doughnuts as we walk down the center of Prince Street amidst a throng of not only tourists but Disir Day celebrants.

Disir Day is a festival of the goddesses and all disir: women spirits and the ghosts of our mother-ancestors. Temporary shrines are stacked haphazardly on the sidewalks, glowing with elf-lights and crowded with seven-day candles, tiny goddess figures, bells and charms, and laughing patrons. Crepe flowers drip from the balconies, adding rainbows of color. I've heard Port Orleans does this for every holiday, and even some outside the Asgardian purview. The stories of Port Orleans at Hallowblot especially titillate, what with the Old Quarter transforming into a giant goblin playground, with masks and costumes and a three-kilometer-long parade.

I keep my eyes stripped for a very specific sort of vendor who's likely to be nearer to the hanging tree, but in a place such as this they might have permanent shops. It's not easy pushing through, and we're forced to a leisurely pace. Street performers clog the corners, and people with plastic cups of icy alcohol stream like private parades between the pubs. If Soren and I had our weapons, we'd be able to cut a better path, but as it is we don't stand out—Soren blends in better than in any place else I've seen. There are every sort of people here, speaking different languages, with every kind of god's jewelry and tattoos and fashion. It seems to relax him, or at least balance out his aversion to crowds. I feel entirely on edge with questions, eyes burning from lack of sleep, while sweat prickles my scalp and the jeans stick to my thighs.

Rathi doesn't help by droning on and on about the history of Port Orleans and how it became so religiously diverse. It was the largest port in New Asgard two hundred years ago, until the end of the Thralls' War, when it divided into the formerly rich and the newly freed. Almost immediately Li Grand Zombi became the first non-Asgardian deity officially acknowledged by Congress, though only as an incarnation of the World Snake. The shock of it drew men from all churches, and Biblists in particular, hoping for similar success. But the voodoo queens had managed the politics by embracing the variety of our gods and finding mirrors in their own spirituality, "while compromise," Rathi says disapprovingly, "was never a Biblist strength."

Rich, coming from a Freyan, Unferth whispers.

He won't leave me alone, either.

It isn't until Rathi, thanks to encouraging grunts from Soren, is speculating on why Port Orleans voodoo is so compatible with Freya the Witch's magic, that I see what I'm looking for. Several piles of wire cages spill out of a storefront, holding rats and sparrows and squirrels.

When I stop, Rathi nearly runs into me but grips my shoulder tightly. "Oh, Signy, really?" He gazes past me at the martyr shop. "I thought you were only going to the hanging tree to speak with the Valkyrie."

"I can't approach the hanging tree on Disir Day without sacrifice." I irritably shrug him off and head for the nearest stack of cages. The tiny white mice crawl on top of each other, whiskers twitching slowly. There's a pair of albino pigeons cuddled together sleeping, and a long gray rat watches me. Soren comes up behind and softly says, "I haven't done this since my dad died."

"I'll be out here," Rathi says, waving his hand at the street itself.

Soren and I duck into the shop. "Weak stomach?" Soren asks.

"Delicate Freyan sensibilities."

Soren's eyes crinkle. "I thought everyone made sacrifice."

"On Yule they hold their noses, but the branch of Freyan Rathi is—all the Summerlings and my family, too—say life is too valuable for such a thing."

"That's the point of sacrifice, though."

"I know."

The shop is livid with animal calls and stinks like bleach and wood shavings and urine. Cages hang from the low rafters, decorated with ribbons and rune flags. There are inkpots and rune brushes, feather fans, penknives and silver throat daggers. A family of four studies the rodent wall as their father points out the coloring on various mice to his two daughters and what the differences represent. A single woman with an iron collar studies a molting crow in a too-small cage. I head for the counter while Soren picks through a stand of prayer cards.

A little man with skin like concrete nods at me from the register, milky eyes fluttering. His left eyelid is tattooed a solid though fading gray. "Lady?" he says in a small, rough voice.

"Do you have any kissing doves?"

"Oh surely, right in the back. How many do you want?"

I glance at Soren as he joins me with a small shake of his head. "Only one."

"I'll take one of the little black mice," Soren says, pointing.

The keeper shuffles behind a violet curtain, and while we wait one of the little girls peeks around her father's hips to stare at Soren. He doesn't smile or even soften his expression. I poke him in the ribs and his eyes pop. It makes the girl giggle and hide. "A smile goes a long way," I whisper at him as the old Odinist returns with a round wire cage holding a gray kissing dove with peach feathers at her breast. He hands Soren a mesh bag and tells him to go fish out his mouse.

As I open my calligraphy bag to pull out some notes, the man cuts his hand between us. "This is no charge," he says quietly, "not for the Vinland Valkyrie and Bearstar. You honor my martyrs by choosing them."

I pause in an attempt to hide my shock. Not at being recognized, but at being recognized and *honored.* I lift my eyes to his slowly, thinking of that Lokiskin pawnshop owner who refused to buy my seax, who barely admitted what I was. I hear Precia say, *You could hold the country in the palm of your hand with your story now.* "Thank you, sir," I manage. "May the finest blessings run through your blood and the blood of your sacrifices."

The keeper pats my hand with his gnarled fingers. "Keep it up, Valkyrie."

I carry my dove before me as we go outside, still stunned. Soren seems unfazed, cupping his mesh bag gently against his chest with both hands. The mouse must be smaller than his thumb. Rathi finds us, glancing mournfully at my dove, but says nothing as we make our way to the square.

The Sanctus Louis temple shines white and tall, with dark stained-glass windows glittering in the thick sunlight. Spreading out from its huge double doors is the green square, with a crooked hanging tree in the center and a marble statue of Odin's wife, Frigg Cloud-Spinner. She's been draped with flowers and plastic beads, her hands holding them as if to weave them into one of her rainbows.

A line has formed, perhaps a dozen people long, before the sacrificial station, where three hooded death priests help people tie prayer cards to the martyrs they've brought, mark them with their rune wishes, and then direct them one at a time to the trunk of the tree, where the Valkyrie waits.

To my surprise, Rathi stays with Soren and me as we move up the line. He's unable to stop himself from cooing at my dove. She cocks her head and blinks at him from one little brown eye. "Hasn't there been enough death?" he murmurs into my ear.

At the long wooden table set up as the prep station, the first death priest smiles out from her green hood. A raven half-mask is tattooed across her face. "Welcome. What prayer will you tie to your martyr?"

Soren steps forward first and quietly speaks to the priest. She uses red ink to create a prayer card for him, tiny as my fingernail, to tie to the tail of his mouse. The rune on one side is *lady* and on the other *youth.* It's a prayer to Idun the Young, keeper of the apples of immortality. Very appropriate for Disir Day. He scoots down to make room for me, turning toward the hanging tree.

There, in the crisscrossed shadows, the Valkyrie of the South finishes hanging a sparrow. She's speaking to the teenage couple as they watch the little bird swing. A red love charm dangles from its claw.

As they back away, Precia unties the sparrow's noose from the branch and hands it to her green-hooded assistant, who then takes it to a ladder and hangs it higher into the tree with the corpses of a few dozen other martyrs. They'll hang for three nights and days before being burned in a fire at the Death Hall.

She stands straight and turns this way to welcome the next martyr to the tree.

And she sees me.

I lift my chin and hold my breath. Here I am in jeans, boots, and a T-shirt, my hair braided in messy loops, while Precia is in full summertime regalia: ankle-length dress the color of the sky, with a wide gold and copper belt and a chain made with silver and brilliant blue glass that cuts across her collar from shoulder to shoulder. From it hangs a diaphanous feather cape, every white feather fluttering individually. Silver cuffs hold the hem to her elbows and wrists, so when she lifts out her arms the cape spreads like wings. Her dark hair is puffed into curls, swept back with mixed-metal combs. True to form, she wears blue and copper earrings so large they swallow everything around them.

She smiles through gentle lipstick and beckons for me with manicured fingers. I bring Soren with me, like a shield.

"Signy," Precia says, "and Soren Bearstar, you honor our hanging tree with your sacrifice," calm and certain, as her assistant and a few lingering people listen. "This is not where I expected to see you," she adds more softly, putting her hand on my shoulder, then sliding it around to half embrace me. She smells of lilac and sharp mint, oils dabbed beneath her ears and on her wrists to keep away the scent of death.

Precia turns her attention to Soren, clucking with approval at his prayer card. She releases me and I close my eyes as I feel the soft feathers brush down my bare arm. My dove bats her wings against the thin bars of her cage.

"Signy."

I open my eyes to Precia's, and for a flash I see *glory* in the rich brown irises.

Shock silences me for a moment. In ten years, I've never been able to read a rune in a Valkyrie's eye before. It raises courage in me and I say, "Precia, I've come for your help. You told me to ask."

Her gaze lingers on mine, cool but interested. She flicks her hand at her assistant, who begins clearing space for us. Soren waits beside his mouse, a tiny dead thing swinging at eye level.

"Paint a prayer card, Signy, and ask." Precia ushers me to the long table, dismissing her death priests with a glance. She spreads rainbow-colored cards for me in an arc.

I choose one that is pale green with silver vines at the edges. "Tell me what you know about my riddle."

She taps a peach-colored fingernail against my card. "We prayed that night, too. Elisa, Myra, and I. We prayed together for an answer, for help managing you because the three of us have always been . . . the ones most behind you." She offers me a pot of dark green ink. I take it without touching her fingers.

"We came out to find you and there it was, emblazoned on the trunk of the New World Tree. It was for us as much as you, Elisa and I thought. That it meant you would always fight us, that your heart is a stubborn one, and one perhaps we should strive to understand instead of dismiss. But Myra said, *That riddle is future tense.* And then you woke up."

"I woke up and ran away."

"You didn't ask us what we thought. You *never* asked. We're supposed to be your sisters."

I draw the rune for *glory* onto my card, and Precia's hand goes still. I add *sacrifice* and *death* and *transformation* into a binding rune. Precia murmurs, "Sacrifice transforms death into its own glory."

"That's what Odin said to me when I was a little girl." I lift my gaze to hers. "Do you still think the riddle's answer is about my being stubborn? Or is it a prophecy?"

Precia's coiffed hair and conservative wardrobe make it easy to forget she's not even thirty years old yet. But the emotion in her eyes is young. "I think you proved yourself against the Vinland herd. I think you were there because of fate, and you were brave; you were a leader, Signy. That's all we need you to be."

"If I went home to the Philadelphia Death Hall right now, you would argue to include me now? Officially?"

"Yes. I already have. But the others—Gundrun and Siri and Aerin, in particular—will not agree until you ask to be one of us again. They argue that you can't have proven yourself if even you don't believe it."

"I have to prove myself . . . to myself."

She nods.

I smile sadly. Unferth said that to me the very day we met. "Do you believe Odin is the one who created the riddle?"

Precia flips over my card irritably. "Signy, really."

"It's not only a riddle but a prophecy. Like Myra said. Future tense. *The Valkyrie of the Tree* will *prove herself with a stone heart.*"

Her mouth curls into a frown. "If the heart is your heart, everything in that riddle was built from pieces of you, from pieces our Alfather could see and understand in that moment."

"I think the answer is the troll mother's heart. The one I'm hunting. Her heart is literally stone, Precia, and when I cut it out of her, I'll have my vengeance. I saw runes in her eyes, too: *stone* and *heart.*"

"She has the worth of a Valkyrie," she breathes.

I knew Precia would understand. "She's my mirror."

"I make myself a mirror to understand the beast."

That my sister made the same leap to Valtheow as I did relieves me like the perfect couplet at the end of a poem. I take a long, deep breath. The air here is thick, heavy. It tastes of rain and wet leaves. "And so I'm faced with two options, Precia."

"Two?"

"Either the riddle is all of Odin, and the answer is with me and me alone, pieces of my heart and the Valkyrie I wanted to be. I've always been the answer. Or the riddle is a prophecy, and the answer the troll mother's heart. A thing to come that Odin could not have seen on his own and asked Freya to look forward into fate for me."

The Valkyrie grasps my face, peers into my eyes. "And you're convinced it's the troll mother. A fated answer from the queen of Hel."

"I dream of the troll mother every night, and she uses runes, Precia. She does what I do; she wears my poem on her stony skin. She recognized me, too, somehow. Her heart is the stone heart of the riddle, and Odin does not see the future."

"But, Signy, the Alfather cast it. If his sister-god looked at Fate for him, he saw her answer and approved of where it would lead you. That riddle is from the god of the hanged."

The certainty in her voice, the firm grip of her hands on my face, makes me wilt against her. "And so he did send Ned Unferth to help me, when it was time."

"What?"

"Last year, at my birthday, I met a poet called Ned the Spiritless, who brought me to the trolls, who taught me about the riddle and, odd-eye, Precia, he . . ." I don't know where to go from there, what detail to give her that will make her understand my connection to Ned Unferth.

"You love him." Precia lets me go so suddenly I have to catch myself on the table.

I gape at her. It must be so obvious.

She says, "There is no room for other men, other loves, between a Valkyrie's heart and the Alfather's."

"Elisa is married!"

"To a man who understands her devotion."

"There are so many stories of Valkyrie and great, epic love," I argue.

"How many of them ended happily? Especially for the Valkyrie in the sagas and ancient poems, the kind of Valkyrie you want to be? They have no happy endings, my love."

It's true, what she says, like a kick in the guts. "He's dead anyway."

Precia softens, touches my prayer card only to flip it over. "Finish your prayer, Signy."

The front of the card reads: *Sacrifice transforms death into its own glory.* The first thing Unferth said to me was that pain wasn't the worth of sacrifice. I think now the worth is in how it changes us. With a shaky hand, I paint the rune *spirit* and cross it out with a jagged line.

Precia blesses my card with a kiss. I open the cage while she gently pulls out my dove. We tie the card to her thin gray leg. I take her in both hands, her downy feathers shivering against my skin, to the hanging tree.

As I hold the dove, Precia ties one end of a green rope to her neck in a simple slipknot and the other end to the branch. I whisper, "I know, little bird, what this fear in your heart is like. Thank you for being my sacrifice."

Birds are difficult to hang, and if you give them their freedom they'll beat their wings and panic, flying against the rope for long minutes before they tire and slowly, achingly, choke themselves. I take a deep breath. Ignoring the chatter of the crowd, the rush of hot wind and sticky sweat clinging to my shoulders and thighs, I close my eyes and picture the runes of my prayer card. I don't let go of the kissing dove, but with a swift, fast tug, pull her down against the rope.

Tears burn in my eyes. They spill out, warm on my cheeks. Beginning in my chest, I feel the relief of sacrifice, the loosening of my ribs and slowing of my heartbeat.

Releasing her with a caress, I allow my dove now to gently swing, like a pendulum marking the wind. The breeze flutters her feathers and teases at my hair.

NINETEEN

THE MOMENT BALDUR'S charity ball officially begins, I'm waiting inside the parlor of the town house. We're to make a grand entrance about an hour into the evening, and as I've been dressed and pressed for quite some time, waiting is all I can do. I sit for a while at the baby grand, plunking out old nursery tunes, trying to distract myself from the whirl of thoughts spiraling endlessly behind my eyes.

Wide-winged fans drive thick air down at the crown of my head. The humidity finds every free strand and curls it against my cheeks and neck. Disir Day is midway through Blissmonth, and exactly six weeks since I sat alone on the death ship beach, watching two hundred paper lanterns rise up and up into the stars. Almost as long since Unferth died.

I tell myself his loyalties don't matter anymore. Precia agrees the riddle itself was approved by Odin, regardless of its being a prophecy, too. And so what would it mean if Freya sent Ned to me? No more than that she wants me to solve the riddle, to meet my destiny. There's no reason to think that just because she stole Baldur's ashes and manipulated Soren's lover, because she may be sending me dreams, that Freya wants anything nefarious from me. Ned Unferth helped me on this path to achieving my destiny; I should accept it and let go.

It's only this niggling question in my heart: how much of Ned's truths were lies?

Soren isn't down yet, and I can't think what could be taking them longer with him than they took with me. I glance at the wide-faced grandmother clock stretched tall beside the door. Five minutes past seven. The manner of this old house muffles the noise from upstairs, though I just left a maid there and saw at least one man moving in and out of Soren's rooms.

I pace around the edge of the Oriental rug that covers a good half the floor. What is the troll mother doing now, as I'm forced to wear a fancy dress and go make nice for charity? *Where is she? Will she dream of me tonight, as I dream of her?* I put my feet down heel-to-toe and breath steadily, imagining the dark red line bordering the rug is Peachtree's tightrope. Pedestrian noise from the Quarter outside and distant music catch a ride on the sticky breeze.

"Isn't this a vision?" says a man in the doorway. He leans against the door frame in a tuxedo with silver fitted vest and bow tie. Sun-yellow hair is pushed behind his ears to curl loose against his lapels, and his face is wide-open, tanned and flawless. Even without the dark foyer for contrast behind him, he'd be a beacon of sunlight.

Baldur the Beautiful smiles, pushes gracefully off the door, and comes to me with his right hand held out, palm up.

Because there's absolutely nothing else to do, I give him mine. He raises it and bows, holding my gaze with his. His eyes are indigo, and around his pupils is a thin penumbra of dark pink. Like the sunset outside. My breath becomes sheer, too light for oxygen. Even seeing him on the pavilion at the funerals didn't prepare me for this contact.

Baldur kisses my knuckles and flutters his lashes as he glances away politely.

It breaks my shock as he must have known it would, and I manage to squeeze his fingers. "My lord Baldur," I say, too husky to sound like myself. He's filling the room with bright ardor, enough to power a city.

"It's such a pleasure, Signy of the Tree." His smile is merry and he drops my hand, planting his on his very fine hip. "I was sorry to have missed you at the funeral."

Despite his words, I feel as though I've been dropped into a summery ocean and have to relearn to breathe. Out of habit I think for Unferth to anchor me: he'd be cutting and hard, but I can't think of anything gloomy about the god of light.

Folding my hands before me in the semblance of calm, I reach for politeness. It's what Jesca would've wanted. "Thank you for what you're doing tonight. Vinland needs it."

"I feel responsible," he says, sorrow eclipsing his smile. "My absence upset so many things, and Vinland paid the price. I would that I could change that."

I shake my head slowly. Odd-eye, he's so beautiful and shining, but his fingers play against his thigh as if he's nervous.

Like a man.

With a leaden tongue I say, "Sacrifice is worthwhile."

Surprise winks across his face and he nods firmly. But immediately Baldur wipes away the brief serious note with a smile. "This dress looks amazing."

The corner of his mouth tells me he's flirting, and my heartbeat picks up again. "Your designer did herself proud, and I appreciate it. Without you, I'd have shown up in a hoodie and giant black boots."

He laughs, too bright for this world.

I struggle to say "I understand you're quite the boxer."

"Soren's been talking about me?" Delight pushes up his golden eyebrows. They distract me for a split second and I notice the pink is fading from his eyes. They truly carry a piece of the changing sky.

"Um, yes. Yes." I'm hopelessly caught up in his beauty.

Empty-headed girl, sneers Unferth.

As if he's here, judging me, I fist my hands and say, "Lord Sun, may I ask you a thing about your father?"

Baldur the Beautiful takes my hand. His own eyes burn too brightly for me to read runes in them. "Of course."

"Do you know . . . all the names of his Lonely Warriors?"

His golden eyebrows shoot up. "Ah, yes, I believe so."

"Was there one named Unferth? Ned Truth-Teller?"

"No," he says immediately. "Though it sounds familiar."

"It's also the name of a character in *The Song of Beowulf.*"

"Ah!" He claps his hands together, and just as he's about to continue, Soren enters, saying, "Baldur, you're here!"

The men embrace, clapping each other's backs and grinning

in the way of brothers. I take a moment to release my shaky breath, to right the world that's tilting under my feet.

They've put Soren in a white uniform that mirrors the berserkers' usual attire: double-breasted jacket with two rows of golden sunburst buttons and a narrow, high collar. The tails of his jacket are almost as full as a skirt and will look amazing if he dances. A thin stripe of yellow lines the outside of his white slacks, and his shoes are so shiny the chandelier reflects back on the toes.

He stretches his neck uncomfortably.

"You look more than worthy of being the Sun's first Berserk," Baldur laughs, throwing an arm around Soren again and turning them both to face me.

Focused on Soren's familiarity, I purse my lips as if shopping. "How can I choose only one?"

"No need for that, pretty thing," interrupts a young woman in a gown that sparkles like it's made of a thousand shards of green glass. She slinks into the room. "I'm here for the Bearstar's escort."

Something in her vivid green eyes reminds me I haven't eaten in hours. My stomach pinches with that hunger, and when the newcomer winds her arm possessively through Soren's, I ungraciously think she must be wearing contacts like Rathi.

Soren lets her hold his arm and doesn't appear surprised, but shifts slightly so he's more between her and Baldur. The woman laughs, revealing strong teeth. "I'm not here to eat him, boy."

"I invited her," the god of light reassures us. "Glory, meet Signy Valborn, of the New World Tree."

Glory's lips never lower down over those teeth as she studies me.

I hold myself still. She's only taller because she's wearing heels. "Glory," I say. "Have you no epithet?"

She leans in. The hairs on my arms rise as her face envelops my entire vision. I don't know what stands in front of me, except that she is no real woman. *Do not quail before predators, little raven,* hisses Unferth.

"I need no epithet," she murmurs.

"Signy." Soren is there beside me, glowering at Glory hard enough she wrinkles her nose at him. "This is Lady Fenris."

Fenris Wolf, daughter of Loki, destined to swallow the sun at the end of the world.

My eyes drop to her neck, where a collar woven from nine silver chains rests. The stories say those chains bind her with all the magic of the goddess Freya and the elves and goblins into this girl's form so that she can be no danger to Baldur. He, at least, must believe it's true.

I force myself to look past her to the god of light. As delicately as I can, I ask, "Shall I ready myself for any more divine surprises tonight?"

Glory barks a laugh, and Baldur bows apologetically as he offers his hand to lead me out. Soren catches my eye and nods once.

But then Soren always prepares for the worst.

+ + +

Pretending it's little deal to sit in a limousine whiter than ivory with two immortal beings strains even my skills at performance. I perch with my knees together and Unferth's sword pressed across my thighs. The housekeeper handed it to me as Baldur swept me out the front door. The sheath is new, made of mirrored silver, with a chain-mail baldric I should easily buckle into.

Glory rubs her bare ankle against Soren's calf to see him squirm and speaks to him in a rough language I suspect is the berserker wolf-tongue. Soren, when he answers at all, does so in Anglish. Based on his answers, she's grilling him on our hunt, occasionally sliding me a wicked glance.

I peer out the tinted window at the passing Port Orleans, relishing the tingle of Baldur's gaze. He hasn't said anything, only sprawls in his corner with a pleasant smile.

The streets are narrow, full of people celebrating the holiday. Light seeps from every window, from the long iron balconies and streetlamps. The limo slowly curves toward the river, which is only a black void between the hotels and convention center. We turn alongside a massive green park. It's Sanctus Louis, and in the center is the crooked hanging tree and statue of Frigg. A brilliant spotlight shines onto her face, making it glow.

I twist to point her out to Soren, but Baldur is staring at my lap with slightly narrowed eyes. Protectively, I grip Unferth's sword and the god looks up at me. "Is there a tiny boar etched into that garnet?"

"Yes, how did you know?"

"*Hringmæl* swords are rare these days." Baldur holds out his hand and I give the sword over eagerly. He inspects the raw garnet, flicks his finger over the ring dangling from the pommel, then caresses the narrow wooden grip and flat crosspiece.

"Do you know it?" Soren asks.

"It looks like Hrunting." Delight peppers his voice. "Is this why you were asking about Unferth and Beowulf?"

"You know its name?" I whisper.

But the limo stops and everyone but me looks outside. Our driver opens the doors and Baldur steps out with the blade. He holds his hand in for me.

Glorious light blinds me and I blink to adjust. We're surrounded by guests and the media, and before us is a mansion. The veranda is lined with massive white pillars and crystal chandeliers hanging between them like fixed galaxies. Taxis and hired cars and another limo fill the circle driveway, and photographers wait in the garden, snapping pictures of the guests in their gala gowns and tuxedos. We aren't the only ones fashionably late, and we're nearly lost in the noise of the crowd and cameras and jazz.

Baldur faces me and gently settles Unferth's sword over my shoulder. His fingers skillfully find the buckle of my baldric and snap it around my ribs. They designed it to act as a belt around the high waist of this red dress and to cut up between my breasts like a necklace. The cold silver pinches but holds the iron weight of the sword firmly against me. I feel as though Baldur is fixing my armor in place before battle.

Beside us, Soren slings his own sword on and touches the small of Glory's bare back. I've no idea how her dress stays on. Divine will? The four of us go together, and Baldur only pulls me ahead of the others at the last moment. We climb the broad steps up into the house.

The foyer would fit the entire Shipworm under its nine-meter ceiling held up by dark wooden beams, and a green marble floor spreads out like a meadow toward the high arch leading down into the ballroom itself. Standing here is like standing in a time-frozen forest cathedral.

It's hot despite the low rush of air-conditioning and crushed with people in every manner of gown and suit, clashing and vying for attention. Here's Precia of the South striding toward us with her wolf-guards behind, in an elegant white gown that seems to be made of spiderweb, diamonds, and soft gray feathers. Her makeup is impeccable, her hair styled beneath a net of silver. She holds her hand to me and I take it, then she kisses Baldur's cheek.

A yell goes up and suddenly we're surrounded by a line of berserk warriors in black long-vest uniforms, hard black tattoos cutting down each left cheek.

They step up and bow to Baldur, but then one smiles at me, turning the attention of the entire line my way. It's Sharkman, grinning, and when he bows to me, it's deeper than to the god. With a happy cry, I release Baldur and go forward, pulling the berserker up and kissing his cheek just where the tattoo cuts. "Sharkman," I say.

"Lady Signy." His voice is inappropriately low.

I glance down the line of berserkers. It's perhaps half of them in full dress uniform. My chest expands and some tension rolls off my shoulders because they are at my side. "Welcome, Mad Eagles."

As one they salute, two fingers over their hearts. Even at attention, Sharkman's shoulders slouch just a little, unconcerned with any threats, and there's Thebes beside him, towering over everyone, and the twins Gabriel and Brick with their thin blond braids. "Captain Darius sent me the youngest and most striking of you."

"To stand at your wings," Thebes manages, blushing in a way that distorts the color around his fire scar.

Sharkman grins that head-swallowing grin.

When I turn to introduce them to Precia, one bright flashbulb snaps, blinding me for a moment. As I readjust I see her waiting curiously, her bodyguards watching suspiciously beneath their wolf-mask tattoos. But Baldur claps Sharkman on the shoulder, and Glory shows the pretty twins her hungry teeth. Soren stands out darkly among the pale Asgardian elite. He looks past me at Sharkman with an expression that's somehow both hard and very sad.

But there's no time now—our arrival is announced, names ringing from an invisible speaker system. The Mad Eagles flank us as we move into the grand ballroom, which is all golden and blue and white with decoration and lights. Star-shaped lamps hang low over spinning, colorful dancers, who make and break patterns across the floor like the pieces of a kaleidoscope. The music comes from a small orchestra tucked into a private balcony overlooking the room. It's a lazy but pleasant melody, full of horns. An elaborate fountain at the far side of the dance floor spills golden liquid I can only assume is mead. Long flags hang from each pillar, brilliant blue with golden letters declaring, HONOR THE DISIR! and WELCOME, QUEENS!

I pick a sight line over everyone's head, to focus on none of the glitter and flashing cameras as the god of light leads us down the wide steps and directly through the dancers. The music slows and ends with a high note, conversations pause, and all the guests turn to watch us mount the dais.

The high table is set against a vast blue curtain like a sky behind it, beside great arching doors that lead out into a colorful night garden. Baldur draws me to the center, with Soren on Baldur's right and Glory on my left. Precia moves to a seat at the far end of the table from me, and the berserkers spread out behind us. Baldur unbuckles my baldric and hangs Unferth's sword—Hrunting—over the back of my chair. He pulls the chair out for me and weaves our fingers together.

Facing the crowd, he raises the hand not holding mine and cries, "Honor to the lady gods on this Disir Day! Honor to the lady beside me, and to my dear friend Soren Bearstar. Honor to the magnificent Valkyrie of the South. Cousins and friends, drink with me!"

Baldur lifts the silver goblet from the table before us, and I grasp mine, cupping it high and proud. We freeze and wait as the partygoers accept sparkling mead in flutes and glass goblets from rushing servants. I imagine the tableau we five are, with wings of black berserkers and the draperies of disir blue falling like water at our backs. I hope they're making a lot of notes on this. It's oh so very showy and grand.

Together the entire company drinks, cheering and calling out *Baldur* and *hope* and *bright blessings.* Baldur orders the feast, and the dancers join those guests already seated at their many round tables. Gentler music springs back to life and I look up to the orchestra ensconced in its balcony. *Is Rathi here yet?* I scan the crowd for him. He's at one of the front tables, sitting with a glittering man who must be Ardo Vassing. They're deep in conversation.

We eat a first course of soup, and Baldur toasts again. There are three more courses to pick at, all while holding myself as calm and relaxed as I can. Glory beside me eats every last morsel, smoothly and methodically, and between my own bites I slide pieces of broccoli and pork onto her plate. I didn't pay gods only know how much for a ticket to this thing, after all.

Being at the high table gives me too much time to watch, to remember the final feast at the circus hall, when Ned pressed his back to my knee, when I saw *chaos* for the first time. By the third course I don't bother hiding the moment I dump my candied potatoes onto Glory's plate.

She laughs and tells me I don't need to worry about my figure.

I study her, remembering that her destiny was manipulated by Freya. The goddess of witches saw in the web of fate that the Fenris Wolf would one day begin the end of the world by swallowing the sun. It was on Freya's word that Glory was bound with the silver chains around her neck, forged by goblin magic and placed there by our gods—her kin. It's easy to forget sometimes that our gods are so vindictive. "Do you hate them?" I ask.

The godling puts down her spoon and leans nearer. She smells like candy. Her dark green eyes fix upon me. "Who?"

"The gods of Asgard." I see *truth* in her wild eyes, too.

Glory slides her tongue against the tips of her front teeth. "Some of them, sometimes."

"They've chained you. Kept you from your destiny."

"Nothing can keep me from my destiny." Her lips curl and she glances past me to Baldur. "He will be so delicious."

"You wish," Baldur says, like a child.

"I'll make certain you enjoy it, boy."

They're so mundane suddenly, cousins arguing over attention or the best seat at Yule.

Nothing can keep me from my destiny.

At the end of the meal, Baldur offers his arm and invites me to dance.

We sweep across the marble tiles. I remind myself what I'm getting out of this—Red Stripe, a powerful ally in hunting the troll mother, and of course charity for the Summerlings—as I put my arms around Baldur and let him turn me and spin me, taking tiny steps, focused on his eyes. They're so dark blue they're nearly black, with tiny points of light reflected in them as if the universe peers through.

He hands me off to Soren for the next song. The berserker dances smoothly but with such concentration it furrows his brow. "You're pale under that makeup," he says. "Are you well?"

"Tired, that's all. Glad to see the Mad Eagles."

Soren glances at the black line of berserkers and I add, "But are *you* well?"

"So many berserkers together make me nervous," he admits with a little wrinkle between his eyebrows.

I reach up and push it out with one finger. He scowls and shakes me away. "They're good men," I tell him, replacing my hand on his shoulder.

"As good as Odin's madmen can be," he says.

An older man with his beard in a seven-strand braid cuts in.

It's the king of Orleans kingstate, his coat heavy with ribbons and medals from the Mediterr Conflict. He tells how glad he is to have our gala in his fine, fine kingstate and I admit admiration for the bursting flowers and heady air. Around us dancers whirl, faceless and pressing in. At least the king doesn't bring up politics. He does tell me everyone is praying for Vinland.

I say, "I'm afraid there's little that prayer can do for Vinland these days." Of course I mean to suggest what we need is money. The point of this entire ball.

He says, "It brings communities together, strengthens them."

I wonder if he believes it. "I assure you, the Freyans at Jellyfish Cove were strong and together when they died with weapons in their hands, not prayers."

The king frowns. "There is always room for prayer."

From behind me, Rathi says, "You're both right." He

touches my bare shoulder, nodding respectfully at the king before he continues. “The wounds on our home are fierce, and etched in bone and blood. The smell of sacrifice is everywhere now, drowning all else.” His fingers tighten on my shoulder. “But the Valkyrie never stay on a battlefield past the gathering of souls. The dead are buried or burned, and the grass grows back. The earth heals itself. None of joy’s children have forsaken Vinland, none of those who live have given up. We’re working—and praying—together, and we will rebuild Freyr’s throne. He will be there again, because we are there.”

The king of Orleans claps a hand on my wish-brother’s back. “You speak like your father.”

Rathi bows. “My thanks.”

“Dance with me,” I say, and turn away into the crowd, bringing Rathi along. He’s warm and smiling back at me, those too-green eyes bright as he spins me onto the dance floor.

“Thank you,” I say.

Rathi turns me under his arm and then back. “Peachtree wants you to pay attention to how I do in a room with at least one person better-looking than me.”

“Surely she knows you’re used to it enough to hide your feelings?”

“Wounded!” He slips a hand from mine to slap it over his heart. The ruby ring on his forefinger catches fire.

I regard him. It might be a curse to have danced with Baldur and let him reframe my understanding of beauty, but as I study Rathi’s short eyelashes and smooth cheeks, the wave of his slick hair that’s not only one golden hue but a half dozen ranging from wheat-colored to sandy and brown, the scar just in front of his right ear and the small indent in his chin, I realize I can't remember anything specific about Baldur's face except those magical eyes. The god of light is too perfect to hold in my memory.

"God, Signy, what *are* you staring at?" Rathi laughs nervously.

I look down at the black horse pin holding his wide silk tie in place. "Oh, you." Forcing myself to meet his eyes again. "I'm thinking I prefer your sort of looks to—to certain gods'."

"Signy—"

"Hrothgar."

He purses his lips and changes course. "You do look remarkably dangerous, but up close your eyeliner is like a raccoon."

Smacking his arm absently, I glance around for Soren. There's Baldur and Glory back up at the high table, but no Sun's Berserk. The red eye of Unferth's sword catches my attention, hanging there on the back of my seat. "Rathi."

"Hmm?" Over my shoulder, he watches the ever-shifting crowd with his confident, relaxed preacher's mask, which makes him seem both approachable and above it all.

"Did you know Ned's sword has a name?"

Rathi frowns. "Hrunting."

I release him and head for an abandoned chair near one of the white pillars. I smooth my hands down my skirt until they're folded peacefully. "What does the name mean?" I ask as he joins me.

"It's the name of the sword Beowulf used to slay Grendel's mother." Rathi raises one eyebrow.

I nod slowly, wishing I had Unferth's flask. "Beowulf got the sword from Hrothgar's poet, right?"

"Yes. The poet, Unferth Truth-Teller, gave it as a sort of peace offering between them. The theory was that maybe Hrunting would work against the trolls when no other weapon would, because Hrunting was tempered in blood. It was a kinslayer. Don't you know all this?"

Unferth whispers, *I killed my brother with it.*

Is it possible my Unferth is *the* Unferth of the poem? He had the sword; he claimed to be a kinslayer; he knew that poem inside and out; he knew so much about me and the Alfather. But Baldur claims there are no Einherjar with his name. Unferth himself said he was only a man.

"Signy."

With both hands on my shoulders, Rathi shakes me just once and ever so slightly. I refocus on his face, all the connections between Unferth and *The Song of Beowulf* knotted in my mind.

"Do you think it could be the real thing?" I glance past him up at my sword on the dais.

"The real . . ." Rathi looks hurriedly over his shoulder, then back at me. He laughs. "Signy, the real Hrunting has to be sixteen hundred years old. That sword is not. There are re-creations of famous swords all over the place, especially at a Viker Festival. Edd Smithson made copies of Gudrun's Helblade every year."

What game was Ned playing? Even if the sword is a replica, if he himself was born twenty-five years ago and took up the name, there must be a reason for it. He put the pieces before me.

Some may be the workings of Fate: my own attraction to Valtheow the Dark's bloody story, the Alfather's love of her. That my wish-brother is named for her husband, the famous Freyan king Hrothgar. But some were woven in by Ned Unferth: He brought trolls into my life; he used the ancient poet's name. He told me my rune scar is linguistically linked to her name—Valtheow, *Strange Maid*—and the troll mother paints herself with that rune in my dreams.

A cold line of fear slides down my back. Red Stripe. One-armed Red Stripe, who Unferth led me right toward.

Beowulf Berserk killed Grendel by tearing off the monster's arm. In vengeance, the troll's mother destroyed the golden hall of Heorot.

Just as my troll mother destroyed Vinland.

Did she follow Red Stripe?

I see Unferth again, ice in his eyes, fingers hard on my elbows, when I told him Baldur was missing. He'd been afraid. Was it not for Baldur's sake, but because he knew the troll mother was coming after her son?

"Sig?" Rathi says.

"I need to go outside," I whisper, pushing away from him and darting through people, rushing for one of the open side doors.

TWENTY

MY SHOES BURY themselves in thick grass and I dash across the circle lawn, past a couple in intimate conversation and a group of old men debating something with flailing gestures. Past waxy-leafed magnolia trees and boxes breaking open with early summer flowers. I duck under a trellis crowded with vines and into a narrow path lined with conical trees blooming purple. At the end is a marble bench. It glows welcome to me.

I sit, grateful to the cool stone seeping up through the layers of my dress, grounding me here in the center of this garden. Against the red silk skirt my fingers are pale sticks, heavy with Unferth's rings. Furiously I tear one off. I throw it into the dark foliage.

If Unferth knew what was coming, it can only be that he was in league with Freya. She sees the future. She stole Baldur's ashes, and told him what to expect. But *why*?

"Hello?"

My head jolts up at the intrusion. A girl stands beside one of the purple trees, certainly not clad for a fancy ball. Her dress is light and cottony, not quite knee-length, her cardigan pale blue, and dusty thin sandals tie up her ankles. She has a mass of dark curls messily pulled into a bun but with tendrils everywhere. A necklace of obviously plastic pearls falls against her collarbone, and there's no makeup to accent her pretty face.

I'm staring rudely, and she sighs before joining me on the bench. "You seem upset," she says.

"I was here to catch my breath, privately."

The girl's eyes crinkle in amusement. "I see."

I smell sharp, sweet flowers I don't recognize, but not like any perfume, and I look more closely into her pale brown eyes. She widens them for me knowingly and tilts her face up to mine. Worked into the tawny wheat flecks in her left eye is the rune *youth*, and in the right, *god.*

A disir! But she's nothing like Baldur and has none of the awesome charisma of Freyr the Satisfied or the wicked magic of my Alfather. She does not even affect me as my sister Valkyrie do. But there's a simplicity to the way she holds herself, a calmness like the breeze cannot touch her, nor heat lick up sweat at her temples.

I breathe slowly out, collecting myself. "I apologize, lady."

Her shrug is graceful but nothing near godlike. "I surprised you."

"Yes."

"What's wrong? Did someone hurt you?"

It pulls a little laugh out of me. "Maybe. Yes? I'm not sure."

"Can I help?" the disir asks, then glances hurriedly away as if she wasn't supposed to offer.

When she looks back, her expression is drawn in peaceful lines. I ask, "Do you know anything about dreams?"

She laughs, a pretty noise like birdsong. "I venture to say I know quite a bit about them."

"How do I tell if my dreams are true ones?"

"Oh." The disir girl strokes her neck thoughtfully. "It's hard to remember, but I think . . . you just know. You can feel the difference, or you see evidence of it when you wake."

"Why would I have true dreams at all? I'm no seethkona; I don't pray to the goddess of dreams."

"Because you're walking along a strand of fate, or because she wants you to."

"Do you . . . know Freya well?"

"As well as any."

"Do you trust her?"

"Oh," she says again. Her head cocks as she thinks. "I trust that she acts for the good of the world."

"For the good of the world."

"She sees everything. The future and the past, and everything in between, all possibilities and outcomes, and she alone can discover which threads of fate knot together best, which will destroy, which will bring peace or strength or happiness."

I ball my rune-scarred hand into a fist. "Does your goddess use men to change the course of the world's fate?"

"There is no other way to do it, than to use us. She gives us prophecy or dreams for a guide, but we are the actors. The gods may not so directly interfere."

It's the Covenant the disir means. Jefferson's Covenant, keeping the gods on a leash.

She touches the back of my hand with cool fingers. "What does she want from you?"

"To kill a troll, I think."

"There are worse things she could ask than that."

We sit quietly, hands together, listening to the distant music from the ball. It's some energetic dance and I think of Baldur's Night again, spinning and drinking with Peachtree until I found Ned in his goblin mask. That brief moment he kissed me back. All his rules, all the truths he would not tell me. *Why, why, why?*

The disir girl says to me, "In the end, it doesn't matter what she wants. Sometimes you must stop thinking about the gods and think about yourself and the people you love. What do you want the world to be like? What can you do to make it that way? You don't need to know what Freya has done or wants done; you don't need to know what Loki or the Alfather or Tyr the Just wants. What is in your heart? Let that be your guide and it will bring you to those moments when you can change fate or the entire world. That's why the Covenant is in place: so that we make our own world."

Though her sad smile has nothing of power behind it, though her pale brown eyes glow only with tiny reflected lights from the party, her words bury themselves in my skin as deep as any charge of Odin's.

This disir girl is right: What Freya wants doesn't matter. Unferth's loyalty and lies only matter because I trusted him. What matters is my god gave me a riddle to solve, and to do that—for myself, not for the Valkyrie or even Odin—I have to find and destroy the troll mother. That is what I want. That is who I want to be.

The heart. The heart is what matters.

I stand. "Thank you for your counsel, lady. Do you have a name? That I may thank you properly at a shrine?"

Every part of the disir girl goes still. "Oh. I had one once. But no one remembers it."

"Tell me and I'll remember."

She shakes her head.

Unwilling to press her, I start to go and am three steps down the tree-lined path when it hits me: *god* and *youth.* Idun the Young, whom Soren prayed to this afternoon, and a name nobody remembers.

"Astrid," I breathe, spinning around.

But she's gone.

My head buzzes as I return inside. I'm desperate to find Soren, to run and whisper Astrid's name in his ear. But Soren is trapped by Glory, dancing. Baldur sits at the high table with a handful of shining guests, eating some pink sorbet. Conversations rise and fall like the ocean waves. Precia and Rathi's preacher friend Ardo Vassing share a plate of the dessert at the round table nearest the dais.

I climb up to Baldur, steadying myself with a hand on the table. "Signy, there you are!" The god's face is bright with anticipation. "I've a surprise for you, if you're ready."

It's a struggle to form my expression into anything resembling pleasantry. "Of course, my lord."

Baldur takes my hand and lifts it. "Friends!" he yells. The music dies on a downbeat, as if they've awaited his cue. Dancers turn to us; faces lift. Cameras flash. Soren and Glory are just below, she with an arm draped around the berserker's shoulders.

The god of light gestures at the Mad Eagles still standing so solidly behind us. Two at a time from either end, they break off the line to jog around the perimeter of the ballroom. Guests titter and whisper, shifting together, some keeping their eyes on Baldur, others watching the berserker progress. When all twelve have reached the far end of the room, they stand on either side of a wide blue curtain, a mirror of the one behind us. Thebes on one end and Gabriel on the other reach out and grip the edge.

"Friends, these are the very good Mad Eagles," Baldur calls. "Those brave warriors of my father who hunted down the Vinland herd, who slaughtered them in a holy frenzy, who brought vengeance on behalf of the dead." He glances at me, squeezes my hand. I lower my eyes to the streak of sorbet melting on my plate. "The berserkers have brought a surprise for all of us." He pauses and, when he continues, sounds amused. "Go ahead and ready your cameras."

My heart clangs like a smith's hammer and I glance down to Soren. A great frown creases his copper face as he stares back to the curtain. I follow his gaze in time to see Thebes and Gabriel tug it away. It falls in slow motion, wafting loose and easy. Behind it is a set of doors. The two berserkers push them back with a massive groan of wood. Wind blows out from the corridor, sweet and burnt.

Red Stripe.

I hear the creaking wheels first, then see the light. It's brighter than the sun, false white UV light glaring out like a spear, making the star lamps of the ballroom seem faded and old.

Odd-eye, what is Baldur up to? Why this production to return him to me?

Captain Darius and four other berserkers walk out, two with massive ropes over their shoulders, dragging the wagon while sweat pops on their foreheads. The rest have long, thick troll-spears pointed at Red Stripe's collared neck.

There are gasps and even tiny screams from the audience. Most push up and move to the edges of the ballroom, shoving over chairs and spilling drinks. They don't realize that the grimace twisting his marble face is *fear,* not fury. The purple gash is still unhealed, trickling with flakes of amethyst.

"What are you doing?" I ask Baldur softly.

Surprise slackens his pretty face. "Giving you your troll. Blood price, Signy, and the stone heart—your riddle! This is a troll of the Vinland herd," Baldur calls clearly. "A monster with a heart of stone. It's Disir Day, the day we celebrate our goddesses and mother-spirits, the day we remember the Valkyrie. There can be no more suited moment or sacrifice: take down this beast and claim your throne, Signy Valborn." His voice rings with excitement and pride.

"He is not the end of my riddle," I say, softly enough for only the god, then I grab up Unferth's sword, swing it over my arm, and push past him, aware of the Lady Fenris's low laughter. The crowd parts for me.

Baldur says, "*The Valkyrie of the Tree will prove herself with a stone heart.*"

Silence answers him, all eyes on me as I stride directly for Captain Darius. They titter and whisper, and a few cheer for the troll's blood to cover the dance floor.

"Lady," Darius says, looking serene despite the monster hulking in stone beside him. His dress uniform highlights the sharp lines of his goatee and leaves his shoulder bare to display his family crest tattoo.

I hold out my hand. "Do you have a knife or dagger?" I ask quietly. He pulls one from the small of his back and offers it hilt-first. I curl my fingers around the warm wooden grip and say, "Turn off the UV."

He snaps around and points at Thebes, who rushes into the corridor. A moment later, the lights click off. Breathing and murmurs fill the space. A camera flashes from the left. Blood roars in my ears, like the ocean in a seashell.

I step before Red Stripe. My shoes are too delicate and

heeled so I toe them off, standing instead in bare feet and all the layers of red silk dress.

Red Stripe's stone body fractures; a web of hairline breaks scatter out from the center of his chest. I see *fate* marked clearly, as if he's a man, and *choice*, and my old friend *chaos* again.

Someone screams behind me. I focus on Red Stripe's eyes, waiting for the little yellow beads to open, to see me. Dust puffs off of him as the fine layer of stone sloughs away, hitting the marble like hail. The other berserkers shift on their feet, putting the tips of their spears against his throat.

"Move back," I order without looking. Red Stripe's head turns to my voice and there is his massive jaw opening, there his blocks of yellow teeth. His bluish lips curve out and he moans. It's like a rockslide, a long rumble, and the floor trembles. I sense movement behind me. "Red Stripe," I croon.

His eyes open and he wrinkles his snout at me. And he roars.

It flutters the banners and grows to shake the crystal chandeliers. I don't flinch, despite the sweet breath blowing past my ear, despite the flashing memory of the troll mother, of the herd crouched about their fire, glancing up one by one to see me charging toward them.

I'm standing in a circle of stone dust, and it tickles my nose and throat. My belly burns with adrenaline, and the eyes of the crowd abrade. "Down," I say. Red Stripe hunkers onto his heels and the knuckles of his single ape-like arm. His beady eyes don't leave my face. Bent this way, those eyes are only two meters off the ground, nearly my height, and I smile for him. "Help me up."

He lifts one knee and holds out his arm. I grip it firmly in my free hand and step up onto his knee. His skin is smooth marble but hot under my toes. I put a hand on his shoulder and manage to turn gracefully toward the audience.

I stand on his knee, nearly encircled by his wide blue arm, and look back out over the audience. At the high table, Baldur the Beautiful gapes and Glory slides her finger across her plate, then licks the last of the sorbet off her skin, her eyes on me. There's Soren, creeping around the side to arrive with Rathi at the edge of my performing circle.

But it's Precia of the South whose eyes I meet. She's come after me, standing in her pristine gown a few meters away. Her head tilts to look up at me. It's anticipation and excitement I read in her face, if it's anything.

"Here is Red Stripe," I call out. "He never did hurt anyone on Vinland and owes the world no blood price. This is no martyr, but a survivor. Like me. He has sacrificed already, his arm, his family, his freedom. In his chest a fire burns. His heart beats as mine does, both of them formed into stone by our losses. Before I would cut out his heart and offer it to the Alfather, I would cut out my own."

I touch the tip of Darius's black knife to my skin, just above the collar of the red silk gown, between my breasts. It sinks through my skin and pain flashes across my chest, in time with my quick pulse. I think of Valtheow.

A hot streak of blood slides down toward my belly.

Precia spreads her arms like wings. "Signy Valborn, the Alfather knows the state of your heart."

Glory the Fenris Wolf begins to clap slowly. It rings out, once, twice, and three times. I tap Red Stripe's shoulder with my forefinger and he lowers his hand to act as a step so I may spring onto his shoulder. I sit and he holds me there against his round head. I raise the knife and unsheathe Unferth's sword.

Red Stripe roars. I do not close my eyes.

TWENTY-ONE

THE TRICKLE OF the old fountain beside me is enough to keep the city sounds at bay, and a humid breeze curls my hair as it ruffles the leaves of the silky dogwood trees enclosing this narrow garden. It smells of honey and perfume from the lilies and hibiscus, and the trellis covered in climbing fuchsia flowers, and under it all blooms the fetid bruise of fertilizer and mud. The neighbors have tall oaks that hang over my fence, dripping their beard moss, and I can barely see the blue sky through all the dense flora. I sit at a wrought-iron table with a sweating glass of iced coffee and the morning paper, which thankfully has stopped plastering the front page with images of me and Red Stripe.

Except now the headline reads, "Thunderer Offers Bounty for Trolls."

Every day in the national, local, and online news we get more information about troll sightings, seemingly random except that they're more frequent. The patterns Soren and I were seeing in Ohiyo are appearing across the country. Bridge eaters clustered on water towers they've never climbed before or calcified into gnarled little gargoyles on the ledges of high-rise buildings all day. Cat wights pour through the suburbs, eating puppies and skinning cats. Even prairie troll packs are migrating south. Theories abound for why so many lesser trolls are showing themselves now, ranging from an unknown mystical purpose to the presence of a high-pitched whistle none of us can hear.

I've been waiting two days since Baldur's ball, ensconced in this cracking old house at the edge of the Garden District, with Red Stripe molding in the garage, three berserkers knocking into the walls like dogs in a cage, and a modest allowance from the Valkyrie of the South to keep us fed. "As long as no one asks," she said, "in which case it's your own savings, of course, or Baldur's."

The morning after the ball she offered to fly with me to Philadelphia and stand before the rest, to declare I'd solved the riddle. *You know the answer; you* have *the answer, Signy. Embrace it.*

But I told her none of it matters until I find the troll mother.

You're as impulsive as you always were! Take this offer, and then go after her with the full weight of your office, if it means so much.

It has to be first, Precia. It's the thing I want. It's the bold, bloody thing, and I'm still Signy Valborn who craves those things. I performed for you, for Baldur and everyone to see, but that's not the end of it. There's truth behind the performance.

Precia regarded me from the breakfast table, delicate silver fork in hand, dressing gown pleated and tied in a perfect bow. Abruptly she stood, swept out of the guest room I'd slept in. Thinking that was the end of the interview, I devoured the rest of my eggs and was halfway through the scalding coffee when she pushed the door open again and presented me with a thin old book. It was the kind with gilded pages and a leather tie to hold it shut. *Valtheow's Lament,* the title read, though several letters were worn away.

Take it, she said softly, pressing it to my hands. *When you are ready, call me.*

We came to this house with its roomy garage and dripping old shingles so I'd have time to focus and find the troll mother.

Too ragging bad I don't know what I'm doing.

Making plans has never been my strength, gathering intelligence and resources never a priority. I want to be the gun fired, the arrow cast, not the general. The information we have is scattered and doesn't seem to fit any design. Why was the troll mother in Ohiyo at all? What was there, and why hasn't she shown herself again after so clearly appearing to the tipster who called? The one thing nobody has reported in days is any greater mountain trolls. We don't even know if the influx of lesser-troll sightings has anything to do with the troll mother, though for my wager it must. It's all connected by choices and consequences.

My best hope is that Baldur has been arranging to get Soren and me into the Mjolnir Institute, which tracks herd movement via satellite. Theoretically, a huge beast like her moving out of her territory should impact prey migration or leave some other widespread sign that their computers and tracking equipment can pick up on.

Rathi's come for lunch both days, mostly to keep my spirits up while I wait. To keep me from running off half-cocked. I must admit it's something I'm prone to do—I've already threatened to go immediately back to Montreal if Baldur doesn't get me into the institute soon—and so I humor Rathi. Together we compared the vivid poetry of *Valtheow's Lament* with *The Song of Beowulf.* The former was composed by a Valkyrie named Christina a hundred and fifty years ago, a version of *Beowulf* from Valtheow's perspective. It's so much fantasy, but we spend hours poring over the two poems, marking the differences, most of which can be written off as the fifteen hundred years between compositions.

For Rathi, I mark all the changes I remember Unferth made when he recited *The Song of Beowulf* for me in Canadia. In particular I describe the language shifts and bridges between dialect and rhyme that I remember.

And I remember I cried when Unferth recited the verses about Beowulf battling Grendel's mother, when she died. If I shut my eyes I can almost hear his voice, hear the rush of the engine so many months ago, when it all began.

Someday soon, I swear to myself, I'll find her. She'll show her tusks again, and I'll be there. The nightmares will end, and I can put all of it to rest.

I close the newspaper and fold it, then drop it onto the

damp ground. I draw my rune scar into the condensation on the side of my iced coffee. It haunts me every night, carved into the troll mother's dream hand, too.

Captain Darius pushes open the screen door and walks softly down concrete stairs to me. He bows shallowly. "I'm going out," he says. The announcement is unnecessary, as he's not in uniform but jeans and a plain blue T-shirt. His tattoo, untarnished by the trimmed Frankish beard around his mouth, will give his identity away if it's noticed, but his uniform would guarantee it and we're supposed to be as discreet as possible. We discovered yesterday, when I ventured out myself with Sharkman, that an interweave magazine is willing to pay a lot for my whereabouts. Sharkman *discouraged* the individual who shouted at us from collecting.

"What do we need?"

"Sharkman says he'll break all the windows if we don't have mead tonight."

I sigh. "He should go be wild in the Old Quarter, get it out of his system." I wish I could. Being pent up in this house makes my blood burn, too.

Darius almost smiles. "There's not enough alcohol or sex or battle in the world to get it out of Sharkman's system. But I'll take the mead out of his pay."

After he leaves, I gather up the paper and my empty glass and head inside. The walls shake and there's an arrhythmic pounding from the heavy bag Thebes acquired and drilled up into one of the ceiling beams in the defunct dining room. To distract myself I change into exercise clothes and join them.

Sharkman works the bag while Thebes goes over some of the hand-to-hand techniques they've been teaching me. The worn hardwood floor is smooth under my toes, and natural light streams in through the bay window. A fan creates a false breeze against the heavy heat, but I'm sweating and thoroughly diverted in no time. It's so hot, unlike the frozen practice ground on Vinland. I'm loose and alive, and I relish the blank blaze that comes over me. Their frenzy stretches out from them, tingling my skin, reminding me of that belonging I felt when we consumed madness together at the funeral.

If only when I stopped the feeling of completeness would stay. Instead, it drips off me like sweat.

Sharkman shoves my shoulder. "Why the frown?" He grins in my face.

"I'm jealous," I say, baring my teeth back at him.

"Oh, you don't have to be, pretty Valkyrie." He presses nearer to me, backing me up until my heels touch the wall. Heat envelops me. He's bare-chested, skin flush from energy. "You can have everything I have."

With a suddenly dry mouth, I lower my gaze to the row of eight horizontal spears tattooed down his sternum.

Sharkman tilts my chin up and puts his lips a breath from mine. The *torch* rune spins in his right eye. "I will let you make the first prick, ink your line across my chest," he murmurs. I sway nearer, thinking, *Yes, this is real distraction,* and kiss him with an open mouth.

"I guess you're not ready to go," Soren says from the entryway.

I stop moving, and Sharkman growls from low in his chest as he pushes off the wall. He stalks away without greeting Soren, snapping his T-shirt up off the floor. We hear him take the stairs hard.

Thebes shrugs at me from the floor, where he's clearly been going through a round of sit-ups.

And Soren says, "Sorry."

I touch my hot mouth and blink slowly. My body feels like it's melting and going rigid at the same time. "Ah, no, it's all right, I'll . . . shower."

The pipes scream upstairs as Sharkman turns on the water. I roll my eyes at the ceiling and think, *Maybe I should wait.*

"We're supposed to be there at one and it's an hour drive," Soren adds.

"Odd-eye!" I crack to attention. "The Mjolnir Institute! He got us in finally."

We go into the kitchen and I fill a water glass from the squeaky tap. Soren sits at the small round breakfast table, sunlight streaming through the fluffy curtains behind his head and casting his face in shadow. There's a black cloth covering his right forearm, like a sock with the foot cut out. It must be protecting the new tattoo he said Baldur was taking him to get. I hop onto the counter and guzzle half the water. It tastes like rust and I'm still so hot. What am I doing with Sharkman?

Whatever you want, apparently, Unferth mutters.

Soren must be thinking the same thing. "Do you love him?" he says, eyes narrowing in confusion.

I laugh. "Love? Odd-eye, Soren, what has that got to do with it?"

He frowns. I suddenly remember the rumpled, pretty Lady of Youth I met, and the plain way he talks about her, the yearning when he stumbles over her forbidden name. I haven't told him yet that I saw her. I want to, but we've barely been alone in this little house. This afternoon, though, we will be for a few hours as we drive to the Mjolnir Institute. Time for him to hear me, and deal with it however he needs to.

"He's very . . . berserker," Soren says by way of explaining his discomfort, but I know it's more than that. Sharkman makes no bones about his dislike of Soren. Last night when I mentioned the institute, Sharkman said, *If you can rely on the Sun's rag-boy,* and Darius sent him away from the table like a child.

"I think that's why I like him," I admit. "He turns my madness on."

"He's got no control."

Thebes comes in. Fortunately, whatever resentment Sharkman has toward Soren, the quiet giant doesn't share. He plods through, twisting his torso to keep his wide shoulders from knocking into either Soren or the cabinets. I pat his arm like I'd pat a big dog—or Red Stripe—as he gets his own water.

"We can feed Red Stripe if you're not back before the sun's at the wrong angle," Thebes says quietly. He's the only one of the three of them who calls the troll by his name.

"Thanks." We feed Red Stripe during the day, as part of the requirements Baldur and I worked out before the god of light would vouch for us to his uncle the Thunderer. Not only must these three Mad Eagles remain here with us as keepers, but we're not allowed to turn the UV lights off unless the sun is shining bright and there's no hope of his escape. But we can't put him in the garden, where he might be seen, which infuriates me: I suspect that old gash from the massacre isn't healing because he's been trapped under UV lights, which long term must have a less healthy effect on him than true sunlight.

The squeal of the water pipes shuts off and I slide off the counter. "Fifteen minutes, Soren," I promise, and dash upstairs.

The hour drive from Port Orleans to the Mjolnir Institute's southern research station is made more pleasant by the convertible Soren's borrowed from Baldur's fleet of sexy sports cars. With the top down, wind blows my hair back, ripping it out of the braids, but the blast against my face, the warm asphalt smell and thickness of it, is so wild I don't mind. I lean my head back and try to relax as best I can as we speed over the massive bridge that spans the huge Wide Water Lake, arcing us down into piney woods.

Soren seems content in silence, though he switches the radio dials frequently, as if searching for something that doesn't exist. I entertain myself commenting on the billboards crowding the highway. They run the gamut from anti-sacrifice rhetoric, with pictures of adorable, big-eyed martyrs being snuggled by children, to greasy fast-food chains and a surprising number of ads for holmgang advocates who specialize in accident lawsuits.

The only stations Soren avoids are news and any talk radio, until I insist we find out what they're saying about the trolls locally.

It's not much different from what's in the paper, except the radio personalities don't bother pretending to be impartial. The show we land on first offers a list of home stores with iron traps on sale and UV flashlights, and the second is a debate between a Freyan and a Thunderer over whether the lesser trolls deserve proper burning and burial or if they're just animals. They bring in a Lokiskin who argues vehemently for the preservation of trollkin and only gets a word in about the Freekin Project's game preserve before she's cut off. The third is advertising their next hour's segment, in which they'll be interviewing Sammy Hanger from Chicagland, who knew me last year on the streets and promises insight into my mental stability in the wake of my performance at Baldur's charity ball.

Soren gives me a clear *I told you so* look and switches back to Allegheny rock music. It's a perfect opportunity to bring up Astrid, but my mood is ragged and I don't trust myself to break the news gently. *After the institute,* I promise myself.

The Mjolnir Institute turnoff is presaged by huge electric blue signs with the logo of the hammer Crusher itself in the hand of a bespectacled, smiling scientist that appear every three kilometers for the twenty minutes leading up to the institute. Ours isn't the only car to exit and drive along the orange two-lane highway, but we are the only ones who take the EMPLOYEES ONLY turn instead of following the visitor signs.

The institute is a sprawling complex with a museum wing

and three research wings, only one of which is open to the public. Soren's directions are impeccable, and we're waved through the gate when he shows his citizen ID. The uniformed guard instructs him where to go and that he'll call in to let our escort know we've arrived.

We park and climb out, heading through the lines of cars to the plain, imposing brick building. To the north and across a chain-link fence is the museum, much more welcoming with its arcing windows and modern steel design and blue banners declaring their current special exhibits.

We wait near the steel door that's the only entrance to this research building. I redo my wind-blown braids just as the door swings open and a young woman in a lab coat hurries out. She's got beautiful thick brown hair loose around her shoulders and narrow eyes and dusky skin. When she spies us she smiles, pushes her glasses up into her hair, and sticks her hand out enthusiastically. "You're Soren, and you must be Signy. I'm so glad you could make it, that I could have this chance. I can't tell you how thrilled I was to find out you and Prince Baldur were taking an interest in getting to the bottom of what's going on here."

I shake her hand lightly while Soren thanks her, and she says her name is Talia Juanson. A gold-braid ring around her forefinger suggests she's probably dedicated to Sif Longhair, Thor Thunderer's wife, the goddess of marriage and peace. She leads us inside after passing us guest security badges to clip on. It's chilly inside, and sterile white. She moves fast over the tiled floor, Soren and I clomping behind in our boots. Talia explains that she's been told to take us to the map room and answer any questions we have, to explain what sort of troll-sign they look for and the wider patterns. "You're looking for the troll mother who drew the herd from Montreal to Vinland, specifically?"

"Yes." I brace for a hundred more questions, but Talia only nods and leads us farther into the building.

We pass other researchers, some in lab coats, some business casual, and a few in uniforms of Thor's Army. Most ignore us, though the soldiers all flick a glance to confirm our badges. The hallway at first is windowless, only breaking for doors or a turn, but we do go straight alongside one row of glass through which we can see men and women at tables sifting dirt and cataloging chunks of rock and obvious bone shards. When I ask, Talia explains there are four research centers around the country, but this is the largest for working with actual specimens because it's considered safer here due to the South's low level of native troll species. They prefer mountains or ice or plains, not the relatively flat piney forests here, where there are few caves and even fewer of the kinds of boulders and rock where they can hide and shelter. The cities, of course, have cat wights and iron wights, but that's due more to infestation than nature.

Talia has to punch in a seven-digit code to access the map room and holds the heavy door for us.

The room is dominated by a huge table displaying a topographical map of the United States and Canadia Territories with tiny LED lights in red, blue, and yellow. The walls hang with additional maps narrowed in on specific locations and computer displays. One wall is entirely made up of the largest monitor I've ever seen outside a movie theater. Talia explains that she can pull up a digital map to show real-time movement patterns up to six months. Mostly they use this to track the migration of prairie trolls, the tiger-like trolls with saber teeth and a taste for human flesh even stronger than the greater mountain trolls'. There aren't many packs of them left, though, Talia says. I detect a hint of regret in her tone and start listening past her words.

It takes fifteen minutes for her to show me the known locations of all herds, even when I ask her to focus on the northeastern parts of the US. We know the troll mother was in Vinland six weeks ago. We know she was in Ohiyo and probably Vertmont, but that sighting was less specific.

Using data from satellite imagery that shows the destruction caused when entire troll herds move, and established deer and pygmy mammoth herd patterns, Talia points to the locations of the only two GMT herds off the ice sheets: one in the Rock Mountains, and one vying against hill trolls for territory in the Adirondacks.

"What about the Vinland herd? Were you tracking them before the massacre?" I ask as lightly as possible.

Talia grimaces and leans her hip against the display table. "We know they were from Montreal, but it's hard to track trolls within the ruins."

"Why?"

"There are so many of them. More concentrated there than any other place that we know of, but they don't hunt near there. They travel far north or east along the coast for food.

Usually bears and wolverines, and they even hunt the icebergs and ocean for whales and seals. We have a harder time tracking coastal herds without physically tagging them, since they disappear under water occasionally, and there have been requests for funding for that for absolutely ages. We only suspect that they keep their hunting away from the ruins because the mothers use it as a meeting grounds."

"Wait." I hold up my hand. "There are still multiple mothers in Montreal? Which one came to Vinland?"

"Oh." Talia looks surprised. "She didn't come from Montreal. We know from descriptions you gave and the Mad Eagles that she's not one of the three mothers known to rule."

Soren says, "We thought the herd was definitely from Montreal. The Mad Eagles' report indicated that."

Talia flips her hand. "Some of them were—all of them, we guess, other than the troll mother. She probably came from high north, where we have no tracking equipment, and drew off some of the sons from the other herds. It's a normal way they cull family groups to keep the gene pool diverse." She flashes a smile. "They're really so very complicated as a species, more so than we give them credit for."

"She . . . was alone before," I say carefully, "but gathered a new herd to attack us?"

"As far as we can tell. But the information is scattered; it's truly a bare guess, not even a hypothesis."

I walk around the table to press my hands along the edge nearest Vinland. I point to the north peninsula. "This is Jellyfish Cove."

Talia pipes up. "It's likely if she left the island she either crossed back over Leif's Channel, since it's the narrowest point to head back up into Canadia, or went south directly to New Scotland."

"I know they *can* go under the ocean. They walk across the bottom, not swim, because they're so dense?"

"Or use icebergs. We've never tagged a greater mountain troll mother and don't truly know everything they're capable of. The Thunderer always cautions us not to underestimate them. Actually . . ." Talia adjusts her glasses. She says in one long breath, "Actually I was wondering if you think maybe I might be able to ask you some questions about your troll or even see him."

"Oh." I glance at Soren and back to her. "I can answer your questions, but I don't know about access."

"It's just I'm writing my thesis about seasonal calcification and migration—really, about how calcification can be affected by temperature, and you've been with yours for a few months, haven't you, and gone with him from cold to this hot? Have you noticed if he wakes more slowly in the heat? Or is there a difference to the texture of his shed skin? I'd like to—"

I hold up my hands. "Stop, Talia. Stop."

She does. And waits. Her eyelashes flutter a little, but otherwise she regains her composure.

"I promise to answer all your questions that I can, but not today," I say. Soren brushes his hand against my back, and I make my voice even. "I'm in the middle of something pretty important—"

"Revenge," she interrupts, then presses her lips shut.

"Yes. Is there anything you can do to help us find her now?"

"I can do some in-depth analysis, call some of my peers at the Ohiyo center who were looking into bird habitats and troll migration. They might have noticed something. Unfortunately . . ." She pauses.

"Yes?"

"Well, there's been so much movement out of pattern this week."

My hopes fall. "All the excess sightings around the country. Are you sure there's no pattern that might be . . . attributed to her?"

Talia chews on the side of her tongue as she thinks. "It will be hard to really mark what's unusual, because it's all unusual. We've been keeping records for fifty years, and with satellites for nearly twenty. This whole situation is unusual." She crosses to one of the computers and types in a series of lightning-fast commands. The wall-sized monitor flares to life, with a detailed map of the Gulf Coast. She flings her arm to it as a string of orange dots appears along the Mizizibi River, clusters especially around the cities of Memphis and Port Orleans. "For example, in the past five days there have been more lesser-troll sightings per capita right here in Orleans and Watauga king-states than in the past ten years put together."

"Could there be more sightings because people are looking harder?" Soren asks.

Talia shakes her head. "We've adjusted for that."

I sink back against the table. "If she culled trolls from other troll mothers—she pulled them to her? Could she be doing that with the lesser trolls, too? Calling them?"

"I suppose so, though I've never heard of it; there's no suggestion in any of the research that mothers cull across species."

"Still. Can you . . ." I approach the monitor. "Can you expand out, still mapping these lesser-troll sightings?"

"Sure. It sticks with the Mizizibi River, roughly, for a while, and then I'm not sure. I'll have to . . . hang on." Talia types more commands into her computer, pulling up additional websites. She hums to herself while I clutch my hands together and try not to pace and grind my teeth.

"I had to access the Ohiyo institute database," she says after a moment. "Here."

Orange dots flare across the country, but they're obviously concentrated in a thick strip spreading north and east along the Mizizibi River and following the Ohiyo River all the way north to the banks of Lake Erie. "Odd-eye," I whisper. This is a highway of rivers and lakes from Port Orleans all the way northeast to Canadia and the Gulf of Lawrence, which connects to Leif's Channel and Vinland. Through both Ohiyo and Vertmont. All along it, there have been even more lesser-troll sightings over the past two weeks than in the rest of the country.

The troll mother could have walked almost wherever she wanted to underwater, unseen, avoiding the sun from Vinland.

Unferth whispers a line from the old poem *The Song of Beowulf.*

From the mere slunk the troll mother, dripping and wet, black fury in her heart.

Soren touches my back. “Signy, look at the dates.” His eyes are on the monitor, not the map. I try to read the list quickly and see what he sees, and Talia says, “Here,” and types in more commands.

The LED lights blink out. “They’ll come on as I say the dates,” she says.

Talia begins a month ago, when the new pattern of excess sightings began. It starts in the northeast, near Montreal and New Scotland, with tiny pockets in major cities around the country. As time progresses, the troll sightings bloom toward the south and west, spilling across the map like a virus. The most intense groupings grow along the rivers from the Great Lakes down the Ohiyo to the Mizizibi, dragging inexorably closer to us here in Port Orleans.

“Did you see?” Soren asks. His palm is hot, burning through my T-shirt to my skin. “Play it again, please, and stop when I say.”

Talia starts the sequence again, and on the date of the Vertmont sighting he says to stop. Then he asks her to continue two days, until we got the tip from Ohiyo, the only positive identification of my troll mother.

“All right,” I say. “Then what?”

For three more days the lights flip on very slowly and make almost no progress south.

Then they explode on the fourth day, and Soren sighs harshly. “See? That’s the day *you and I* started down toward Port Orleans, Signy.” He turns me to face him, hands hard and hot on my shoulders. The spear tattoo is rigid on his dark cheek; he hardly moves his mouth as he says, "We followed the troll mother to Vertmont and Ohiyo, but after that this pattern pauses, and then started up again heading south. Just behind us. If this . . ." He waves a hand at the map. "If this is tracking the troll mother, it means she waited for us in Ohiyo, and then tracked *us*. She's not just hunting you in your dreams. And she's already here."

TWENTY-TWO

AFTER EXTRACTING FROM Talia a promise of temporary silence about our discoveries and a printout of the latest lesser-troll sightings in Port Orleans in return for allowing her a personal visit with Red Stripe, we head home. My toes curl and tap in my boots as I analyze the possibilities. If the troll mother's here, if she's been hunting me, I should draw her away from the city and its residents, but it's also possible the huge population has been a cushion of safety because she can't find me here without revealing herself.

And suddenly I have questions for her, not only this black need to cut out her heart. I want to know why she came to Vinland. What choices did she make—as it's clear she does make her own choices—that led her there? If she wasn't from Montreal and if she truly followed Soren and me here, it has nothing to do with Red Stripe. That is both a relief and horrifying, because then what if it was only and always to do with me?

If Freya and Odin set me on the path toward her, did they

set her onto me, too? *Your heart,* she said, as if she recognized *me,* had been looking for *my* heart. And what about Unferth? Where does he fit in?

There must be a solution to this puzzle. A refrain to this poem.

After ten minutes of silent driving along the red highway, Soren says, "Maybe she has nightmares about you, too."

I shiver despite the heat and bright sunlight, and ask him to pull off at a rest stop.

It's white with a pink tile roof, sheltering soda machines and candy dispensers, toilets, a Skuld shrine for travel blessings, and a stand of brochures advertising swamp tours and the Old Quarter and the Mjolnir Institute we just visited. While Soren buys a honey soda, I wash my face in one of the rather wretched sinks, then stand outside in the sunlight. It dries the water as I lift my chin, eyes closed. The evaporation is slow and prickles. What does it feel like to have your skin turn to stone?

Shaking out of the thought, I plop onto a bench. I bend down to grab a sharp chunk of gravel and carve *nihtmaera,* an Old Anglish word for nightmare, into the surface of the picnic table. I turn it into a binding rune and try to match it to my scar. It nearly fits.

Soren slides in across from me and adjusts the sock on his forearm before putting his elbows on the table. He doesn't even open the soda can but regards me placidly while condensation forms against the aluminum.

I take a deep breath and pluck the front of my sundress off

my chest to let air slip down. Dogs bark and cars rush past; the wind bends the pine trees lining the highway.

Finally I reach over and pop the top of his soda for him. He lifts his eyebrows. Instead of bursting out with my thoughts on what we should do next about the troll mother, I say, "I met a disir in the garden at the ball."

"A disir!"

I rub my finger over *nihtmaera*. "It was Idun the Young."

The flash of heat rips down my arms and face; I jerk my face away. When I peek again, Soren's hands are flat against the picnic table, his brow creased, but otherwise he hasn't moved. "She was there?" he whispers tightly when I meet his gaze.

"Yes."

Soren knocks the soda can over with a sharp swipe. Carbonation hisses as the liquid glugs out. He watches it for a long moment and then says, "I'm sorry. I'm . . . sorry."

I cover his fist with my hands and slowly pry it open. I draw the rune *love* in his palm.

"How does she look? Is she . . . well?" he says, so quietly I nearly can't hear it.

"Pretty, and healthy." I catch his eyes. He looks down.

We remain posed with our hands together while the breeze and sun dry the spilled soda into a nearly invisible patch against the wood. Soren's shoulders heave then, and he withdraws his hand.

"Soren, how is she Idun the Young? I saw it in her eyes, her godhood. I know you aren't supposed to say more, that it was breaking enough trust to even tell me her name. . . ."

His glower is severe. "That's why Freya stole Baldur's ashes, or arranged for it, to get Astrid there and make her the Lady of Apples. That is what she wanted."

"There was no other way?"

"Astrid . . . agreed. She knew it was the right thing to do, and always . . . always was devoted."

"To Freya?"

"To Freya, and Baldur, and the world and . . . her own heart. She's *so good,* Signy."

I scowl. "If Freya wants me to kill the troll mother, she'll get that, too. Everything she wants."

He nods. "Freya didn't get everything she wanted. I was supposed to forget Astrid, too. It would have destroyed me. I would not be the man I am without her in my life. It would change me as much as cutting out my frenzy."

"Odd-eye, Soren. I should have tied her up and dragged you to her."

He laughs sourly. "I'll see her in a few weeks."

"You will?"

"Four times a year, at the heavens' holidays, I'm allowed to spend one day with her."

"What a curse."

"A blessing compared to what it might have been." He covers his chest, as if it pains him, and stands up. "Can we go? I'm too hot; I need to move."

I follow him back to the car, where he insists on driving, as it will give him a thing to focus on to stay calm until he can practice his meditation.

As we head back into the city, I wonder if I've been too selfish. What if I'm not Freya's endgame, but Astrid was? What if Vinland and I and the massacre were all just consequences to her plan? Did she give us up for Astrid to become Idun the Young? Were we casualties of war? Maybe my riddle was to position me for vengeance. Maybe Freya did this *for* me.

And that would mean Unferth did it for me, too.

I think of his dangerous teeth, of that hidden smile behind his eyes, when his lips never moved at all. And I wonder if I'm making it all up, inventing meaning in her actions and in his, because I can't stand the thought that he was her pawn, that he only betrayed me.

I invite Soren to stay for dinner, but he shakes his head and says darkly, "I can't control myself right now if your Sharkman pushes me."

I lean across the gearshift and kiss the corner of his mouth. His hands tighten on the steering wheel and he very carefully remains still. I say, "If you change your mind, you're welcome. Always welcome wherever I am, Soren Bearstar."

He nods once, slowly, and I gather the rolled-up map from the backseat and climb out.

When I enter, I go straight into the garage where Red Stripe is chained. He's crouched more comfortably in this airy room, despite the restraints, than he's been in weeks. His calcified expression is merely uneasy instead of twisted with rage or pain. I set my map down and take a harsh cloth from the bucket of salt water in the corner. Darius, reading a book in the only chair in the room, glances up but says nothing as I wring out the water and put the cloth against the gash clinging to Red Stipe's back and side. I lean in, scrubbing at the purple crystals that are his hardened blood. I should have asked Talia if she could guess why he's not healing well, and wonder if maybe it's the heat as she mentioned. But then, he was in the cold of Halifax for two weeks at least, and it didn't heal then, either.

When I've scraped off the blood crystals as best I can, I stroke a finger along his short tusk and whisper, "It won't be much longer."

"Lady?" Darius says.

Putting my back to Red Stripe's hard marble chest, I lean into his arm, which props him up like a pillar. And I look at Darius. He's back in his uniform now, the long black vest and black pants, black boots. It leaves his arms bare. The left shoulder is marked with a family crest tattoo: a rampant eagle spreading its wings, in its claws a round-shield divided into quarters: two are blacked out, one holds the rune for *strength,* and in the last is a crossed hammer and anvil. Beneath the crest is a small phrase in medieval script.

"What does *not a leader, but a man* mean?"

He puts his book upside down against his knee. "It reminds me that when dealing with such power as turns in my chest, with the god of madness, I must be a man first before I can expect anyone to follow me. My father used to say it, and I had it added when I was made captain."

"You must have been young."

Darius shrugs. "Young but strong, Lady Valkyrie."

"Strong," I murmur.

"That isn't something you need to worry about. I saw your strength when you charged at the herd, all alone."

I push away from Red Stripe. "I wasn't thinking about it. It was just what I had to do."

He nods as if to say, *Of course.*

"Darius," I whisper.

The captain sets his book on the floor and leans his elbows onto his knees. He regards me intensely but only waits.

"The troll mother is here. Near here, at least." I take a long, shaking breath. "I think she followed me, and maybe even somehow was in Vinland because of me and my riddle. I can't explain how, but the goddess Freya is involved, and I suspect she's capable of manipulating nearly anything."

He nods once, slowly. "What would you have us do?"

I push my temple against the hard, smooth surface of Red Stripe's knee until it hurts. "I want to go out tonight and see if I can find out about where she might be. Through the lesser trolls. If I can find some iron eaters, maybe I can bargain with them. There's so much water here she could be hiding in—the Wide Water or the ocean, or any of these massive swamps. If I can't narrow it down, we'll have to do something to draw her out."

"Which would be more dangerous."

"Exactly."

"We'll go with you. Sharkman and I, and leave Thebes here with Red Stripe."

"No, I should go alone."

The long look Darius gives me makes plain his disagreement.

"You'll scare them—especially iron wights, Captain. Probably I'll scare them, even if I'm gentle. But I'll fare better on my own with getting them to talk instead of run."

"This sounds more like madness than bravery."

I throw him a half smile. "I'm better with madness."

"As am I," says Sharkman as he clomps down the stairs. "You see? We belong together."

I laugh, and it feels good.

Sharkman gives me the smile that earned him his name.

TWENTY-THREE

NEAR MIDNIGHT I slip out the front door in jeans, boots, and my black Mad Eagles hoodie despite the warmth that lingers in the night air. Thebes is on guard duty in Red Stripe's violently bright garage, and he whispers "Good luck" as I strap Unferth's sword over my shoulder.

I spent three hours with my berserkers going over the maps of troll sightings in Port Orleans to pinpoint the best possibility for me encountering the least dangerous iron wights. The majority of the sightings are near the river and bridges, of course, or near highway overpasses and up north by the Wide Water. Darius suggested I avoid deep water if I'm truly uninterested in danger, and we isolated a seven-block area south of here between the trolley tracks and river where there've been sightings of mostly iron wights. So that's where I'm headed, and alone in order to be less of a threat to the curious little trolls. There are some cheap silver rings in my pockets to bribe them with, and a handful of colored paper clips I found in a kitchen drawer. My other pocket is full with a cell phone, at the captain's insistence. Just in case.

The night is quiet but for the harsh-pitched cry of frogs and muffled traffic, and I jog down our dim street to an avenue with better lighting and four lanes divided by a grass median. It's lined with scraggly oak trees and a strange blend of very nice antebellum houses and sorry ranches on concrete foundations with sagging porches. I start at an easy gait, Unferth's sword quietly slapping my butt as I go. I count the blocks, and after nine take a left onto Sanctus Charles, which is busy even at this time of night. I follow the trolley tracks for two blocks before heading right, toward the river, again, this time on a narrower street in the center of these localized iron wight sightings. This one is quiet and dark thanks to fewer streetlamps. One side is lined with gorgeous three-story town houses, the other with short chain-link fences and single-family homes. Even in the dark it's like two cities crashing into one another.

I tuck into the shadow of a tree as a cluster of five men spreads out across the street, sweeping their UV flashlights up the sides of houses and into the branches of trees.

Hunters after the bounty Thor promised yesterday, on account of all the extra sightings.

Once they've passed, I step off the sidewalk to cross the street. On my left the houses are replaced by a two-meter-tall whitewashed brick wall that glows in the dingy streetlights. I slow my pace and hop onto my tiptoes to see over it.

Darker gray and white rooftops peer at me from the other

side, some peaked or curved, others entirely flat. They're decorated with stone flowers and urns, some with false windows or wrought-iron crowns. Mausoleums and family crypts.

I sink to my heels. It's one of Port Orleans' cities of the dead. An entire block of marble and stone that wasn't marked on my map. This should be the center of that iron wight territory Darius identified. What better place for small trolls to hide under the sun?

With a running start, I leap to grab the top edge of the wall and drag myself up. I roll onto my side across the flat top and catch my breath. Right before my face is a crumbling mausoleum, tucked against the wall, stained gray by rain and weathering. A lush green fern grows from the top corner. I sit to dangle my legs down into the cemetery. No streetlamps invade the city of graves, but it looks like there's a lane around the inner perimeter and two that cross in the middle to create four smaller blocks of crypts within the larger block. Trees grow near the center and along the lanes, casting additional shadows in the dim moonlight.

I hop down into the cemetery.

My boots hit the dirt hard, and I crouch with my back against the cool brick wall. I'm hidden between two mausoleums. The breeze smells like wet stone and mud, and down here the city sounds are muffled.

I touch the cool marble to my right, skimming my fingers down it. This place reminds me of the death ship beach, though crowded and claustrophobic. I wish I knew who this cemetery is dedicated to. Most like it's for Thunderers, who are often buried whole-bodied in stone graves like this, or in crypts beneath one of their rock cathedrals, waiting in peace for the day Thor Thunderer summons them to his side, to travel with him to his far mountain home. But in a city like Port Orleans, there might be shared cemeteries, with portions assigned to Freyan ashes or Biblist internment or foreigners or anything.

My neck prickles. I tug the cowl of my hoodie down over my forehead and go out into the narrow lane. Moonlight shines on the rows of thin mausoleums, exactly like a row of town houses but small and gray. The tiny death homes are worn, the poems and epitaphs faded from their marble faces. What few markings I recognize are messy and eclectic: hammers carved into the lintels, or circle snakes or crosses, lambs and flowers. Long grass squeezes out a living between them, and a few of their doors are crumbled or missing and replaced with plywood. This is no cared-for graveyard like the one at the Death Hall; it's old and forgotten even in the heart of the city.

But not everything has forgotten it.

There's a scratching like rats in the walls. I turn slowly, see nothing but leaf shadows.

Wind brushes the edge of my hood, caresses my cheek. On my right the proper entrance appears, its iron gate locked tightly, with the name of the place arched over: *Garden Cemetery No. 1.* In cursive script, almost impossible to read backward, it promises, *All the dead are welcome here.*

A modern orange sign is tied to the bars. I pull the bottom away to read it. CLOSED FOR REPAIRS.

Putting my back to the gates, I walk directly down the overgrown lane toward the center.

Stone scrapes stone, like one of the tomb doors is opening. My lips part and I suck in a quick breath. They're here; I was right. There the sound comes again: the scratching, the claws scrabbling across marble roofs.

I scan the black shadows between tombs, the short iron fences that mark family vaults, the sudden splashes of color from the plastic bouquets set about the place.

There's a growl at my back; I swing around but nothing stands behind me. I hear it again, a low growl and skittering claws, followed by high-pitched giggling.

All the shadows move. There! The golden glint of reflecting eyes.

Cat wights.

Skit. They're less conversational and will hardly care for the paper clips and rings I brought to trade. Cat wights want to play, rather like their feline namesakes, and won't think twice about biting off my fingers. "Good evening," I say gently, firmly, as if I've nothing to fear.

For an answer, a chunk of marble the size of my fist flies out from between two mausoleums. I shift my leg and it hits the lane. Another follows. Then a hail of pebbles, and with them comes more laughter. Snickers and babbles surround me. I block my face, pummeled briefly by the hard rain.

"I'm not here to hurt you," I say, pulse quickening. I hold out my bare hands, spread them.

There's a chorus of hoots in reply. Not only cat wights but

also the iron eaters I was expecting. I recognize the calls from Chicagland. There must an entire troop here at least, and probably a whole pack of cat wights. This might be on the verge of going very, very badly.

"I only want to know if you've seen the troll mother. I've brought metal to trade." I dig into my hoodie pocket and pull out a handful of rings and clips. They scatter on the gravel.

More hooting, and the cat wights hiss. A greater shadow moves suddenly away from a tomb and slinks, hyena-like with long legs and a hunched back, into the moonlight. A prairie troll. I suck in air, lift my chin against sudden fear. Saber teeth glow as it opens its mouth and hisses at me, rising onto shorter rear legs. They're man-eaters, and where there's one, there's another. "Ssssnack," it whispers.

I take a step back but glance over my shoulder so I don't run into another. *Rag me.* I consider fumbling for the cell phone, but the Mad Eagles won't get here for ten minutes. By then I'll either be fine, or dead. *More like madness than bravery.*

Behind me iron eaters cling to a tomb with their huge eyes and gnarled baby faces. As one, they laugh, displaying blocky teeth. I turn in a careful circle, hands flat out from me, and back toward the iron wights: there's more chance of surviving a flat-out run through them than past the prairie troll. How is it there are these huge prairie trolls and nobody saw them in the city? And why was this a center of iron wight activity but also full of cat wights? Though with the cemetery closed to the public, they could hulk here all day long without being discovered.

The prairie troll swings its head left; I follow the look but see only three more of its kind stalking nearer from the thin copse of trees huddled around the crossroads in the center of the graveyard. I step back toward the wights, and back again. I unsheathe my sword. There's no use pretending this is going to end peacefully.

The prairie trolls slink nearer, their shoulders knocking and tongues lolled out more like hyenas now than ever. Cat wights hiss from the shadows, and my peripheral vision is full of laughing iron eaters clinging to the walls and roofs of the dead city.

My heel catches on a patch of gravel and I stumble back into the sharp corner of a mausoleum.

It grunts.

Horror burns through me, leaving only ice in its wake. Turning, I raise my eyes to a greater mountain troll as it shakes free of its mausoleum shape.

I bite back a whimper. That troll was shaped like a house and all right angles a moment ago! I remember with a shock Unferth saying in Montreal that the troll mothers use rune-work to hide their sons in plain sight.

Every tomb in this entire yard could be a massive, bone-crunching troll.

A hand grabs my shoulder and there's the sharp prick of a knife at my throat. Somebody has me from behind.

Unferth whispers, *Bad timing for you, friend.*

Except this time it's not in my head.

I knock my hood back as I spin around. A line of pain slices across my throat.

He stands there, shock painted over his sharp face, knife up and glinting with my blood. Like me, he's all in black, tight against his body for slipping through shadows. *Signy,* he mouths voicelessly.

I open my mouth but have no words. My hands tremble; my heart is a wild monster in my chest.

Ned the Spiritless takes a hesitant step toward me. "You're bleeding," he breathes, and the knife in his hand lowers.

One of the prairie trolls growls, bunching its legs to leap. I raise Unferth's sword to defend myself, but Ned grabs my wrist and jerks me behind him. He faces the prairie troll as it stands two meters high on its rear paws, long tail flicking like a serpent behind. "Down," Ned orders. "Now. This one is for me, not you."

"*Cat-man,*" it whines. Two of its pack snicker, and the iron eaters hoot like monkeys. The greater mountain troll I disrupted hunkers quietly, almost indistinguishable from the other tombs.

Odd-eye, the iron eater at the Vertmont locks said *cat-man,* too.

Cat wights dart out and weave through Ned's legs, rubbing his knees, one or two of them reaching up to tug at his pockets, at the hem of his shirt.

I back up again, stunned at the sight of him, but more so at his familiarity with these creatures, the casual way he strokes the triangle ears of one, gently bats another away from his hip.

Ned lifts his colorless eyes to mine and wipes his knife against his forearm before sheathing it against his thigh.

He's *here.* Pale and slim, listing to the side as always, hair braided into a topknot to keep it out of his way. I don't know whether to scream for answers or touch him, prove he's here and he's mine. I shake my head, breath tight.

"Signy," he says. "Are you all right?"

I keep silent, afraid of what I'll do.

Ned frowns. "Signy." He waves away the cat wights, nudges them off with his boots. They swarm away from him and he walks to me, trailing trolls in his wake.

"I saw her kill you. *I saw her eat you.*" I fling his sword onto the ground. It hits concrete with an ugly clang.

Ned brings a finger to his lips. "Hunters are everywhere. Would you bring the city down on us? Have them all massacred, their packs and families?"

"They massacred mine! Why are they even here?"

Ned nods. "Witnesses. Nothing like this has happened in hundreds of years."

"Nothing like what?"

He doesn't respond except to twist his lips.

The trolls slink back into the shadows, curling into stone vases and pressing against curved roofs.

I stamp my boot. "Tell me, curse it. Is she in here, too? Where is she?"

Instead of answering, Ned crosses the distance between us, grabbing me up in his arms.

My eyes shut themselves and I clutch him, holding tight

around his neck, my cheek against his rough jaw, sucking in huge breaths of him and the scent of my own blood. He hugs me, his fingers digging into my sides as if he'll hook them through my ribs. His breath is cool on my ear, and he presses his lips to my temple, to my cheek.

Gasping, I shove back but seize his face. The moonlight does little to illuminate him or mask the strain in the corners of his mouth. I put my thumbs under his eyes and stare into them, into the gray-glass irises.

Truth.

"I don't know if I can trust you, Ned," I say in a voice so low it doesn't sound like my own.

His eyes drift closed. "Finally."

Confusion settles me somewhat. My natural state when I'm with him. It convinces me he's real, at least, and I slide my hands down from his face. "What happened? Tell me how you're here, alive?"

"Not here," he says, picking his sword up off the ground. "Somewhere we can talk. Besides, I need a drink."

We walk through the dark streets of Port Orleans. Ned moves in his off-kilter way, profile straight and sharp but missing the usual slight sneer from the corner of his mouth. He looks tired.

He glances at me, too, and I catch the tentative nature of it. Whatever happened to him has changed him, too. My Ned Unferth was never tentative about anything.

Or, I think as force myself to look away, I never knew him at all.

We find a dirty pub in the corner of a town house that blazes with neon beer signs. Ned stomps to the bar and gets us pints that slosh thickly over the rims. I use a fistful of napkins to mop off the tall round table I find, but mostly the paper sticks, so I unfold and spread them out like a tablecloth. Ned smiles tightly at my fastidiousness, clunking the glasses down.

Lazy jazz plays off a jukebox, harsh with static, and most of the other patrons hunker over their own drinks or bet at the pool table in the rear. We're the only blond, pale-faced people here, which is surprisingly uncomfortable for me. It makes me think of Soren, and with a sharp longing, I wish he was here for a buffer.

Ned drinks a fourth of his pint in the first go, then curls his fingers around the glass. "I can't tell you everything," he begins.

I sip surprisingly smooth beer and wait.

"But not because I don't want to. I truly cannot."

I flick my fingers but refuse to tell him it's all right. Let me be the recalcitrant one now.

He takes another drink. "I wasn't dead. I woke up after it all, in a stone dugout, hidden under leaves. She buried me; she hid me."

"Why? I saw your sweater—I thought they were eating your bones, Ned."

"She knew better than to kill me. She knew what I was."

"And what was that?" I manage.

"Her ally."

"Her ally! She killed people. Your friends. My family! Rome and Jesca are dead."

His eyelids don't even flicker. "I know. I always knew."

"Always knew *what,* exactly?"

"That when the sun was lost, the trolls would come."

I grip my hands together in my lap. "That's what you were afraid of. When I told you Baldur was missing, that's what it meant. The trolls were coming."

"Yes."

I shove away from the table. *"Odd-eye."* My boots hit the ground. Like I'll attack him, or run as far away as I can get.

"Signy." He catches my elbow. "Signy, wait please." He pulls my arm against his chest and I avert my face, unwilling to look at him.

"You could have warned them," I say.

His fingers tighten and I notice the bartender eyeing us. It would serve Ned right for me to make a scene, hand him over. But probably he'd hurt somebody. I shake my head a little and pull myself free of his grip.

"I wanted to, Signy, but I couldn't. I wasn't allowed."

The urgency in his tone makes me listen. But I glare. "You weren't allowed. You can't tell me! Why not? Who? Who forbids it? Freya? It was the goddess, wasn't it? She gave you the prophecy about the sun being lost. She told you to find me."

"I . . . can't . . . say." But he doesn't avoid my eyes, staring hard as if he wants me to know I'm right.

“Skit, Ned, then why are you even talking?” I cry, flinging my arms out. “Why did you bring me here if you were just going to tell me rag-all?”

He glances up at the ceiling helplessly, revealing the shiny, nearly invisible scar that hugs his neck under his chin. Like a noose. When his eyes lower back to mine, *truth* throbs in the rainy irises, and I taste an edge of laughter like bitter, bitter rage. I say, “Ask the right question and you’ll answer? Is that it, *Truth-Teller*?”

“Always,” he sighs.

I’m tired of being the one responsible for riddling out his truth. Wearily I say, “The Alfather didn’t send you to me.”

He says, “He’s a student of history, not the future.”

“Stop beating into the wind, Ned.”

“I’m trying to be direct.”

“Well, you suck at it.”

“And you’ve gotten better,” he snaps, then drains the last of his beer.

I grind my jaw. “Tell me where the troll mother is.”

“Here.”

“Where here? Tell me.”

“I don’t know where, exactly. But I . . . I do know she’s looking for you. Waiting for you to make a move where she can get to you. You must be careful, though. She wants to kill you, Signy.” He says it like it will be a surprise. “As much as you want her.”

I shrug as flippantly as I can. “Tell me things I don’t know, Ned Unferth.”

He's quiet, lips pinched.

"Why does she want to kill me? What have I done to her? Is she the first troll mother, and her heart is the first heart? Did Freya set her on me? Are you all in league? What is it they want?" Every question comes faster, a deluge I barely control.

Nothing.

"Tell me why you came to find me last year. Tell me why you set me onto her trail, why you told me the answer was a troll's stone heart."

His hands tighten around the glass of beer. Ringless, his fingers seem longer but vulnerable. I threw one of those rings into the foliage in that moonlit garden three nights ago.

I say, "Tell me or never speak to me again."

Now his mouth twists into a wry, bitter smile.

Frustration makes me pound my fist on the table, shaking my pint. Suddenly I'm glad for this slice across my collarbone, itching with dry blood and painful when my hoodie scrapes against it. Not quite over my heart like the tiny cut I put there myself, but near enough to be an unavoidable reminder that I already know what Ned the Spiritless will do to me.

"Why didn't you tell me you were alive?" I ask in nearly a whisper.

He reaches across the table and drags my beer to him, tearing the paper napkins stuck to the table. "I didn't deserve to."

Shock dries my mouth, freezes my tongue for a moment. It's a struggle, and tears bleed into my eyes, but I harden my voice. "But I did. I deserved better than to mourn you and miss you and blame myself for your death when you were alive and—and *her ally.* You were supposed to be mine."

"Maybe . . . it's . . . the same thing."

"Here the gutless son of the sword-widow," I say. A line from *Beowulf.*

He sets down the beer, eyes glazed and staring at the caramel slosh.

I stand up. "Goodbye, Ned Unferth."

Before he can respond or not, I leave.

TWENTY-FOUR

I LET MYSELF cry like a child all the way home, grateful for the easy grid of streets and the darkness.

My little house is easy to spot by the tall iron fence molded like wheat stalks and the ghostly blooms from the dogwood trees in the back. Sharp white light escapes through a slit in the heavy curtain blocking the square windows high in the garage door where Red Stripe is hidden. Inside, I suck away my tears as I hurry through the hall to the garage and whisper to Thebes, "I'll stay until morning and talk to you all then."

He hesitates, but I go straight to the calcified troll and sink down to the floor, my face against his stone knee. Thebes's large hand settles on my head and then he leaves, more quietly than any of the other berserkers seem to move.

When I'm alone, I bury myself in Red Stripe's cold comfort, my chest aching from the fury and wildness and just plain *relief* that Ned's alive. I hold myself tight, shaking and hissing sobs through my teeth.

My tears turn the pale blue marble of the troll skin darker, like patches of lichen.

She catches me from behind in her claws and pulls me against her chest, cradling me gently. She's soft and cool, humming a lovely tune that has my eyes drifting shut. Until her claws dig into my chest. I scream as she cracks open my ribs like double doors. My heart is on fire, but she takes it in her massive hands and eats it.

I wake up.

My eyelashes stick together, but I smell coffee. Somebody is poking my cheek and I grimace up at Sharkman. There's no grin on his face this morning. "Why were you crying?" he demands softly.

Darius crouches just behind him, holding two mugs of coffee. Rain hits the tiny windows; moisture drips through the crack at the bottom of the wide garage door. "Did you locate her?" he asks.

I sit up. My first vicious thought is I should have tied Ned up and dragged him here and given him to Sharkman for interrogation.

My fingers curl as if he's here now, and I make fists, wanting to hit him because I'm hurting so much.

"You were bleeding," Thebes says from the three steps leading up into the kitchen. "Last night when you got home."

The three of them glower at me to various degrees, and I

unzip the hoodie, then drag it off my arms. Rusty dried blood stains the collar of my tank top. I can't quite see the gash from Ned's knife, but my exploring fingers find it. My entire chest is warm. The pain is a dull burn.

"That's a knife wound," Darius says.

Without ceremony, Sharkman pulls me to my feet and half carries me into the house and up the stairs to the bedroom he and Thebes are sharing. He plunks me down onto one of the twin beds and digs through his military-issue duffel bag for a box of first-aid supplies. I untie my boots and remove them, then fold my legs up by the time he kneels before me to wash off the wound.

"I'd really like that coffee Darius brought me," I say ungraciously.

"Coffee after." Sharkman rips open an alcohol swab and swipes it against the cut. I yelp.

He's quick and methodical, decides there's no need for stitches or a hospital, but suggests I change my shirt so Thebes doesn't get light-headed again. I do as he lurks in the doorway lasciviously.

In the kitchen Darius and Thebes are dancing around each other in the narrow space to fry bacon and toast, though it's nearly lunchtime. I reach across the counter to the old rotary-dial phone and call Soren and Rathi and ask them to come over.

Two cups of coffee and brunch later, Soren arrives with Rathi on his heels. My brother goes a little white when he sees the slash across my chest but eyes the berserkers instead of asking.

We gather in the empty dining room where the heavy bag

hangs. Darius and Rathi drag chairs in from the kitchen, but the rest of us sit in a circle on the floor. I immediately catch Rathi and Soren up, and say instead of finding out the mother's location I discovered several packs of wights and trolls hiding in an old cemetery.

Rathi loosens the orange and gold sunburst tie at his neck and sets his coffee on the floor. "Did you alert the authorities?"

"Which ones?" I ask. "The army? The jarl? The Valkyrie of the South?"

"All of them?" he suggests.

Sharkman laughs. "They will demolish the cemeteries or cause a wide panic."

"And what will you do differently?"

I say, "Find the troll mother, kill her, and they'll disperse. They're here because of her."

Rathi says, "You know that?"

"Yes. Ned Unferth confirmed it."

Soren's eyes instantly go to my shoulder, where Hrunting usually hangs. Sharkman curses and Rathi smiles. "He's alive?"

"He was in the cemetery with the trolls. Talking with them. Protecting them." I cut my hand through the air, eyes on Rathi. "He is no friend of ours."

"How do you know he told you the truth?" Darius leans back in his chair. It creaks gently.

"He always told me the truth. No lies pass his lips," I say, as bitterly as possible. "It's what he doesn't say you have to worry about."

"Signy." Rathi gets off his chair and crouches in front of

me. “What did he do to you?” His eyes lower to the wound on my chest.

Sharkman hisses, “That complete bastard.”

“Stop, all of you.” I put a hand on Rathi’s wrist. “I’m fine. I will be fine, I promise. I can handle Unferth; I always have. The point is that I did not find her exact location—we only know she is here. But she’s also definitely looking for me. Unferth admitted it. She wants me, but we can’t take the fight directly to her, and so we need to move. We need to find a safer place and be on our way there by the time the sun sets.”

“We should tell someone, Sig,” Rathi insists. “Thor’s Army. We should have machine guns and heliplanes and walls of swords.”

“Guns don’t work well against trolls,” Thebes says quietly.

“Bombs would,” Darius says. “You can blow them to pieces.”

“I need her heart,” I say firmly. Soren catches my eye. He knows she wants mine, too, that she said *your heart* to me.

Sharkman grins. “Where’s the fun in killing them from a safe distance, anyway? Getting up close and personal is what berserkers were *made for.*”

“This is about me and her. I will face her and take her heart.”

“Do you think you can kill her on your own?” Soren asks quietly. “In your dreams of her, you die.”

Rathi makes a noise of protest. I keep my eyes on Soren. “I am going to face her.” There’s no point arguing it, especially since I know better than the rest of them how impossible it is.

None of them were there when I charged her, when she *laughed*. None of them felt the cracked ribs or the grind of dirt in my raw hands, the sheer panic when my arm was useless or the pain that burned through me. None of them were there when I thought, *This is my end*. I take a deep breath. "But I don't want to be alone. I'm asking you all to go with me."

The brief silence as all five men study me is broken by Darius casually suggesting, "Move nearer the Wide Water?"

Thebes shifts his mass and it's like the whole room shifts with him. "We can find a warehouse or commandeer something."

"I'd rather be as far from the city as possible."

"It's all swampland, isn't it?" Soren says.

"Swamps are never good for combat or hunting." Darius stands up. "I'll get one of the maps."

I nod. "It does need water access, for her."

"Wait." Rathi runs his hand through his hair as he does when upset. "I . . . have an idea."

Surprise turns all our heads toward him.

He directs the thought at me, bottle-green eyes bright and discomfiting. "What about a private island?"

Sharkman starts to laugh.

Ship Island is a barrier island twenty kilometers off the coast of Mizizibi kingstate. Rathi points out the long, crescent finger of it on a map, explaining that Hurricane Camille destroyed its center, dragging about forty percent of the landmass back into the ocean. There's the remains of a Thralls' War military fort on the western island, and a working dock. It used to be a kingstate monument, but there hasn't been money to rebuild the campgrounds or facilities since the last major hurricane seven years ago, and Rathi's mentor Ardo Vassing decided to buy it. For a private retreat or to fix it up for national tourism, the preacher hasn't decided yet. All I can think is that the Bliss Church of Freyan Worship must be significantly richer than I imagined.

And it's incredibly convenient.

We break up the meeting for Rathi to speak with Ardo about the island and Soren to call Baldur and ask for the use of his yacht, though Thebes, whose family comes from Massadchuset fishermen, recommends we rent a trawler because it has something called a displacement hull that might make it better at bearing Red Stripe's weight. We considered leaving the troll behind, but I have an idea that if we allow him to decalcify once we're in position, he might be able to hear or sense the troll mother coming, the same way she's gathering all these lesser trolls to her. He may be our only early warning system.

The berserkers start to pack up and make lists of anything they think we'll need for an island siege. I go wake Red Stripe to feed him. The troll's wound is better but still seeps purple crystals. I clean it and take the new pot of ink Rathi brought me yesterday to paint *whole* and *son* around Red Stripe's chest.

I don't stop. With the troll awake and witness, I paint runes down my arms and in spirals around my legs. They're all the runes I know, in a vast, chaotic poem. I close my eyes and paint a line by memory and touch just under the red streak of blood Unferth gave me: *Where is my heart?* I strip off my tank top and write *daughter of Odin* across my belly.

It's been too many weeks since I wrote poetry, since I let my mind rest and explored the words of my heart. Since I prayed to my god.

I don't want to die; I don't want her to kill me, but I won't leave her. I chose this destiny a decade ago, with the Alfather beside me, and I won't run away from the consequences of my choices. That's what destiny is, I told Rathi weeks ago. I have to prove to myself that I can be the kind of Valkyrie I want to be *and* be accepted by the world. No matter how many other answers there might have been at one point, now, today, it means holding her stone heart in my hand. Whatever that heart is, whether magical or only a heart.

Hangatyr, my god of sacrifice, accept my sacrifice, this is my choice, my choice, my choice.

This is the throne I will build: a throne of trust and love, a throne of choices and blood.

My choice. My blood.

Signy Valborn, death-born, outside herself, inside the world, strange strange strange girl.

My poetry is war paint, great swathes of black against my skin, gouges and scars of prayer, marking me for the sacrifice.

Myself to myself.

The ink tickles me, tightening as it dries. The runes wrinkle and I let my brush wander, spiraling and circling, sometimes becoming a word, sometimes only a pattern.

Outside, a crow calls twice. Another answers. I think of the ravens Thought and Memory, snickering at each other. My shoulders relax; I breathe evenly. I'm not afraid.

"What is this?" Sharkman asks, clomping down the three stairs into the garage.

"Prayer."

Sharkman holds out his hand for the brush. I give it over and offer Sharkman my back, lifting my hair off my neck.

The cool brush licks my skin in assured, smooth strokes. I shiver. "What are you writing?"

"A poem."

"Will I be embarrassed if my wish-brother sees it?"

"Does he like limericks?"

I laugh and he grunts. "The letters will be shaky."

"Give me my brush back." I reach for it and he catches my hand. He turns me around and spreads my fingers.

Sharkman traces the binding rune on my palm with heavy black lines. As the ink dries, he holds my hand. I raise my eyes to meet something hostile and dangerous in his. *Madness* glows sure and tiny in his left iris, like stars caught in the blue.

"I will not let you die, Valkyrie," he says.

"I am not planning to die, berserker."

Sharkman leans over me, around me, as if he can surround me from all sides. "I will do what I have to do."

It sounds like a threat.

+ + +

I go upstairs to wash off my poem, to repeat the words I remember as they rush down the drain. *Choice, my choice, a throne of choices and blood.*

Soren follows me, and while I pull out a T-shirt wrinkled from being balled in the small drawer of the bureau, he plants himself in the center of the room. His shirt is that orange color he favors, and the sock on his forearm is white today.

"What's the tattoo?" I ask, wringing the dress in my hands.

He ignores the question. "Do you think Freya wants you to die?"

"Maybe."

"I don't like it."

"Who does?"

"No, I don't like you accepting it."

"I haven't accepted it—it isn't as though I'm just going to stand there. I plan to fight. I plan to fight *hard*."

"But if you think it's inevitable, that will change how you fight. If you've given up."

"I haven't, Soren."

"Baldur could have Thor Thunderer here in an hour and we'll all go together. You'll have more backup than a few berserkers."

"This is about the Valkyrie I am, who I want to be, and my blood revenge. I can't set an army on her."

"Because it would be too safe? Because it wouldn't *feel* like revenge?" That line in his brow has returned, and the corner of his jaw shifts as he clenches his teeth.

Soren must be absolutely furious.

He grinds out, "Explain it to me in small words, Signy, because I don't understand."

I take a step back. "Why are you pissed?"

"You're playing into her hands, you're being stupid, and you're going to get yourself killed."

"Stop, Soren, stop." I drop the shirt and hurry to him, taking his hands. His skin is slick with sweat. "Soren." I touch his buzzed hair, his tattooed cheek, and put my palm over his burning heart.

He sucks in a huge breath and shuts his eyes.

It hits me, first Sharkman and now this: my friends love me terribly, and their grief will be a screaming storm if I die.

I know what that grief is like.

I throw my arms around Soren. He balks for a hot moment, then hugs me back. I lay our cheeks together and softly say into his ear, "I have to do this because I want to serve the god of the hanged, and this is how I prove myself to myself. I face myself; I face destiny with my eyes open. And moreover, it's *right.*"

"I don't trust your god of the hanged, or his cousins."

"You don't have to."

Soren groans.

"What would Astrid say?"

His dark eyes sadden, but his mouth pulls into a tight smile. "She'd want to know if we have a sword her size."

"I knew I liked her," I say, nudging him away so I can shower.

✦ ✦ ✦

Downstairs, Rathi is arguing with Soren over the keys to the Mad Eagles SUV. He's rolled up the sleeves of his pin-striped shirt, and his tie is unknotted. The moment I enter the kitchen Rathi whirls to me. "Signy, tell them I'm going with you."

"I want you safe."

"I don't care. The island was my idea, and you couldn't have gotten it without me. And, regardless, I have to be there with you." His hair is ruffled, and with his loose tie, with his sleeves rolled up, he's more like my old wish-brother than he's been in a long while. But it's not excitement coursing through him; it's desperation.

"Why?" I ask, stepping nearer.

His entire face twists with grief. "I wasn't there when my parents died. You know what that's like, Signy."

Soren gets my attention over Rathi's shoulder, and when I glance at him, he nods. Just like Astrid, Rathi wants a sword his size. I squeeze his hand. "All right. All right." I rise onto my toes and kiss him. Rathi leans his forehead against mine.

I can't help thinking we need our King Hrothgar to make the cycle complete.

The semi-trailer the Mad Eagles transported Red Stripe in from Halifax is parked in an abandoned warehouse lot fifteen minutes away. Sharkman and Rathi go get it while Darius, Soren, and Thebes make a run for extra camping supplies. I wake up Red Stripe and feed him again, and by the time he's rubbed down they've arrived with the transport. I join Darius and Thebes in the foyer, where they're going over a long checklist surrounded by hard weapons boxes and backpacks, nylon bags of tents and tarps, folding chairs, gas cans and batteries, and a camp stove, plus our suitcases and crates of food. Once we're on the island, getting back to a city for something we forget will be rough.

It's three hours till sunset when we're all ready but for loading Red Stripe.

We stand in a circle for a moment, as if waiting for somebody—me—to give a rousing speech about our mission and purpose. I stare at Rathi, the sheath strapped over his shoulder incongruous with his loose tie and the shine of his loafers. Soren stands in an orange T-shirt and jeans, his father's sword in his relaxed hand, and the three Mad Eagles are broad ravens all in black, steel glinting from hips and shoulders and boots, and shields against their backs like massive dark halos.

"Where's *your* sword?" Soren asks me.

Everybody stares at the empty sheath hanging from the baldric strapped across my chest. They all know Ned's alive, and so what can I say?

Darius offers me his sword, hilt-first.

The doorbell rings.

We all freeze. I jerk forward to swing it open, ready to scare whoever it is away with the circle of large, well-armed men behind me.

Ned Unferth stands there, holding Hrunting in his hand.

TWENTY-FIVE

IN THE GLOOMY evening light, Ned gives me a tight smile and lowers his sword until the tip nearly skims the porch. He's dressed in the same dark shirt and black jeans as last night, a knife strapped to his thigh and another in his belt.

I step aside to let him in, pressing my spine to the doorway so he doesn't have to brush against me. But he ignores everyone to stop under the lintel and face me. "I need to talk to you," he says.

There's a rumble from the Mad Eagles and Rathi says, "It's Ned Unferth."

I keep my eyes on Ned's. "We were leaving; we have to go."

"Signy, you have to—" He reaches for my elbow and I jerk it away so hard it smacks into the wall.

Thebes and Sharkman have Ned in an instant, dragging him inside and away from me. He doesn't fight as they throw him past all our gear and into the empty dining room. Sharkman pulls Hrunting out of Ned's grip and hands it to Darius. We follow the berserkers.

Ned sits slowly up and wipes a trickle of blood from the corner of his mouth. "Call off your dogs, little raven," he says.

Sharkman kicks him down again.

"Stop." My voice is hard and doesn't shake.

Rathi pushes past me and kneels beside Ned, offers him a hand up at the same time he glares at me. "What is wrong with you? He's still a man."

"Yes, Signy," Ned says, knocking away Rathi's hand. "What's wrong with you?"

I clench my fists. The three Mad Eagles array themselves behind me and Soren goes to the window, where he crosses his arms over his chest in disapproval. I say, "Ned knew about the Vinland troll attack before it happened, and *he did nothing.*"

Rathi's hand slowly falls, along with his face. He looks from me to Ned. "You did?"

Ned nods once and manages, somehow, not to sneer.

"Why?"

"I had my reasons."

"Don't lie to my brother!" I yell, leaping forward. Darius catches me around the waist and I struggle out of his arm.

Ned holds up his hands. "I came to— Signy, send them away; let me talk to you."

"Whatever you have to say you can say to them. I'll only tell them later. That's what trust is."

He stares at me, as if his eyes hold any power over me anymore. Then he sighs. He scoots back to lean his shoulders against the bare wall. "She's coming for you. Tonight."

"And she knows where I am because you told her."

Ned grimaces. "One of the prairie trolls found her and told her. Just like I found you because the cat wight who followed you home last night told me. They're watching this house even now."

"And before that?" I grip my hips, fingers bent so hard against my jeans I think they might break.

From the floor, Ned gives me a parody of a smile. "Yes. I knew you would come to Ohiyo after her."

"You called in the tips to get me there. For her."

"To get both of you together again!"

"In Ohiyo!"

Rathi inserts himself between Ned and me. "What happened on Vinland? How did you know about the attack?"

"It doesn't matter right now, Rathi." I face him, breathing hard. "He has nothing to do with what happens next."

"You're wrong, little raven," Ned says. "I have everything to do with it."

"Don't call me that anymore."

"What would you have us do, Signy?" Soren asks quietly, his first words since I opened the front door. He walks over to me and slips his hand against my back. I lean into the comfort.

Ned sees it, and his colorless eyes narrow at Soren and me.

"We should chain him up in the garage and get to the ship," Sharkman suggests with a malicious grin.

I stare down at Ned to consider it. He tilts his head back to meet my gaze and I am struck again by how tired he appears. His eyes pinch at the corners; his mouth is flat and pale. Even his braids seem limp. I step over his legs and crouch so I'm straddling his thighs, and I take his head in my hands. "Tell me, Ned Unferth. Why I shouldn't do what he says and leave you here, chained."

"Because." His jaw works under my hands. I brush my thumbs along his cheeks and his eyelashes flutter. "I can help you kill her."

Pressing his head into the wall, I release him. "Why should I believe that's what you want?"

He grasps my wrist with rigid fingers. "You know me, Signy."

I twist my hand around in his and grip his wrist, connecting us strongly. "If you are lying I will let Sharkman pull you into pieces."

"I'm not," he whispers. "I swear it, though my word has always been my curse."

"No more riddles, I said."

"By swearing to you now, I foreswear my former self. That is as plain as I can make it," he hurriedly adds, voice hollow.

Soren crouches beside me. "There's no risk to taking him with us. We want the troll mother to come to the island, so even if he's leading her, that works for us."

I lean my shoulder against Soren's. "Let's go."

In the garage, I unhook the troll chains from the iron posts buried in the concrete foundation. Sharkman opens the garage door and the semi-trailer is parked in the gravel driveway, rear doors open like a gaping whale. Sharkman slides the ramp into place and latches it, then lifts two of the heavy troll chains so they don't drag while I lead Red Stripe up into the metal container. I chain him under the UV lights rigged to the top corners of the trailer but don't turn them on. The roof itself was cut away so while they drove in the afternoon, sunshine would pour inside. Now early evening sky glows pale blue, but the sun is too low in the west to cast its rays upon us.

For the ninety-minute drive to Bay Louis, where our ship awaits, Sharkman will pilot the semi, Ned's knives and sword in the passenger seat, while the other four men are spread between the SUV and Soren's truck with all the gear. I'm riding in the trailer with Red Stripe and Ned, and when Darius paused as if to suggest otherwise, I gave him such a mean look he only sighed and passed me a knife from his boot.

With two water bottles, I follow Ned up the ramp into the trailer. Sharkman shoves the ramp up behind me. Metal shrieks against the trailer floor. The outside lock rings into place.

I'm alone in shade with Red Stripe and Ned Unferth, and I feel a weight settle onto my shoulders. I sink onto the floor, back against the corrugated metal wall. Red Stripe squats as far from the rear doors as possible and hums at Ned. He picks his way to the troll as the engine roars and we jerk into motion. I watch him rub Red Stripe's arm, pat his chest, and give the left tusk a friendly tug. "It's good to see you, too," he murmurs. Red Stripe moans softly, a contented sound like a cat's purr.

Ned's hand is dark against Red Stripe's pale marble chest. He touches the healing gash.

I say, "If you'd been here, been alive, you could have taken care of it."

Ned grunts and carefully walks over. He puts his back to the metal wall an arm's length from me and sits slowly. The hiss of his breath as he adjusts for the pain in this thigh is so familiar I close my eyes and press the back of my skull into the wall.

We sit in silence until the truck stops slowing to make tight turns, stops moving in fits and starts from traffic lights, and instead picks up speed. A highway must rush beneath us, vibrating the entire trailer. I look up through the missing roof to the sky. By the time we reach the ship, it'll be violet with sunset. Will she find us fast enough to come tonight?

"Signy."

I roll my head to him. He's drawn up his good leg to balance his elbow on the knee and looks at me. "What do you want, Ned?"

"It . . . doesn't matter anymore. What matters is that you listen to me now."

"I listened to you for five months, and at the end of it my home was destroyed, my heart broken."

He falls quiet again. After a moment I shift to face him completely. "Tell me what's different. Tell me why you came to warn us now, when you could have last night. You could have said then that she'd come faster, that the trolls would give our location away. But you said you couldn't help, wouldn't tell me anything."

"I changed my mind," he says dismissively.

"Oh, no. You do not get out of this so easily. What really changed?"

"You," he snarls. "You—always *you* changing me."

"Me!"

Fast as a cat he pulls me against him. I raise my hands to shove him away, but then he's kissing me.

Startled, I gasp into his mouth. He scrapes his teeth on my lips and my eyes flutter closed. From those teeth down to my belly there's a hot, tight cord. Ned kisses me harder and his arms crush me and it's like being buried alive.

I reach for his face as a lifeline. He slows down, mirroring my gesture with his hands on my jaw, gentle and caressing. His mouth and tongue grow tender, kissing the aching places on my lips where his teeth bruised. I slide my arms around his neck and hold on, thawing against him with a little moan.

He tilts my head to reach farther inside me, to draw everything I have out through my mouth. It stops being a kiss and instead becomes a poem.

That's the moment I pull away.

Ned whispers a sigh, and says, "So."

My wits dance around, trying to form back up into thoughts and words. "So," I repeat.

"Now it doesn't matter; now everything is over." He leans back against the wall, closes his eyes. "I have forgotten my promises; I have forgotten how to care if I live, forgotten my gods, forgotten what even a thousand years of dying is like."

"Because . . . you . . . kissed me?"

"Because I kissed you."

I draw away from the weight of that riddle and stretch down onto the floor of the trailer. The speed and engine vibrate through my bones as I take long and measured breaths, trying to compose myself, refusing to touch my hot mouth. "I don't understand," I finally whisper.

"I'm going to tell you a story. You've already guessed some of the pieces."

I turn my head but his eyes remain closed, his head back against the metal wall, crushing his braids, and he's touching his own hot mouth. His hand drops away and he says, "I was born when men did not dedicate themselves to gods but to kings."

"To kings!"

"Don't interrupt until I finish, or I may never finish."

I clench my teeth, fist my hands at my sides.

He continues in a hollow voice, with nearly none of the rhythm I expect from him. "My mother called me Edolfr, and I was the son of Einrik the Widow-Maker, a king. But I was only a second son and so allowed to be nothing more than a poet, until my brother slew my father for his crown and I was forced to challenge him for our father's blood price."

His face twists and his hand clenches. "I killed him, avenging my father, but that made me a kinslayer, and I did not argue when the people, when my father's and brother's men, called me to hang myself for Odin at the summer sacrifice."

Now I do press a hand over my mouth. It's the only way to remain silent, to stay still. Lines from *The Song of Beowulf* tease at me, lines about Unferth the Poet, the kinslayer. His sword.

"I hung, Signy, but the Alfather did not want me then, and so I did not die. I had paid my blood price but couldn't remain where my father and brother had died. And so I left my home to serve another king, who did not care of my past but only of my poetry and counsel. That is where I met her, Valtheow the Dark, the king's wife and Valkyrie-born."

"Ned!" I sit up, clutching at my chest. The knife wound smarts. "She lived *sixteen hundred years ago.*"

He holds out a hand for my silence. "And she was *everything* a Valkyrie should be. Strong and vicious and mad, like a great ocean storm in a tiny, dark creature. She read runes and fought me in poems, ruled that place more surely than Hrothgar could. She is the one Beowulf came to serve, and she was the reason the trolls were there at all. In the end she was too dark, too mad, for her own good."

I draw my knees up to my chest and hold myself tightly together. "What happened, Ned? How did you— That was so long ago!"

In the darkness, his eyes glint like elf-gold. "That damned berserker Beowulf lost my sword at the bottom of a lake, and I did not have it to defend my king when our enemies came. I died truly. Only this time it was at my king's side, fighting with Hrothgar in defense of our hall. That was an honorable death, and the—the Valkyrie came for us." His eyes drift closed. "Dancing out of the stars, screaming and bloody, they came."

"Odd-eye, you said you aren't a Lonely Warrior."

"I," Ned says, fist pressing hard into his wounded thigh, "I am a kinslayer, and not worthy of such glory. Yes, I was taken to the eternal battlefield. I fought every battle again and again, but we who are dishonorable, who deserve no grace, we do not drink nor feast with the others. We only fight, long battles that last not merely a day but days and days, until every last one of us has died again. We are kinslayers and oath-breakers, who have broken the greatest covenants of warriors and men. When we wake, my dark brothers and I, it is only to fight again, starved and thirsty, weary on our feet. I am no Einherjar." His voice hushes in a way I've never known.

Sadness drags down my shoulders and mouth, and Unferth sees it. "You understand. It was so long, so many centuries of fighting and dying again and again. There is nothing in the nine worlds that could be pleasant for so long, without peace, without variation. Nothing."

I reach for his fist and cover it gently.

"Do not be kind to me, Signy," he murmurs. "Not until you've heard it all. In life I lost my father, killed my brother, and was plagued by pain, by trolls and hardship. In death there was no reprieve, not ever. And so when I woke one morning into comfort, into a meadow of sun-warmed flowers, with a breeze blowing against my face that smelled of sweetness and the sea, not blood and vicious rot, I would have agreed to anything to remain."

Elf-kisses rise on my neck, my arms, for here is a familiar story rhythm. I know what comes next in my cold, knotted guts.

"A woman lay beside me, beautiful and soft, caressing my cheek and lips with her shining hand. I'd never known such bliss, such freedom from the pain in my bones and my heart. She looked at me, and said, *Truth-Teller, I want you to do something for me, and as a reward, this will be your heaven.* Her eyes were the color of the moon and half her face shadowed—exactly half, split down the middle."

"Freya the Witch," I whisper.

"Yes." Ned's shoulders tuck together and he shudders. "The queen of Hel and magic had plucked me from my death and brought me to her bed. I immediately said I would do anything for her. It curved such a smile across her face I might've died again in her arms."

I crawl nearer him and take both his hands. I squeeze them in mine and raise his knuckles to my mouth. Ned watches me and does not pull back. "Freya took me to an icy country, pointed to a lonely troll mother as she crept through the moonlight, hunting polar bears. *In this mother's heart rages the fire of all trolls, the heart of stone. In one year, you will find the Child Valkyrie and tell her this is the answer to her riddle. You will tell her nothing of yourself or of me. You will teach her and guide her, prepare her for the troll mother. She will face her destiny and end your suffering.*"

My hands are shaking and I'm glad for the pretense of comforting Ned so I can grip him tighter. He smiles grimly. "Freya said, *If you speak of this to the Child Valkyrie, if you give her any of my truths or change her destiny, if you distract her or if you* love *her, Ned Spiritless, you will lose heaven. She is meant for someone else.*"

"Someone else!"

He turns his hands to wind our fingers together. "She gave me my sword back, that had been lost in the mere, and everything I needed to acclimate to sixteen hundred years of change. I read and learned; I focused on the history of the Valkyrie, on new poetry and legends about them. And you, of course. I looked up Signy Valborn in old newspapers and online. Then the final thing Freya the Witch said to me was *You will know you are finished when the sun is lost from the sky and the troll mother comes for the Valkyrie's heart.*"

Ned closes his eyes again and we ride in silence.

The troll mother comes for the Valkyrie's heart.

A mirror riddle. My mouth is dry.

Freya wanted the troll mother and me to come together, and so she dragged Unferth out of Hel and offered him heaven. It was all her. Where does my god fit in to all of this? "How did you know what Odin calls me? Little raven?"

Without looking, he says, "I told you the truth of that. Even Valtheow was called Hrafnling when she was young. It is no secret name for you, but what the god of the hanged calls his favorites. A lucky guess on my part."

"A lucky guess determined the whole course of the past half year." I let go of him. I press the balls of my hands into my eyes.

He says, "I should have confessed it all when you told me Baldur was missing. I should have. The sun was lost from the sky, and so I knew the trolls would come."

"You were forbidden by a goddess to warn me, to warn my family. I don't know what I'd have done with a challenge like that."

"But I know." He touches my bottom lip with his thumb. "You would have rung the warning bells; you would have evacuated; you would have made certain a hundred berserkers waited for the herd, to save your family, your home."

I take his hand, drop it into my lap. "Maybe."

"Most definitely, Signy, for you are brave where I am not, you are wild and a little crazy and you would have told Freya to hang herself and assumed you could find another way out of Hel when the time came, or maybe not even thought of yourself at all. You're not as selfish as you presume to be."

"Ned," I whisper.

"I told myself that when you met the troll mother, that would be the end of it. You would be the Valkyrie of the Tree, and you wouldn't need me. Freya would overlook my feelings for you because the job was finished, and I could enjoy the heaven she'd prepared."

"But that isn't what happened," I whisper.

"No. I woke up buried under leaves, as if the troll mother had tried to keep me safe. She was alive; I was alive—you hadn't killed her. She heard the heliplanes coming and charged back to the valley. I tried to follow, but was too late. It was over, and I barely found her again. I convinced her to wait, to bide her time until the berserkers were gone, that she could only get to you when you weren't with them." Ned's speaking faster and faster, losing all semblance of storytelling. "But she was desperate—I don't know what Freya did or said to make the troll mother want your heart as fiercely as you want hers, but she *does,* Signy; she wants to kill you. Or worse."

"Worse!"

"Make you like her, Signy. Turn you into a monster."

I scoff.

He glares at me but keeps pushing. "I went to Vertmont and Ohiyo to draw you out in those hills, to get you away from Vinland, where all the attention of the world was turned. She came after, slowly because of the wights crowding around and making it harder for her to hide. But she's calling them, because her heart is the heart of all trolls. She saw you in Ohiyo, and after that it was all I could do to keep up with *her.* She's only been waiting in the swamps for a sign of exactly where you are."

"Why did you come tonight? Why are you throwing your heaven away now, after everything?"

His eyes drop to my mouth and he sucks air through his teeth. "Because you are glorious. I see in you something I haven't seen since Valtheow. And I want it more than a thousand years in heaven. I want to be as brave as you. I know I should have warned you on Vinland, and there's no forgiveness for that. I'm acting now, before it's too late again. Not because I have anything to gain." He laughs that one barking laugh. "But because it's what *you* would do. Because it is *right.*"

Because it is right. The same reason I gave Soren.

I wrap my arms around Ned, to give myself something to cling to, to feel his breath on my neck. His hands make fists against my back and he buries his face in my neck.

After a moment of silence, I ask, "Was it truly so horrible?"

"Being dead?" His voice is muffled, warm against my skin.

"Yes."

"Perhaps it wouldn't be to everyone, but oh *yes,* I despised it. I thought there was nothing I would not have agreed to, in order to be free of that killing field."

"I'm sorry," I whisper.

"For *what*?"

"All your pain."

"Odd-eye, *don't be kind to me.*" He pushes me away.

I lean back onto my heels. "If you'd had kindness before, none of this would ever have happened."

"Our gods are not forgiving."

"Maybe sometimes they're wrong. You shouldn't have been punished for hundreds of years, not so long. Not forever. It gave you no chance to grow or change or find redemption." I put my hand on Unferth's chest. He's sharp and hard and surrounded by this bitter pain, but inside he's a poet. He's good. I know it. I see it. *Truth* in his eyes.

"You'll bore a hole in me with that look," he mutters.

"I don't need a hole there to see what you're made of."

He lowers his eyes and whispers poetry from *The Song of Beowulf:* "And, gold-adorned, the queen stepped forth."

I hold his hand and lean my head on his shoulder for the rest of the drive.

TWENTY-SIX

THE CITY OF the dead spreads out around me, marble glowing like pieces of the moon fallen to earth. I sit cross-legged, facing a woman with black hair in two thick braids down either side of her face, hollow cheeks, a smile carved to hold laughter.

We speak of family and the old television I watched with my mother and father on those rare weekends when they decided satisfaction meant snuggling under blankets just the three of us, when we never got dressed or even brushed our teeth, but only ate sugar toast and the most activity was tickle torture during commercial breaks. I tell the woman those were the times I first felt wild, when I shrieked and cried for relief but begged them not to stop. She says her first encounter with madness was at a wedding, a night made brilliant by bonfires and drums.

I tell her, *I'm waiting for you on an island.*

And she says, *I'm coming.*

It's sunlight that wakes me, warming my face.

Grass tickles my hands and cheek. I sit up. The sun is high. I fell asleep on the scraggly grass mound on the northwest edge of Fort Massadchuset. Salty sea air ruffles the wisps of hair around my face and I wince into the light.

We arrived last night after midnight, under a low, oblong moon, and it was only the UV lights we'd torn off the semi that let us find the long boardwalk reaching out from the narrow island into the sea where we could tie the trawler off. Red Stripe had to climb over the boat and plop into the water. I rode on his shoulder as he struggled up the steep sand bank in the darkness toward the fort. Cold ocean soaked my jeans and I was crusted with pale sand by the time we made it to the brick wall and around to the only entrance to the fort. The berserkers were there, affixing the UV spotlights in ways that gave us light but didn't bar Red Stripe from the arched doorway. The sally port, Rathi called it, unable to hide his admiration for the construction. All I saw were bricks.

I took Red Stripe through the three-meter brick tunnel into the inner courtyard and trudged back down the long dock to help the rest unload all our supplies. And Ned, of course. Sharkman led him by a slipknot noose around his neck. It pinched my heart to see it, knowing what I knew, but I allowed it to happen and climbed up the narrow turret stairs to the grassy roof of the fort with a spear and handheld light to keep watch in case she was right behind us.

After an hour or so my eyes burned for sleep as I scanned the black waves and shoreline for any oddities, and Soren relieved me. I curled up right there to dream.

Now in the daylight I can see the whole of the fort and island and can't imagine a more perfect place.

It's probably three or four kilometers from tip to tip, curved toward the mainland like a young moon, all white sand and rough green grass and inner saltwater bogs. No trees, no tall dunes that a greater mountain troll might use for shelter or shield. We control the fort, the only permanent structure other than the boardwalk connecting the sides of the island and the flat wooden patio with its falling-down picnic tables and old restroom facilities.

The fort itself is a great circle of concrete and brick, sunk down into the ocean floor at the inner edge of the island. Rathi told me on the ship last night it was built to protect the mainland against the Anglish during the War of 1812 but not completed until the rebel army took control during the Thralls' War. It had thirteen cannons at one point, and you can still count the crumbled mounting platforms. I stand on one of the grass embrasures and could walk the entire perimeter if I wished. Down in the half-circle parade ground the Mad Eagles have set up a large baby-blue tarp on tall poles next to one of the three turret stairs. Soren perches on a folding stool under its shade, sipping coffee and watching the three berserkers work out. The folding chairs lean against a brick furnace with a small hearth and chimney.

Red Stripe shelters below me, under one of the brick archways lining the parade, and Sharkman tied Ned up in a sublevel storage room rather like a cave.

A soft yell draws my attention back to the Mad Eagles. They

stand in a line in the center of the grassy parade ground, exercising. As I watch, they cry out again in a single voice, moving in unison through a series of defensive postures. Their swords shine in the sun.

I slide down the steep grass embrasure and land on the brick footpath that runs around the inner circumference of cannon mounts. There's a more modern metal rail, filthy with salt and rust, to keep tourists from pitching over into the inside.

Even the seven of us should be able to hold this place against the troll mother, especially if we have warning from Red Stripe. But he's given no indication yet that he's aware of anything the rest of us aren't, and so we can't rely on him. As I go carefully down the dark turret stairs, the sense of my dream rushes back to me. The woman in Valkyrie braids who spoke with a smile of the Alfather's madness. The sense that we were old friends; the comfort between us had been gentle and warm. And yet, I know in my heart it was a dream of the troll mother. I told her where to find me.

I join Soren under the mess tarp. He silently points to a package of toothbrushes sitting on the plastic folding table, and then to the ten-gallon water jug hanging from one of the poles. He doesn't take his eyes off the Mad Eagles. "The toilets outside don't flush, but Thebes and I made a compost on the other side of the building first thing."

Not looking forward to that, I quickly brush, counting out the supplies piled beneath and atop the table. There's boxes of protein bars, a bag of oranges, a cooler, honey sodas, and bottles of wine. Toilet paper. I rub at the flaking salt still clinging to my skin from my swim, wondering if we'll be here long enough that I have to worry about tampons. I grab some of the toilet paper and head out of the fort, down the creaky boardwalk to the facilities. Outside the fort, the sun glares off the white sand and tightens the salt on my skin. I've got to change out of these clothes.

When I return, I use my tank top and the hanging water bottle to scrub my face, then ask where my stuff is. Soren points to one of the guardhouses. "You're in there, and Rathi and I are sharing the other. Unferth is still tied up in that powder magazine. The Mad Eagles set tents up in the casemates with Red Stripe."

It's a good thing he points to the low black arch leading down off the parade grass when he mentions *powder magazine* and to the proud brick arches that completely surround the rest of the parade when he says *casemates.*

I thank him and head into the casemates: the hallway of linked chambers underneath the circle of cannon mounts. Green slime stains the corners of their vaulted brick ceilings, and a thin white layer of sand and salt streaks everything, even the slate floor. In the cool shadows Red Stripe is hunkered down, back to the bright parade ground. His spine and shoulders are calcified, but I see his arm moving slowly as he traces the cracks between the bricks. His eyes turn to me when I approach and scratch behind his ear. "There, Red Stripe," I say. He grunts contentedly.

The guardhouse walls where I find my suitcase and sleeping bag were whitewashed at some point; a naked wooden checkout counter and a few sagging shelves mark how it was a bookstore once. I strip and dig out jeans and one of the Mad Eagles T-shirts that have become a staple of my wardrobe.

When I emerge back into the sun the Mad Eagles have circled up into a complicated battle-ring, and there's Soren still drinking coffee. No sign of Rathi.

I pick my way barefoot across the meadow and then pad down the concrete stairs into the blackness of the powder magazine. Ned lounges against the crumbling wall with his hands tied together. He eyes the berserker logo just visible on my shirt. "Do as the Romans do?" he asks lightly.

"I can find one for you, if you're jealous."

He shrugs one shoulder as if it matters not at all, wincing at the light behind me. "Am I free to leave this cage, Signy?"

I crouch to untie his hands. "Unless you'd rather I bring you a chamber pot. We've got toothbrushes and water and TP at the mess." As I turn away, I toss back over my shoulder, "Probably no hot chocolate, though."

Sun and humidity curl the wisps of hair escaping from my messy braids. I join Soren, accept a tin mug of hideous camp coffee, and pretend not to watch Unferth harvest morning necessities from the table and stroll out the fort. His limp is bad, likely from being bound on a cold stone floor all night. But his shoulders seem relaxed, and just before he vanishes I see him glance up at the sky. Maybe he's relieved to have told his story. He held on to it for so long.

I undo my braids and use my fingers to untangle them, thinking of Ned's fingers on my scalp, and I watch Soren watch the Mad Eagles move through a complicated series of defensive postures. "Why don't you join them?"

"I'm not one of them."

"Neither am I, but I've worked out with them."

"It's different."

"Sharkman makes it different, you mean."

"No." He glances at them again, not bothering to hide the confused longing. "I've never been good with other berserkers. And now that I denied Odin, most of them hold it against me. You saw, back at the base. He didn't even want to let me in the gate."

Abandoning my hair, I smack his shoulder. "Let's go, then."

He hesitates for only a moment.

We warm up quickly, with the system he showed me in empty hotel weight rooms, and by the time Unferth is rooting around in the mess to make more coffee, we're sparring with two of the Mad Eagles' practice spears.

Though I know Soren goes easy on me, I sink into the rhythm and feel I'm doing well, until the Mad Eagles gather to watch. Darius folds his arms over his chest and Thebes crouches like a mountain beside him. Sharkman glares hot daggers at Soren, and Ned brings his tin cup of coffee nearer. I try to ignore the audience, but the moment Unferth drinks he sneers and spits coffee onto the ground, then overturns his cup. I laugh and Soren disarms me, shaking his head at my lack of attention.

In the ensuing quiet, tension draws us all together as Unferth stands there, free and casual.

I grab up my spear from the ground and toss it at him. He drops his cup to catch it, and I take Soren's spear, lifting it in challenge. Unferth lowers his chin and smiles. I rush to find my footing, forgetting everything else.

I attack wildly. He slows me down with careful blocks, wielding his weapon like a troll-spear. The jar of spears colliding shakes up my arms and I use my feet to hold the butt in place, dodge, place the spear again, dive through his defense, and shove instead of whipping it about to get in a lighter hit. Unferth staggers but goes low and pushes me back with a hard angle against my waist.

The sun beats down. It's been two months since I fought in this style, and Unferth knocks me down again and again, but I turn fast and am on my feet before he can pin me. Little flashes of surprise on his face fill me with satisfaction, no matter how often I hit dirt. Practicing with Soren has helped tremendously.

Finally, when he knocks me to the ground, I stay there, breathe hard, and stretch my hands and feet out as far as I can. My shirt sticks to me and my scalp itches, my head spins and the tips of my fingers throb with my pulse. But the air rushing in and out of my lungs is clean, dragging all the darkness out of me. It finds each crevice, every fold inside where doubts hide, and tears it out.

Unferth crouches over me, the spear tilted against his shoulder, and says, "Have you gone soft while I was away?"

"*Away?*" I sneer at him, but it turns into a laugh.

His annoyance melts as he watches me smile, and my insides seem to evaporate in a burst of bubbles. He holds down his hand and I take it, letting him pull me up against him. We part slowly, as friends, and I know the Mad Eagles will see it, will understand as far as I'm concerned he's part of our team.

Darius begins to speak, but Sharkman turns fast and gets right in Soren's face. "Our turn, *berserker.*"

He makes the word into an insult.

As if he's been spring-loaded, Soren throws immediately into Sharkman.

My guts knot as Unferth and I back up out of the way. Unlike our spar, this is vicious and fast. Like dogs, Soren and Sharkman dart in to engage, punch, and grapple, then fling apart. They circle and leap back in with jabs and grunting. Sharkman knocks Soren's head to the side, and Soren connects with Sharkman's stomach in a heavy blow. They break apart again and Sharkman shakes his shoulders, then strips off his shirt. The column of horizontal spear tattoos ripples as his chest heaves.

Soren pauses, and I'm about to insert myself when he slowly removes his T-shirt, too, and sinks back into his boxing stance. Sharkman growls and bares his teeth, face flushed.

The meadow is silent but for the smack of flesh and hard grunts and the occasional explosion of breath. Soren takes a few hard hits, then goes on the defensive; he dodges and blocks, occasionally knocking back, while Sharkman pounds harder and faster, and my throat is closing up. I think I have to throw in myself to get this to stop, if Darius won't, and *all the gods curse them.*

Just as I think it, Soren lunges in and grabs Sharkman by

the neck and chest, and there's an explosion of heat. I spread my arms to catch myself when it hits me. Thebes sways, and even Darius falters back a step.

Sharkman drops to his knees.

Soren lets go, expression stricken, and turns away. As Sharkman falls forward and barely catches himself with his hands, Soren heads fast to the mess tent, grabs a bottle of water, twists it open, and pours it over his face.

And Rathi, standing in the doorway of the second guardhouse in miraculously pressed pants, shirtsleeves, and a vest that shines with pink-and-orange-flowered embroidery, says stiffly, "If you've all finished determining your place in the pack, maybe we should discuss the battle plan."

Soren raggedly insists on checking the perimeter of the island first, though we can see everything from the wall of the fort. Worried, I go after him, padding carefully barefoot along the boardwalk until he leaps off into the shallow dunes. I roll up my jeans and track after him, around the edge of an inland pond that shimmers with tiny waves, toward the far western tip. Whitecaps beat at the southern curve of the island itself, but to the bay side the water is clear green, calmly lapping the beach.

Soren sinks to his knees at the edge of the water and lifts great splashes of it up to his face.

The sand sinks away under my toes. Sunlight warms my neck and arms, and the air smells like fish and salt water. Soren looks up at me, shoulders dripping and seawater glistening in his buzzed hair. I notice the new tattoo on his forearm that's been covered until now.

It's the outline of a skinny, twisted apple tree growing from roots that encircle his wrist. The branches weave and tangle up toward his elbow in delicate lines, only the phantom of a tree with tiny apples sketched in like promises.

"Are you all right?" I ask. "What did you do to Sharkman?"

He strips off his orange T-shirt, rubs it over his face, and tosses it onto a tuft of grass. "I drew off his frenzy. The power of it, even though we weren't berserking. That's what happened, at the end of the fight. I reached it and just took it away."

"Odd-eye, that's incredible."

"I shouldn't be able to," he says darkly. "I'm not their warleader. That's how they assign captains."

"It isn't about seniority?"

Soren rolls his wide shoulders with discomfort. "Just power. Madness, and the one in charge needs to be the one who can control the rest of the men. Just in case."

"Could you do it to Thebes and Darius?"

"It's possible." He doesn't sound convinced.

"When I decide to take over the world, you'll definitely be my first call."

"If you survive the next few hours." Soren's gaze stretches toward the mainland, reminding me sharply of what's coming. We should head back now, but it's so lovely here for these last few moments of peace. I wonder if the troll mother is under the water yet, if she made it that far.

“I’ll survive,” I say, and kick a huge splash of water at him. He doesn’t waste energy blocking it but lets it fall all over him, completely darkening his jeans.

I grin.

His hand snakes out and he grabs my ankle, shifting up with his shoulder to knock my hip and send me crashing back into the ocean with a yell.

The water barely softens the blow of my other hip against the beach. Laughing and wincing simultaneously, I dunk back all the way, lying back into the sloping sand. I rub sweat off my arms, scrub my face, and pop my mouth and nose out enough to breathe while I work my fingers through my hair and let it all loose.

I let the gentle sway of the tide move around me, for one moment lost in the quiet roar of the ocean.

When I sit up, Soren has dragged a large hunk of driftwood to the water and straddled it. I stay in the ocean, enjoying the cool silk of it sliding over my legs. Leaning back with my elbows on the soft sand, I breathe as deeply as I can and hold it, then I tell Soren everything Ned told me.

His glower grows fiercer the longer I talk, and when I say Freya’s name, he moves his mouth like he wants to spit but can’t. I flick my fingers against the surface of the sea and say, “We have to go back and make a final plan. I know she’s coming tonight.”

“Because of things Unferth said? We can’t trust that. Not if the troll mother is coming, and he’s done so much for her, for hundreds of years.”

I shake all the water from my hands and stand up. With water sluicing off my jeans I look straight at him. "I love him."

Soren tilts his head up, wincing away from the bright sky. "There's nothing Astrid could do to make me stop loving her."

Relieved that he understands, I smile. "I'm sure Ned Unferth could manage *something* unforgivable if he tried hard enough."

"Probably that's part of what you like in him. You both reach for impossible things."

As he joins me on the bank, I lift my chin and adopt an air of haughtiness. "Naturally."

"I'll dump you back in the sea," he threatens, and I swing an arm as high as I can around his shoulders. It occurs to me that everything I've been through is worth it for earning a friend like Soren Bearstar.

He must agree with me, for he puts his arm around my waist and lets us walk like that for a few minutes before his usual reticence kicks in and he withdraws. We're nearly back to the fort, me cursing my playfulness because wet jeans are the most awkward thing in the world, when I see Ned himself waiting for us on the boardwalk. Soren casts me a careful glance and murmurs, "I'll see the others are gathered and ready," before walking through the sally port.

I stare at Ned while Soren clomps down the boardwalk. He leans off his bad leg and holds an open bottle of wine loose in his hand. He takes a drink. "You and Soren enjoy your bath?"

"Quite," I say with relish.

He twists his mouth. "He'd make you a good consort. Possibly he's even who Freya had in mind when she made me promise not to love you myself," he says more casually than I've ever heard him bother with.

I laugh. "That's not likely. Soren . . ." My laughter trails away and I stand there, stunned. *He was supposed to forget Astrid.* "Do you really think so?" I stoop beside him.

His shoulders jerk in a shrug. "Why else would she care who I loved?"

My instinct is to shove him over, to act out because he keeps dancing around that *word.* "It isn't Soren you have to worry about."

"*Worry about,*" he sneers.

"Sharkman is the one I kissed."

Ned hisses through his teeth; exactly what I wanted him to do. I smile, and he cusses. "I do not like this, little raven—Signy."

"It's hard being the one not in the know. The one teased." I skip back from his reach.

He doesn't chase. "Not being the one you're kissing."

It hangs between us in the sticky air. I swipe the bottle of wine. "You know you'll have to cut back how many nights a week you're drunk when I'm the Valkyrie of the Tree. I can't be surrounding myself with bad role models."

He studies me, slowly sucks in his bottom lip as if he's tasting a last drop of wine. "I'll consider it," he murmurs.

I offer the bottle back to him. As he takes it, our fingers brush together, and I slowly smile.

✦ ✦ ✦

The seven of us gather in the questionable shade of the mess tent to eat protein bars and talk. Sharkman and Soren sit at opposite ends, and Rathi folds his hands and bows his head like he's in church.

I describe my dream this morning, my feeling that the woman was the troll mother despite her lovely Valkyrie appearance. That if this mother is the first troll mother, perhaps this was her face before Freya put the heart into her chest.

Ned's lips tighten as if he disagrees, but he only says, "We should be ready before twilight. I've seen her walk under cloudy skies and rise when the sun still burned in the west."

"Is that because of the heart?" I ask. "If I'm right, it lets her use rune magic like the ancient Valkyrie could, like Odin and Freya do. That might be one reason why it's my riddle's answer—so I take that power from her, to use it myself, or . . . give it to Odin."

"That's just a story," Rathi scoffs. His eyes are dark and warm as the earth. It dawns on me he's not wearing his contacts. "You're forgetting the *fossil record*."

I laugh. Rathi sniffs and regards me with the familiar brown eyes from all my best memories.

But Ned says, "This troll mother isn't the original troll mother."

"What?"

He only gazes at me as if I should already understand.

"How do you know?" asks Darius.

Ned twists his mouth, and his hand tightens on his knee, knuckles whitening.

Impatiently I say, "He knows because he's the original Unferth Truth-Teller. Raised from the dead by Freya to lead me to the troll mother. Ned, are you sure? I thought she *told you* this troll has the heart from—"

Sharkman surges to his feet. *"Freya!"*

"You knew Hrothgar Shielding?" Rathi interrupts. "Of the great Freyan kings? You were at Heorot?"

Darius quietly says, "Beowulf Berserk."

Rathi stands up to, too, towering over Ned, and the sunlight gilds the smooth waves of his hair. "That's why your version was different in places, like I've never seen or heard before. You wrote the poem!"

Of course my wish-brother resisted the legend of the first troll mother being true, but he believes this with only scant linguistic evidence.

"Sang it. I sang it," Ned snaps. "When I was a poet, when I was a man, we didn't murder poetry by carving it onto stone. It lived in the air or not at all."

There's a long silence as everyone studies him.

I rub my rune scar. "Ned, how do you know this troll mother isn't the first?"

He slowly turns his gray eyes to mine. "The same way she knew me, when she saw me. We are old friends."

"Grendel's mother?" Darius asks.

Sharkman says firmly, "She died. Beowulf killed her."

Suddenly I know. My rune scar. *Strange Maid.* Ned told me

the answer months ago. And again last night: *In the end, she was too dark, too mad, for her own good.* I splay my hand and thrust to my feet. "Rag me," I whisper. "*Valtheow.*"

My troll mother. My mirror self, the monster of my dreams. Writing my name again and again, carved into her stone chest. But not my name. *Her name.* Valtheow.

I push through the men and look down at Ned. *Truth truth truth* flickers against his pupil. "You lied," I whisper, hoarse and shocked.

He says numbly, "That poem was the worst thing I've ever done."

"*What?*" Rathi demands.

"He made it all up," I say. "What happened at the mere. The story of Beowulf."

"No. Most of it is true." Ned blinks, staring at a thing from the past. "The berserker killed Grendel. But it was Valtheow who destroyed the mother and saved Heorot."

Darius puts his hand on Thebes's shoulder as if to steady himself. Sharkman's face is blotchy around the spear tattoo on his cheek. Bright sunlight pours down through the tarp, turning everything a haunted blue.

"He's our greatest hero," Thebes rumbles.

"But why?" Rathi whispers. "Why lie about that?"

"Grendel's mother had the heart," Ned says, his voice hollow. "The magical stone heart from the very first troll that Signy was talking about. It's what made Grendel's mother so powerful. The trolls had passed it down, mother to daughter, over the ages."

I sink to my knees beside Ned's camp chair. "Valtheow took it."

He says, "Because she made herself into a mirror of the creature, she recognized the heart. She felt its power and coveted it. She ripped it out of the troll thinking she could control it. Thinking she was strong enough alone. She wasn't. The heart destroyed her, turned her into a monster in truth."

"You lied to protect her legacy," I say.

"I had to, didn't I?" he begs. "I couldn't let anyone know; I couldn't make *that* her immortality. She was magnificent, but she . . . fell. She lost herself to the worst parts of her nature: vengeance and passion and the darkness that had always drawn her." Ned grips my wrist. "Signy . . . you're drawn to those things, too."

I push up and away from him as my heartbeat thunders in my ears, counting that old eight-point rhythm like Odin's own pulse.

"It's happening again," Rathi says ominously. "We have all the pieces: berserkers and Valkyrie, the poet and his king named Hrothgar. A troll mother. Even a one-armed troll-son."

"This isn't Heorot," Ned says irritably.

It's Thebes who rubs his scarred temple and says, "I hope it goes better for us."

TWENTY-SEVEN

AS THE SUN slides in its arc across the clean blue sky, I stand outside the fort at the edge of the ocean.

Valtheow.

My palm tingles when I think her name, and I rub the rune scar. My Valtheow the Dark, transformed into the troll mother who destroyed Vinland, who nearly crushed me in her arms.

I shudder and close my eyes. I can't hold my fingers still; I can't stop the chills screaming up and down my spine.

I can't tell if this is bliss or terror.

Her aquamarine gaze was so sharp and clear when we met, and in the dreams, too. She was a Valkyrie but fell completely into monstrousness. Could the same happen to me? *Signy, you're drawn to those things, too.*

But how can I take my seax and shove it into the heart of Valtheow the Dark? Won't that be like cutting out my own heart?

A strangled laugh falls out of me as I remember putting my seax to my chest at Baldur's ball and saying, *Before I would cut out his heart and offer it to the Alfather, I would cut out my own.*

Soren, as if sensing the rising panic, comes and takes me gently by the neck to go with him and check that all the weapons are ready and placed where we can easily get to them.

"This changes nothing," I whisper to him. "I still have to take the heart. Make her pay."

"Work," he says, "and distract yourself."

Sharkman and Rathi sail to Mizizibi for some heavy nets and a second generator so we can reposition two of the UV lights to shine south over the island. We expect her from the north, to rise directly out of the water, and I take off my jeans to wade with Darius around the circumference of the fort, since the piece of the wall that dives into the ocean is the most likely place the troll mother could surprise us, if she stays underwater that long. Darius checks for weak spots, especially around the small drainage holes where the brick meets the concrete foundation. I draw invisible protection runes with seawater and spit, and imagine them being more than prayers, more than poetry, but feel silly.

When I have the heart, my runes will have true power. I can have everything I wanted when I was younger.

Is that what Odin always wanted? He must have known what happened to his Valtheow, whom he loved, whom he spoke of in such passionate terms. And when Freya offered him this prophecy, he knew I was Valtheow's perfect heir.

What could I do with that power?

Anything.

I splash out of the ocean and tear over the sand into the fort. Inside my little guardhouse I press my forehead against the edge of the slit window that opens up along the eastern side where the sally port is. There's nothing but wild beach and grass billowing in the wind, a few wispy clouds clinging to the horizon. We have maybe an hour until twilight, almost three until full dark. Until my hero, my dark enemy, arrives.

I'll never survive her. I'm not strong enough; I'm terrified of her: she's not only an impossibly old troll mother but a Valkyrie with all the strength of runes and centuries behind her.

What am I?

My throat closes; my mouth suddenly waters profusely.

I'm going to throw up.

"Signy."

I whirl and it's Ned. I swallow, shaking my head. He helps me lower to my knees onto the cool slate floor. I spread out onto my stomach and press my cheek to the stone, my palms. I breathe deeply and think of the New World Tree. I think of the bright pearl of Odin's mad eye, and the laughter of his ravens, so like the echo of seagulls crying outside.

Ned rubs gentle lines across my shoulders.

Until my stomach settles, until my pulse calms, I remain silent. I breathe. I pretend I can feel the oxygen spinning out to all my cells, filling my veins and arteries, out to the tips of my fingers and toes. I know what I need to know. Nothing can make me bigger or stronger, but I've got my weapons and my friends, and we're as ready as we can be. I roll over. Ned kneels beside me. *"Nu is se ræd gelang eft æt Þe anum,"* he says.

Now our plan depends upon you alone. Words from King Hrothgar to Beowulf before he went hunting Grendel's mother. I look into those rain-colored eyes.

He says, "The heart, it will call to you, too. You're so like Valtheow, and even younger and less experienced."

I open my mouth to curse at him for mirroring my fears, but he shakes his head sharply. "You don't know how to kill, and she'd fought in battles. She'd sacrificed men with rope and knife since she was a child. It was different then; life was different, and its value different. Here in this new world you all place so much more value on individuals and choice, no matter the talk of destiny or Freya's web of fate. *Wyrd bið ful aræd*, you like to say, that line from 'The Wanderer.' *Fate is inexorable.* But you don't believe it. You think you can change your destiny."

"*Ned.*"

"You're brave, Signy, but so was she. You're drawn to the darkness and power and blood, and so was she. She succumbed. She turned into a monster, don't you understand? You have to be *stronger than Valtheow.*" His hands grope at the air but find my hips. The simple connection relieves me, offers up the answer I need.

I grab his collar and drag him down to me; I push him over onto his back and roll onto him and do what I've dreamed of: I put my thighs against his, our hips together, our chests and lips together. I prop myself on my elbows and stare into his eyes from barely a breath away. *Truth* spins in his starry gray iris. "I don't have to be stronger than Valtheow; *we* do. All of us. I have you and Soren and the Mad Eagles and even Rathi, and none of you will let me fall. You can't. I need you."

"*Me.*"

"I love you," I whisper. "And I hate you. Both things stick in my heart, grounding me here. That's the complete truth."

His hands cradle my neck, thumbs flick along my jaw, and he says, "I don't deserve it."

"Make yourself deserve it; rise up to meet me if you want me." I press my cheek to his shoulder and curl around him like he's the earth. His heart pumps hard under my ear.

"I'm afraid," he says, an echo in my ear. "Of her."

I put my arms around his neck and pull him tight.

"She won't forgive me."

"I do." I kiss him. I open my mouth and force my way in, to show him there's nothing between us now, to show him I understand. His hands crawl down my hips. I scramble at his shirt, tugging it up, but I don't want to stop kissing him. He rolls on top and pushes my face away to separate us so he can tear his shirt off. It catches on his braids like always and I laugh. He laughs, too, half a little snarl with his teeth, and I feel it straight down to my rocks. I tug at him and he shoves my shirt up, making my spine burn and arch. I don't know where to put my hands and so I try to put them everywhere, and I open my legs to let him closer even though there are still clothes between us. Just the weight of him between my thighs makes me groan, and I clap my hands over my face because I'm too loud but I don't know how to stop. He kisses my first rib, climbs his lips up the second and third. I bend under him; I grab his back. His skin is rough under my hands. I have the absurd thought he needs to eat more; he's too whip-tight and the scars raking down his flesh curl my own fingers into claws.

His teeth dig into my shoulder, my neck. I gasp and suck at his ear, I taste the salt at the hollow of his throat, and I feel so messy.

I try to get my hand in his pants but can't—quite—turn my wrist the right way, and he gets in mine first. Surprise and severe pleasure crack my head back against the ground so I see blobs of light and leave my eyes shut. I bite my lip until he kisses me again, slow and deep with his mouth, and with his fingers. There's nothing for me to hold on to. So I just let go; hands rigid and splayed out, I open up with my whole body and try not to moan and hiss and beg too loudly.

Hot satisfaction melts me into the floor. I reach for his braids, pulling, and whisper his name as I try to remember how jeans unbutton with tingling fingers. He helps finally, muttering things I don't care about like how there's no pillow or even a door, and everything is too hard and cold. But he lies back to pull me on top of him. Then Ned Unferth says "prophylactic," and I rear back and stare with horror, not because that matters right now, but because it is absolutely the least poetic thing I've ever heard fall out of his mouth.

I flatten my hands on his chest and laugh silently, shaking so violently his eyes go wide like there's something wrong with *me.* He scowls and I don't hear what he says next because his stomach flexes under me and he sits, pulling me into a close embrace. I curl in a ball, giggling and shivering, half undressed and holding on to the waistband of his jeans like my life depends on it.

TWENTY-EIGHT

THE LIGHT COMING through the east-facing window of this guardhouse is violet and low. Twilight. "I need a phone," I say. Ned's entire body tightens and I untangle myself from him, hurriedly grabbing my shirt, my boots, and my seax.

I find Soren sewing two pieces of old leather armor together and borrow his cell. Dialing the Port Orleans Death Hall, I jog back to the guardhouse, where Ned is still on the floor but clothed. At the proper moment I put in Precia's private extension and she says, "Hello?"

"Precia."

Ned sits up, leans on his elbows.

"Signy." Her voice through the line is fragmented and thin.

"The troll mother is coming tonight. I wanted to tell you, she's Valtheow the Dark, who stole the stone heart from Grendel's mother, but she lost herself and its power corrupted her. She became a monster and . . . I'm going to take the heart, too. I wanted to tell you, in case."

"Signy!"

"I love you. And I love Myra and Elisa and all of you. That's all. But you believed in me, and I won't forget that."

Ned is on his feet, glaring at me. *Don't give up,* he mouths. I shake my head harshly. "I'm as strong as you all made me," I say into the phone, holding Ned's eyes.

There's silence on the end of the line, and the distance between us rushes and crackles like a bonfire.

Suddenly, outside, Red Stripe cries out. It's a bark that shakes the foundations of the fort.

He barks again. And again.

"What is that?" Precia asks, startled.

"Her. I have to go."

"Signy, I know where you are," she says, but I hang up.

Red Stripe howls. The troll mother is coming. I hear the Mad Eagles scramble outside, Darius yelling something.

"Here." Ned catches my wrist and offers me his sword, hilt-first.

"No. I won't leave you weaponless again."

"Take it, Signy." He butts the pommel into my stomach. "It's a gift from your poet."

"You'd better be at my side with spears, then," I say fiercely, taking the sword.

Out in the parade ground, Soren tosses me a hard leather vest with metal plates sewn into the lining. I thread my arms through as I dash after him up the spiral staircase to the cannon mounts. We climb the battlement and face southwest. The Mad Eagles will be going out through the sally port to wait on the beach while Rathi mans the UV lights.

The waters of the bay are still, a lustrous purple under the evening sky.

My chest is heavy, but my spirits are light and excited. The ocean licks at the red bricks below me, and the setting sun casts a fuchsia and hot orange rainbow against the sea, a wavering line like a spear pointing from it to me. To the place where she emerges, rising out of the ocean with kelp snaked against her moon-white head and shoulders.

"*Valtheow!*" I cry.

The troll mother roars back. Her trumpet echoes across the sandy island. Low and longing, it reaches for me, curling around my ears, and I shudder when it fades.

She continues walking up the beach, too graceful for her size, like the earth itself growing up where the ocean touches shore. Necklaces of iron and bone fall down her stony chest, and she wears a belt hung with charms and steel. Those scars cut in patterns over her bulging shoulders, and the rune-like ones: this time *transformation* and *darkness.*

Behind her, the ocean seems to roil with whitecaps and foam, as if she can force the tide to rise.

I keep pace with her, striding along the circular embankment above her.

Soren follows me, and Ned the Spiritless joins us, both with swords and spears. Soren offers me a spear. The Mad Eagles wait in a spreading line at the top of the beach. They won't engage her without me if she doesn't force them to.

"Signy," Ned says urgently. He points with his spear to the roiling tide. It's cat wights and bridge eaters. They hide just under the dark water, glaring up at us, clawing at the sand and snarling, spreading their teeth.

I can barely look at them, for the troll mother's marble skin captures all the dying light, and her shifting muscles are a kaleidoscope of color, like the northern lights dancing against her stone flesh.

She lifts her face and meets my eyes with her aquamarine ones, so fresh in my mind from last night's dream. *I'm waiting for you.*

I'm coming.

"Valkyrie," she grates now, just as she did on Vinland.

Even in the warm night, the hairs on my arms rise.

"Valtheow," I say.

She opens her mouth and laughs again. Her marble shoulders roll and her spiral tusks gleam. All that bulk of her, the gnarled, bulbous troll form, all wild boar and elephant and great ape sculpted together from the finest marble, it retains so little humanity. Only her eyes, only the way her shoulders shift when she reaches up for me, only the rune scars scoured into her flesh.

Soren murmurs, "I feel her heart. I feel the madness burning like a sun."

My blood is on fire, too, pulsing with something like glee as I stare at her, as I think of Valtheow the Dark and how I've adored her. And here now I am going to destroy her, tear her stone skin off her bones and take her heart. For the Summerlings I want her to die; I want to let her bleed for hours; I want her to suffer. The desire builds inside me, a scream and a roar and a great broken river.

I could still lose myself.

The sun vanishes.

The troll mother spreads her arms.

"Signy Valborn," Ned says. With a hard hand he jerks me to him and kisses me; he bites my lip hard.

I gasp. He sucks at my pain and presses his hands against my face. "Strange Maid."

And he leaps off the grass embankment with a cry, flinging himself at the troll mother.

He slams into her with his sword, sinking it low in her chest. She curls around, roaring and flinging him away, but shows her back to me. I follow Ned, spear and sword in hand, and when I hit her it's like hitting a solid steel wall.

I stab with my sword and slide down her, hit on my feet and dart away. There's Ned swinging around, and we harry her together, one on each side. She swipes at us, claws glancing off my shoulder. I use the momentum to spin and plant my troll-spear hard, catching the butt under my boot, and Ned drives her toward it with a harsh cry.

There's shrieking and motion all around me: the wights are on shore now, racing through the evening shade, meeting up against the Mad Eagles and Soren.

The air crackles with berserker heat.

Red Stripe roars from inside the fort, chained and trapped and safe.

The UV lights flash on, cutting off the trolls' exit. They're trapped with us on the beach or must return to the sea.

I slash at the troll mother, but the blade glances off her ribs.

She charges at me, so heavy the island shakes. I run; I can't survive her crushing strength, but the sand slides under my boots and I hit the ground. I roll; there's Sharkman dragging me up. The troll mother swings out and slams her fist into his skull. Bones crack and he flies off. I stumble and reach for him—

Claws dig into my back.

Screaming, I tear a cat wight off me, but another scrapes at my calves. I've lost my spear and sword, and unsheath the seax. I slice one's head near off. Darius appears, hacking with a battle-ax in one hand and a sword in the other. Purple and black blood splatters his face and beard.

There's Soren driving his sword into her, being smacked away, and then Thebes on her back just as another handful of wights leap for me.

"Call them off!" I scream at her. She spins to me, too quick for her size, and Thebes gets his arms around her head. Darius runs at her wildly. They grab parts of her, pulling at her arms with all their mad strength. But she bares her massive fangs and throws Thebes off.

Darius stabs her in the eye with one of his knives, ripping it away, flinging gore in a wide arc.

A wide swath of light flares suddenly, and I throw up a hand to block it. UV lights sweep the sandbanks. Wights shriek and flee, diving for the ocean again or into the inland pools. It's Rathi and Soren, lugging the lights and aiming them to make a tighter perimeter. A circle of sunlight.

The troll mother heaves to her feet.

She throws Darius, bashes Thebes in the side.

Sharkman doesn't move off the sand. Blood stains the white sand in scarlet ribbons, stark under the spotlights. *No, no, no.*

My breath rattles. I should see his spirit; I should be able to gather it up and take it to the Valhol, where heroes belong.

The troll mother roars.

I turn to her with a scream, blood on my face and my hair straggling out of its braids, purple ichor staining the front of my jeans. This is what battle looks like. This is the true costume of a Valkyrie: smeared death.

With that stain of blood, I draw *Strange Maid* onto my thigh.

Valtheow the troll mother stares back at me. The same battle raiment of blood and pain coats her body. Her shoulders heave; so do mine. Her mouth spreads over spiral tusks into a wicked smile; so does mine.

Before me stands the monster that I might become if I push toward death, toward screaming and violence and pain, the raw pieces, the blood and skit of hanging, the broken, flawed beauty I thought was the strongest core of my god.

She is the answer to my riddle because I was *always* on the path to her.

But I've found something stronger.

Here's Soren standing before me, his father's blade bare in his hand, *hero* burning in his dark eye like a brand.

Here is Ned Unferth, staring like he wants to devour me. Here's Rathi Summerling with old-brown eyes, and Darius and Thebes, and Sharkman crushed on the sand. I whisper *Precia* and *Myra Quick* and *Elisa of the Prairie. Siri* and *Alanna* and

Gundrun and *Aerin* and *Isabeau.* The names of my sisters. I whisper *Astrid,* too, and my wish-parents' names, *Rome* and *Jesca.* They all tether me here. I belong in this place that I've made. I'm strong enough to bear the weight of the troll mother's stone heart because of these people.

I look up at the troll mother. Lesser trolls shriek from outside the UV circle.

"Valtheow, I want your heart," I say firmly, glad my voice rings out boldly.

She smears blood off her stomach and writes a rune between her breasts: *Strange Maid.*

The troll mother roars again, louder than a hurricane. Soren winces and Ned presses his fists to his ears, blades sticking out like spikes.

The roar spreads out like an explosion, a mushroom cloud of noise, shoving back at everything. I dig my boots in, but the lesser trolls scatter. Thebes crouches over Sharkman's bloody body to protect it. Darius and Soren brace themselves. Rathi screams. Ned falls to his knees, back bowed.

At the center of it, the troll mother shivers and shakes. Her roar lifts into a scream and she flings aside her arms.

It's a woman there. White as the moon, with black hair falling in strings about her face, thick with stone dust and salt. She's naked but for iron and bone necklaces, a belt of steel that hangs with claw charms and silver rings and strips of fur. Tusk bracelets curl around her forearms, and her fingers end with thick, twisting nails. Her skin is cracked, and purple blood seeps between her teeth.

I tighten my grip on my seax. "Give it to me."

"You take it," she says, her voice a grating thing, too big and low, like it comes from the earth, not her mouth.

When she charges me, she's a meteor of rage and fire. Terror blazes down my spine, but I don't move; I don't run. Her feet shake the earth; her searing white body becomes my entire world.

I scream at her, teeth bared, bones shaking, because I am the Valkyrie and she is the monster.

She reaches me and I drive my seax into her stomach with both hands. Valtheow grasps my wrists, locking us together with the seax in between. Her grinning mouth is near mine, her breath hot and sour as a back alley. Those bright eyes blaze with power, and runes: *stone heart, death maid.* I jerk at the seax, but her grip is perfect; her claws dig into my skin.

Her blood pours over my hands and I'm bleeding, too—purple and bright scarlet together.

The blood hardens.

I bash my forehead into her face, there's a flash of wicked pain, and she lets go of one arm. She slaps her hand onto my cheek, smearing our blood across my face.

The runes in her eyes turn black.

Hot pain bows my spine. My knees go weak.

"Signy," she murmurs, drawing me into her embrace. The pommel of my seax presses into my diaphragm. Her arms are hard and cold, and there are her lips on my cheek, on my lips. "Take it," she whispers.

I hear my name from Ned and Soren, from Darius. But all I can do is hold on to the seax, force my legs to stand.

There is a pounding in my ears, that eight-count rhythm of Odin's pulse, and with every beat my bones grow colder. My fingers stiffen. I can't blink.

Darkness surrounds us. But our mingled blood glows like lava.

"Take it," she whispers again, hissing the words into my open mouth. "Swallow it. My heart that was her heart, passed from the first mother to her daughter, to her daughter and then to me. Now to you, daughter of Odin, greatest of Valkyrie."

But I cannot move.

I use all my strength just to close my eyes.

It's bright in my own mind, and here is the roaring of my own blood. My skin turns to stone, but inside I recognize myself. I am strong; I *have* changed my fate before. This stone heart cannot destroy me.

"*No,*" I say, lips cracking.

My stone skin shatters and Valtheow shoves me back with a scream.

I hit the hard sand, dazed. My hands are coated with dark troll blood.

The troll mother looms over me, huge and bulbous and monstrous again. There is no sign of Valtheow. Her massive, moon-bright body blocks the last of the bright violet sunset, the first evening stars. She is my entire world.

And here are Soren and Ned appearing beside me to drive

her back. Their swords together are like fangs, my warrior and my poet.

The UV lights are gone, bulbs blown out, and lesser trolls swarm around. The Mad Eagles and even Rathi bat at them, cutting and slicing.

Ned cries out as the mother cuffs him away; his sword flies. But Soren shoves his sword into her throat. He lets go of it, buried up to the hilt in her chin, and swings to grab up Ned's lost sword. With it, he slashes at her belly, at her thighs and groin. His dance is so fast he's a blur of steel, hacking at her, dodging her claws. She bleeds from every limb; from her chest and sides bright purple blood spills.

He stabs her again, all the way through, with a cry like a lion.

I get up as she struggles to remain standing. There is a gaping wound that gushes in the rhythm of her heart, where my seax remains lodged.

I reach into the wound and tear my blade free.

The troll mother falls.

My heart rages and sings, but my mouth is a line; my eyes do not burn.

Soren pins her to the mud with two swords; his breath harsh, hers like a sigh. Ned staggers to us, catches himself on her great shoulder. He leaves a violet handprint like a bouquet of flowers.

I kneel at her head, and I kiss her brow.

"It screams," she whimpers.

"It's supposed to," I return. I climb onto the boulder of her chest, push aside iron necklaces, chains of bone, and with both hands I thrust the blade of the seax down into her again.

She crumbles beneath me, chunks of marble and bone falling away, in a puff of sweet breath. The moonlight finds rainbows in her breaking flesh: amethyst and emerald, ivory-white and lines of pink rubies, trails of gold, the oily sheen of obsidian. Up to my elbows in sticky dark blood turning to powder and tiny sharp crystals, into flakes of glass that cut my knuckles, that bleed my wrists.

It throbs in the center, small as a pinecone. A sharp rock of fire, hot to touch. I gather it in my palms and cradle it to my chest. It reaches hot fingers through my skin, teasing at my breastbone, calling at my heart with tingling pleasure.

There is no poem I know to describe it.

Like sunlight and kisses, like Ned's tongue on my skin.

I close my eyes, let my head fall back.

This is the line between death and life, the line between fire and air. It whispers to me as the Tree whispered to me: here is the first heart, forged by elf-queens, by Freya herself, the goddess of magic and dreams. It whispers that we will be glorious; together we will transform the world into anything I like.

I controlled it moments ago. I could do so again. I've defeated it; I'm strong enough. Stronger than her.

A smile spreads on my face. The heart whispers *yes yes yes.*

I want it forever, hardening my skin and beating in my breast. With it I cannot die; with it I can save everyone.

I will be the greatest Valkyrie.

Pleasure rolls through me, and these tiny licking tendrils

of power. "Yes," I say, allowing them to hook into my heart. I bring the beating stone to my mouth, where it is warm and silky-soft.

"Signy Valborn."

My name rings out.

My name.

Again and again.

"*Valkyrie. Sister.* Signy."

It's all of them, their eight voices from eight points in the sky. Precia and Myra, Elisa, Siri, Alanna and Gundrun and Isabeau and Aerin.

I open my eyes. They're all here, in a circle around us: me and the troll mother, Soren and Ned. Starlight horses cast such a shine to push back all the shadows, to keep the lesser trolls at bay. My mounted sisters watch with bright runes in their eyes, hair in braids but for Myra, who keeps hers short and spiky. They wear silver corselets over armor and T-shirts, over pantsuits and summer dresses, with leather boots or loafers or high heels or, in Alanna's case, house slippers. They came when I needed them, dropped everything. Undignified but ready.

Precia dismounts, rushes to me with her fine dress tossing up sand. She kneels and thrusts out a gilded jewelry box. She opens it, and the inside is empty but lined with dark green velvet.

The heart burns my fingers as I set it inside and shut the lid.

THE VÁLKYRIE OF THE TREE

It was the night before the summer solstice, and I was Signy Valborn, the Valkyrie of the Tree.

My Death Hall was a grand old hall of stone and sweeping buttresses in the center of Philadelphia's historic district. Heartwood pillars rose toward the ceiling, and in the very middle a massive black pillar carved like the trunk of the Tree spread branches that were truly rafters out across the ceiling in a web. Green banners hung, painted with silver binding runes. My throne was carved into the base of that central pillar, soft and gleaming with inlaid marble. Before it, squatted a short altar for laying out a body. Most days concentric half circles of pews waited empty for a congregation, and wisps of evergreen incense sharpened the air.

But that night I'd had all the pews pushed away, had torches and a thousand green candles lit. It was like a cave on fire.

In an intimate ritual at the foot of the New World Tree, I had finally, irrevocably, been named to the Council of Valkyrie. In attendance were only the Alfather himself, my sister Valkyrie, everyone I loved who still lived in the Middle World, and the entire country through the wide black lenses of television cameras. We preceded the solstice, not for any concern that Thor Thunderer, whose holiday it was, would mind, but in order that Soren could attend before rushing to see his Astrid for this single night.

After I spoke my name, and the Valkyrie spoke it back to me, Odin Alfather kissed my mouth and locked an iron chain at my neck. The small heart shimmered inside the delicate iron and steel setting.

I led everyone into the sanctuary for a wild reception. I kicked off my shoes and tied up my skirts and walked to the barrels of mead and street-shine. I climbed up onto one and held out my arms so the feather sleeves dripped off my elbows like wings and called, Welcome to the New World Death Hall; if you don't dance here you might as well be dead!

The bluegrass band took their cue and in a blaze of banjo and tin drums and fiddle I dragged Soren Bearstar onto the wide floor in front of my throne and dared him not to move his feet.

I danced with everyone except Ned Unferth, who shot me a look that clearly said, I have already died, and so what have I to fear from your hall? *Even the Valkyrie of the Rock and Gundrun Graycloak danced with me, even Captain Darius Strong. I ached when I thought of Sharkman, who had loved to dance as wildly as me.*

Only the Valkyrie tapped and poured from the kegs and barrels, because we serve death, and the mad passion of death is what filled that sanctuary like heavy humidity. We passed out plastic goblets dripping with golden mead, and tiny shots of shine, and

Elisa surreptitiously hid bottles of water where guests might find them.

My bare feet slapped the marble floor, I let my braids loose, and I showed the world my teeth and my laughing, while the stone heart in my necklace winked pink and blue and violet as if alive, kept cool on my skin by the silver and iron entwined around it like lace. A collar of power created to contain the heart by the Alfather himself.

The band cried poetry.

I sank into my throne, carved smooth and small into the wide, round pillar at the center of the sanctuary, an epic column of limestone and shale that reached up to the spanning roof like the Tree itself. It fit me now, like it was grown for me, for my hands to reach the raven-beaked ends of the armrests, for my knees to bend where the seat bent, for my feet to rest firm and flat on the floor. I gripped it and closed my eyes. Whirlwind music and talk flew in every direction, teasing at my smile.

I drifted until my heartbeat found the pace of the celebration, until I breathed with the rhythm of it. Until my party became a song and the lyrics whispered under it all, or above it all, like the constant drum of the ocean against the rocky shore of the death ships, high north on Vinland.

The queen walked out, gold-adorned.

I dipped my finger into my goblet of mead and smeared the sticky stuff onto the still-healing tattoo over my heart: a horizontal spear, Sharkman's ninth, in honor of him who would never complete his own. The tattoo remained slightly raised and stung when I touched it. I wished it always would, a tiny sacrifice of pain to remind me.

Everyone else was present.

There was Rathi Summerling in green for me, arm around the son of the Philadelphia jarl, laughing and talking fast. There Soren dancing with Precia of the South, earnest and sure-footed while she teased him. There Siri of the Ice not-quite-smiling, with a line before her as she doled out shine to any who answered her riddles. Baldur the Beautiful slid behind the bass to pluck one string at a time while the player smiled so wide it was a grimace. Thebes Berserk loomed with a goblet of mead while a tipsy death priest flirted so hard it turned his fire scar white. Brick and his brother Gabriel laughing behind their hands. Myra Quick and Elisa's modest, strong husband admiring Myra's newest pauldron design.

And there was Ned, watching me without a smile, in that muslin shirt I made him put on, slacks that slouched at his ankles because they weren't meant to be worn with tired old boots. He tugged at the end of one of his braids, a slick eyebrow raised. I ran my fingers through my free hair. Come fix it, *I mouthed.*

No fixing you, *he mouthed back.*

Come here anyway, *I wanted to say, and pull him onto my throne and make him kiss me right there in front of everyone, right where it could never be taken back.*

A soft caress on my ankle startled me and I glanced down at a small gray cat. She flicked her tail at my knee, looked over her shoulder as she sauntered away. Toward the garden.

I followed.

My Tree was lush with summer and the green and yellow elflights I had wound through the branches. Red, pink, and yellow papers were tied among the leaves, each one a prayer from a citizen, like flowers budding on the limbs of fate. I walked over cool grass, past marigolds and extravagant lilies, falls of iris and rocket clusters of coneflowers. All the colored lights trembled in the wind, casting rainbow shadows on my hands and on the snaking black roots of the Tree. I sank into the crook of two roots, hands against the rough, damp bark, and breathed in the perfume all around me. My Tree. My throne.

The riddle was gone, grown over with gnarled, ropy bark, a scar there on the Tree that would slowly fade as my lifetime faded.

"There remain strands of the future where you do not get all you desire, Signy Valborn."

She perched on the thick root beside my shoulder, ankles crossed. The colored shadows mottled half her face so it appeared ruined, burned, melted, and weeping with blood and pus. But her cool gray eyes fixed on mine, threaded with scarlet like the loom of fate itself always impressed upon her sight.

I whispered, "My poem began with a god in a tree, and here it ends with the same."

Freya, the goddess of dreams, the Witch and the Weaver of Destiny, laughed just like the troll mother, "ha ha ha," her teeth white and her mouth pretty. She said, "I am not here for your ending. Yet."

"Why are you here, then, at the foot of the New World Tree?"

"I see roads diverging from this moment, and I've come to choose one to follow." The goddess smoothed the velvety skirt over

her thighs. She wore a long dress off her shoulders and a medieval girdle that looped low against her hips, all of it too heavy for such a summer night. But I saw no gleam of sweat, no curl or frizz in her loose, waving hair. In fact, she glowed pale and cool like the moon. Like the troll mother. Even her hair and the ruffle of her dress seemed carved of stone. "Will you ask?" she murmured at me.

Fear trickled down my spine. "What paths do you see?"

"One: you destroy that heart at your throat. Two: you wear it until it is taken from you violently. Three: you give it to me now."

"You want it. That's what you've always wanted."

She smiled a cruel smile. "Never."

"Tell me what you want now, lady moon, and maybe I will do it."

"You, little raven, do exactly what you're told?"

I shoved my back against the rough bark, the warm damp Tree alive where she was still and cold. "Try me."

"Destroy it, for it was never meant to be in the world like this. Destroy it and it will never ruin your daughters."

"Why did you make it if only to wish it broken?"

"That is what hearts are for." Her gaze skimmed away from me, back toward the Death Hall. "You know my words are truth*."*

"Are you threatening Ned?"

"He's mine, little raven. I rule all the unsung dead, and he made promises to me."

Words burned like bile at the back of my throat. I swallowed them. I whispered, "He will not remain unsung, no matter if he dies tonight or in fifty years. I am a Valkyrie and I choose. You cannot use him against me."

"But you would miss him, if he were gone again."

"Yes."

We were silent, the goddess and I, while a breeze played through the branches above, hinting at stars and the changing paths dancing around us like elf-lights.

I said, "The Alfather forged this necklace for me. I am his, and he wants me to wear the heart. To discover what I can do with it. I have it from his own mouth, Freya."

"Yes, my love craves power in you, but he does not see the future." Her sigh tilted toward petulant, and I glanced at her, startled. The goddess pursed her lips. "Some day, Signy, you will come to me to ask a thing, and I will say no. Because of this. Because of tonight."

She leaned nearer to me then and kissed me. I felt her breath in my mouth, sharp and sweet like a flower. I gasped and the heart blazed against my skin. Its tendrils curled through my ribs, searching for my own heart, making pleasure and madness burn through my body.

"Can you resist its song forever?" the goddess of dreams murmured into my ear. "Will your daughters? Will your priests and lovers?"

I didn't want to resist. But I grasped the stone and said, "Tonight."

"That is all you will have, a thousand tonights and a thousand tomorrows, always tempted, always choosing for the rest of your life, Signy."

"That is everyone's destiny," I said. "Always choosing."

I pushed to my feet. I held my hand to her, and she took it as she gracefully stood. She remained near, her cool presence and my wild, hair-raising passion pushing off each other like magnets.

"Everyone's destiny," the goddess intoned, transforming my words into reality. "Always choosing."

"Maybe someday you'll convince me to do it." I drew chaos *onto her chest with my finger. It glowed as green as death against her white, white skin. She drew* destiny *onto my cheek.*

Together we passed through the garden, back into my sanctuary, where my family drank and cheered and danced.

# ACKNOWLEDGMENTS

I'D LIKE TO thank everybody who's still my friend after the writing of this book. I swear, it won't happen again.

Most especially I want to thank my editor, Jim Thomas, for not giving up on me. I know I made your life exponentially harder for a few months in 2013.

Thanks to everybody at Random House: Michelle Nagler, Nicole de las Heras, Mallory Loehr, and especially Jenna Lettice for all the legwork; Aisha Cloud, Rachel Feld, Nora MacDonald, and the publicity and marketing teams; and Tracy Lerner and everybody in library marketing. (Paul Samuelson and Mary Van Akin, I hope it wasn't me who drove you away! You were so great to work with.) Jennifer Prior and Alison Kolani for their painstaking detailed work. I am constantly blown away by the things you all do for my stories.

My agent, Laura Rennert, I wouldn't have succeeded without your dedication and faith in what I was trying to do.

Maggie Stiefvater, we survived!!!!

Brenna Yovanoff, knowing you got over your revision PTSD helped me keep pushing.

Myra McEntire, xoxoxoxoxoxoxoxoxoxoxoxoxoxo give me your moonshine.

Stephanie Burgis, I wouldn't have climbed back on my horse without you.

Tara Hudson, Sonia Gensler, Josie Angelini, Anna Carey, Amy Plum, Julie Murphy, Rae Carson, Kate Johnston, Chris Kennedy, Emily Kennedy, Robin Murphy, Lydia Ash, and everybody who listened and nodded and filled up my wineglass.

My entire family: thank you for only gently rolling your eyes as I worked on this book at Disney World.

And Natalie, you lived it with me, what can I even say? I don't deserve you. ♥

ABOUT THE AUTHOR

TESSA GRATTON has wanted to be a paleontologist or a wizard since she was seven. Alas, she turned out to be too impatient to hunt dinosaurs, but is still searching for someone to teach her magic. After traveling the world with her military family, Tessa acquired a BA (and the important parts of an MA) in gender studies. While in school she studied Old English and translated *Beowulf*—leading her on a wonderful journey through the sagas, which in turn inspired her to create the United States of Asgard. Tessa lives in Kansas with her partner, her cats, and her mutant dog. You can visit her online at tessagratton.com.